the
BIRD
and the
BLADE

the BIRD and the BLADE

MEGAN BANNEN

BALZER + BRAY

An Imprint of HarperCollins*Publishers*

Balzer + Bray is an imprint of HarperCollins Publishers.

The Bird and the Blade

Copyright © 2018 by Megan Bannen

Map copyright © 2018 by Jordan Saia

All rights reserved. Printed in the United States of America.

No part of this book may be used or reproduced in any manner whatsoever

without written permission except in the case of brief quotations embodied in

critical articles and reviews. For information address HarperCollins Children's

Books, a division of HarperCollins Publishers,

195 Broadway, New York, NY 10007.

www.epicreads.com

ISBN 978-0-06-267415-9

Typography by Michelle Taormina

18 19 20 21 22 PC/LSCH 10 9 8 7 6 5 4 3 2 1

First Edition

For Jenny and Kathee

CONTENTS

CAST OF CHARACTERS

JINGHUA
a slave girl

WEIJI
Jinghua's brother, a ghost

KHALAF
prince of the Kipchak Khanate

TIMUR
Khalaf's father, khan of the Kipchak Khanate

ZHANG
chancellor of the Mongol Empire

THE GREAT KHAN
khan of the Yuan Dynasty and ruler of the Mongol Empire

TURANDOKHT
the Great Khan's daughter and heir to the empire

HULEGU
ruler of the Il-Khanate, brother of the Great Khan, enemy of
Timur Khan

ABBAS
a Persian merchant

MAZDAK
a camel trader

QAIDU
descendant of Genghis Khan, enemy of the Great Khan

THE

MONGOL EMPIRE

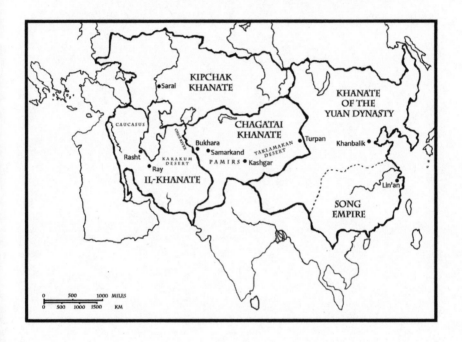

PROLOGUE

The City of Sarai, Kipchak Khanate

Autumn 1280

THE FIRST TIME I DREAM OF my brother's ghost is on the night I meet Khalaf.

In the dream, I'm sitting at a lacquered desk in the women's quarters practicing calligraphy when someone pulls aside the curtain. I look up from my work to find Weiji standing at the door. He still wears his battle armor, its hardened leather plates smeared with blood. His head is half severed from his body, a downward stroke that leaves a pulpy chasm running from his shoulder to his heart.

I drop the paintbrush in shock. Ink drips and bleeds over the paper as Weiji steps across the threshold. The curtain swings shut behind him. He reaches for me with skeletal hands.

I'm hungry, Jinghua, he rasps, his voice hardly a breath. *Feed me.*

I wake in the slaves' *ger* of Timur Khan's tent city, where I lie on a thin mat, sweating fear and revulsion. My brother's words haunt me in the darkness, like the phantom lights burned into one's eyes after fireworks have burst.

Feed me.

I'm a slave. It's not like I keep a stash of food under my mat. The only way I can honor Weiji now is to steal from the Mongols' stores. If I get caught, I could be killed, and then who will feed my brother's spirit? We'll both haunt the earth forever.

The pendant I wear under my shirt weighs uncomfortably against my breastbone as I tiptoe over the other slaves, through the door, and out into the open air. Overhead, the stars glint like ice crystals in the frigid night. I snake my hands up inside the long sleeves of my *deel* to keep them warm as I creep between the white felt *gers* that glow like evenly spaced moons across the steppe.

Sarai is a strange mobile city—"city" being pretty loose with the language—that moves up and down the Volga River depending on the time of year, so the food stores are kept on large covered carts. I head for one full of peasant fare for the servants—barley, cabbage, fruit—and that's just as well, as far as I'm concerned. The Mongols can keep their nasty cheese curds to themselves.

There's a snoring guard posted outside with a skin of the fermented mare's milk they call *qumiz* at his feet. I'm certain my pounding heart will wake the man as I sneak by him, but he wheezes through sleep-slackened lips without pause.

What little light there is disappears altogether as I climb over the huge wheels and into the cart like a monkey. I feel my way through the sacks from memory even though I arrived here only eight weeks ago.

And what have I done in those two months? I've scrubbed plates with sand and cooked horseflesh and served food and fetched supplies from the carts. Basically, I've done nothing. It's pathetic. *I'm* pathetic.

Feed me, my brother's nightmare voice echoes in my mind. My grief for him, dulled by two years of loss, sharpens to a point as I think of the pathetic ghost I saw in my dream.

I reach for one of the baskets where the apples are stored. I've only tasted apples a couple of times since my arrival, but I think Weiji might like them.

Suddenly, the cart trembles beneath my feet, and I hear someone climb up the back. Panicked, I squint my eyes and look for a place to hide, but the cart is crammed with bags and supplies, and there's no time to conceal myself.

"I'm sorry," I tell Weiji, my failure as cold as the hint of winter in the air.

A stranger enters the cart. He's not the guard but a young man I've never seen before holding an oil lamp. He cocks his head to the side, taking me in, noticing my guilty hand on the apples. I stare back at him, mute. I'm as good as dead.

"Hello," he says. He takes a step closer, holding the lamp out to see me better, and now I can see him better, too, a typical Kipchak Mongol wearing a plain wool *deel* belted with red silk. His face and hands are scrubbed clean, but his clothes are dusty, as if he's been on the road. His hair is braided in loops behind his ears, and on his head he wears a fur-lined leather cap with flaps hanging down the back of his neck. The whites of his eyes are remarkably white, as if he were lit up from the inside.

"You're a slave?" he asks, but it's not really a question. I fall to my knees and bow before him, praying that he'll have mercy on me. I'm not sure what happens to thieves in the Kipchak Khanate, but it can't be good.

The young man takes another step forward, and the upturned toes of his boots enter my field of vision. "What are you doing here?" he asks.

"I was . . . I was . . ."

He sets the lamp down on top of a covered bin and crouches to my level. "Stealing?" he finishes for me. I'm baffled by the fact that he's not yelling, but if anything he's soft-spoken.

"Forgive me, sir," I plead to his feet.

"Are you so hungry that you would steal?" he asks gently, and I'd swear that even the flicker of the lamp's flame grows still in his presence.

"It's not for me," I explain. My eyes are still downcast, but I sense him listening—really listening to what I have to say.

"For whom, then?"

I wipe my face with the prickly wool of my sleeve. "For my ancestors."

"And are they slaves here as well?"

He doesn't understand. I dare to look up at him and find a face that is not unkind. "They're dead," I tell him, feeling a fresh stab of grief.

He studies me for a moment. "And they need to be fed, these ancestors?"

"Yes, sir."

"What will happen if you don't feed them?"

Really, you don't realize how loud most people are until you encounter someone who very distinctly isn't.

"They could lose their way," I tell him. "Their souls might become confused or angry. They might haunt the living . . ." My voice trails off. Misery swells in my chest. It kills me that Weiji might be one of these ghosts. I'm fluent in Mongolian, but my words are hopelessly inadequate to explain something so large.

"I see," says the young man. He rises, steps around me, and starts to rifle through the apples in the basket. He takes one, holds it up for inspection in the dim light, and puts it back. He does this a second time, then a third. Finally, he finds one that is acceptable, and he repeats the process until he holds three perfect apples. He returns to crouch in front of me and holds up one of the apples before my eyes.

"Did you know that if you have a spherical, reflective object, like this apple for example, and a light source, like that lamp, you can calculate the exact point on the surface from which the light will be reflected back to the observer?"

"I . . . no?" is my bumbling response. I have no idea what to make of this boy.

He sets the apples in the bowl created by the bowing of his *deel* between his knees, and he takes a dagger from his belt. I shrink away from the blade, assuming that he's going to punish me at last. Instead, he lightly carves a figure in the wooden board beneath us, a circle with two lines jutting outward to meet at a point beyond the circumference and a cross within the circle that connects the points where the two lines touch the outer edge.

I begin to understand it, to see how light can be measured and calculated. My flaccid mind stretches like a cat waking up from a nap in a square of sunlight.

"Ibn al-Haytham's theorem is all about optics, you see," he explains, "creating an equation to the fourth degree. It's sheer, beautiful mathematical genius."

He smiles at me. It's not a huge smile, not bright or toothy, just a turning up at the corners of his mouth, a slight crinkling of his eyelids, the hint of a crescent-shaped indent in his left cheek. For the first time in over two years, I believe the world is not an entirely terrible place simply because this one decent person lives in it.

He takes one of the apples and holds it out to me, his hand flattened like a platter. "For your ancestors," he says. The sheer kindness of the gesture inspires an aching lump in my throat as I take the fruit from his hand.

"Thank you."

He offers me another apple in the same way. "And for you. We must also feed the living."

The lump in my throat blossoms into tears. I can't even manage a thank-you this time, so I just nod.

"'God does not judge you according to your appearance and your wealth, but He looks at your heart and looks into your deeds.' So please don't cry." With that, he crunches into the third apple and rises to his feet. He slides the dagger back into its scabbard, retrieves the lamp, and tells me, "Come along, fellow thief. It's easier to climb out by lamplight."

I wipe my nose. "Won't we be caught, sir?"

"You let me worry about that," he assures me, but I stay where I am. His expression softens. "I would not leave you alone in the dark, little one."

He thinks I'm a child. As diminutive and flat-chested as I am, I can't blame him. My legs feel tingly and weak when I stand, but I follow him out of the cart.

"Hello, Buri," the boy calls as he hops down and claps the dozing guard on the shoulder.

My heart stops as I hit the ground behind him. What is he doing?

The guard snorts awake, sees the young man, and jumps to his feet, knocking over his stool in the process. "Prince Khalaf, I didn't know you had come home."

"Only just," says the boy.

Who is Prince Khalaf.

Prince Khalaf.

His name hits me like a loose ceiling tile clattering on my head. I lean against the back of the cart, hardly able to stand.

"I'm afraid I have a confession to make, Buri," says the prince. "I have stolen into the khan's stores and absconded with three apples."

The guard stares at him quizzically. "Apples, my lord? Since when does the khan's son eat the servants' food?"

Prince Khalaf shrugs. "I like them," he says. "Not to worry, though. This loyal servant caught me in the act and made sure the damage was minimal." He looks to me with those bright eyes. "Excellent work. You may return to your quarters now, I think."

"Yes, my lord." I bow my head and scuttle off between the *gers* as quickly as I can, leaving the whole mortifying scene behind me.

Khalaf, each footstep says as I hurry away, and layered beneath it is the memory of Chancellor Zhang mocking the sounds of the Mongol language: *Pilaf. Kumar. One of those unpronounceable Turkic names.*

Once I've returned to the slaves' *ger,* I kneel on my mat, take the thong from around my neck, and set the pendant down in front of me. It's so pale that it glows faintly, its subtle shape blurred by darkness. We had an entire room dedicated to our ancestors back home. Now I have only this broken piece from an incense burner.

And I have two apples as well, I remind myself. I offer them both to Weiji.

Afterward, I lie down and watch the smoke from the brazier billow out of the hole above. But in my mind, all I can see is Prince Khalaf of the Kipchak Khanate smiling back at me.

PART ONE

THE FIRST RIDDLE

The City of Khanbalik, Khanate of the Yuan Dynasty

Autumn 1281

1

A GUARD WAVES TIMUR AND ME through the north gate of Khanbalik without question. Apparently, we don't seem like the sort of people who threaten the safety of the Great Khan of the Mongol Empire, which is hilarious when you think about it. Timur Khan of the Kipchak Khanate isn't a threat to the Great Khan? Really?

Granted, Timur is the *overthrown* khan of the Kipchak Khanate, and the Great Khan's brother, Hulegu Il-Khan, is hunting him down like a dog. But still.

My body sags with relief as we take our first steps inside the city. Again, the irony is not lost on me. Timur leans his great bulk too heavily on my bony shoulders as we walk. He needs to eat. So do I, for that matter. The constant need to eat also weighs too heavily on my bony shoulders.

Maybe it's the fault of my empty stomach, but I suddenly remember in stunning detail the sight of Khalaf crouched before me in the cart last autumn, holding out an apple, the instrument of my doom. That apple would taste fantastic right about now. But I have no apple or any other food for that matter, so I keep us moving.

There's so much to see as we trudge ahead: fine houses with red-winged rooftops, lush gardens, and a staggering number of silk-clad pedestrians. And since Timur and I have only one decent set of eyes between us—my own—it's up to me to search the faces around us on the street.

"Slow down, girl," Timur says. The hungrier he gets, the more he tries to mask it with rough authoritarianism. The hungrier I get, the more I want to yank him by the beard. It's not pretty, but there you have it.

"We're never going to find him here," I say as I wipe a ticklish strand of hair out of my face. Even caked in sweat and dust, the baby-fine wisps defy gravity.

"Don't be a pessimist. We'll find him."

"Says the man who can't see."

A year ago, I would not have dreamed of speaking so insolently to the khan, but months of traveling in exile and deprivation by his side have bound us together in surprising ways. He may once have ruled over his own sprawling piece of the Mongol Empire, but, from my perspective, he's just my grumpy old goat.

He stops to glare at me and, while I know he can't see me clearly, I wither. Even gaunt and impoverished, the man has eyebrows that can command armies. It's his son I'm talking about here, and my . . . well, I'm not entirely sure what to call Khalaf in relation to me, but it's big and important and much larger than my selfish irritability. I bow my head and say, "Sorry." Timur folds his arms. I roll my eyes and add, *"My lord."*

He nods and lets me lead him again. As I'm calling him *old goat* in my mind for the thousandth time, he squeezes my shoulder and says, "It'll be all right, little bird. Just keep looking." My heart cramps as hard as my stomach.

The streets of Khanbalik are wide enough for seven horsemen to pass abreast, but I still feel penned in like a rabbit in a trap. As the sun wheels toward the western walls of the city, a constant, low-grade worry eats at my insides.

I'm pretty sure I'm going to die.

I know, we all die, but *my* dying feels imminent. It's breathing down my neck like an eager, wet puppy.

A sedan chair floats by on the shoulders of six slaves, its silk curtains as opalescently pink as a sunset. It reminds me of home, the way the elite rode through Lin'an in sedan chairs just like this when there was still a Song Empire and I lived in it. I stare after it longingly until a young man brushes past me, waking me from my reverie. He's humming a familiar tune under his breath: *"Mòlìhuā."* Jasmine flower. I turn my head as he walks away, and my entire body freezes.

It's Weiji.

My brother's gait, his frame, even the rakish tilt of his black cap, the way his thick braid sways behind him—all of it as familiar to me as the song he's singing. I'm about to run after him, to shout his name, when Timur tugs my sleeve.

"What?" he asks, hopeful. "Is it him?"

I glance at Timur for an instant, just enough time for the boy who could not possibly be my brother to disappear into the crowd. Irrational disappointment weighs me down, heavier than Timur's thick arm. "No, my lord," I answer, squinting into the crowd. "I don't see your son."

We head south toward the Great Khan's palace just because that seems to be the direction in which most people are moving, but my mind keeps drifting to Weiji, who's been dead for nearly three years. He began haunting my dreams the night I first met Khalaf, but the possibility that I could see my brother's ghost here in the living world gnaws at me. *It wasn't him, Jinghua,* I try to reassure myself, but it feels like a lie. In all honesty, I want it to be him. I want my teasing, obnoxious brother back.

The growling of my stomach distracts me, and since I haven't been ashamed to beg for months, I pull Timur toward a food cart that wafts of duck-filled heaven. "Try to look pathetic," I whisper to him. It's more for the sake of formality. He's looked effortlessly pathetic for some time now. To the dumpling vendor, I plead, "Sir, could you offer a meager bite to hungry strangers?"

The man snorts. "Why would I give anything away when I can make a full week's profit at the execution?"

I feel like I've swallowed a brick. Timur's grip stiffens on my arm.

"What execution?" I ask, dreading the answer.

"Another prince tried to answer the khatun's riddles and couldn't. Just this morning he beat the drum in the market square to announce that he was mad enough to enter the contest; then he failed just like the rest of them. Turandokht Khatun is having him executed tonight."

"Who is it?" I ask. By now, Timur's hand on my arm has become viselike. "The prince to be executed. Where is he from?"

"Balkh? Kerman? Sarai?" The man shrugs. "Who knows and who cares? It's great for business." He pushes the cart ahead so that we can no longer keep up. Timur and I come to a halt and let the growing throng of people buffet us like a paper boat on a river.

"Sarai. He said Sarai." Timur's voice thickens.

"He also said Balkh or Kerman," I say, trying to remain calm. "I'm sure it isn't your son, my lord."

Timur goes alarmingly silent. My own anxiety is growing by the second. Our combined losses form an army of misery and grief in our wake as we follow the stream of people heading south until we find ourselves packed into a crowd at the northern end of Khanbalik's market square. At the far edge sits the imperial compound, its roof tiles gleaming in the twilight like the iridescent scales of a fish. Between us and the palace stands a dais with several white taffeta pavilions at its feet, all heavily guarded by the Great Khan's red-and-black-clad warriors. The gong in the bell tower glints in the torchlight on the southeast corner of the square, while the drum tower looms like a giant sentinel on the southwest corner.

In my mind, I try to picture Khalaf climbing the steps to beat the huge drum over our heads. It's hard to imagine him doing anything so dramatic as that. Maybe he didn't.

I hope he didn't.

A dignitary draped in gold silk steps out of one of the pavilions and puffs his way to the top of the bell tower. Recognition bowls me over. It's Zhang, a man I've known since before I was a slave, back when he came to Lin'an three years ago. I don't want him to see me as I am now, so I shrink into Timur's bulk as if the old goat could hide me. I know it's unlikely that anyone would take notice of one puny girl in a crowd this size, but I feel like a bug just waiting to be squashed by a boot.

The crowd hushes as Zhang unfurls a silk scroll and reads a proclamation.

"As chancellor of the empire, I speak for the Great Khan, the Son of the Eternal Blue Sky. No prince shall be allowed to wed Turandokht Khatun who shall not previously have replied without hesitation to the riddles that she shall put to him. If his answers prove satisfactory, she will consent to his becoming her husband. But if the reverse, he shall forfeit his life for his temerity. This the Great Khan has sworn to the Earth and to the Eternal Blue Sky."

A simmering wave of anticipation ripples through the crowd. I can feel Timur's worry streaming off him, matching my own unease.

"The prince of Hormuz has this day beaten the drum, faced the trial, and failed. According to the Great Khan's sacred oath, let him be put to death!"

The prince of Hormuz. Not the prince of the Kipchak Khanate. Not Khalaf. Tears of relief prick at my eyes. "Thank the Eternal Blue Sky," Timur breathes as he sags against me. It's an odd sentiment from a Muslim convert, but I'm not going to nitpick.

The funeral procession appears out of the palace gate beginning with a swarm of shamans dancing and jingling and beating on their drums. As they spin back and forth, their many-colored ribbons fly out all around them. The bells and mirrors sewn to the ribbons clink and flash firelight from the torches. They hold their drums high before them, beating them so hard I can feel the reverberation in my chest, mimicking my heartbeat as they make their way down the aisle that cuts through the crowd.

Just behind the shamans, eight slaves carry in a magnificent sedan chair curtained in silk brocade, girded by a unit of the Great Khan's personal guard. They tote it up a flight of stairs to the dais, where they set down their burden. Two of them pull back the curtains to reveal within a haggard man whose beady eyes are nearly lost in the tired folds of his face. Once, he was fat. Now he is clearly wasting away.

"Is that the Great Khan?" Timur asks me.

"I think so."

"How does he look?"

"Unwell, my lord."

Timur clicks his tongue against the roof of his mouth, and I know what he's thinking. If he had made an open play for the throne of the empire, he'd now be in a position to rule the world. Instead, he's a beggar, as haggard as the Great Khan but a lot poorer. Hindsight is a curse.

I should know.

The crowd kneels before the sickly man on the dais, and I follow suit, yanking Timur down with me. "Fanatics," he mutters as his knees pop. I know how he must hate bowing before the Great Khan, but I shush him so he doesn't get us both killed before we manage to find Khalaf.

Lines of the Mongol elite file in and kneel on cushions inside the pavilions. Grim-faced warriors surround another sedan chair held aloft by eight more slaves, as nameless and faceless as I have been. They carry it to the top of the dais, setting it to the right of the Great Khan. When they pull back the curtain, there is an audible gasp from the audience. Like the sun bursting through the thick clouds of winter, Turandokht Khatun steps out.

The pale, pregnant moon crests the top of the city walls and bathes her so that she appears to glow. She wears a long robe of rose silk with cuffs and edgings embroidered in gold thread. The open red-and-gold brocade jacket over the robe shimmers in the moonlight. There is a tall, cylindrical headdress strapped to her head, two feet tall, oxblood red, adorned with gold brooches and a fine peacock feather at the top that billows sinuously in the breeze.

All that finery, and she would be just as breathtaking if she wore no more than rags. The skin that hugs her round cheeks is taut and perfect. Her dark eyes shine with intelligence. Her full lips pout beautifully below her tiny nose. Everything is in proportion, every feature of her face an homage to beauty. She stands erect before the people of Khanbalik, as exquisite as an ornate sword.

This is the girl Khalaf intends to marry. It's uncharacteristically mercenary of him, but desperation does that to a deposed prince. He needs to save the Kipchak Khanate, so he's going to try to marry the most powerful woman in the empire. I know this, but looking at Turandokht now, it's hard to think of my own feelings for Khalaf as anything other than laughable. She's more than simply lovely. As she towers over her father, there's no escaping her dazzling self-assurance, the power that practically oozes off her skin. What am I compared to Turandokht? Nothing, that's what. I have always been nothing in comparison to her. Khalaf isn't blind. He'll see that, too.

"All rise!" Chancellor Zhang calls out, after which people get to their feet, buzzing with excitement. Clearly, something unusual is going on.

"What's the big deal?" Timur asks as he struggles to his feet. "She's just a girl."

Just a girl? I swear, the man never learns. I catch a snippet of conversation from one of our neighbors and translate it from Hanyu into Mongolian for him. "It seems this is the first time Turandokht has personally attended an execution."

"Very big of her," Timur comments drily.

"My lord," I warn him. He grumbles, but he cuts the snide remarks. For now.

Turandokht surveys the assembly before her and waits for the world to go still and silent before she speaks, her alto voice cutting through the air like a bell.

"Today marks the failure of the twentieth prince to prove himself worthy to rule beside me. And yet I continue to hear arguments in favor of my marrying for the peace and security of the empire. Do you not see that my marriage would lead to the antithesis of peace? Should I bear children at great risk to my own life? And what then? None of us is ignorant of such stories of ambition from every kingdom, from every land. We have witnessed what fighting happens between father and son or brother and brother."

"I hope you're listening to this," I mutter at Timur, who harrumphs in response.

"Some of you would have it that the heirs of Genghis Khan's son Ogodei are the rightful rulers of the empire. You forget how Ogodei stole his sisters' lands. You forget that he attacked his sisters' people and sent his men to rape every girl over the age of seven from sunup to sundown before he sold them into slavery."

I've never heard this horror story before, and I glance up at Timur to see if it's true. He looks uncomfortable. "Ugh!" I hiss at him in disgust. He shushes me.

"Some of you believe that the descendants of Genghis's son Jochi are the rightful heirs of the empire, but they have colluded with the disgraced line of Ogodei to ruin our peace—*your* peace. This is how the matter of succession is handled by men."

I sense Timur's outrage flaring like a lit rocket behind me. Jochi was his grandfather. "Don't do anything," I murmur over my shoulder. "We need to find your son." Timur exhales audibly, blowing hot air over my head, but he keeps his cool.

"It is the descendants of Genghis's youngest son, Tolui, who have united Zhongguo, north and south, and brought the Persians back into our fold," says Turandokht, as ethereal as a goddess from her marble dais. I grit my teeth at her use of the word "Zhongguo," as if the Yuan Dynasty had the legitimacy and superiority to equal the Song.

"Tolui's heirs have brought you peace and prosperity," she continues. "As Tolui's grandchild, I am not moved to violence, if only men would desist in assaulting my liberty and leave me and my father to the ruling of this empire. Today, I renew my vow to our gods that I will marry no man so unworthy of you, my people."

I hate that what she's saying makes sense. I hate the fact that, if Khalaf's life weren't at stake or if my brother weren't dead, I might even be sympathetic toward her. Most of all, I hate how much I envy her—her beauty, her power, her intellect, everything she has that I don't. My jealousy of her is like a tiger; it could devour me.

She glides to her chair and lowers herself onto the seat, placing a hand on each chair arm like a hunting bird on its perch. "Let the prince of Hormuz pay the price for his pride," she declares, and it chills me to think she might one day say these same words about Khalaf.

The sound of another shaman's drum comes from the palace as the gates spit out the prince of Hormuz flanked by six Mongol warriors. He's painfully young, with delicate lips and large hazel eyes. Behind him come four executioners, two of whom carry a long shroud between them and two who lead four fine horses. Turandokht's face is devoid of emotion as she nods her head at them. The prince closes his eyes. His lips move in silent prayer as the first two masked men situate him in the center of the shroud. One of them pulls up each end, completely enveloping the boy, while the other sews him inside with an efficient flicking of needle and thread up and around the fabric. Once he is secured inside his shroud, they ease the prince down until he lies on the ground.

"Don't look, little bird," Timur murmurs, his beard tickling my ear.

But I watch it all.

The prince of Hormuz screams in agony as the other two masked men lead the horses over the sewn-up heap on the ground to trample the boy's body. There is the sick percussion of hoof against flesh and bone, and the conflicting cheers and cries of protest as the prince's body stills at last. Zhang rings the bronze gong beside him to signal the boy's death with a solemnity he enjoys a little too much.

There is no way I am going to let Khalaf end like this. No earthly way.

2

FOR A FULL HALF HOUR AFTERWARD, Timur and I are stuck, packed in like rice in a rich man's bowl. "We've got to find Khalaf," he growls. "And when we do, I'm going to strangle the life out of him."

I give a humorless laugh. "That kind of defeats the purpose, doesn't it?"

"It's the difference between stupidity and justice. Don't quibble with me, girl."

There's a commotion near the drum tower, a series of gasps and exclamations. "What is it?" Timur asks, but with very little interest. Really, nothing matters at this point but Khalaf.

Khalaf, whom we have not found.

Being without him these past few weeks has planted a constant, dull longing inside me, so entrenched I can feel it in my spine. You'd think the bustling streets of Khanbalik would alleviate the loneliness, but the ache is more acute here. It's just so easy to imagine him studying the architecture or trying to identify the trees of the Great Khan's arboretum.

A tall man nearby shakes his head and says, "Unbelievable. The prince of Hormuz not dead an hour, and there goes another one."

I jump up, but I still can't see anything. It's not until heads move and bodies turn in just such a way that for one instant, I see him—Khalaf—standing at the base of the wooden stairs leading to the top of the drum tower. Dread robs me of breath. My pulse pounds in my ears.

"It's him," I tell Timur, my voice floating high, completely unmoored. I grab the old man's arm and yank him toward the tower as Khalaf ascends the steps.

"Go!" Timur bellows, pushing me forward. I spring ahead to swim through the crowd without him. Angry protests fall in my wake as Timur does his best to follow.

Khalaf reaches for the mallet tethered to the platform.

"Move!" Timur shouts. I'm not sure if he's yelling at me or the people in my way or both. I'm almost there, close enough to see Khalaf swing back the mallet.

"No!" I scream as I burst through to the front of the crowd just in time for Khalaf to bring the mallet down against the taut skin of the drum. He beats it three times—*Boom! Boom! BOOM!*—so loud it bounces off the palace walls. My cry outlasts the echo of the last percussion by half a second, long enough for Khalaf to hear me. He turns and looks down.

For the span of several breaths, we stand ten feet apart, he above and I below. We stare at each other as if the rest of the world has disappeared. I've crossed deserts and mountains to find him, and now here he is, a thousand times cleaner than I've seen him in months, with his hair combed and braided into glossy loops behind his ears in the Mongol style. He's wearing a robe of pale blue silk rather than his customary plain wool. He may as well be the sun clothed in the sky. Seeing him in the flesh, alive, hones my pent-up loneliness into a point that jabs me hard right underneath the breastbone.

And all I can think to say is *"Cān jiàn Diànxià."*

Hello.

A very formal hello.

A crevice of incredulity deepens between his eyebrows before he rushes down the stairs. He takes me by the arms, and I can feel the heat of his hands through the fabric of my threadbare sleeves. It takes every ounce of decorum I can muster to stop myself from throwing my arms around him and burying my face in his neck. Given what happened the last time we spoke, that would not be a wise move.

"What are you doing here?" he asks, bewildered, as he pulls me away from the crowd to the foot of the tower. "Is my father with you?"

"I'm here," Timur answers for himself, pushing past the onlookers.

Shouts strike up from the pavilions. Turandokht's guards are coming for the man who beat the drum.

Khalaf releases me and looks at Timur in horror. "You followed me? What were you thinking? Hulegu Il-Khan's men were looking for us not fifteen hundred *li* west of here in Ordos. I barely escaped capture, and I've had to stay off the trade routes ever since. It's taken me ages to get to Khanbalik. I'm certain our enemies must have arrived by now. It's incredibly dangerous for you here."

Timur's face falls into its familiar, stony scowl. So much for family reunions.

The sound of marching footsteps approaches quickly, and the crowd begins to part to make room for a unit of guards coming to take Khalaf away.

"You have to go," he tells us.

"Like hell," says Timur. "You're coming with us."

"It's too late for that."

"I am your lord and khan, and you will do as I say."

"I'm trying save you," Khalaf says, his frustration on full display. "And the Kipchak Khanate. And . . . and her." He turns back to me as the guards arrive.

"What man is it who beat the drum?" one of them asks.

"I did," Khalaf answers, but he's still looking at me.

I don't know what to do. I'm terrified that if he takes his eyes off mine or if I tear mine from his that he'll be lost to me for good.

"Only men of royal blood may offer for Turandokht Khatun," the guard says, eyeing Khalaf doubtfully. "Any commoner who beats that drum dies on sight."

"Then it's too bad for you that I was born a prince," Khalaf replies.

Timur curses when he hears his own words coming back to haunt him. There was a time when I would have said that it served him right, but those days are long gone. The guard rolls his eyes and tells his companions, "We'll let Chancellor Zhang sort this out." To Khalaf he says, "You will come with us, please."

Each of those statements is a death sentence. If Zhang is the one sorting this out, they may as well run their lances through Khalaf where he stands.

"Don't do this, my lord," I plead with him.

"Sir?" the guard asks.

"I'm coming," Khalaf says, but he hasn't turned away from me. There's fear in his eyes, and his fear is my fear. "Will you do me the honor of taking care of my father if—"

I put up my hands to stop him from finishing that sentence, as if my preventing him from saying the words will erase the possibility of his death. Inside, I rage against the idea that his life could end here, now. I resist it as hard as I've fought against my own death. Harder even. "I will," I tell him. "I promise."

He holds out his hand, the one that offered me apples, that gave me a dagger, and I put my hand in his. His thumb strokes my skin just once, the same gesture that led in a roundabout way to his dumping me and Timur in the Chagatai Khanate. I don't care that the feeling it inspires is why everything has gone wrong from Sarai to Khanbalik. I want his thumb to stroke the back of my hand for the rest of my life.

"Forgive me," he pleads.

"There's nothing to forgive," I assure him, doing my level best not to start bawling. I know full well that he's not apologizing for the fact that he just entered a contest that could very well end in his death. He's referring to what happened back in the Chagatai Khanate the night he abandoned us. He has only one thing to be sorry for. I have a million.

"Sir." The guard is out of patience with the lengthy goodbyes.

Khalaf presses my hand one last time before releasing me. He throws his arms around Timur, hugs him fiercely, and kisses him on each cheek. Then he lets go of his father and walks away with the guard. Timur and I stand there, gaping in powerless misery at the back of his head, when, suddenly, he stops and turns back to look at us.

At me.

"Sir," the guard spits, grabbing him by the upper arm. Khalaf pulls himself free. His face tightens as if he were in physical pain, and my whole chest tightens right along with it.

"'And wilderness is paradise now,'" he says. He holds my gaze, begging me with red-rimmed eyes to understand his meaning before the guard jerks him away. This time, he doesn't turn back.

I feel as if someone has reached down my throat, ripped out my backbone, and left me a hollow shell.

"'And wilderness is paradise now'? What is that? What the hell is that supposed to mean?" Timur asks me, grasping at hope that these words contain some hidden message, something that's going to save Khalaf from death.

"I don't know, my lord," I answer, and it's true. Those may have been Khalaf's last words to me, ever, and I don't understand what he was trying to tell me. I look to Timur for guidance, but he has devolved into his mountainous state, the unmoving posture he assumes when everything has gone to hell. The people who witnessed Khalaf's entry into Turandokht's trial are staring at us, and I remember the promise I made to him only moments ago to take care of his father. I tug on Timur's sleeve and say, "We should get out of here."

"What's the point?" Timur replies in a dead voice.

For Khalaf's sake, I am grimly determined to hold it together. "Your son is still alive, and we are still alive. It's not over yet." I pull him away from the onlookers, closer to the dais, so that we'll have a decent view as Khalaf faces his trial.

"I can't see much," Timur admits, looking out over the crowd.

"I know, my lord," I tell him, anxiety hanging from my bones like wet sheets. "I'll be your eyes as best I can."

From our new vantage point, I see a small procession making its way to join Chancellor Zhang. It consists of only three old, pompous men.

"There are three men climbing up the bell tower," I narrate for Timur. "They look like scholars."

"The judges?"

"I think so."

Another guard unit escorts Khalaf to the foot of the dais as if he were a dangerous criminal. Do they think he'll flee? And what would they do to him if he did?

"There he is," I tell Timur.

"How does he look?" The man sounds desperate. I know the feeling.

"Calm" is my answer, but it doesn't come close to describing him. Even from this distance and even though Khalaf is dressed in remarkably humble clothing compared to the imperial court, he is radiant. I imagine the other princes who came before him, dripping with jewels, touting their carved bows and brilliant scimitars, each trying to outglorify the next in riches and luxuries. I'm certain Khalaf puts them all to shame. He doesn't need to act the part. He *is* the part.

I'm giddily tempted to race into the center of this spectacle, grab him by the arm, and yank him all the way to Lin'an. If we wouldn't be killed on the spot, I just might try.

The rest of the players are already present. Turandokht and the Great Khan sit on their ornately carved chairs. The dignitaries kneel once more on their cushions. Chancellor Zhang smiles smugly beside the judges from his lofty place in the bell tower. He clears his throat and begins the trial.

"On behalf of the Yuan Dynasty and the entire Mongol Empire, I welcome you to your death, sir," he says. The snake. "You have signaled your intent to wed Turandokht Khatun at a most auspicious moment, as we are already gathered together to witness the failure of another man much like yourself."

"Are you the prince who would marry my daughter?" asks the Great Khan. His voice is weak and brittle, his mouth a crooked line, livid against his clammy skin.

"I am, Son of the Eternal Blue Sky," Khalaf answers. His voice lilts with his Kipchak accent, so intimate and familiar to me in a city full of strangeness and strangers that I wish I could snatch the sound out of the air and tuck it into my pocket.

"You are young," says the Great Khan. "Not as young as the last one, but young all the same. How old are you?"

"I am nineteen, my lord."

"As a Mongol, I have the decency to abhor death, and I don't wish to see another this night. Go home."

I hear Timur's intake of breath, which matches my own. For one blissful second, hope surges in both of us, until Khalaf replies, "Son of the Eternal Blue Sky, I have come to Khanbalik to face Turandokht's riddles, if it please you."

His self-condemnation flattens me, and there's nothing I can do about it.

"It does not please me." The Great Khan leans forward. "Do you know war? You appear strong enough. Can you fight?"

Khalaf's stance widens. He nods, and there's something in the simplicity of the gesture, some physical grace that conveys the fact that he is deadly when armed. "Yes, my lord. I have known war, and I am able to fight."

"Then let me advise you to give your life honorably on the field of battle in the cause of expanding our glorious empire to all the nations of the world."

"He's got that right," Timur mutters.

"As I understand it, my lord," Khalaf answers, "Turandokht Khatun merits the sacrifice that I am willing to risk."

It hurts—physically hurts—to hear these words waltz so easily from his mouth. She merits him.

I don't.

From her high place on the dais, Turandokht shakes her head. "Have you come to Khanbalik to kill yourself?" she asks Khalaf. "If not, you must understand that should you persist in battling my intelligence, you will die."

"My khatun, you freely admit to your intelligence. Do you not see that a wise king must treasure such a gift in his wife and the value a great intellect would bring to any kingdom?" The softness of Khalaf's voice stands in stark contrast to Turandokht's grandeur, and yet it's strong enough to bounce across the market square and crush me.

The Great Khan inclines his head. "Well said. Forgive me, I did not catch your name . . . ?"

I feel Timur stiffen as Khalaf replies, "Does my name matter?"

"We do not, as a general rule, allow beggars on the throne,

though you are no beggar, I think. Enough. Where is your kingdom? What man is your father?"

"If I solve the riddles, and it is discovered that I am no prince, you may break my body and rip my flesh from my bones."

Khalaf has just made the most solemn of Mongol oaths. His words comprise a sacred, unbreakable vow. I can't believe this is happening, that he cares more for his principles than his own life.

Zhang laughs. "Look at him. He's like a pig that's willingly crawled onto the block to be butchered."

I want to wrap my hands around that man's neck and strangle the life out of him, but my abhorrence of Zhang wraps itself up with my own self-loathing. I may want to rip the smile from his face, but at the end of the day, he's no worse than I am, is he?

"If you truly wish to die, let it be so," the Great Khan tells Khalaf. He reaches out a palsied hand and sets it on Turandokht's wrist. "He's beyond reason, Daughter. Offer the trial."

Zhang tsk-tsks at Khalaf. "The men who were the prince of Hormuz's executioners tonight will be your executioners tomorrow, sir, and it will be your body sewn into a bag and trampled."

The memory of the other boy's execution floods my mind, morphing into images of my brother's bloodied ghost. Zhǎngxiōng, *please*, I beg Weiji's spirit. *Don't let Khalaf die like this.*

Turandokht's fine features look as if they have been carved out of ice, and even that is lovely. She gives Khalaf a long, hard look. He returns her gaze with his own beatific Khalaf-ness.

"The first riddle, then," she says.

Timur sucks in a breath but doesn't release it. Terror makes my heart beat so hard in my chest that I'm finding it hard to breathe, too. I hate this powerlessness, this inability to act. Nothing I do helps Khalaf or Timur or Weiji or anyone I've ever cared about. It's like I'm going through my whole life with my hands tied behind my back.

Zhang unfurls a silk scroll and reads the same edict we heard just an hour ago. When he's finished, he rolls the scroll up and neatens it on the palm of his hand before addressing Khalaf. "You will have seven minutes to answer each riddle," he explains. "Should you fail to answer correctly each riddle by the end of seven minutes, you shall forfeit your life. Do you understand?"

"I understand," Khalaf answers, his soft voice incongruous in the expansive market square, the beating heart of a city that is the beating heart of the empire.

Turandokht says, "The first riddle is this:

> *"She is the dragon with an iridescent wing*
> *Stretched taut across the bleak and yawning void*
> *To whom the hollow human heart must sing*
> *When, with it, like a cat with prey has toyed.*

> *"She only lives in shadow's heavy hue*
> *When, invoked by man, is night her reign.*
> *So every dusk gives birth to her anew,*
> *And every dawn destroys her once again."*

"Seven minutes," Zhang announces.

As Khalaf bows his head in concentration, my mind spirals, thinking of all the things I could have done to stop this from happening, of all the little missteps along the way that led to this. But it was a long road that brought us here, and, to be honest, I'm not sure where the road began or at what point I put my foot on the path and took my first step toward disaster.

Toward this.

PART TWO

HOPE

The City of Sarai, Kipchak Khanate

Autumn 1280

3

THE ROYAL FAMILY DINES TONIGHT IN the khan's enormous *ger*. It's late autumn in Sarai, Timur Khan's tent city on the Volga River, north of the Caspian Sea. The fire in the brazier keeps the room warm within the *ger*'s luxurious brocade-lined walls. It's no palace, but the gold-plated support beams encrusted with gems and pearls lend a certain opulence to the scene. Beyond the door, however, the bland steppes make me long for the green hills beyond the West Lake back home.

There are four place settings at the table, one more than usual, and I can only assume that the seat across from the khan is meant for Prince Khalaf, the boy I met last night in the cart. The very idea of facing him again spins me into a panic.

Timur Khan hunkers on a low divan wearing his permascowl,

one enormous hand fisted on his hip, the other holding out a porcelain dish containing a bit of washed, pale sheep's lung for his goshawk. The bird sits on a wooden perch, grasping the rod with fierce talons. The khan doesn't look up as I set a platter of stewed lamb before him. I dissolve into the background, taking my station against a beam alongside twelve other slaves. I'm so nervous that my knees feel like they could give out at any second.

The khan's oldest son, Prince Miran, enters the *ger*. The goshawk flaps her great wings as he passes, and the slave next to me stifles a laugh as the prince trips in surprise. The prince glares at the bird before eyeing the extra place setting on the table. "Are we expecting company?" he asks his father as he sits.

"No," the khan answers, setting the bird's dish down on the embroidered muslin that covers the table. Prince Miran frowns. The two men sit in silence until Prince Khalaf enters the *ger*.

Last night in the cart, the apples, his kindness . . . it all seemed unreal. But seeing him here in the khan's home brings reality into sharp focus. I hold my breath and press my back against the beam. He walks by me without a glance and sits across from his father. I let out my breath and will myself to become invisible.

"Good evening, my lord," he says to the khan, and to his brother, "Miran."

He still wears a plain *deel* and trousers, but this is a cleaner set of clothes than what he wore last night. He also has a distinctly foreign turban wrapped around his head. His dress is so modest that he makes his brother, who is not particularly showy, look like a canary in quilted brocade. Prince Miran seems surprised to see him, and not in a pleasant way.

"Khalaf, I didn't realize you were here. When did you get in?"

"Late last night. This is a magnificent bird, Father. Is she new?"

"Your friend Nasan captured her from the nest for me," Timur Khan answers.

"May I?" Prince Khalaf gestures to the khan's leather glove resting on the table, and his father nods. He slides his arm into the glove and offers it to the bird, making soft clucking noises with his tongue. The goshawk obliges, stepping onto the boy's forearm.

"Look at the pattern of her wings," he marvels. "It's as if God wrote a page of the Qur'an on her. She'll bring you good fortune for that, Father."

I tend to think of Timur Khan as more mountain than man, but while to all outward appearances he remains as hard and massive as ever, I detect something resembling approval hiding beneath his beard.

Prince Miran's lips thin, and he taps his cup. A slave steps forward to fill it. The older prince dips his hand into the *qumiz* and flicks a drop into the air, an offering to Tengri, the Eternal Blue Sky, before he guzzles the rest.

The khan's second son, Jahangir, arrives as Prince Khalaf places the bird back on her perch and removes the glove. If the youngest son's somber attire makes Prince Miran look a bit showy, it makes Prince Jahangir look like a peacock. The man struts to his chair with his embroidered green-and-blue silk *deel* glinting in the lamplight. Unlike the khan's eldest son, he makes no attempt to hide his lack of enthusiasm at seeing his younger brother seated at the table.

"What's he doing here?" he asks his father with a jerk of the head in Prince Khalaf's direction. I can't help but think of my own brother poking his head around the curtain of the women's quarters to tease me, but there was at least a sheen of affection in his taunts.

Weiji.

Last night's dream of my brother's ghost, the grinding pain in his voice, comes crashing in on me. The thought of him haunting the earth makes me heartsick. I try to shake off the memory and focus on the family drama unfolding before my eyes.

Prince Khalaf seems more amused than put out by his brothers' greetings. He's much younger than they, and here by the brighter light of the brazier and lamps he looks even younger than I thought him last night. It makes my chest ache harder.

"You're late," Timur Khan tells Prince Jahangir.

"Oh, are we standing on ceremony for the runt? Nice turban, by the way." The khan's second son lounges like a cat on his divan, drawing a dish of yogurt toward himself.

"Father sent for me," Prince Khalaf explains.

"For what?" Another slave steps forward to fill Prince Jahangir's cup. Like Prince Miran, he flicks an offering to the Eternal Blue Sky into the air before taking a drink.

"Is there tea?" Prince Khalaf asks.

A pit of dread opens wide in my stomach. The Kipchaks have developed a taste for whipped tea in the Song fashion, and that means the Song girl is the one assigned to the task.

Me.

I bow my head and shuffle over to the tea service to retrieve the pot and the pressed cake and the whisk, and I will my hands to stop shaking. *Please, please, please, don't see me,* my mind begs Prince Khalaf.

And he doesn't. He never glances in my direction. I should be relieved, but for some unfathomable reason, I'm a little disappointed as well. I suppose it's depressing how insignificant I am, that his kindness to me was nothing special.

You are an idiot, Jinghua, I tell myself brutally.

As I break off a chunk from the tea cake, I can make out the familiar dragon seal still visible on the compressed leaves, trace it with the tip of my finger. Homesickness surges within me. My father could whip tea into the most beautiful green-white froth with nary a watermark on the utensils. Me? It always comes out a sad, yellowed mess. I can't help but wonder what my father would think if he could see me now.

What choice do I have? I ask him. *What choice did you leave me?*

My father's judgment, even in death, tastes bitter in my mouth.

The khan places both his scarred hands on the table as I point the steaming water from the pot and send it splashing messily over the crumbled tea. "I have sent for Khalaf so that we may all discuss a matter of the utmost importance to the future of the Kipchak Khanate," he says, "a matter that threatens to destroy us."

That gets everyone's attention, even the slaves', and we're not supposed to pay attention to anything. I raise my head to listen and wind up overfilling the cup, the water spilling over the sides like a fountain. I pour off the excess, burning my fingers in the process.

"I've had an emissary from Hulegu Il-Khan," Timur tells his sons. "The il-khan has sacked Baghdad and is demanding a tribute of eight hundred thousand dirhams from us."

Prince Miran lets out a breath, and Prince Khalaf nods grimly.

Frankly, I find Mongol politics bewildering. The Song Empire had an elegant bureaucracy with the emperor unequivocally at its head. The Mongol Empire, on the other hand, is an incomprehensible mishmash of khans and governors and random nobles who war against one another while the Great Khan oversees his own khanate in the east. The only thing I know about Hulegu Il-Khan is that he was sent by the Great Khan to recapture parts of Persia that had stopped paying their tribute to the empire.

"Eight hundred thousand dirhams? How much is that?" Prince Jahangir asks.

"Based on the exchange rate to the standardized *sukhe*, that's about one thousand six hundred silver ingots," says Prince Khalaf.

"And Khalaf should know"—Prince Miran sulks into his cup—"since he was the one who created the monetary standard for all the currencies of the empire when he was only twelve years old."

"I was fourteen," Prince Khalaf says quietly. "And the Great Khan's finance ministers simply adopted the Kipchak standard for the rest of the empire. That's all."

Brilliant, I think as I whip the prince's tea with grim determination. The concoction looks even more sickly than usual, as if I've managed to stir my fear and resentment into it along with everything else.

"And how do you think we should respond to the il-khan?" Timur Khan asks.

"I think we—" Prince Miran begins.

"I am asking Khalaf."

The room goes still, palpably so, like someone blew out all the lamps at once. Even I notice the change in mood, and that's saying something given my current focus.

"What? Khalaf?" Prince Jahangir seethes while Prince Miran bites his lip with infuriated impotence. "You're giving precedence to the Beardless Wonder? You can't be serious, Father."

"He's been tested in two battles," Timur Khan points out. "He's proven himself."

"Minor skirmishes," Prince Miran protests. "And the boy has spent most of the past five years learning the Eternal Blue Sky knows what in Isfahan."

Timur Khan waves away his older sons' comments while Prince Khalaf stares back at him in silence.

The tea is as ready as it's going to get. I stare at it for a long moment before I will my feet to move and my hands to remain steady and unshaking as I set the cup in front of the prince. His quiet, even presence radiates off him as I lean in, and I wish for the millionth time in the eighteen hours since I met him that he were not quite so wonderful.

Timur Khan asks simply, "Prince Khalaf?"

I step back, melting into line with the other slaves, but I feel as though I left my stomach on the table beside the prince's hand. Prince Khalaf remains quiet and watches the steam billowing out of his cup.

"My lord," says Prince Jahangir, nearly choking on his anger as he reaches for a bit of lamb. "Khalaf is a child and he's flowery and he's up to his ass in books. How is that good for anything?"

"There is as much to be learned about war from books as there is on the field of battle," Prince Khalaf says at last. "Frankly, I prefer books. So if you'd rather I didn't share my opinions on the matter at hand, I'll happily return to my studies."

The boy rises from his divan as if to leave, and for one dizzying moment I am both panicked and relieved.

"Sit," Timur barks at him. "I called you here for your learned opinion, and I will have it."

"You know I don't relish matters of state, Father."

The khan leans forward. "Then it's too damn bad that you were born a prince."

Prince Jahangir gives an ugly laugh as Prince Miran takes

another drink. After a moment, Prince Khalaf releases a breath and sits obediently. "I'm assuming we can't afford to pay off the il-khan?" he asks.

"We can't afford to pay tribute to the Great Khan *and* Hulegu, no," Timur Khan confirms. He scratches at his beard and mutters, "Frankly, I'd like to signal our absolute refusal of the il-khan's temerity by gutting his emissary and sending the little prick back to his master wrapped in his own shit-filled entrails."

Jahangir cheers, "Hear, hear!" and Prince Miran sneers at him. I've been watching the pair of them for the past two months trying to figure out which one could be considered smart enough to rule the Kipchak Khanate. Seeing them now, side by side with their brother, there's no contest. Miran's lack of grace and Jahangir's oafishness become ridiculous beside Prince Khalaf's quiet intelligence. This boy is clearly the rightful heir to the Kipchak Khanate, a fact that twists up my insides, like someone is playing jump rope with my intestines while I watch.

"I have not finished." Timur Khan scowls at his older sons. "I would love nothing more than to throw down the gauntlet, but the il-khan has the Great Khan's support, and his army outnumbers our own by a hefty margin."

"He has two hundred thousand men," Prince Khalaf adds, curling his fingers around the cup. I suck in a sharp breath of air that saws into my chest. "And Baghdad is the epicenter of Muslim culture: art, scholarship, libraries. As a Muslim convert, Father may be obligated to avenge this act."

"So what do you propose we do, O Great Scholar Khalaf?" scoffs Prince Jahangir as his older brother taps his cup for another refill of *qumiz*.

"Excellent question," says Timur Khan. "What do you propose, Prince Khalaf?"

The young prince regards the gems and pearls of a support beam as they reflect the flickering firelight. His hand still hugs the cup, and I can't help but notice that even the shape of his hand on the cup is lovely. It's the same hand that held out an offering of kindness to a slave, a nobody. Me. His soft voice presses against my conscience. *"God does not judge you according to your appearance and your wealth, but He looks at your heart and looks into your deeds."*

Prince Khalaf replies softly, "We declare war."

"Hark the genius child," Prince Miran slurs.

Prince Jahangir crosses his arms over his chest. "We should have tried to arrange a marriage between the Great Khan's chit and one of us. I said so all along. The il-khan wouldn't have dared strike at us if we were so strongly tied to the Great Khan."

Even this small reference to Turandokht makes my resentment of my current circumstances rise biliously up the back of my throat.

"Khalaf," says the khan, "please explain to your brother why that plan is fucking idiotic."

"It's not idiotic," the boy sighs, finally betraying a hint of frustration with his family.

"You're right. I said it was *fucking* idiotic. Now tell him why."

Prince Khalaf traces the rim of his cup with his finger. "Because many in the empire believe Father holds a stronger claim to the throne than the Great Khan does. So it's highly unlikely that the Great Khan would wish to marry his only daughter to one of us since that would invite our family to take over the empire. Besides, the competition over her hand in and of itself could lead to war with another nation—*has* led to war, in fact. Look at what happened to the Song. They're dead and gone now."

The reminder of all that I've lost, spoken so casually, stings like a wasp. I'm the only person in the room who truly comprehends what happened to the Song Dynasty, but unlike Prince Jahangir, I'm not at liberty to explode in a rage.

"So we recruit heavily from the kingdoms and tribes of the Kipchak Khanate, and we fight off Hulegu Il-Khan and his milk-blooded army?" the khan asks his youngest son.

Prince Khalaf lifts his cup at last. "I can't refer to an army of two hundred thousand men as 'milk-blooded,' but I see no other way, my lord."

I imagine the way the porcelain feels in his grasp, the heat seeping into his skin. I can't tear my eyes away.

Look at what happened to the Song, he said. I try to cling to the words and the hate they inspire, but my mind fills instead with his smile, his outstretched hand, the guilelessness streaming off him. Try as I may, I can't bring myself to hate him.

"Are we agreed?" Timur Khan asks.

Prince Jahangir sighs and nods. Prince Miran grunts, "Fine."

"Then it sounds like we have a plan, gentlemen," the khan declares, pushing back from the table and templing his thick fingers.

The Kipchaks are going to war. And men die in war.

Dammit. Just, dammit.

When Prince Miran taps his cup again, I grab the carafe from the slave beside me to pour *qumiz* for him. The royal family takes no notice, but I can feel the other slaves staring at my back with a mixture of awe and horror. I bump hard against Prince Khalaf as I pass him, knocking into his arm and sending his tea splashing to the table and floor and all over the sleeve of his plain wool *deel*.

4

OVER THE FOLLOWING WEEKS, THE CITY of white *gers* grows and spreads into a far-reaching grid across the landscape, dotted with herds upon herds of the stocky mares favored by the Mongols. When the day finally comes for the Kipchak army to depart, most of the women and children of Sarai come to see them off, myself included.

I watch Prince Khalaf ride among his men, the sun glinting off his conical helmet. The quiver of arrows at his horse's flank points upward to the Mongols' Eternal Blue Sky, although he prays to a different god from most of his tribesmen.

Is he praying for his life now? I wonder as I watch him ride away.

For two months, I try and fail to resign myself to my lot in life. For two months, I try and fail to appease my brother's troubled ghost. For two months, I try and fail to scrub the memory of Prince Khalaf out of my mind the way I scour burned meat from the bottom of a pot.

Emphasis on the word "fail."

My brother haunts my dreams at night, while the memory of the prince's kindness invades my waking thoughts until, nine weeks after the Kipchak army leaves, I wake with a terrified lurch to the sound of hooves pounding into the encampment. Shouts cut through the night air. I race alongside the other slaves to the grazing pasture of the imperial *ger* just in time to see Prince Khalaf swinging down off his mount.

Prince Khalaf, back from the war with Il-Khanids.

Prince Khalaf, who is not dead.

His lip is swollen, and there's dried blood on his face from a gash through his left eyebrow, but he's very much alive. I'm more elated than devastated to see him still in the world, and I berate myself for both emotions.

Timur Khan strides out of his *ger* wearing a quilted *deel* hastily tied around his waist, and the men go quiet.

"What's this?" the khan asks.

The prince removes his helmet and tucks it under his arm. "Father, we've come from—"

"Are we victorious?"

"No, Father, we—"

"Then why are you here?" the khan demands.

"I'm trying to tell you—"

"You just told me that we are not victorious. That means you should be either fighting to the death at this moment or dead. So let me ask you again, why in the name of God and the Eternal Blue Sky are you here?"

The khan's voice grows in anger until the last word cracks like a whip. Everything stops. Slaves and nobility are standing side by side with the city of *gers* at our backs, all of us silent, all of us watching and waiting. It begins to sleet.

Prince Khalaf opens his mouth to answer but promptly shuts it again. For a moment, I think he might start crying. He gazes back at his father with wet eyes and doesn't utter a sound until he's regained his composure. "May I speak now, my lord?"

When Timur Khan's only response is a flinty glare, the prince continues. "We woke one morning to find that many of our allies had accepted a bribe from Hulegu Il-Khan and had fled in the night. We were left with thirty thousand fewer men, and we were already outnumbered to begin with."

He pauses, but his father says nothing.

"It was a slaughter. I ordered my unit to cut through enemy lines so that we might make it back to Sarai in time to warn our people and to get you out of the city before the il-khan and his forces arrive." He gestures to the six men behind him and announces hoarsely, "This is all that remains of your army."

Nothing but sleet hitting mud greets this news. The silence is staggering, as if the world were holding its breath. The entire Kipchak army has been obliterated, and one of the only men left standing is Prince Khalaf. I'm not sure whether to laugh or weep.

"You left the field of battle?" the khan asks his son.

"Yes."

Without warning, the old man backhands the boy across the face, splitting the prince's lip and nearly knocking him to the ground. I gasp and take a couple of steps forward, but what can I do to help? Nothing. I'm nothing. And I shouldn't want to help the boy in the first place.

Prince Khalaf staggers, rights himself, and stands erect before his father. "You would prefer me dead, my lord?" he asks.

I cringe at the old man's silence. A father's disapproval can cut like a knife.

"I suppose we could have fought to the death," the prince says, "but it would have made no difference to the battle, none whatsoever. And I thought the Kipchaks might prefer to be warned so that they could flee before Hulegu Il-Khan's forces come to burn their homes and rape their women. Even now, the Il-Khanids are hot on our heels. The only reason we were able to move so quickly to get here is because we are so few."

My mind reels, trying to grapple with the fact that my circumstances, which were already terrible, have just taken a dramatic turn for the worse. Timur Khan still says nothing.

"And I believed—I still believe, in fact—that I ought to do everything within my power to protect my khan," the prince persists. "So, by your leave, I will ready my men to escort you into exile."

Exile.

He's leaving, and he's going to carry away my hopes—my whole life—with him.

He turns away from his father and begins ordering the evacuation, wiping at his lip with the back of his hand. Blood shines on his skin, dark and slick in the torchlight.

"Miran? Jahangir?" Timur Khan shouts at his back. "Where are my sons?"

Prince Khalaf stops. He turns his head to the side, revealing a profile shining with rain. He shakes his head before he walks on, the mud sucking at his boots.

Sarai bursts into a frenzy of escape, spreading so quickly through the *gers* that within minutes, the only people left standing in the pasture are myself and Timur Khan, both of us glazed over and inert.

What am I going to do? I have no idea where to go from here. *Think, Jinghua,* I beg myself. *Think!*

I drift aimlessly between the *gers*, where the slaves are stealing what they can before they run. For a moment I'm tempted to escape, too, an idea so visceral I can taste it like honey on my tongue. But where would I go? Home? I may as well walk to the moon.

My mind is divided in two: the enormous chunk that is blind with panic and a tiny corner that is still functioning. That tiny corner reminds me that I cannot stay in Sarai, where I have no friends and no one to help me, that I am roughly sixteen thousand *li* away from my home in Lin'an. It directs me to follow Prince Khalaf, my one and only ticket to freedom, at any price. It whispers seductively that if I follow him, there's still a possibility, however slim, that I could make my way home. My panic asserts that a girl traveling with a band of Kipchaks is begging for trouble, but my logic tells me that maybe, just maybe, I could pass for a boy.

The functioning portion of my mind grows, flexes a muscle, moves aside the panic. I enter the slaves' *ger*, cast off my *deel*, and tie a thick strip of muslin around what passes for my breasts. The shapelessness of the quilted, heavily lined boy's *deel* I put on over my trousers hides what little femininity I had to begin with. The original owner of these clothes was probably a good two years younger than I am, but I'm drowning in fabric.

What are you doing? This will never work! my shrinking panic says in one last death gasp, but there's a certain freedom that comes from having nothing to lose. Steady now, I pack two changes of clothing and an extra pair of shoes inside a blanket that I tie to my back. I braid my hair into two loops, one on each side of my head in the style of Mongol boys, before I head back to the pasture.

I find Prince Khalaf at the center of all the noise and activity with two other men, tying supplies to their horses. I hover near him, wringing my hands, unsure of what I'm going to do or say and still worried to death that he'll recognize me as the apple-stealing thief I am. Finally, he notices the idiot whinging behind him.

"Yes? What is it?" He sounds more weary than snappish. I don't think he has any idea who I am.

"I'm here to serve you, my lord," I tell him, or more precisely, I tell my feet.

He pauses in his work. "You're a slave?"

We've had this conversation before, but he doesn't remember. "Yes," I tell him.

"Can you cook?" he asks.

"Yes."

"Can you shoot?"

"Yes," I lie.

"Can you ride a horse?"

I look up at him, trying to decide how to answer. The sleet has tapered to a freezing drizzle, and he wipes the condensation from his tired face.

"I don't usually fall off, my lord," I tell him doubtfully, and even that's a stretch.

His exhaustion-glazed eyes stare at me before he nods and then calls out to one of his men. "Nasan!"

I recognize the tall, narrow-faced man who finishes hoisting a *ger* frame onto a cart and hurries over to where the prince and I are standing. He's a little older than the prince and he's dressed like a soldier of rank, but he doesn't seem to mind taking orders from the younger man.

"My lord?"

"This boy will help you pack up what we need from the stores.

Put him to use." He claps Nasan on the shoulder before returning to the carts and horses.

Nasan looks at me with a face devoid of expression. He meets my eye and nods. I nod back at him. I have no idea what I'm doing or how I'm going to pull this off or even why. I only know that I have to follow after this prince, and so I push everything else to the back of my mind to worry about later. For now, I lead Nasan into the carts. He chases off slaves who are pilfering food, prodding them out with the blunt end of his lance. We spend the next hour packing up dried meat and cheese curds and pressed yogurt and pots and spoons among other, more important items.

When we're finished, we haul what we have managed to scavenge outside. The icy drizzle comes to an end as dawn peeks over the horizon. The few Kipchaks who remain in Sarai gather by the horses with mists of steam drying off their bodies. I shuffle uncomfortably in the small pool of men, my head bobbing through their sea of shoulders, unsure what to do with myself while the men check and double-check the packing to make sure it's secured to the horses.

Timur Khan hasn't moved since Prince Khalaf told him his oldest two sons were dead. He has turned to stone, his thick eyebrows forming a heavy line over his eyes.

The prince speaks with Nasan for some time, their heads close together. Then Nasan walks over to Timur Khan and bows before him. The growing light of morning gleams off his shorn head as the two braided loops and front forelock of his remaining hair dangle from his bowed form.

"Might I offer a suggestion, my lord?" he asks.

Timur Khan makes a sound that is little more than a rumble. Nasan takes this as permission to speak.

"As you know, there are few trade routes through the Caucasus Mountains, and most of them are treacherous."

"Are you seriously suggesting we escape by heading straight into the Il-Khanate?"

"Exactly, my lord. The il-khan will have cut off the trade route east to the Yuan and will expect us to head north or west."

"So we go south, directly into the lion's mouth, and hope that his army doesn't follow?" The khan's voice begins to regain life.

"I doubt he could bring an army through those mountains, my lord. And once we're past the Caucasus, we can head north and west around the Black Sea to the Bulgarians. They have no love of the il-khan either."

Timur Khan nods grimly. Any fool would know the route is Prince Khalaf's idea, but maybe the prince hopes it will sound like a good plan if it doesn't come from him. Whatever the case, the exile party heads south, taking me along with it.

5

IT'S HARD TO IMAGINE HOW THE Kipchak horde I saw sprawled across the grassland outside Sarai just two months ago could have been reduced to this handful of men riding beside the khan and his son. They look like children's toys against the vast backdrop of the steppes, woefully incapable of defending their leader—much less me—should the Il-Khanids catch up to us.

I spend the long days staring at the horizon we leave behind, willing the il-khan's army not to appear and terrified that it will as a light snow falls all around us. After five days of hard riding, with me rattling around the back of a wagon beside sacks of dried meat, we catch our first glimpse of the peaks in the distance. It feels like a turning point two days later when we enter the new terrain without Hulegu Il-Khan materializing to our north.

I'm freezing in the mountains. I've had few opportunities to spend time outdoors and certainly not while fleeing for my life in the company of eight men. Frankly, I'm not sure which is worse, the mountains or the men. At least a mountain doesn't bring out its private business to pee. The only one with any sense of propriety is the prince, who disappears from time to time into the trees.

And speaking of pee, I am coming to realize that I did not quite think through the ins and outs of what it would mean to masquerade as a boy. Urination has become a furtive endeavor, and it involves my having to hold it in for long chunks of time until we stop somewhere and I can scurry off into the woods without getting left behind. Then there is the fact that I get my period on our fourth day in the Caucasus. The extra shirt I packed now serves a very different function than originally intended. So for me, at least, our slog through the mountains is a new kind of hell.

The reason that few trade routes run through the Caucasus Mountains is because the Caucasus comprise the worst terrain in the history of horrible terrains. Plateaus of frost-coated steppes disappear into narrow gullies between looming mountain peaks. All around us, the world is dense with trees and shrubs. Oak and hornbeam give way to birch and pine as we climb higher and higher, and then birch and pine give way to oak and hornbeam as we descend lower and lower in an unending cycle of trees and altitudes.

Somewhere along the way, we cross into the Il-Khanate, although it's hard to say exactly when. This area between the

Black Sea and the Caspian Sea has been hotly contested between the Kipchak Khanate and the Il-Khanate for decades. I can't for the life of me figure out why anyone would want to live here, much less fight over it. As far as I can tell, there's nothing here but mountains and snow and trees and mud and more mountains.

The route cutting through the Caucasus grows so narrow that we ditch the wagons after a week and load up the horses and ourselves, too. I am now carrying a bag of stinking curds, and I feel like a peasant woman hauling a fat, sleeping toddler on my back.

We're a quiet lot, nine of us traveling together on a hard road. The six soldiers who accompany the prince and the khan were all in Prince Khalaf's *tumen* since he was in charge of tens of thousands of men on the field of battle, and most of them were in his own *arban* of ten as well, which would make them almost family. They're the ones who cut through enemy lines to reach Sarai. Nasan, ever the loyal friend, looks only to the prince for orders and guidance, but the rest of the men shift their eyes between the prince and the khan whenever Prince Khalaf gives a command, as if they're ascertaining Timur Khan's approval, too.

I collect their names: Farit, Kamil, Rustam, Almas, Ildar.

No one has asked me for my name, I notice.

Another week passes and I'm marching behind Rustam, a boy soldier maybe a year or two older than I am. I watch his shoulders slump with each passing step. I suppose his dead are walking alongside him, weighing him down with grief. That's nothing new for me. The burden of my ancestors is heavier than the overstuffed pack I carry on my back. Even so, I almost feel badly for him until I nearly collide into his backside when he stops to pee.

I have seen more penises in three weeks than I thought to see in a lifetime. I shudder, completely mortified, every time a man urinates. My mother must think me a disgrace, wherever her spirit resides. She used to sit by a courtyard window and embroider silk, her body still and lovely, her only movement the deft flick of hand and wrist. She was so effortlessly womanly. She had little patience for my sulking and my lack of grace, but being in her presence had been easy and uncomplicated. What I wouldn't give to be home beside her now, to appreciate her as I never did before.

My eyes dart to Prince Khalaf far up ahead of me where he walks at the front of the line side by side with Nasan. It's hard to see around Timur Khan's enormous bulk in the middle of our formation, so I have to tilt my head to catch a glimpse of him, the prince who is, if not the complete cause of all my sorrow, at least a small instigator of it. I feel nothing for him in this moment. Nothing at all.

And that's a good thing.

The only positive news is that Prince Khalaf's plan seems to have worked. The Il-Khanid army hasn't followed us through the mountains. But positive news is pretty relative at this point.

The Kipchaks brought me along to cook, but so far I've done nothing. We've kept our fires low and lit them only at night. I haven't even been the one to hand out rations. Nasan has seen to that. All I've done is walk and walk and walk.

Finally, Prince Khalaf calls for a day of hunting and foraging to bolster our stores after losing the wagons, and the men give a faint cheer in the understanding that tonight there will be a decent fire.

I guess I'm cooking. *Hopefully, I won't poison anyone,* I joke to myself.

As the men break off to hunt, the prince holds out a bow and half a quiver of arrows to me. It's ludicrous, the fact that he's handing me a weapon. I almost burst out laughing.

"You said you could shoot," he says in response to my hesitation.

"I can, my lord," I lie.

Timur Khan curses. "Then if you see something tasty to eat while you're out there pissing in the forest, shoot it."

"Yes, my lord."

When I reach for the weapon, the prince leans in and murmurs, "Please don't shoot any *people*, though."

He's kidding, but it is emphatically not funny. I scuttle away into the trees with the bow and arrows before I can bring any more of the khan's scorn upon myself. The old man has hardly spoken a word since Sarai, and I don't particularly want to be the one who inspires him to speech. My experience is that he doesn't usually have anything nice to say.

I don't hunt, obviously. How could I? I'd probably wind up shooting out my own eye by accident. Instead, I climb a tree. It was something I used to do as a little girl to get away from my family, to think and dream in the quiet of the courtyard garden, in the time before I was a slave. Well, here is the perfect tree, and I may never have this opportunity again. Plus, I desperately need to do some thinking.

I've been operating under the assumption that slaves have exactly zero choices in life. Now, cold and exhausted, a girl disguised as a boy, tottering after the losing end of a battle, I have to second-guess that assessment. It seems to me that I've made some choices—some very *bad* choices—that have led me to this moment.

I catch myself singing under my breath. It's a nervous habit. Half the time I don't even realize I'm doing it until I'm well into a song. But this is a particularly bad venue for an audible nervous habit. For all I know, our pursuers are out in these woods, and my tuneless humming might have led them straight to us. I bite my nails to keep quiet.

I don't go back to the camp when I should. I don't know why I watch the sun set through tree branches that stretch up to the sky like arms and fingers. I don't know why I sit stiff and frozen for hour after hour, my back growing sore against the trunk as the moon rises and spins slowly through the leafless tree branches above. I'm not really planning to escape. It's just that I can't bring myself to go back yet. It's not as though anyone will come looking for me.

Maybe I hope they will.

Maybe I hope I matter enough, that's all.

It's funny. While to all outward appearances my life has changed drastically over the past couple of years, there are some things that stay the same. Like my complete insignificance, for example.

My breath slows, and I close my eyes.

"He's going to kill us," I say, although I can't remember why.

"Not if we don't get caught," says Weiji.

My brother sits on a branch across from me. I can just make out the familiar features of his face in the moonlight. It should be day, though, shouldn't it? Why is it night?

"But what if he does catch us?" I ask.

"He won't if you shut up."

We perch, each of us on our respective branches, and listen to the wind in the trees.

"Zhǎngxiōng? Older Brother?"

"What?" he asks, clearly annoyed.

"I want to go home." The memories of the ancestral altar, the feel of a beautifully crafted chair beneath me, the taste of tea on my tongue—they all threaten to overtake me like a river overflowing its banks. There's no end to the damage it could do.

"I want to go home, too," Weiji answers.

"Then let's go," I beg him. "Please."

His wound snakes down his body, forming a slow channel from his shoulder to his heart, a black chasm in the darkness.

"'Are we buffaloes,'" he says in a voice that is not his own, "'are we

tigers / That our home should be these desolate wilds?'"

Before I can say or do anything, he steps off his branch and plummets to the ground below.

I open my eyes to find myself frozen to the core and more uncomfortable than I can bear. The dream quickly disintegrates in my memory. I remember only Weiji telling me he wanted to go home, and it leaves me feeling hollow and depressed. I have no idea why he's showing up in my dreams nearly two years after his death, but it can't bode well. And I have nothing to offer his soul.

I climb down from my perch and reluctantly head back to camp, inventing a lame story in my mind about following some promising tracks that led to nothing.

A muffled shout from the direction of the camp brings me to a halt. I look around, suddenly aware of how very dark it is. Another cry reaches me, rattles my insides with trepidation. I walk forward a few paces, and when nothing jumps out to attack me, I keep walking. As I get closer, I don't know what I'm hearing, but I know it's not good.

I stop again and listen.

Another cry, sharper than the last. The faint clank of metal. Men killing men.

The memory of the violence I have seen and experienced floods me, fills my entire body, threatens to drown me with fear.

Maybe if I just stay here and wait, it will end, and I won't have to deal with it. Maybe everything will be over before it even begins. Maybe I was right about having no choices, that I won't have to make any.

But standing here and doing nothing is a choice, too.

I look around me at the moon-glazed trees, the way the ethereal light reflects off the dusting of snow on the peaks beyond. This is a world of ghosts and night. I don't want to be alone in it. What good would it do me to have my choices taken from me here, now? I will my feet to move forward.

The skirmish grows louder with each step. My heart pumps hard in my chest and my limbs go jittery. My pace is slug-like as I press on, praying the whole way that whatever is happening will be over and done with by the time I arrive. I have no such luck. The battle is still going when I reach the campsite and hide behind a completely inadequate shrub.

It isn't the Il-Khanids attacking the Kipchaks. It's just a bunch of ragged bandits out to rob a nicely outfitted envoy, not that they know or care whom they're robbing. In the end, it doesn't matter whether it's enemy soldiers or a band of criminals with swords and knives. Death is death in all its ugliness, regardless of who delivers it. Several of our men already litter the ground, and the bandits have what's left of the Kipchaks completely surrounded. I try not to look at the bodies, although I can't help but recognize what remains of Nasan, even with half his face and his brains strewn across the ground. I have to bite back the horror that threatens to overwhelm me as I peer out from my vantage point. That's when I realize that Prince Khalaf is the only Kipchak left standing.

I don't know much about war. I haven't had many opportunities to see men fight to the death, thank heaven. But even I can see that Prince Khalaf's skill in battle puts most men to shame. Outnumbered five to one, with an *uurga* in one hand and a dagger in the other, he dodges every blow or blocks it with the *uurga*'s long handle while wounding an opponent with each strike of the dagger's blade. It's almost like he's dancing. If it weren't terrifying to behold, it would be beautiful. His *deel* is blood-darkened, and I have no idea how much of it is his and how much belongs to his assailants.

At first I don't understand why he never moves from his spot, why he never seeks the advantage when he has the chance, until I realize that he is ruthlessly defending a lump of humanity that I can only assume is his father sprawled on the ground behind him.

I was mistaken. It's definitely not nothing that I feel for him. His love for his undeserving father gouges my conscience even as I think the words, *Let him die. He's not worth it.*

Prince Khalaf lassos one of the men around the neck with the *uurga* and pulls the leather loop tight when another bandit finally slips past his guard and slices into his shoulder with a long knife. The boy who gave me apples cries out in pain.

Logic abandons me. I nock an arrow, pull the bowstring taut, and release. The arrow flies through the moonlight and lodges itself in a tree three feet to the side of the bandit.

What on earth are you doing, Jinghua? the voice of reason asks somewhere in the recesses of my mind, but my instinct ignores it. My instinct nocks another arrow and sends it hurtling toward the bandit and into another tree. It's pathetic, but in that instant Prince Khalaf has the distraction he needs to strike three men in one breath.

"Halt!" calls one of the assailants, and his remaining men fall back, some of them stumbling with shocked surprise over their own dead as well as ours. I drop the bow and make a run for it, but two of them catch up quickly and drag me roughly to their captain.

"It's nothing but a little slave," one of the men points out. He hawks and spits in my face. If I weren't exactly what he says I am, I might have the dignity to wipe it away. But as it is, I just shiver, my mind blank with fear.

"Put him with the rest," orders the leader, jerking his head to the bandits' growing pile of spoils. "Not that he'll fetch much."

I have just been stolen for the second time in my life. *You're an idiot, Jinghua,* I excoriate myself. *You are such an idiot.*

A bandit pushes me past one of the dead men lying on the earth, polluting the soil with the blood that pours out of the hole in his neck. I can see bits of bone and muscle, too, and the man's lips pulled back in pain and fear. I collapse to the ground and retch. The bandit kicks me, knocking the breath out of me, but I don't care. I retch again, and strings of vomity snot stream from my nostrils. My guard has to roll me with his foot the rest of the way to the stolen goods.

"A *gerege!*" shouts one of the thieves, waving a thin gold tablet around for all to see before his leader takes it from him for examination. It's easily the most valuable item in our possession, a passport issued by the Great Khan. It guarantees safe travel and lodging across the major trade routes of the empire.

And now it's been stolen, too. I let my head fall against the earth in dejection.

Idiot.

The leader approaches Prince Khalaf, who is hauling Timur Khan to his feet. The old man has a black eye and lump on his forehead, but aside from that and a general ragged appearance, he looks none the worse for wear. The prince hoists his father's arm over his good shoulder, and he stands there with the khan hanging off his neck, panting at the bandits and staring them down with fierce eyes.

"Many thanks for this, my friend," the leader says, holding up the *gerege*. "I suppose I should kill you now, but I would sooner kill a fine painter than an artist like you. It's a rare treat to see a Mongol with such skill in hand-to-hand combat."

Timur Khan spits a bloody mixture at the bandit's feet.

"Well said," the bandit commends the khan, then returns his attention to Prince Khalaf. "To reward you for the astonishing size of your balls, I'll give you a choice. You can keep either your bow or your tent. You pick."

It's a terrible choice. Without the bow, he'll be dead within days. Without the tent, he'll be dead much sooner. And either way, I'll be on a bandits' wagon headed toward a slave market.

Any hope I had foolishly entertained about returning to Lin'an dissolves like blood into soil.

"Take the tent," Timur Khan tells his son.

"I'll take the boy," Prince Khalaf answers instead, nodding to me.

The bandits turn to look at me with curiosity, and it takes my numb mind a moment to wrap itself around what Khalaf has just said.

The boy.

Me.

He's choosing me.

No slave market. No brothel. It almost tastes like freedom. My whole body aches with abject gratitude.

"That wasn't a choice," the leader tells him.

"But it's what I choose."

The bandit laughs. "Then it's my lucky day. The bow and tent are worth five times that useless little runt."

"What are you doing?" the khan asks his son, but the prince ignores his father and continues to stare down the bandits' leader as one of the men grabs me by the arm and drags me over to the Kipchaks. Unbelievable. I couldn't make this scenario up if I tried.

"We'll take the tent," Timur Khan insists.

My panic lasts only a moment, because the leader informs him, "It's not your choice, old man."

We stand there for an hour under guard while the rest of the bandits rob trinkets from our dead and load up all our supplies.

How utterly bizarre to think of Prince Khalaf, Timur Khan, and myself as "we."

The prince has not looked at his father once through any of this, nor has he looked at me, for that matter. He continues to watch the dismantling of our hope for survival as he presses a torn-off wad of his *deel* against the wound on his shoulder. I shiver in the dark beside him.

I'll take the boy, he said. In my mind, I cup those words in my hands, fold them carefully, and place them inside the hollow pendant I wear.

For your ancestors.

We must also feed the living.

If kindness were a dagger, my heart would bleed itself dry. I doubt this soft-spoken, saintly boy will ever comprehend the staggering odds he just defied to earn my undying loyalty. Now I'm as powerless and directionless as a twig carried along on a swollen river thanks to him.

"Rotting carrion," Timur Khan curses, "Why did you bring a *gerege*? That made us an easy mark."

"It wasn't mine. And it doesn't matter anyway since it's no longer in our possession." Prince Khalaf looks drawn and pale.

"It's not too late. Tell them now. You want the tent."

"Not another word, Father. Not a word." The prince sounds angry, even if his voice is as soft as ever. The khan, who is khan no more, grunts but shuts his big mouth.

6

THE HORIZON HAS GONE PINK BY the time we watch the bandits disappear into the forest. Once they're out of sight, Prince Khalaf slumps against the tree trunk behind him and turns ashen.

"It's a shoulder wound," his father says. "You'll be fine . . . except for the fact that you chose a useless slave over a bow or a tent."

"You can't see," the prince says, his voice uncharacteristically cold.

"What was that?" Timur Khan snaps.

Prince Khalaf repeats clearly, "You. Can't. See."

The khan goes still and icy.

"You claimed it was your old hip wound keeping you out of the war with the Il-Khanids," says the prince. "But that wasn't it at all, was it? How long has this been going on?"

"You know nothing."

"I know you fired an arrow through Nasan's head. I know my friend is dead because of you and your pride." Grief and anger roughen his voice.

I've been so busy contemplating my own dire circumstances that it takes me a moment to realize I'm listening to a conversation that is none of my business while gawking at what's left of the Kipchak royal family. In my defense, it's hard to focus on social niceties when grappling with the fact that I am now stuck in the middle of a mountainous forest with no food or shelter, having given my steadfast allegiance to a beggar prince and, by association, his unpardonably rude father. I discreetly step away, although where I'm going is a mystery to me.

"I was hit on the head," the khan insists.

"I was the one who hit you on the head. I had to knock you out so that you wouldn't do any more damage," Prince Khalaf informs him.

I walk toward a thick stand of trees that lines a nearby stream, hoping the burbling water will drown out the conversation. I leave a long pause behind me, but as I hit the trees, I hear Timur Khan bark, "You!"

I freeze. It's like he fired the word into my back. I turn around to find him glaring daggers in my direction. He sure looks like he can see to me.

"Yes, my lord?"

"Tend to the prince's wound."

Is it possible to blanch and flush at the same moment? I answer, "Yes, my lord," at the same time Prince Khalaf protests, "I can tend to it myself," which makes the situation all the more mortifying.

"No, you can't," says the khan. "Your worst wound is on the left shoulder. I can tell by the way you're listing. Because I am not blind."

The prince remains silent.

"Perhaps if you were to sit by the stream, my lord?" I suggest, gesturing to the water beyond the trees that outline the clearing of our camp, or rather what remains of our camp.

Prince Khalaf sighs, but he moves in the direction of the stream. As I turn to follow him, Timur Khan shouts, "Boy!"

I walk a couple of paces before it occurs to me that he's referring to me, and I wince. Clearly, I'm not so good at this masquerading business. I turn around. "My lord?"

"If you so much as split one hair on that boy's head, I'll plunge my hand into your chest cavity, wrench your organs from your body, and take a bite out of your still-beating heart before your very eyes."

The thing is, I think he could and would do that. I find it difficult to swallow for a moment. "Understood, my lord."

"And keep your precious Song hands off him."

"Yes, my lord," I answer, although this will be difficult given the fact that I am about to attend to his son's shoulder, may the gods and ancestors help me.

I find the prince kneeling by the stream as if in prayer. His back is to me and he doesn't turn around when he hears my approach. He just says, "Leave me. I need a minute."

I mull over this command. On the one hand, a prince has just told me to leave him alone. On the other hand, a khan has ordered me to tend to this boy's wounds and has threatened to eat my still-beating heart if I screw it up. It's no contest. I step gingerly around to Prince Khalaf's front side and look down at him.

He's crying—and he begins to cry harder when he realizes I can see his tears. He turns his face away from me, but he can't hide the wet tracks streaking down his cheek, the grimace of his mouth, the shaking of his chest.

So the last remaining prince of the Kipchak Khanate is not entirely perfect after all. That's something of a relief to my staggeringly imperfect self, but his vulnerability makes him more human now, more likable. And I don't *want* to like him.

Then I remember his voice saying, *I'll take the boy,* and my heart hurts. I may not want to like him, but I do like him. Very much.

I crouch in front of him. "My lord?"

He turns his face away further.

"My lord, let me tend to your wound." I've let my voice go too high. I sound like a girl, but I doubt he notices.

"Don't tell him," he says, his face still turned away, and I know he means his father.

A memory of my own father surfaces in my mind. *She doesn't shine at all, does she?* he said to my mother. *Do something with her.* My heart clenches even harder.

"I won't, my lord," I reply.

"Don't tell him I cried."

"I won't."

"Miran, Jahangir, and now Nasan, all my men, not to mention my country. What am I going to do? I don't know what to do."

He looks to me as if I know the answer to his riddle.

I'm your problem, not your solution, I think with a pang of regret, but I certainly can't tell him that. All I can do is give him empathy with my sad, sorry face. He wipes the sleeve of his good arm across his eyes and nose, takes a few deep breaths, and pulls himself together.

"I'll need help getting this off," he says, getting down to business. He gingerly unties the belt around his waist, moving with a troubling stiffness.

"Here, allow me, my lord." I realize suddenly that I'm about to see his naked torso, that I'm going to have to touch him. My mortification pulls up a chair and settles in for the long haul. Touching a man other than my brother is as alien to me as holding a sword.

Even before I make contact, I can feel the heat of the prince's body radiating from him. With unsteady hands, I finish untying the red silk belt, which falls away to the ground. I'm halfway through undoing the clasps along his shoulder and under his armpit when I realize that I've stopped breathing. I suck in a breath of air as quietly as I can so I don't pass out as I grasp the front flap, and although I'm not touching his body at all, I can sense the hard shape of him beneath the wool as I peel it back, helping him shrug out of the right sleeve.

The left side is worse, just as Timur Khan said. I wonder if the prince might be wrong about his father's eyesight. He grits his teeth as I remove the other half of the *deel*, but a groan of pain escapes his mouth. When I finally get the first layer off, he's gone a sickly pale color and he's panting.

There's more blood than I realized, because most of it got trapped between the outer *deel* and the raw silk tunic beneath. The strength of the silk managed to stave off much of the attack, but without a knife I won't be able to cut through the fabric to remove it. I'll have to get it off over his head, and I'm thinking that this particular method is going to make the prince pass out in pure, hellish agony.

He takes a deep breath through his nose and says, "Let's get it over with."

"May I remove your turban to get the tunic off?" I ask, my voice hardly above a whisper. I have no idea who has the right to remove what in the Muslim world, but I'm pretty sure that if he knew I was a girl, I wouldn't be allowed to touch him like this, and I definitely would not be allowed to remove clothing.

Of course, the Mongols have their own way of incorporating others' religions into their own. Even so, I have to chastise myself for stomping all over his beliefs like this. Besides, I know for a fact that this whole scenario is completely forbidden from my own standpoint, whatever his beliefs are.

The prince nods even as the memory of my mother shakes her head in utter disapproval in my conscience. It's not like he can take it off himself, I reason. I doubt he can reach his left arm higher than his shoulder at this point.

I unwind the cloth around his head, and a thick sheath of glossy, black hair tumbles down his back. It's glorious, actually, the kind of hair a woman would wish for, the kind of hair *I* would wish for instead of the baby-fine mess I was born with. I fold the turban cloth and carefully set it down on the driest patch of ground I can find.

As the sun rises higher, wisps of steam billow off his tunic. I help him work his right arm through the armhole and slowly scrunch the fabric upward to take it off over his head. The heel of my hand brushes the bare skin of his ribs, and his body responds, jerking away as if I've tickled him.

"Sorry," I say, mortified.

"It's all right."

His tunic is wadded up in my hand, halfway between his waist and his shoulder, revealing the lean, taut muscles of his stomach and a strip of hair running along his breastbone. My cheeks burn with embarrassment, and I have to remind myself to keep going.

As we get his right arm out of the tunic, I can see that his arm and shoulder are badly bruised, but even so, everything up to this point goes more smoothly than I would have thought. And then I realize that the silk around the left shoulder wound is stuck to his skin and clotted thickly with blood.

"My lord . . ."

"On the count of three."

I nod, and because I know he can't manage it, I take his beautiful hair in my hands and pull it gently over his right shoulder. My face burns even more hotly, if that were possible.

"One . . . ," he says. "Two . . ."

I rip off the tunic before he gets to three, thinking the element of surprise might help.

It doesn't.

He cries out and falls forward, pressing his head into the silt loam of the stream bank. He's making awful sounds with each breath, but he does manage to avoid weeping. I'm not sure what I should do. Should I help him up? Should I let him recover for a few minutes?

"My lord?" I ask tentatively.

"What's going on over there?" Timur Khan yells from the camp. "That slave had better not be as worthless as I think he is."

Oh, heavens, I hope my still-beating heart remains in my chest cavity after all this is said and done.

"It's all right," Khalaf calls back, even though he looks anything but all right. With audible effort, he manages to push himself back into a kneeling position with his right hand. Fresh blood is seeping out of a straight slit in his shoulder. I cover my mouth at the sight of it.

"I'm sorry, my lord."

He hasn't quite caught his breath to answer, but he shakes his head.

"Shall I clean it now?" I ask.

"Yes," he breathes.

I cup the cold mountain water in my hands and pour it on the wound. He moans again, but gasps for me to keep going. I pour clean water from my cupped hands over the wound until blood no longer stains the skin on each side of the wound and my fingers go numb with cold.

"Don't tell my father you're doing this." His voice is nearly as ashen as his face.

"What, my lord?"

"Washing the wound with water. Most of my people believe that water is a sacred spirit. My blood pollutes the water."

This boy is a saint. How could his blood pollute anything? "That's a Mongol belief, isn't it?" I say. "I thought your father was a Muslim now."

"My father is many things," he answers in a threadbare voice. "I keep a needle and some sinew in the pocket of my *deel*. Can you stitch it up?"

"I think I can, my lord. I know how to sew." *Badly,* I add in my head.

"That's all this is," he tells me. "It's just sewing."

I riffle through his pockets until I find the needle and sinew, and then I warm my fingers in my armpits for a minute before beginning. At the first jab of the needle, he stiffens and breathes hard through his nose.

"My lord?"

"Keep going. Just keep going."

I choose my pace carefully, quickly enough to get it over with and slowly enough to get it done right, not that I know what "right" is in this situation. I try not to think too hard on exactly what it is I'm sewing together. The prince keeps his breathing slow and even.

I understand that her embroidery is also dreadful, my father's voice says in my mind. I push it away. This is not embroidery. I can do this.

"I owe you thanks," the prince says.

I pause in my work.

"Don't stop," he commands, adding softly, "please."

I keep working. "You don't owe me anything, my lord."

"You helped me when I needed it most, when you fired your arrows. We'd be dead if it weren't for you."

The enormity of the night presses down on me. "It was nothing," I mumble.

"It wasn't 'nothing,'" he insists, but I don't respond. "I thought you had run off."

"I'm still here."

Forever. A slave to my dying day. I don't want to think about that now, so I focus on the stitching, on the needle and sinew moving in and out through skin and muscle. My hand moves with the same cadence and rhythm of my mother's hand if not as elegantly.

"I'm the one who should be thanking you, my lord," I say impulsively before I immediately regret having said anything at all. I wonder if he can hear the crushing shame in my voice.

"It was nothing," he says, repeating my words back to me, and even in his pain and exhaustion, he manages to smile at me, that same smile from the night we met. At this moment, I loathe myself. I am lower than dirt, truly I am.

"What's your name?" he asks.

It makes sense that he would ask this question at some point. But nothing's as it should be anymore, and here I am, floundering at how to answer the most basic question of all.

"Baraq," I answer. It was the name of one of the slave boys back in Sarai. They actually called me Adelma in Timur Khan's palace, but that's a girl's name, and I'm not supposed to be a girl.

He turns his head to look at me, taking his shoulder slightly out of my reach with him. "And what did your mother call you?"

I gaze back at him for some moments, feeling like he's stripping away all my bristly, hard parts one by one until I'm left with nothing but my infinite weakness.

"Jinghua," I tell him.

My real name.

A *girl's* name.

Every salty word and phrase I know screams inside me, haranguing me for my carelessness. *Please, don't let him know how to speak Hanyu,* I pray. *Please, please, please.* I try to keep my face steady so he won't detect my panic.

"Jinghua," he repeats. Badly. His intonations are off, and it sounds like he's calling me "quiet flower." I nod anyway, and, despite my nerves, I feel like I might cry, hearing something resembling my own name from someone else's lips. It's been months. If he suspects my true gender, he doesn't let on, to my infinite relief, which I also hide from him.

"Jinghua," he says again, his voice heavy with exhaustion, his eyes bottomless. "My name is Khalaf. It's nice to meet you."

I nod again like I'm mentally incapacitated. He shifts his body to sit on his rear. He pulls up his knees and rests his battered head on them, letting his hair stream down his right side. I resume my stitching.

"It's nice to meet you, too, my lord," I finally think to say.

"Khalaf," he corrects me, his voice muffled by his knees.

"Yes, my lord," I answer. I can't and I won't call him by his name to his face. But in the safety of my own mind, I'm already his friend, and I call him Khalaf.

Khalaf walks before me back to our campsite. There's no way I'm walking in first, just in case Timur Khan still wants to wrap my intestines around my throat or yank my teeth out or something else along those lines.

I need not have worried. The khan has spent his time constructing a rough awning out of the *deels* of our dead, which he has draped over a boulder on one side and a couple of saplings on the other. He's already underneath the shelter, asleep. He coughs and sputters, "Milk-blooded il-khan," before continuing with his snoring.

Khalaf staggers into the shelter without a backward glance. He lies down beside his father, and I suspect he's already asleep by the time he hits the ground.

I step close to the shelter, but I'm not sure if I'm allowed inside. Plus, I can smell the blood on the *deels* the khan used. Heaven forbid the man wash them first. So, despite the fact that I'm sore and exhausted, I spend the rest of the morning chasing away the vultures while I tug the wool *deels* from the bodies of the two least damaged former humans littering the field of skirmish. I take the robes down to the stream to wash them as best I can, and may Timur Khan and his Mongol beliefs about blood and water be damned. I'm not going to spend the rest of my days in a tent that reeks of death.

As I dunk the fabric in the icy water and slap and scrub it on a stone, I get lost in my thoughts. Thinking probably isn't the best course of action right now, but I can't turn off my mind. I can't even begin to consider the larger philosophical ramifications of my choices, so I decide to contemplate more basic issues: where we'll find food, how we'll get out of the mountains, where we'll go. Or, more accurately, *if* we find food, *if* we get out of the mountains, *if* we find somewhere to go.

Those are big "ifs."

I also contemplate the fact that I am somehow still among the living.

The only reason Timur Khan isn't dead is because he is ludicrously lucky. The only reason Khalaf isn't dead is because he is brave beyond all measure. And the only reason I'm not dead is because I was singing in a tree like an idiot.

7

I DECIDE THAT IF I'M GOING to think of the prince as Khalaf, I may as well call the khan Timur, if only in the private recesses of my mind. Why not? He's no better than I am now, is he? And it gives me a nice, petty thrill every time I think it: Timur.

In the beginning, Timur—oh blessed, smug contempt—is stoic, but as the days of trudging along rough paths and through thorny gullies stretch into a week with little to eat but bitter herbs and roots, he becomes sulky.

"Rally our forces," he says in a nasal, mocking voice. "Fight off Hulegu Il-Khan and his milk-blooded army. Brilliant."

Khalaf heaves a long-suffering sigh. "We made that plan together, Father." He doesn't mention his brothers by name, but their deaths hang heavily in the air.

I don't think Khalaf is more than eighteen or nineteen years old, but he's starting to look older. There is the wound on his shoulder, which is slow to heal, and the weight of the world that pushes down on the burgeoning frame of his body. He's the one who has to find food, since I have no idea what food looks like here and Timur claims that he is a khan and shouldn't have to fend for himself. Maybe Khalaf is right about the old man's eyesight after all.

"This was your idea," Timur accuses Khalaf as he yanks his fraying brocade *deel* from yet another thorn bush.

"If you had had a better plan, you were welcome to have shared it." Khalaf's voice is, as ever, soft, but it's lacking its usual serenity.

"And how is your idea holding up, young mustang? Are you finding your books and your learning helpful now?"

"More helpful than complaining, I should think," Khalaf replies, and he picks up his pace, marching several steps ahead of us. Since I have no desire to lag behind with Timur, I scramble to catch up and follow behind him on the narrow path that winds its way to nowhere in particular.

"This is a rutting goat path," Timur grumbles some time later. "We're traversing the world on a path meant for rutting goats."

"Apropos," Khalaf utters, so softly that Timur doesn't hear him. "For one of us at least."

And so I trudge along for hours between a wounded prince and an old goat.

Khalaf and I stand on the path waiting for Timur, who has gone off into the trees to relieve himself. The old goat is absent an inordinately long time.

"Everything all right?" Khalaf calls into the forest.

"What do you think?" is Timur's response, his terse grunting muffled by trees and distance. I don't know how the man can spend so much time pooping. We've found barely enough food to keep us living. I guess our steady diet of roots and herbs disagrees with him.

"Well, I'm sitting," Khalaf tells me as he plunks himself down on the grass by the side of the track. "I have a feeling we're going to be here for a while."

I follow suit, and several minutes of awkward silence pass between us. At least, it's awkward for me. I doubt Khalaf has been awkward a day in his life. He does look weary, though, and I'm sure his shoulder must be bothering him. Even so, I decide to take this opportunity to ask some questions with Timur out of the way. If I'm going to throw my lot in with the prince, I may as well be armed with at least a little bit of knowledge.

"My lord, there are a few things I don't quite understand," I say, remembering to pitch my voice low.

Khalaf breathes a laugh through his nose. "A few things?"

"I've heard you say that many believe Timur Khan has a better claim to the throne of the empire than the Great Khan does. If that's the case, why isn't he the Great Khan?"

The prince rubs at his eyes. "We'd have to go back nearly a hundred years to answer that question."

I look at him expectantly. He's worn-out, but when he sees that I'm awaiting his response, he relents and begins the lesson.

"Genghis Khan had four sons: Jochi, Chagatai, Ogodei, and Tolui. Before he died, he tried to settle the matter of succession with them. In Mongol families, when a father passes away, each son receives a certain portion of livestock as well as an allotment of grazing land. For Genghis, the empire was simply an extension of that tradition. Each son would get his own khanate to rule, but in addition, one of them would be Great Khan to oversee the administration of the empire and take responsibility for foreign affairs with his brothers as advisers. When Genghis gathered the four sons to discuss this, he called on his oldest son, Jochi, to speak first, which singled out Jochi as his choice to succeed him. Chagatai, the second son, protested and declared outright that Jochi was a bastard, literally. The two brothers brawled right there in front of their father. And because neither Jochi nor Chagatai could accept the other as Great Khan at that point, Jochi nominated the third brother, Ogodei, for the position, and Chagatai agreed. But the two oldest sons of Genghis Khan would never forgive each other, and my father, as Jochi's grandson, is not overly fond of the Chagataiyids either.

"What about the youngest brother?" I ask.

"Tolui was the prince of the hearth. For Mongols, the youngest son keeps the hearth fire burning and protects the home. So

Tolui inherited the Mongol homelands where Genghis first rose to power."

"Does that mean you're the prince of the hearth, too? Is that why your brothers were so angry when your father called on you first to discuss the war with the Il-Khanids?"

It isn't until after the words have left my mouth that it occurs to me how inappropriate the question is. Khalaf looks at me like I've grown a third arm out of my head.

I cringe. "Forgive me, my lord. That was forward of me."

"Not at all," he murmurs. It seems that he is, in fact, capable of feeling awkward. "Electing Ogodei as Great Khan brought a temporary peace among the brothers, but in the long run it wasn't the best choice. Ogodei was a drunk, you see."

"So he was the Great Khan but not a great khan."

Khalaf gives me that look again, his eyes narrowing as if he needed to bring me into better focus. It gives me the sensation that he can see right through me. I drop my gaze and add, "My lord."

"Khalaf," he corrects me. "You're a remarkably good student, Jinghua, very . . . clever."

You are remarkably stupid, Jinghua, I tell myself. I'm a slave. I'm not supposed to be clever. Of all people, it's Timur who comes to my rescue with a loud grunt from the trees.

"Father?" Khalaf calls.

"Leave me the hell alone," Timur shouts back.

I use the distraction to shift Khalaf's focus back to our history lesson. "So, the third son, Ogodei, became the Great Khan.

What happened after that?"

"Ogodei ruled for over ten years, and when he died, his son who succeeded him was also a drunk and a disaster. So the heirs of Genghis Khan's youngest son, Tolui, staged a coup d'état about thirty years ago. The current Great Khan is Tolui's son, and he sits on his throne today because his family overthrew Ogodei's line. However, Genghis Khan's law clearly states that all family members must agree on the election of a Great Khan, and my father did not agree to this election."

"Did your father rebel against the new Great Khan?"

"He didn't like it, but he felt that the empire would be stronger if all the khanates were united, at least on the face of things." Khalaf looks off into the trees where his father disappeared ten minutes ago and adds, "Much good it's done him."

"And what does Hulegu Il-Khan have to do with any of this? Why did he attack the Kipchak Khanate?"

Khalaf tears his attention away from the trees, but his worry for his father is still plastered over his face. "Once Genghis's heirs turned against each other, the Muslim kingdoms to the south of the Kipchak Khanate stopped paying tribute to the empire," he explains to me, "which is why the Great Khan sent his brother Hulegu to bring them back in line by force. Hulegu is now il-khan, which means he acts as the Great Khan's regent in Persia and Iraq. Hulegu has also been chipping away at the borders of the Kipchak Khanate, so he and my father have had several run-ins already. The il-khan's sacking of Baghdad was the last straw.

Hence, the war. Hence, here we are."

And I thought my family had problems. What kind of mess have I gotten myself into?

"Won't the Great Khan intervene?" I wonder aloud.

"I doubt it," says Khalaf, looking even more exhausted. "My father played nicely with the Great Khan in the eyes of the outside world, but he has always been more than happy to break a few rules if it benefitted himself and the Kipchak Khanate. At the end of the day, Timur Khan is Jochi's grandson, and everyone knows that he would gladly rule the empire if anyone let him. And between you and me, much as I hate to admit it, he's probably the best qualified for the job."

"Damn right," says Timur, who now stands over us like a monstrous giant in the mountains.

I didn't hear him sneak up on us, and it's clear from Khalaf's pained grimace that he didn't either. "Shall we move on?" he says as he rises to his feet.

We hike through the unending Caucasus range, losing track of the days, growing ill with cold and hunger, trudging along in silence, until one morning Timur just stops. He comes to a halt on a bluff overlooking a plain in the distance, and between us and that plain is a series of gulches filled with brambles, an impenetrable wall that stands between us and the will to live. Khalaf and I stand behind him as he sits down like a defiant elephant and refuses to move.

"Would that I had died with them," Timur says without looking at either of us. He has turned to stone, as massive and immovable as the boulders that litter the mountains, moss-grown, unmoving.

The word "them" plants itself, takes root, and grows between Khalaf and his father.

Them.

Miran and Jahangir, the brothers who never came home.

It's a reminder that my own brother never came home either, a fact that stings every single time I think of him. I touch the pendant under my shirt.

Khalaf kneels beside his father and places a hand on his shoulder. "There's no use agonizing over our misfortunes. We have no choice but to submit ourselves to the will of God. If He has the power to pluck the crown from your head, does He not also possess the power to restore you?"

Timur stares blankly at the rough terrain that stretches before us. The impenetrable landscape sneers at me, telling me that I have no one to blame but myself for this. Gaunt with hunger and guilt, I sway woozily on my feet.

"'For truly with hardship comes ease,'" Khalaf continues, his voice like a soft blanket, his outlook stunningly hopeful. "I have faith that He will lift us out of this deplorable condition."

"I'll await that day right here, then," Timur says. "You can take your faith and find a way out of this hell. Personally, I prefer death to such an existence."

Khalaf looks to me with helpless eyes, but to be honest, I can see Timur's point. My feet throb and bleed in their ill-fitting boots, and I'm so dehydrated I can't even muster tears. A feverish wave washes over me as I tumble to the ground. I lie in the rough grass and watch the pinkening clouds spin overhead. Khalaf gazes down at me. It's a pretty good way to die, really: sunset, clouds, a prince (even if the prince in question is looking green around the gills these days). Not many people could boast of such a death.

Khalaf turns his head toward Timur. I watch his larynx move under the smooth skin of his neck as he says, "Maybe there's another trail that will give us access to the plain. Why don't I go see if I can find one."

"Knock yourself out," Timur answers as I slip into my feverish mind.

I'm singing.

Jasmine flower.

A vague series of images flashes before me: a porcelain duck atop a green-glazed lotus blossom, the hills rising over the West Lake, the swift current of the river rushing past.

My brother stands at the door, haloed by the red silk of the curtain behind him. He gazes longingly at the portrait he holds in his hand. When he turns it toward me, I see a girl's perfect face staring back at me with cold, reptilian eyes.

Let me pluck you down, *I sing,* and give you to the one I love.

I'm draped across the bumpy terrain of Khalaf's knees. He's cradling my head in the crook of his arm. I assume this is part of the dream, but then he pours cool water down my throat. I sputter and choke on it.

I crash through the water's surface as if it were a wall of ice. I'm drowning. Drowning.

My arms thrash.

"Shh. You need to drink." He wraps my arms up in his and murmurs to me in the kind of voice a man uses with a feral dog or a jittery horse. My body goes slack. I'm as helpless as a baby.

Timur's craggy head comes into view, blocking out the sun that shines around the edges of his wild, matted hair.

"We should ditch her. She's dead weight at this point."

"You'd leave this poor little bird here to die alone?" Khalaf asks.

I barely have the mental capacity to follow the conversation, much less join in. I swallow the trickle of water that Khalaf squeezes into my mouth from a damp cloth.

"She's not a little bird. She's a slave," says Timur. "And not a very pretty one at that. There'll be girls enough to bed when we get out of this mess."

They're calling me "her" and "she." I've been caught. *"Wǒ de tiān nǎ,"* I groan in Hanyu. *Oh, my heaven.* I ease back into the dream. There's a garden behind my eyes with a little hill and a footbridge over a creek, and peach blossoms bobbing on a sunny day. I slide my slim fingers between the lotus blossoms of the goldfish pond. The scent of jasmine rides the breeze. My brother, Weiji, is somewhere nearby, hiding, waiting for me to find him.

Jasmine flower, I sing.

I can no longer see Khalaf, but I hear his unmistakable voice. "She stayed with us when none of the other servants would. She came to our aid when we were under attack. She risked her life for us."

For you. I don't know if I've said this in my real voice or in my dream voice.

"*You* saved us," says Timur. "Not her. She was nowhere to be found until the end. And she was pretending to be a boy. I don't trust her. We should leave her to fend for herself like the lying dog she is."

If Khalaf answers, I don't hear him. I taste sweet water in my mouth and I watch the bamboo in my family's garden sway in the wind as I sing.

Jasmine flower
Your willowy stems clustered with sweet-smelling buds

8

WHEN I WAKE, IT'S NIGHT, BUT no one has erected the makeshift tent. I'm lying by the embers of a small fire that cast a glow against Timur's sleeping bulk across from me. Beside him, Khalaf is sitting up, staring off to his right. Here, in the middle of nowhere, half starved and swathed in ragged wool, he still manages to look poised. I doubt his brothers could have carried this off. He has a serenity about him they never had, that most of us will never have. By now, the other princes would have grown as rough as Timur has, and it would have been impossible to discern them from common beggars. Khalaf doesn't look like a beggar to me.

I can't even let myself think how he looks.

His hair still hangs loose down his back. He's got the topmost portion knotted behind his head to keep it out of his face. That's when I realize that the soft cloth beneath me is his turban. His generosity, his kindness, the very *goodness* of him are almost as infuriating as his father's gruff insults.

When he turns his head and notices I'm awake, I feel that dagger-in-the-heart sensation again and try to push it away.

"Hello," he says, the first word he ever spoke to me back in Sarai.

"Hello," I reply. My voice is scratchy, my throat dry.

"Can you sit up? There's fruit to eat."

I push myself up, but even that small motion makes my head spin. My eyes widen as I discover a pile of quinces and late-season pomegranates heaped on the ground beside me. Khalaf turns his head away again, maybe so that I can gorge myself in relative privacy.

"Go slowly," he urges without looking at me. "It'll take your stomach time to adjust to having decent food in it again."

"Thank you, my lord." My mouth is already full of half-masticated quince.

"Khalaf."

I'm too busy chewing to answer. Oh, my heaven, I have never eaten so well. I will treasure this fruit all the days of my life, however long that may be.

"You lied to me," he says, his face still turned away, his profile lit by the flickering light.

I stop chewing. There's no point in playing dumb. I swallow

and say, "I didn't lie to you exactly."

"Fine, then. You deceived me."

I consider this. "Yes," I agree. "I deceived you."

He turns back to me, his expression inscrutable. "Why?"

"Would you have taken me with you if you had known I was a girl?"

"Of course not. This is no place for a girl."

"This is no place for anyone."

"You shouldn't be here," he insists.

"Where else would I go?"

He has no idea how deep this question runs for me. He hugs his arms across his chest and brings his right hand to his mouth, flicking at his bottom lip with his thumb. "I should have known," he chastises himself. "Now that I'm looking at you, you're very clearly . . ." He clears his throat and brings his hand back down, folding his arms tighter in front of himself. "Female," he finishes.

"Forgive me, my lord."

"You were that girl with the apples. It didn't occur to me until now, but that was you."

"Yes." I dip my head, partly because I'm ashamed of myself and partly because I'm pleased that he does remember me after all.

"Do you need to make an offering to your ancestors?" he asks, his cool tone replaced by a gentleness that inspires pointless, stupid tears to pool on the rims of my eyes.

In my feverish state, I had returned home and played hide-and-seek with my brother. Waking up in the present, thousands of *lǐ* from Lin'an, feels like losing Weiji all over again. I blot my eyes dry with my sleeve and answer, "I will soon. Thank you, my lord."

He nods. After a brief silence, he says, "When we lost the war with the Il-Khanate, all the other servants fled, but not you. Why?"

His eyes probe my face. The expression isn't suspicious exactly, but it's clear he believes there's more to my story than simple loyalty. And really, why *am* I here? I keep asking myself the same thing, but I haven't found a decent answer to tell myself yet, much less him.

"You gave me apples," I reply. It's true enough.

"You've risked life and limb and shared in our anguish because of apples?"

"Cruelty is easy to repay, my lord. Kindness is another matter."

He looks off into the trees, mulling this over. I suspect he doesn't buy it, not entirely. "I wish you would stop 'my lord'-ing me" is all he says.

I taste the sounds of his name in my mouth, feel them floating on the surface of my teeth. *Khalaf.* It begins with an explosion and ends in a whisper.

"You are a prince, my lord, not a slave," I tell him.

He gives me a humorless laugh. "Tell that to heaven."

I can't help but raise my eyebrows at this uncharacteristic hint of bitterness, a gesture that doesn't go unnoticed. He sighs and says, "Forgive me. God has shown me the steep pass, and I must climb it, much as I may not want to."

"The 'steep pass,' my lord?"

He tilts his face toward the heavens and recites a passage, I assume, from the holy book of his faith.

> *"And what will apprise thee of the steep pass?*
> *[It is] the freeing of a slave,*
> *or giving food at a time of famine*
> *to an orphan near of kin,*
> *or an indigent clinging to the dust,*
> *while being one of those who believe and exhort one another to*
> *patience, and exhort one another to compassion.*
> *Those are the companions of the right."*

"There," he says to me, "if I am not a slave as you say, perhaps it is because I have been set free by the compassionate as all slaves should be. That is the will of God."

He eyes me on the word "compassionate," as if I am the one who could free him from his misfortune. What can I say to that? It's easy to speak philosophically of slavery when you're only wearing the yoke metaphorically. I take a moment to finger the duck's head pendant to make sure it's still there before changing the subject. "My lord, where are we?"

"I don't know. It's an oasis of some kind. I found a trail that leads out to the plain, and this was at the end of it." He nods in the direction behind me and says, "There's a fountain."

I turn around and find, to my amazement, a three-tiered

fountain brimming water over its edges, tinkling and dripping. I can't believe I didn't notice the sound until now.

"And there's an orchard all around us," he tells me.

I can see now that we're camped in a grove of trees, the fruit uplit in the firelight. I suspect that it will look positively miraculous in the morning light.

As I begin to break open a pomegranate, I'm tempted to ask how I got here. I also *don't* want to ask how I got here. Or how they figured out I was a girl. The answer to both these questions is likely more humiliating than I can bear at this moment. Instead, I say, "How is your shoulder, my lord?"

"Better. May I ask you something?"

I nod. Does he really think I can tell a prince no?

"You have welts all over your back," he says.

Oh, my heaven, he has seen way too much of me. A combination of worry and humiliation makes me want to hide under the nearest rock, although it's clear he has no idea how cleanly he has hit the mark. I remember in vivid detail the sensation of my hip bumping against him, the way the tea sprayed all over his arm, the exact moment my life turned so hard I lost hold of it altogether. And I'll never get it back.

"That wasn't a question," I answer stiffly.

"They're not old scars. That happened recently."

"Yes," I say, wishing he would just leave it alone.

"Who did that to you?"

I regard him, his smooth cheeks lit by firelight, his eyes as innocent as those of a newborn fawn. The smartest person I have ever met is, in many ways, the most ignorant, too. It makes me wistful for the naive girl I used to be.

"The head servant beat me, my lord," I tell him.

"Why?"

My disbelief in his callowness deepens. This boy is as green as grass. "I bumped into you. I made you spill your tea."

He gapes at me like I slapped him in the face. "And you were beaten for that?"

"Of course, my lord."

His long stare—the pained eyes—make me look away.

"I'm sorry, Jinghua," he says. "I'm so sorry."

I shrug it off, because I can't begin to accept an apology from a boy who owes me nothing. I continue to eat, my eyes cast downward. Neither of us speaks until Khalaf finally breaks the silence.

"What were you singing?" he asks.

"My lord?"

"You've been singing the same song over and over for the past two days. You don't remember?"

So Khalaf or Timur carried me here. One or both of them saw all or part of me naked, and I've been singing in my delirium. My stomach turns as it digests a cocktail of fruit and mortification. I slow the pace of my eating as instructed, and I shake my head.

"No, I guess you wouldn't remember, would you?" He licks his lips and begins to hum a tune. Music is, perhaps, not his gift, and it takes me a moment to recognize the melody. He stops humming and asks, "Do you know it?"

"Yes." I pop a pomegranate seed into my mouth and focus my attention on the fruit staining my hands red.

"What is it?"

"'Mòlìhuā,'" I answer shortly, wishing he'd leave it alone. It's a song that reminds me of home, and thinking of it makes me all the more homesick. I pluck another seed from the pith and poke it into my mouth.

"'Mòlìhuā'?" he repeats.

I nod.

"Is that Hanyu?"

I nod again.

"Will you sing it?"

I choke on the seed, coughing so hard that I launch it from the back of my throat across the fire. It hits the ground, bounces once, and skitters across the dirt, stopping at Khalaf's foot. *Smooth, Jinghua. Real smooth.*

"You want me to sing?" I ask.

"Yes."

"Now?"

He picks up a long, sturdy stick by the fire and pokes at the embers, sending up little tendrils of flame. "If it pleases you," he says.

"Won't I wake your father?"

Timur picks this exact moment to let an earth-shattering

snore vibrate through his mighty nostrils and out the cavern of his open mouth.

Khalaf laughs, a genuine laugh. It's a wonderful sound accompanied by white teeth and squished eyelids and a dimple that is deeper than I realized. "I don't think he'll notice," he says, still smiling.

When he smiles his whole face lights up. I may as well go back to being a baby cradled in his arms, I'm that helpless.

So I sing for him.

At first, my voice wavers horribly like an old lady warbling to her cats. I stop, take a deep breath, close my eyes, and begin again.

Mòlìhuā . . .

As I sing, I return to my feverish dream, laughing, hiding from my brother in the garden back home when we were very young. He chased me from bush to bush, but he could never catch up to me.

Jasmine flower.

It's as if Weiji is captured inside the song, and if I just sing it long enough, I'll be able to keep him here with me. But when the song ends, I open my eyes and find myself irrationally crushed to be sitting in the middle of nowhere, thousands of *lì* away from a home that I will never see again and a family that no longer exists.

"What does it mean?" Khalaf asks me in the silence that follows.

The desire to be alone, to nestle my memories back into place, fills me. But since there is nowhere to go, I translate for him, halt-ingly, having to think over the words in my head as I go.

Jasmine flower
Your willowy stems clustered with sweet-smelling buds
Fragrant and white, everyone praises your beauty
Let me pluck you down
And give you to the one I love

He says nothing at first. He just cocks his head to the side and rubs his lip again. I am coming to recognize this gesture as Khalaf's Thinking Face.

"So that's the song, then," I babble like a lunatic, squirming under the intensity of his gaze. There's a thick chunk of quince pulp stuck between my back teeth, and I'm itching to pull it out, but obviously I can't at the moment without looking like an even bigger idiot.

"That's lovely."

"Is it?" I ask faintly.

"Not just the poetry of it. I mean, your voice. It's very beautiful."

No one has ever used the word "beautiful" in association with me, and now I have to add this to the list of reasons why my life is inextricably intertwined with Khalaf's. I stare across the fire at him with an incongruous mixture of gratitude and resentment as he holds my gaze a few moments longer than is comfortable. This would all be easier to bear if he weren't quite so lovely himself.

He turns his concentration back to the fire and begins to poke at the orange coals with the stick as Timur's big-barreled chuckle cuts through the air like an unwelcome guest at dinner.

"You're right, Khalaf," he says. "She is a little bird."

9

FOR FIVE DAYS WE HEAD SOUTH in a steady descent, each of us hauling as much fruit as we can carry. The path opens up onto a lush plain just south of the Caspian Sea, and whereas the mountains were cool, the air down here is warm and muggy.

I haven't seen a town in so long that I had almost forgotten that such things exist, as if the world had become a wilderness bent on killing us and nothing more. Now here we are sitting in the shade of a tangerine tree just outside a niceish town where actual people live normal, everyday lives while the late-afternoon sun scorches the earth. The air seems impossibly hot for spring, although my weeks shivering in the mountains may have changed my perspective on temperature. I suppose I should be thrilled to find myself back in something resembling civilization, but I've got a bad feeling about this. If poverty is a great equalizer, civilization tucks rank and propriety right back into place—as Timur quickly proves.

"Just because Hulegu Il-Khan didn't follow us through the mountains doesn't mean he didn't figure out where we went," Timur says to Khalaf. "This could be dangerous."

"I know." Khalaf is burnishing his bottom lip with his thumb. I kick myself internally for being jealous of that thumb. I wonder if my circumstances would be different if Khalaf had been an ugly egg instead of a wonderful human being.

With nice lips.

I mentally kick myself again.

"We can't go in there looking like paupers," Timur adds.

"Beggars can't be choosers, Father."

"We aren't beggars."

"Aren't we?"

Timur waves his son's comment away with an impatient huff. "We need money."

Oh, I've got a *really* bad feeling about this.

Khalaf is either too naive or too exhausted to understand what Timur is getting at, because he rubs his tired eyes with the heels of his hands and sighs. "What we need is shelter, followed closely by fresh water and food."

"Which one acquires with money."

"We don't have any money," Khalaf says, his exasperation making a rare appearance.

"Sure we do." Timur looks to me, and I feel as though my entrails have suddenly liquefied.

"What?" Khalaf asks, catching up. "Jinghua? You want to sell Jinghua?"

My name, twice over, feels like a bludgeon.

"No, I want to sell this fine garment I'm wearing," says Timur as he clutches at what remains of his *deel*, which is crusted with filth and rent by brambles. "Yes, of course we're going to sell her."

The eloquent Khalaf rendered speechless is as terrifying as the very prospect of being sold. Again. I'd be flattered that this is shocking to him, that my going away would make him unhappy or, at the very least, uncomfortable, if my own self-preservation hadn't just sent me into a mad panic.

Timur grins at his son's discomfort until Khalaf finally asks, "How can you even contemplate such a thing?"

"She's a slave, isn't she?"

"No, she isn't just a . . . You can't sell her like a . . . like . . ."

"Like what? A horse? A camel? Chattel? That's what she is."

Chattel? I'm *chattel*?

"But—" Khalaf begins.

"There are far prettier slaves in the world, boy. You need to let this one go."

Khalaf's ears turn red either from anger or embarrassment, possibly both. If I weren't teetering on the edge of disaster, I'd find Timur's insinuation humiliating, too. "It isn't like that," Khalaf insists.

"Oh, isn't it?"

"No. It isn't."

I'm hardly listening by this point. My mind has whirred into action, trying to figure out how I'll escape and where I'll go. The running part is easy enough—Timur is too slow and (probably) too blind to catch me, and I doubt Khalaf would hunt me down. Where I'll go is another matter. And there are so many things left undone, so many loose threads tangling into impenetrable knots.

"We owe her our lives," Khalaf argues. "You can't sell her."

"We can sell her and we will sell her," says Timur.

I want to kick myself as I stand here, watching two men argue my fate and powerless to do anything about it. I could have ended all this back in Sarai. I could have been halfway home by now.

But I already know that isn't true, even before I'm finished thinking it. Who am I kidding?

Timur folds his arms. "If you had chosen a tent or a bow back in the Caucasus, we wouldn't be at the edge of death toting around a third mouth as it is."

Khalaf draws himself up, squares his shoulders. He looks very regal in the gesture, and it would be an impressive sight if his father were not quite so enormous. "I won't allow it," he says.

"What did you just say to me?"

"I said—"

Timur takes one aggressive stomp toward his son, bending down so that he's nose to nose with Khalaf.

"Am I or am I not your khan?" Timur demands.

Khalaf says nothing. He draws a long breath through his nostrils, but it never reappears. He remains silent with his breath pent up inside him.

"Answer me."

"Yes, my lord, but—"

"Cancerous lamb's balls, stop thinking with your rocks and start thinking with your head! The Eternal Blue Sky knows I've paid enough tutors to fill it to bursting. That slave is our one and only asset." He points at me as if he could skewer me with his thick forefinger. "We are going to liquidate that asset, and we are going to buy food and shelter, the need of which you have already so astutely pointed out, so that we can regroup and figure out our next steps. We need money. She is money. Do you understand?"

Khalaf looks to me with damp, wild eyes, as if I could do anything to help him or myself. But the only one who could help either of us is Khalaf. And Khalaf is doing nothing.

"Do you understand, boy?" Timur repeats.

Khalaf's dignity and poise have melted into anguish. He looks to me and then to Timur and then back to me again, and nowhere can he find an answer that will suit. Shit all over the girl you believe to have saved your life or disrespect your father: it's a moral dilemma par excellence for a philosophical prince.

He regards his father smoldering above him, inches from his face, and he bows his head. "Yes, my lord," he says.

Well, what did you expect? I ask myself brutally. *Kindness isn't an eternal font. At some point it has to run dry.* Given the circumstances, I have no right to feel hurt or offended, but I do anyway. Khalaf's defection bruises me badly.

You have nothing left to lose, I urge myself. *Just run.*

But it's too late to run, because a stranger is standing at the edge of shade cast by the canopy of the tree. The man smiles with congeniality, although I can't imagine why. What a scene we must make, all of us ragged and filthy.

The man speaks to Timur in a language I don't recognize, and Khalaf answers cautiously. Of course he knows whatever language this is. He probably picked it up in his spare time when he wasn't busy defining financial systems for an entire empire or mapping the trajectory of a comet across the heavens—he's done that, too.

"So sorry to disturb you," the man says in accented Mongolian, his teeth glowing in the shadows of the canopy as he walks nearer. He's an older man, though not as old as Timur. He wears a blue vest over a pale yellow kaftan and a turban around his head like Khalaf. "You'll have to forgive my intrusion. I didn't see you there at first, but may I say you have the right idea? There isn't a decent shade tree in the village, let me tell you, so I always come out here when it gets this hot."

"You're welcome to join us, sir, if you don't mind the company of weary travelers," Timur says civilly enough, but both he and Khalaf widen their stances, their bodies wound tight for battle just in case. They look remarkably unruffled, united side by side as if they hadn't been at each other's throats moments ago.

I imagine that I look like a three-days-dead corpse, but no

one's paying much attention to me anyway. To hell with all of them. My ridiculous hurt feelings have quickly transformed into seething anger and resentment. Let the khan and his bookish son get caught by the il-khan. I'm running the first chance I get.

"You look as if you've traveled a great distance," the man comments, stepping forward. He adds politely, "If you don't mind my saying."

"Not at all," Timur answers stiffly. "Perhaps you can tell us what town this is?"

The man raises his eyebrows. "Certainly. You've reached Rasht."

Timur glances at Khalaf, who shakes his head. I haven't heard of Rasht either, so I guess that makes three of us who have no idea where we are.

"You must have come a long way if you haven't heard of it," the man says.

"We have," says Timur. "We were traveling with several other merchants through Circassia when we were attacked by robbers. They left me and my son alive, but they abandoned us in our current state of misfortune. We wandered here without knowing where we were going."

And me! I want to scream. *I'm still alive, too, you stupid egg!*

"Dreadful." The man shakes his head. He certainly *seems* nice—nicer than the jerks I'm traveling with, at any rate. "You must stay with me until you have recovered your strength."

"We cannot trespass on your kindness, sir," Khalaf tells him,

but the stranger is so effusive in his sympathy, so cordial in offering hospitality, that it would be prohibitively impolite to refuse
his invitation. The man ventures out into the heat to notify his
household, and we follow. I still seem to be along for the ride, at
least for the time being.

As Timur steps forward to speak with our host, Khalaf drops
behind with me, slipping a quince into my hand.

"I won't let him . . ." But he can't bring himself to finish.

"Yes, you will," I say, glaring at him. "You said as much."

He glances warily at his father's back. "I'm sorry. I'll figure
something out. I promise."

"What do you care?" I toss the quince away and watch it roll
across the dusty street, even though my stomach screams in protest. I plant my feet on the ground and glare down at them.

It wasn't my intention, but I have now put Khalaf in a position
where he has to choose between dealing with me or following
after his precious khan.

"Jinghua," he pleads, standing between me and the two men,
who are walking farther and farther away. I hate the fact that he
reminds me of Weiji in this moment, the way my brother always
had to navigate a world in which our father would never approve
of him. I feel the burning itch to cry scratching at my eyes.

"Son!" Timur barks, calling his loyal dog to his side. Khalaf
pauses for a heartbeat before he catches up to his father.

He's so sure I'll follow.

He's a fool.

But if he's a fool, then so am I. I keep telling myself I have a choice, that I could either do what I crossed a continent to do or I could run. But a familiar voice echoes in my head: *You're a slave now, my dear. You don't have a choice.*

So, in the end, I shuffle after the Kipchaks.

Who's the loyal dog now? I chide myself.

Stupid Jinghua.

Stupid, stupid Jinghua.

10

THE MAN'S NAME, WE LEARN, IS Abbas. His home is small and spare, but I get the sense that his life is simple rather than impoverished. It can't be too impoverished, at any rate, since he keeps several slaves. Abbas orders one of them to give me a clean kaftan. Khalaf must have tipped him off that I'm a girl, since it's a female slave who gives me one of her own plain, black garments. She pinches me when she forks it over, and the memory of who I was puffs itself up like a peacock. I gore her with a glare so fierce that her eyes go wide and she backs away, giving me a wide berth for the rest of the evening.

I do my best to wash weeks of grime off my skin in the small alley behind the house before I slip on the kaftan. Even though wearing clean clothes feels like heaven, it's not nearly enough to overcome my rancor at my new predicament.

Me. The asset to be liquidated.

I hear Timur's bluster before I even step across the threshold, which irritates me even more. "An education is all well and good, but nothing replaces experience," he contends, his voice dripping with derision. "You can't win a war because you read about one in a poem."

Timur and Khalaf are finely groomed again, and their new kaftans practically glow in the lamplight. I let the dishes speak my bitterness as I serve them. I clatter the teacups and rattle the pot. Khalaf gives me an apologetic glance, but he looks away when I scowl at him.

"And yet poetry, philosophy, the study of the stars, these things give you wisdom," Abbas answers. He grins madly, enjoying the debate. "The man who is wiser than his opponent will always win the battle."

"The man who can shoot an arrow with accuracy from a galloping horse will win the battle."

"That is certainly very helpful." Abbas chuckles. He turns to Khalaf to ask, "What do you think, sir?"

Khalaf the traitor sits quietly on his cushion, frowning down at the steaming cup in his hands. And here I am serving him his damn tea yet again.

I saved your life, you ingrate, I think at him. *You owe me.*

"'Seek knowledge,'" he answers Abbas, "'for through knowledge doors will be opened to you and never closed.'"

Timur sighs to the heavens, and, for once, I share the sentiment. The Kipchaks are about to sell me back into slavery, and Khalaf's quoting poetry. I bite back my tongue so hard it nearly bleeds, I'm that livid.

"Was that Nizami?" Abbas asks. "How does the rest of that verse go?"

It's as if our host has lit a lamp inside Khalaf. He recites a passage, his voice soft and reverent:

> *"Seek knowledge, for through knowledge doors will be*
> *opened to you and never closed.*
> *He who is unashamed of his learning pulls pearls from*
> *the water, rubies from the rock,*
> *While a man who is ashamed of his learning is assigned*
> *no knowledge and knows nothing.*
> *To be keen of mind but slack of effort is to sell pottery*
> *from a lack of pearls,*
> *While many a dullard, through his being taught,*
> *becomes a leader of men."*

Abbas's smile widens, and he turns to Timur. "That," he proclaims, his finger pointed upward to his god, "is wisdom."

Khalaf drops his gaze to his lap, trying to hide his pleased smile. It must be nice for him to be in the presence of a father figure who approves of him for a change. I'd be happy for him if he weren't about to sell me out to gain the approval of his real father, who doesn't deserve it. Stupid egg.

"You are very learned for one so young," says Abbas. "Here, you must speak with my man, Mustapha, who has an excellent mind. Mustapha!"

An Arab slave standing against the wall steps forward and kneels before Abbas.

"Give him a subject, sir," Abbas tells Khalaf. "Ask him any question. I promise you, his answer will merit your praise."

The Arab turns his attention to Khalaf and waits for his direction.

"We've heard in our travels that the Il-Khanids have overthrown our Kipchak brothers, Mustapha," Khalaf says casually.

"Indeed, sir," answers the Arab. His voice is high and light. It belies the largeness of the body beneath his white robe, like a great limestone brick.

"It's a sort of puzzle, isn't it, how the Kipchaks might regain their khanate again? I wonder if there is a solution to it."

Even though I'm angry with him, I can't help but wish Khalaf would be more careful, that he wouldn't take such a risk as to speak openly about the Kipchak Khanate. If the Arab suspects anything, he shows no sign of it. He pronounces, "The solution to that problem lies in the Great Khan's own city, Khanbalik."

"Khanbalik? Do you think the Great Khan would help the Kipchaks then?"

"No," answers Mustapha. Abbas laughs good-naturedly.

Khalaf obviously doesn't find it amusing. "Perhaps you could elucidate?"

"Forgive me, sir," says the slave. "It is not entirely correct to say that the Great Khan will not help. Rather, he might be coerced into aiding the Kipchaks if one managed to win his daughter."

Turandokht, once again. Her specter haunts me as regularly as my brother's ghost, and far more malevolently.

"A man would woo Turandokht Khatun at great risk," says Abbas. The sound of her name makes me grit my teeth.

"How so, my lord?" asks Khalaf.

Mustapha takes up the tale. "Two years ago, the Great Khan made a contract with the Song Dynasty to marry his only daughter—his only living child—to one of the Song princes. The daughter refused to consent to her father's wishes. She would neither eat nor drink. She grew quite ill. The Great Khan relented and destroyed the contract, but it wasn't enough for Turandokht. She demanded that, henceforth, any man wishing to marry her would have to pass a test of wits and, if he was unable to succeed, forfeit his life. If the Great Khan didn't agree to these terms, she would starve herself to death."

Mustapha doesn't mention what happened to the Song Dynasty, but I know. The Song declared war on the Great Khan and the Yuan when Turandokht refused our prince. And now the Song Empire is no more, and the Khanate of the Yuan Dynasty stretches from the Mongol homeland in the north to the farthest reaches of what was once my home in the south. I keep my face as blank as ever while my blood boils in my veins. I've lost everything—everything—to Turandokht. Even the sound of her name makes me ball my hands into tight, furious fists.

"Honestly, can you credit that?" Abbas hoots. "The pride of young girls these days!"

"I admit I'm astonished," Khalaf says. "Did her father consent to this?"

"He took an oath before the Eternal Blue Sky."

Timur remains remarkably impassive through this conversation, and that, in and of itself, is suspicious.

"What sort of test must one pass?" Khalaf asks.

"A series of riddles."

"Riddles? Really?"

I want to throttle Khalaf for being intrigued, and I want to throttle myself for caring enough about him to want to throttle him.

"Yes," Abbas interrupts, "the kind that result in a young man losing his life. Literally. Turandokht has executed at least ten princes to my knowledge for failing her challenge, and if the rumors are true that the Great Khan is gravely ill, who knows how many more will step forward."

Here, Khalaf looks sharply at his father. I suddenly recall a moment right before I came to Sarai when Chancellor Zhang mentioned something about the Great Khan being "under the weather." I didn't think anything of it at the time. Now Zhang's words make me feel like a game piece strategically placed on a *xiàngqí* board.

"Mustapha," Abbas continues, "I praised your great knowledge and wisdom, and here you are filling the boy's head with dreams of conquering the Ice Queen. Only a man of royal lineage might face that challenge."

"Forgive me, my lord. It was only that the young gentleman asked how one might save the Kipchak Khanate. And I'm sure you would agree that saving the Kipchak Khanate at this point would require desperate measures."

Our host grins. "I dislike losing arguments with you, slave."

"Indeed, my lord." Mustapha bows before returning to his place behind his master.

Timur slurps his tea while Khalaf rubs his bottom lip and eyes his father sidelong. I suspect we're thinking the same thing. The Great Khan of the Mongol Empire may be dying, and if a man in a small city like Rasht knows about it, how much did the khan of the Kipchak Khanate know four months ago, when he and his sons decided to go to war?

I guess we all have something to hide.

I stand against the wall, homesick and heartsick, trying to figure out how I'm going to get out of being sold so that somehow, some way, I can leave all this behind me and go back to Lin'an.

Despite the hospitality of our host, Khalaf is so exhausted from our trek through the Caucasus that he falls asleep right there on Abbas's tasteful rug. The entire process takes about half an hour as the older men talk of trade and war and past battles. Ever meticulous in matters of formality, Khalaf fights against it, but he slowly sags toward the floor until his eyes close and his lips sag. His beardless face looks startlingly young, his soft lower lip vulnerable.

The innocent, dutiful jerk.

Timur gives his offspring a look of annoyance, and Abbas laughs.

"Let him be," the host says with a dismissive wave of his hand. Timur grunts his assent, to which Abbas laughs again. "Your son has a gifted mind, sir."

"My son cares too much for learning," Timur replies as I pour out another cup of tea for him. His voice sounds gruff, but as he regards his son, his face takes on a different expression, one he would never let Khalaf see: he looks genuinely worried.

"Would you have him soldiering, then? With your forgiveness, he doesn't seem the type. Does he do well with a bow?"

"He fights beautifully with anything—a bow, a lance, an *uurga*, even a saber. I've never seen a more talented warrior."

"I see."

Two thoughts cross my mind simultaneously. One is that Timur, despite all evidence to the contrary up to this point, is fiercely proud of Khalaf. The second is that, as the conversation goes on, Timur is sounding less and less like the merchant he supposedly is. I step on his toes and glower at him as I walk past to call his attention to it, although I can't fathom why I even care at this point. It does no good anyway. He just ignores me.

Abbas sits back to ruminate before speaking again. "Perhaps it is his reluctance that makes him so."

"I'm afraid I don't follow you," Timur says.

"He does not rush into violence. He thinks first. Therefore, if he must act, if he must use force, he does so with wisdom and clarity."

"Perhaps," Timur answers doubtfully.

"It is the same with all great men. The man who craves power is the one you cannot trust with it, but the man who is reluctant to lead becomes the greatest ruler of all."

"A great ruler of men is the one who fosters the most love and obedience."

Abbas sets his teacup down carefully. "True. But it's easier to foster love and obedience when ruling is a sacrifice rather than a pleasure."

Timur strokes his mustache and lets his hand fall down the length of his beard.

"Where will you go once you have rested here?" asks Abbas. "Although, of course, you may stay as long as you like."

"You are very good." Timur dabs at his mouth with a napkin, an incongruously delicate gesture. "We may head west toward the Bulgarian kingdom. We'll have to sell our slave, of course, although I don't think she'll bring enough to buy a horse, much less two."

"You wish to sell your slave?"

"Yes. Would you happen to know of a trader nearby who might

wish to take her off our hands?"

I can't believe how casually two men can discuss the selling of me when I'm standing right here. The other slaves stare at me and shuffle their feet uncomfortably. I grasp a tray until my knuckles turn white, and I try not to cry.

"I wouldn't sell her just yet," advises Abbas, halting my panic.

Please, I beg the universe.

"You think we should hang on to her?" Timur asks.

"I'll supply you as best I can—"

"You are too generous. I could not accept so much."

"I am happy to do it," Abbas assures him. "Hang on to your slave. You may have need of more funds down the road, and you can sell her then. What possessed you to bring a female slave with you to begin with?"

"*I* didn't bring the slave."

"Ah." Abbas grins. "Your son is young yet. All the better to keep her with you, then, if he has a use for her."

A "use" for me? If the man hadn't just saved my life, I'd shake him till his teeth rattled. As it is, Timur nods his reluctant assent, and I can't believe my luck. I've won this volley, and I give him a smug look when our host isn't paying attention.

After a moment, Abbas says, "It's a sad circumstance that brings you here, sir, but I'm glad of the company."

"Thank you for your hospitality. When our goods are restored to us, I won't forget you, sir." It's amazing how civilized Timur sounds when he puts his mind to it.

Abbas inclines his head graciously. "Sadly, you are not alone in your misfortunes these days. As your son said, the khan of the Kipchak Khanate has had to flee his own country. His pursuers are relentless. They look for him throughout the Mongol lands, even as far as Mosul." The man locks eyes with Timur. "Even here."

Oh. That is bad. That is very, very bad.

"I see," Timur says carefully. His body tenses the way it did when Abbas first found us under the tree outside town.

"The reports say that all his sons are dead. All of them," Abbas emphasizes. "Can you imagine?"

"That is a grave misfortune, indeed."

Abbas nods gravely. "Hulegu Il-Khan is a vindictive little upstart, and his sacking of Baghdad is unforgivable, as is his attack of the Kipchak Khanate. If the Great Khan is dying, as rumor has it, this move against the Kipchaks bodes ill for us all, especially now that the il-khan has troops lined up near Constantinople to stop Timur Khan from seeking asylum across the border of the Il-Khanate. I tell you, if Timur were yet living, I'd tell him to cross the Oxus River to the east and seek asylum with his cousin Qaidu in the Chagatai Khanate. The free Mongols are hardly high society, to be sure, but they owe allegiance to no one but themselves, not even the Great Khan."

The man's tone is light and chatty, but the meaning is clear. Our escape route west has just been cut off, which means we now must head in the opposite direction.

And the opposite direction is going to take me closer to home. I have to clamp my lips to hide the unseemly grin that wants to spread across my face.

Timur's tension eases. "I'm sure Timur Khan would gladly receive your counsel, sir," he says. "You are very wise."

Abbas's smile thins.

"I don't know about that. Timur is a direct descendant of Genghis Khan, and I have no love for the Mongols, if you'll forgive my saying so." Abbas smiles fondly at Khalaf, who is now drooling on the carpet. "But his heirs—or one of them, at least—showed great promise."

11

ABBAS HAS ARRANGED FOR OUR TRANSPORT to the Chagatai Khanate with a camel trader whom he finances, a man named Mazdak. We meet up with him at the Shah Abbasi Caravanserai in Ray, a city to the south of Rasht that sits on the trade routes running between the Yuan and the rest of the Il-Khanate. It's a logical place to begin our journey, since the caravanserai provides lodging for all the traders coming and going through the city. But the bazaar is set up just outside, and it's all so very public. Anyone could spot Timur and his son here, especially since they're bickering with each other. They stand side by side, facing forward, each inclining his head toward the other as he speaks.

"Did you know the Great Khan was dying?" Khalaf asks his father in a low voice.

"I do now."

I play the good slave and stand behind them as befits my station. I can hear every word, clear as a bell.

"What about four months ago, when you and your sons made a plan to fight the Il-Khanids? Did you know then?" Khalaf presses.

"Would it have changed anything if I did?"

"Is that a yes?"

Timur turns his head to face his son. "No, it isn't. And I don't like your tone."

"Is there anything else you haven't shared with me?" Khalaf asks, his face still turned away from his father, his tone frosty. But that's when Abbas arrives with Mazdak to make the introductions, and the conversation comes to an abrupt end.

The trip between Rasht and Amul, where we will cross the Oxus River into the Chagatai Khanate, will run anywhere from six to eight weeks, depending on the weather and how often we stop to sell and trade. For the most part, it's a day's journey between caravanserais, but there are times when we'll have to sleep under the stars, especially in the desert. I'm not really looking forward to that. Even though it's spring, the temperatures are sure to be frigid once the sun goes down despite the daytime heat.

We walk on foot beside the camels—the stinking, obnoxious beasts I have already come to loathe—as Mazdak leads us south toward our first stop, the Dayr-i gachīn Caravanserai. We're not an hour on the road when Khalaf comes over to walk beside me. We move in silence, which is good, since I don't want to talk to him.

"You're mad at me," he says at last.

What can I say to that? I am mad at him. And yes, I'm aware that makes me a hypocrite.

"You have every right to that anger," he goes on, "so please believe me when I say that we are not going to sell you. We owe you our lives, and we need every friend we can get. You may live under our protection—however little that may be worth—for as long as you please. This is my promise to you. I will never go back on that promise. Do you understand?"

No niceties. No preface. He cuts right to the chase, a paragon of sincerity and honesty with eyes that make me want to either crawl under a rock or burst into song. In a way, it was easier to be angry with him. This? I have no idea what to do with this. The only thing I can manage to do in response is nod.

"Good," he says. "Thank you."

Thank you. Who tells a slave *Thank you*? His kindness makes everything so incredibly difficult. Not that I believe he'll be able to override his father on this point, but it's a nice gesture. At least I can rest easy in the fact that Timur won't try to sell me before we cross the border into the Chagatai Khanate—*if* we make it that far—and in the meantime, I can get three thousand *li* closer to home under Khalaf's protection, maybe even nearer. I just need to figure out exactly where and when to cut and run after that.

Because I definitely can't follow Khalaf all the way to

Khanbalik—if that is, in fact, his ultimate goal as I suspect. He was as hopeful as a puppy with the promise of table scraps when Mustapha mentioned Turandokht's riddles back in Rasht. For now, ostensibly, we're heading first south and then east in search of an old ally named Qaidu, but since I'm a little fuzzy on the details, I decide to ask for more clarification.

"My lord?" I say, but he's looking behind us again to make sure we're not being followed. It must be contagious, because I look, too. While we may not be able to see our enemies, I know that Hulegu Il-Khan moves somewhere behind us, and Turandokht Khatun waits before us, and here's little, insignificant me, slowly squeezed between the two like a pressed flower.

"Who exactly is Qaidu?" I ask him when he turns back to me.

He glances behind us one more time for good measure before answering. "Qaidu is the grandson of Ogodei, Genghis Khan's third son, the one who was elected Great Khan when Genghis passed. When the coup happened, Qaidu fled to the Chagatai Khanate, and he's been staging regular attacks against the Great Khan ever since. My father was more than happy to assist him in carving out a chunk of the Chagatai Khanate for himself. They're old allies, my father and Qaidu. The Kipchaks supported Qaidu when he needed it most. We're hoping that he'll return the favor."

My mind is still trying to sort out the complexities of the Mongols' family tree when Khalaf changes the subject. "That song you sang in the Caucasus, 'Mòlihuā.' Your name is in the lyrics."

"It is?" My mind runs through the verse trying to scrounge up my name, which is most certainly not there.

"Mòlìhuā," he says. "And your name is Jìnghuā. It's the same word, right?"

"Oh, my name is pronounced 'Jīnghuá,' my lord," I correct him.

"And that's not what I'm saying?" He looks a little embarrassed, which is frustratingly endearing.

"I'm afraid not, my lord," I admit.

"What am I saying?"

"You tend to call me 'jìnghuā.'"

He cringes apologetically. "I have a hard time hearing the difference. Is what I'm saying bad?"

"It's not bad. It means something like 'quiet flower' when you say it." For a moment, I'm tempted to tell him that my name actually means "illustrious capital city," but I imagine it would seem like a strange name for a humble slave girl, so I keep it to myself.

"Quiet flower," he repeats in Mongolian, mulling it over. "That seems appropriate."

He smiles that small smile that got me into so much trouble in the first place. A pathetically stupid giggle escapes my throat, and I have to fight the urge to slap a hand over my mouth.

"Does 'huā' mean 'flower,' then?" he asks.

"It does."

"So 'mòlì' means 'jasmine'?"

"Yes, my lord." I'm oddly pleased that he figured this out. "Mòlìhuā. Jasmine flower."

"I am now a student of Hanyu, it would seem. How do you greet someone in Hanyu?"

"Why?" I ask.

"We're heading east, aren't we? Who knows how far we'll go?"

"And you want to learn Hanyu?"

"I want to learn lots of things." He makes an expansive gesture with his arm, indicating the whole world. "At the moment, I'd like to learn how to greet someone in Hanyu."

He can play off this urge to learn Hanyu as casually as he likes. I'm on to him. He's thinking about what the slave Mustapha said back in Rasht. He's thinking about going to the Yuan, to Khanbalik. He's thinking he's smart enough to face Turandokht's riddles.

And, really, why shouldn't he go to Khanbalik? He's the one person in the world who could answer Turandokht's riddles, isn't he? That makes him more than a boy, more than a prince. That makes him a weapon. In a way, he's *my* weapon, and I take some satisfaction out of that.

"Greeting someone in Hanyu is complex," I explain. "It depends on the person, on the relationship."

"Well, how would I greet you?"

"You wouldn't."

"Which only goes to show how little you know about me. Fine, then, how would you greet me?"

"*Cān jiàn Diànxià.*"

He tries to repeat the phrase, but he botches the intonations. It sounds like he's saying, "bashful silkworm, Prince." I laugh another fluttering, stupid laugh, which quickly disappears when I consider how fluttering and stupid I sound. I remind myself to guard my feelings, but his eyes are shining, and how can I guard myself against that? I may as well sail the ocean on a river gondola. I'm going to drown in this boy.

"*Cān jiàn Diànxià,*" I correct him, and he repeats it far more successfully this time. I nod with approval.

"Is that how you would greet a friend?"

"No."

"How would you greet a friend, then?"

"*Hǎo jiǔ bú jiàn, xiōngtái,*" I tell him. I have to walk him through the intonations several times before he finally gets it.

"*Hǎo jiǔ bú jiàn, xiōngtái,*" he says, almost perfectly. "How was that?"

"Very good, my lord."

"*Hǎo jiǔ bú jiàn, xiōngtái.*" He smiles again, wider, dimple and all, and I know that it's me he's greeting as a friend, even if he has no idea that he's calling me something along the lines of "brother."

Oh, Jinghua, I think, my unguarded heart singing in my chest, *how on earth did you manage to get yourself into such a mess?*

Dayr-i gachīn Caravanserai is a huge brick structure built in a square with a circular tower at each corner and a semicircular tower on each side of the south-facing entrance. The white gypsum roof glows brightly in the fading light of dusk. Inside, there's a mill, a bathhouse, large kitchens, and a mosque. The well at the center of the courtyard is salty, but there are two cisterns that collect rainwater for drinking.

When we stable the camels, I notice low, raised platforms built into the wall, presumably for sleeping. For one depressing moment, I assume that I'll have to camp out here for the night with the spitting, biting, stubborn camels, but it turns out Mazdak prefers to stay close to his inventory, and I get to sleep in the vaulted antechamber of our room. Not too shabby.

I lie on the floor, wrapped in a warm blanket furnished by Abbas, and consider how my fortunes have changed. A week ago, I was recovering from starvation and dehydration. Now I'm heading east toward the Yuan in the company of, maybe, the nicest person I've ever met. Granted, his father wants to sell me somewhere along the way, and Hulegu Il-Khan might catch us yet. Even so, I can't help but feel hopeful for the first time since we fled Sarai. Maybe I didn't mess everything up. Maybe the decisions I've made are solid.

Maybe I can go home.

That night, I dream my way back to Lin'an. I'm standing at the window in the women's quarters that gives the best view of the West Lake. It's late morning, and the fine mist that cloaks the Six Harmonies Pagoda begins to dissipate. The scene looks like a painting, a work of art come to life. I hum under my breath, free of all cares.

A harsh voice calls my name and rends my peace in two.

Jinghua.

One moment I was alone, and the next, Weiji stands beside me. His wound is rotting in mottled shades of black, green, and white. His eyes have been picked clean by carrion birds, leaving nothing but empty sockets. The stench of his putrid flesh shreds the floral scent of the air, filling my lungs with my brother's decay.

I wouldn't get my hopes up too high if I were you, he tells me, his mouth a cavernous black void that expands farther and farther until I fall into it.

Timur and Khalaf have decided to hide in plain sight by masquerading as a pair of traders, selling Abbas's wares in the market of each town along the way. What's hilarious is how well Timur takes to the merchant's life. The man is a born salesman.

"Feel the weave on this," he tells a veiled, chaperoned woman two days outside Ray. "I have it on good authority that the prince of Mosul clothes his own daughter in this very same muslin."

"Hold it up to the light," he instructs a man looking at glass-ware. "Not a single imperfection. The glassblower's hands are truly a gift from God."

Not that Timur gives a rat's ass for his customer's god, but the sucker pays too much for the glass anyway.

When Khalaf gives a discount to an old widow in Damghan, Timur lectures him. "No, no, no. You let that lady run all over you. When they start getting shirty, just walk away. They'll practically beg you to take their money at that point."

"You know this is just a cover, right?" Khalaf says to his father under his breath.

"Why bother doing anything if you're not going to do it well?"

Khalaf raises his eyebrows in amusement. "That almost sounds like wisdom."

"That's because it is. Watch and learn. There's not much difference between being a salesman and being a khan."

Timur is so good at selling from caravanserai to caravanserai, no one seems to notice that what he's actually doing is hiding.

At first, Khalaf glances over his shoulder every five minutes while we're on the road, expecting Hulegu Il-Khan to come riding up behind us at any moment, but as the days stretch on with no sign of the Il-Khanids on our tails, and as the landscape changes from the sultry green on one side of the Alborz Mountains to the barren scrub on the other, Khalaf peers behind us less and less. I wonder if we're rightfully hopeful or simply waiting to fail. We have so much time to fill with waiting or hoping. Hours of it. Days of it. Weeks of it.

The deserts and mountains connecting the network of oasis towns comprise our classroom. The lessons begin simply.

"How do you say 'sun' in Hanyu?" Khalaf asks me in the beginning.

"How do you say 'bird'?"

"How do you say 'mountain'?"

Hours. Days. Weeks. He learns as we travel from Sabzevar to

Nishapur to Merv, piecing together words and phrases like a child stringing fat wooden beads on thick twine.

Khalaf takes off his turban in the afternoon heat, pulling his sleek hair in a knot behind his head. He has traded in the green silk Abbas gave him for a plain, woven, mustard-colored tunic and black jacket.

"How do you say 'I'm so hot that I have sweated off half my body weight'?" he jokes as he takes off the jacket, but now I'm thinking rather shamelessly of how his tunic clings to his sweat-dampened torso, which grows harder and leaner with each passing day. I don't even try to turn off that train of thought anymore. Just because I think it doesn't mean he has to know I think it.

"How do you say 'Shut up'?" Timur interjects. He sits atop a camel like a king surveying his land, whatever he can see of it with his weak eyes. Frankly, I suspect that's exactly what he's doing, thinking, *If I play my cards right, this could be mine, too.* Men: nothing teaches them, not even a near-death experience.

"'*Shăguā,*' my lord," I answer.

"Good," says Timur. "*Shăguā!*"

He thinks he's telling us to be quiet, but "*shăguā*" means "silly melon." Khalaf has learned enough Hanyu by this point that he giggles. He actually giggles. It's adorable. He's adorable. It's becoming a bit of a problem for me, this adorableness, this adorability. A few weeks ago, I was furious with his willingness to go along with his father's plan to sell me. One apology later, I'm a doe-eyed idiot. I need to be more careful of him. Of me.

Ever since I patched him up in the Caucasus, I've been thinking of him as a friend, which in and of itself is ridiculous. But now he seems to consider me a friend, too, and I don't know what to do with that sensation or even what to call it. The only word that comes to mind is "affection."

Sometimes, in the middle of a lesson, Khalaf squints at me, as if he can really *see* me. He may as well peel back the skin over my heart to examine what lies there. I suppose he never expected to find companionship in a scrawny slave girl with round cheeks and oversized lips. Who could blame him for that? I certainly never expected to find anything like Khalaf in the world.

Affection. Or something like it.

It's utterly foreign to me and runs against everything I was taught to understand about what happens between men and women.

Back home in Lin'an, before the Mongols came, I expected any day to find out that a prospective groom's family had approached my family about me. My parents would have taken me to a place where the groom could see me, and he would decide if he wanted me.

I lived in mortal fear that this faceless prospective groom would not want me.

But if he did, the arrangements would be made, and there would be an elaborate ritual of giving and receiving gifts until, at last, we would be married. He would introduce me to his ancestors, and I would be part of a new family and owe obedience to new parents and produce sons who would honor me when I died. That was supposed to be my future, my life, all decided for me. That was the natural order of the universe.

And affection between myself and my husband would grow like a sapling into a tree, slowly, over time.

Affection is supposed to be a result of marriage, not a precursor to . . . what? What happens between a prince and a slave? I blush even to consider it. And I can't imagine Khalaf, in all his decency and propriety, doing anything that is less than decorous. I can't imagine myself doing anything less than decorous either, not along those lines at least. I may be a slave, but I was raised to be modest. I don't see that changing any time soon.

Then again, it wasn't decorum that brought me to the Kipchak Khanate in the first place.

It's exhausting work, traveling across the world, and Khalaf bears the brunt of the heavy lifting, being the most able-bodied among us. His shoulders broaden by the second under the labor of packing and unpacking and chopping wood for the fire when there's wood to be had. There is a word that describes those shoulders that is something akin to "adorable" but far more complicated.

He is so very nice to look at.

I, however, am not.

I wonder what he would have thought if he had been the prospective groom eyeing me anonymously in some public house in Lin'an. Would he have nodded his approval?

Or would he have run for the door?

12

WE'VE BEGUN THE WEEKLONG JOURNEY ACROSS
the Karakum, a desert that stretches out so flatly in all directions
that I have to hike a long way if I want to relieve myself in relative privacy. As I make my way back to camp, Timur's voice drifts
clearly to me where I stand downwind from him and his son.

"I hate to interrupt your language lessons with a slave girl," he
tells Khalaf, "but do you think you might spare me a moment to
discuss what we're going to do once we cross into the Chagatai
Khanate?"

I squint into the distance. I can see them seated across from
each other next to the fire, but I don't think they can see me
where I stand in the darkness.

"You are my lord and father. You know perfectly well you have my attention whenever you want it." I can hear Khalaf's strained tolerance in every syllable he utters.

"Good. Because I'd like you to stop paying attention to a language you don't need to know and a girl you don't need to be associating with. I'd like you to turn your attention back to your khanate and your duty."

"Forgive me, my lord," Khalaf replies. I've noticed that he calls his father "my lord" when he's irritated with him, which brings a smug grin to my face. "I assumed the matter was settled. I assumed that we would seek asylum with Qaidu in the Chagatai Khanate."

"You assumed incorrectly."

This is news to me. I assumed the same thing since it was Abbas's suggestion, and he's the one who sent us on our way.

"We're heading for Khanbalik?" Khalaf asks, and I detect intrigue and excitement in his voice, confirming my suspicions. He wants to face those riddles. Surely Timur can hear it as well.

"Rotting carrion, are you mad? No. We're going home."

So: Khalaf wants to get himself killed in Khanbalik, and Timur wants to get himself killed by returning to the Kipchak Khanate. They're both out of their minds, and I'm stuck with the pair of them in the middle of a desert. At least I can sympathize with Timur's desire to go home. Khalaf? I don't know what to think about him.

"You want to head north?" he asks his father in a tone that conveys serious misgivings.

"Once we cross the Oxus," Timur confirms.

"From where?"

"Samarkand. We'll raise an army among the eastern tribes and march west to Sarai."

And I thought my plan to get back to Lin'an was preposterously optimistic. Timur's delusions of grandeur put me to shame. They're also stomping all over my own hopes for the future. This is not good.

"Father, we can't do that," says Khalaf. "You know we can't."

"Explain."

"We've been on the run from Hulegu Il-Khan for three months. We know he was looking for us near Rasht, but he hasn't caught up to us, has he? So where is he?"

"Sitting arrogantly in my rightful place while our country goes to hell," answers Timur.

"No, he's figured out which way you went, and he knows you well enough to guess that you'll try to take the Kipchak Khanate back from the east. He didn't follow us through the desert because he's assembling troops on the Kipchak-Chagatai border. And where is the best road between those two points?"

"You don't seem to understand." Even from where I'm standing in the distance, I can see Timur dismiss Khalaf's rational argument with a wave of his huge hand. "This is the plan."

"The best road is the one that heads north from Samarkand," Khalaf says, standing his ground, answering his own question.

"Are you with me or are you against me?"

Khalaf's head goes back, and I know he's offering up one of his long-suffering prayers to his god. "I'm trying to give you counsel."

"I asked you a question."

For a moment neither of them speaks, their profiles still.

"What if we were to go to Khanbalik?" Khalaf suggests.

I knew it. I *knew* it. Each one of us is fostering an impossible hope, and each hope opposes the other two. We are a trio of lunatics.

Timur snorts. "And do what?"

"Appeal to the Great Khan. He can't support Hulegu's move against us, even if the il-khan is his brother. He may be willing to support us with troops."

"He's dying, and it sounds like his daughter is running the show. As far as I can tell, the empire is in chaos right now."

"Then go to Qaidu and ask for help," Khalaf says, his patience wearing thin in his voice. "He owes you."

"No. We head north. We muster troops around the Aral Sea. Then we march on Sarai from the east and take back what's ours. Is that clear?"

"So you're avoiding the Great Khan *and* Qaidu. Why?"

Timur lets out a great sigh and rubs his eyes in a gesture that is surprisingly similar to Khalaf's own eye rubbing. "You are just like your mother sometimes."

Khalaf sits up straight and pulls a curtain of cold distance between himself and his father, so frigid I can feel it even from my vantage point. It's never occurred to me that Khalaf had a mother, just like me, and that his mother appears to be out of the picture, just like my own. It's never occurred to me that he might long for his mother as much as I long for mine.

"What does my mother have to do with anything?" Khalaf asks. I've never heard him speak quite so coolly.

Timur snorts. "You wouldn't understand."

"Try me."

"Your mother has nothing to do with anything," Timur snaps. "She's gone. I'm here. I'm your father. We head north. We take back Sarai. We rule the Kipchak Khanate. Is that clear?"

There's another pause, another moment of still silhouettes in the night before Khalaf bows his obedient head and says, "Yes, my lord."

My thoughts are a whirlwind of confusion and worry and contrary opinions, and since this seems like an incredibly bad moment to return to camp anyway, I step farther into the darkness with our campfire burning like a beacon in the distance behind me. I need to straighten out my own thinking.

I kneel on the sandy ground, take the thong from around my neck, and set the duck's head down before me. I saved a spoonful of lentils from dinner in a small bundle of cloth, which I now pull from my pocket and offer to my brother, who haunts my dreams with increasing regularity. I hope Weiji likes lentils, because I have nothing else with which to honor him in the desert. For my own part, I am sick to death of them.

Sand oozes up my robe and shimmies into my boots as my

knees sink into the earth, but I'm used to that now. Everything is full of sand these days. For the past two nights, I've slept on the desert floor under the open, starry sky, so cold I've had to cuddle up to the least offensive camel. Every morning, I wake to find myself achy and covered in a thin layer of sand. I thought the Kipchak Khanate was brown and dull, but so far, the lands of the Il-Khanate are even drier and dustier. Rasht wasn't bad, I suppose, but nothing compares to the green hills of Lin'an, a world bursting with life and color, a world I didn't adequately appreciate until it was gone forever.

I remember every detail of my home, from the wooden ancestral tablets and the thick odor of incense in the family shrine to the silk landscape paintings in the women's quarters, the scent of each flower in season wafting inside through the windows overlooking the garden, all of it so visceral that I feel as though I could grasp it with my hands.

I just want to go home.

I *am* going home, or I'm going to die trying.

But even as I think the words, it already feels like a lie. I can tell myself I have options, but really it all boils down to one choice:

It's either Khalaf's life or mine.

And that's a choice I don't know how to make.

Mazdak is off tending to the camels when I return to camp, and the tension between Khalaf and Timur lingers in the air. I sit across the fire from them to take apart my plait, which has become a tangled mess.

If I were a lady of quality in this part of the world, I'd get to wear a veil, which might help protect my head from the regular onslaught of desert winds. As a slave, I have no such luck, and my already pathetic hair must suffer for it. I brush through the tangled strands with my fingers. It's a time-sucking ordeal. My hair is not cooperative.

At some point, I notice that Khalaf is looking at me from across the fire with the strangest look on his face. His eyes are glassy, and his mouth is hanging open a little. I pause, my fingers embedded in my hair, and ask, "Are you unwell, my lord?"

The question seems to take him off guard, as if he'd forgotten that I have a voice. "Yes. I mean, no. Um, no, I'm quite well. Thank you."

Both Timur and I stare at him. I don't think I've ever seen Khalaf stammer. The prince glances at his father, who gazes back at him with flinty eyes.

"I'll just go see what Mazdak is up to," Khalaf says, rising to his feet and dusting himself off before he makes his way toward the trader and the camel herd.

Which leaves me alone with the old goat.

Timur claps his huge hands together and rubs them briskly. "This seems like the perfect opportunity to get to know each other. Let's have a nice little chat, shall we?"

That sounds like about as much fun as a public impalement.

"You wish that I 'get to know you,' my lord?" I ask.

"It's more that I'd like to get to know *you* . . . ah, what was the name again?"

"How would you like to call me, my lord?"

"Ha! Very good!" he says with a not entirely pleasant smile on his face. He studies me and repeats, "Very good."

Timur forcefully reminds me of Chancellor Zhang, who came to Lin'an two years ago, who knew me in the time before I was a slave. He once assessed me in a similar way: *Good. Yes, that's quite good.*

It's not a comforting thought.

"Thank you, my lord," I tell the old goat.

Timur nods, takes a gargantuan bite of lentils, and speaks with his mouth full of food in a manner full of false congeniality. "It's easy for a man to forget who he is when lesser men are not there to remind him."

"Then it's a good thing that I am here, my lord, to remind him of who he is."

"Yes, it is, isn't it? Although, flat as you are, you are not a man. And, forgive me, little slave, why exactly is it that you are here?"

It was hard enough to answer that question when Khalaf asked me the same thing. The best response I can cough up for Timur is "Maybe it's the will of the gods."

"You and I both know that is a steaming pile of shit, so let me ask again. Why are you here?"

It is so hard not to hit this man.

"The prince has always shown me great kindness."

"The prince shows everyone great kindness. It is one of his worst traits. And you've just handed me another steaming pile of shit. That's two piles of shit now, and my hands are full. So one more time, slave, why are you here?"

I bow my head, trying to hide my fear and fury from him. In all my dealings with Khalaf, I forgot what a threat Timur is to me. What did he say, back in the mountains? *We should leave her to fend for herself like the lying dog she is.* And he wanted to sell me in Rasht, and still wants to sell me somewhere along the way.

"Look at me," Timur demands. My fear aside, it makes me seethe, the way he speaks to me when he's no better than I am. Angry tears threaten the rims of my eyes. I swallow my resentment.

"Look up, girl!"

I look at him, doing my level best to keep my face cold. The old khan glares at me for a long, long moment before he barks with laughter. It isn't a nice laugh. "Oh, so it's love, is it? And here I thought you were a spy. That's disappointing."

I feel as if I've been punched.

"It isn't . . . I'm not . . ."

"Oh? You're not what?"

In love with Khalaf? A spy? What are we talking about anymore? My cheeks burn, but I take a breath to compose myself. "I'm repaying a kindness, my lord. That's all."

"And how will you repay that kindness? With your life?"

"If I must." And I think that just might be true. How strange to admit it out loud, especially to the old goat.

"But your life is worth very little," he points out.

"It's worth a great deal to me, my lord."

"Good. That should help us all stay alive a bit longer." His faux congeniality dissolves, replaced by a cutting look. "Just so you remember who you are and who he is."

"I'm not likely to forget that, my lord," I inform him, letting myself enjoy a private moment of self-superiority over Timur, who knows exactly nothing about me.

"Because there are entire nations relying on him now, whereas there is no one relying on you."

"Except the prince and yourself, my lord, and possibly Mazdak. Or were you planning to cook your own lentils and wash your own pot?"

Liquidate that, you stupid egg.

Timur laughs again, and this time, he sounds genuinely amused.

"You know, you're not much to look at, girl, but I'm starting to think the boy's not so foolish as I thought. I'm suddenly rather taken with you myself."

"That's because you are a lecherous old man, my lord," I mutter, since the gloves appear to be off.

"That I am, girl," he agrees, setting down his bowl and stretching his arms behind his head. He waggles those incredible eyebrows at me. "That I am."

13

FIVE TIMES EACH DAY, KHALAF AND Mazdak kneel side by side to pray, Khalaf on his sash and the camel trader on his unfurled turban. When water is at hand, they wash their faces, their hands, their arms, and even their feet before beginning. When we're traveling across long tracts of desert and need to preserve water for drinking, they scrub themselves with sand.

Sometimes, Timur joins them. I had always assumed he just pretended to be a Muslim from time to time to placate the people over whom he ruled, but he seems to know what he's doing. They're very ecumenical about religion, the Mongols. They treat it like a buffet, taking a little of this and a little of that as it pleases them, even Khalaf to a certain extent.

The more who join in, the lovelier and more impressive are

these prayers, these choreographed dances for their god. In the larger towns dotting our eastward escape route, I watch scores of men perform the ritual together. I don't understand it, but it's beautiful all the same.

I learn that the five daily prayers are called *Salat*. Khalaf's day begins not at sunrise but when the sun sets, and he prays *Maghrib*. Between sunset and midnight is *'Isha*. *Fajr* at sunrise, *Zuhr* at midday, *'Asr* in the late afternoon, and the cycle begins all over again.

"That's a lot of praying," I tell him.

"If praying were a burden, I suppose one might see it that way. But praying is like food. If you don't eat, your body starves. If you don't pray, your soul starves. And so I pray to feed my soul."

His soul must be a bottomless pool. One could live a lifetime and never fully explore the depths. Then again, time is something we have in infinite supply as we flee across the Il-Khanate, walking for days on end beside the camel herd, waiting for Hulegu Il-Khan to catch up to us.

"Are we still headed to the Chagatai Khanate to find your father's ally, my lord?" I ask after watching Khalaf scan the horizon one morning. "What was his name again?"

Khalaf glances at me, midscan, and I wonder if he can sense my faux ignorance. "Qaidu," he says, and after a long pause, he adds, "Yes, we're going to find him."

I don't believe he's lying to me exactly. I think he intends to chip away at his father's resolve to return to the Kipchak Khanate until he's won him over. So *We're going to ask Qaidu for help* has a lot in common with *We're not going to sell the slave girl*. That means I can rest assured that we're going to make it to Samarkand at least, if we're not caught by Hulegu Il-Khan first. After that, I'd better have a plan in place, because Samarkand is still hell and gone from Lin'an.

I'm lost in my own thoughts until I realize Khalaf is giving me that squint, the one that makes me incredibly nervous. I change the subject back to Hanyu verbs.

Little by little, Khalaf's lessons expand until one day I find that I'm as much his student as his teacher. One moment, Khalaf is asking me to explain words like "soul" and "God" in Hanyu; the next, he's relating my answer to a poem by a man named Attar:

> *Let love lead your soul.*
> *Make it a place of refuge,*
> *Like a monastic cave, a retreat*
> *For the deepest core of your being.*

Another day, when I'm teaching him the names of birds in Hanyu, he steers us toward the poet Rumi.

> *Yet with his call the fowler oft essays*
> *To bring the errant hawk within his reach;*

So, when men wander in life's devious ways,
The Dervish too may utter human speech,
And in mere mortal words immortal truths may teach.

The following day we talk as much about Saadi as the grammatical rules of Hanyu. One poem in particular, "Guardians," stands out. I'm sure Khalaf's selection is random, but the meaning forms a painted backdrop to the play of my life that unfolds inevitably with each eastward step we take.

Lost is the difference of king and slave
At the approach of destiny's decree;
Should one upturn the ashes of the grave,
Could he discern 'twixt wealth and poverty?

Nizami's tragic *Laili and Majnun* takes us within sight of the Oxus River, the border between the Il-Khanate and the Chagatai Khanate.

And there, of different tribe and gentle mien
A lovely maid of tender years was seen
Her mental powers and early bloom displayed
Her peaceful form in simple garb arrayed
Bright as the morn, her cypress shape, and eyes
Dark as the stag's, were viewed with fond surprise.

With each line he quotes, I marvel at the staggering breadth and scope of his mind. It's like he reads something once and the words write themselves indelibly on his brain, ready to come forth at his command. He translates the verses into Mongolian and, sometimes, tries to translate them into Hanyu as well. And if I thought Khalaf's voice was impressive in everyday speech, it becomes a thing of magic and wonder when it's wrapped around verse.

I think he must miss learning as much as I miss home. So now I am his university. And he, I realize with a sick dread in my stomach, is my universe.

It happened in little fits and starts through the deserts of the Il-Khanate and then in an overwhelming rush as we near the Chagatai border, like water breaking through a dam. I'm drowning in a flood of Khalaf, and I don't know what to do about it.

I'd like to recite the poems I know for him. I think Khalaf's hungry mind would sop up Su Shi or Lu You. But it would probably seem odd that a slave girl could recite poetry, that she could write it beautifully with a brush on parchment. And yet the more I get to know Khalaf, the more I want him to know me, too. It's a hard line to walk, wanting to be known while remaining unknowable.

Mostly I stick to songs, of which, thankfully, there are many. Li Qingzhao wrote verse after verse, full of beauty and longing, set to the songs even a peasant knows: "Cassia Flower" to the tune of "The Silk Washing Brook," "Spring in the Women's Quarters" to the tune of "Beautiful Nian Nu." I sing one poem and then another from Li Qingzhao's hand to my lips. At first, it's awkward, walking alongside Khalaf and singing to the open sky, but I love the words, the sound of music in my throat. With each note, it becomes less awkward, until I'm no longer nervous but eager.

"Will you sing something today?" he asks.

It's never a command. He never pushes.

"Would it please you to sing?"

Yes, it does please me.

The memory of my mother shaking her head at me, of her reminding me that a lady does not sing, the way she always scolded me—it all begins to fade. When I sing, I'm free of my past, and the present relinquishes its stranglehold on me, if only for the duration of the song.

The music has a similar effect on Khalaf. When I sing, he stops looking behind us every five minutes. When I sing, I think he forgets Hulegu Il-Khan, Turandokht, the riddles, his duty to his father and to his khanate, all his earthly responsibilities.

> *Creatures of the same species*
> *Long for each other. But we*
> *Are far apart and I have*
> *Grown learned in sorrow.*

Sometimes, when I finish a song, he rubs his lip, mulling over the words he's managed to pick out before asking me for a better translation. Sometimes, he just watches me with brown eyes gone soft and glassy. Sometimes, the way his eyes settle on my face, tracing a line from my eyes to my lips, makes me long for things I shouldn't want and can't have.

Sometimes, I let myself suspect that his eyes linger on my lips for reasons that have nothing to do with music.

As we ride, I catch Timur inclining his head in our direction, trying to parse out what we're saying to each other. He calls Khalaf to him from time to time. They argue, or I should say, Timur argues. Khalaf remains as unflappable as ever. Mazdak glances at them, too, but if he suspects anything, he doesn't let on. When the arguments peter out, Khalaf always walks back to me, leaving his father's frown deepening behind him.

14

IT'S BEEN EIGHT WEEKS SINCE WE started out from Ray. We've been following the west bank of the Oxus River northward for a couple of days toward Amul, where we should be able to cross into the Chagatai Khanate and breathe a sigh of relief.

Well, Khalaf and Timur can breathe a sigh of relief. My troubles are increasing with each step we take. I'm not close enough to Lin'an to run away. I can't go to Khanbalik with Khalaf. And I won't go back to the Kipchak Khanate with Timur.

I'm so focused on my own problems that I fail to notice when the Kipchaks send Mazdak and the camels ahead while Timur haggles over something with a local peasant. Both Timur and Khalaf stand so close to the water's edge, they practically dangle their toes in the water. Me? I hang back. And by "hang back" I mean that I'm standing a good twenty paces away. I'm not going anywhere near the water. I'll cross that bridge when I come to it. Literally.

As I watch Mazdak grow smaller and smaller on his northward trek, I call, "My lord?" to Khalaf. He turns to look back at me, shielding his eyes from the midday sun with his hand. "What are we doing?" I ask.

"Mazdak's taking the herd to cross at the bridge in Amul," he calls back. "The three of us are going to ferry across here."

Ferry.

As in, a boat.

In the water.

I catch sight of this "ferry," a ramshackle fishing boat that looks like a toy floating in an ocean, and terror explodes within me.

"How much for three to cross?" Timur asks the peasant.

"Five dirhams," the man answers.

"Too much. How much for two?"

"Three," Khalaf insists.

Panic grabs hold of my lungs and won't let go. I stagger away from the river in a jittery haze.

"Jinghua? Where are you going?" Khalaf calls behind me.

I find a tall thicket of shrubs and desert grass behind which I can cower. I cover my head with shaking hands and try like mad to breathe, but I can't calm down.

I hear his feet swishing through the sand before he comes to sit beside me. "So, it would appear that you don't like rivers," he says.

His turban is off, and the wind blows bits of his hair against my arm. I scoot a few inches away from him.

"Is she coming or not?" Timur yells from the bank.

"She's coming," Khalaf calls back.

Like hell, I think.

"We can't go over the bridge," Khalaf explains to me. "We're technically still in the Il-Khanate, and Hulegu may have guards posted on the bridge, even if he seems to have lost interest in hunting us down. If we ferry across, we're less likely to be recognized or caught. And then we'll be safe in the Chagatai Khanate."

I start to cry into my kneecaps.

"You have to come," he says.

"They won't wait forever," Timur shouts at us.

"You don't understand," I wheeze at Khalaf.

"You're right. I don't understand. So why don't you help me?" His tone is gentle, but I've known him long enough now that I can hear the tinge of impatience in his voice, which makes me cry even harder.

"Jinghua," he says, breathing out my name in an exhausted sigh, his stiff posture caving in. He changes positions to squat before me, cocking his head so that he can catch my eye. His face is as kind and earnest as that very first day we met, if a little exasperated. There are times when I resent the hell out of that kindness.

"I can't," I cry. Snot is dripping out of my nose and running down my tear-fattened lips.

"Why?"

I remember my mother's face, blanched by fear, as she asked, *Where's the boat?* I can still recall with perfect, terrifying clarity the way my body crashed through the water's surface when I hit it. I shake my head at Khalaf. I can't say it.

He reaches out a hand, hesitates, then touches my arm with his fingertips. The tenderness of the gesture cracks and breaks the wall of grief I've been building up inside myself for two years. I'm weeping torrents of misery, sinking in it, drowning in it. He curls his fingers around my forearm and squeezes gently as I cry like a baby. A moment later, he sits beside me again and wraps me up in his arms like the wailing child I am. I toss propriety out the window and press my face against the warmth of his chest, pouring my sorrow into him.

"My mother drowned," I sob into the safe folds of his tunic. "And then I drowned, too. I drowned."

I've never said it aloud, never told anyone what happened to me.

"Do you need an engraved invitation?" Timur calls from the riverbank.

"In a minute!" Khalaf shouts back angrily, adding, "My lord!" probably in the hopes of placating the old goat. To me, he says softly, "There are no words for this. I'm so sorry, Jinghua. But you didn't drown. You're still here. You're still living."

He doesn't press for more, doesn't ask for particulars, and for that I am eternally grateful. I finally muster enough dignity to pull myself away from him, missing his warmth as I soon as the air hits me. I'm sure my face is puffy and hideous.

"I can't do this," I tell him.

"I won't let you fall in," he promises me.

My fear begins to relent. Damn his brown eyes.

"LET'S GO!" Timur booms.

"I don't even want to get wet. Please don't let me get wet." I hate the sound of my own voice.

He makes an exasperated face and nods his head from side to side as if he were haggling with a market vendor. "I'll do my best," he says, not very reassuringly.

"All right," my mouth agrees while every other fiber of my being is screaming in protest.

I close my eyes and keep them shut tight as Khalaf guides me to the boat, which wobbles sickeningly under my feet as I get in. Fear grips me, and I squeal like a pig going to slaughter.

"Good God," Timur says in disgust.

I sit between Timur and Khalaf as we float across the water. A fortress of musky male torso blocks my view of the river (and the banks and sky, for that matter), or at least it would if I could bring myself to open my eyes. Khalaf's body is wrapped around me from the back, and Timur's body is a solid wall in front of me. I can't stand the man, but that doesn't stop me from burying my face into his thick back, my head rising and falling with his breath. I can hear his heart, feel it thudding against my cheek.

"This is ridiculous," the old goat mutters as we slide across the water. His deep voice vibrates my skull.

"Jinghua?" Khalaf whispers into my ear.

My entire body is shaking.

"Jinghua, what's your favorite color?"

"I don't know," I tell Timur's spine, wondering at Khalaf's incredibly bad timing. What's my favorite color? I'm facing death, and he wants to know my favorite color? What slave stops to ask herself, *Hmm, what is my favorite color?*

"Don't be ridiculous," he says. "Everyone has a favorite color."

"I don't," Timur informs us over his shoulder.

"You're kind of missing the point here, Father," says Khalaf.

"You have a favorite color? Are you a man or are you five years old?"

"My favorite color is blue, for your information."

"Why blue? What's so great about blue?" Timur asks.

"It's the color of the heavens, and so it is the color of peace."

Timur growls in disgust from the back of his throat, a sound so similar to one my mother used to make when she was irritated that it makes me want to break down weeping all over again.

"Yellow," I say, my voice muffled against Timur's kaftan.

"What was that?" Khalaf asks me, his breath tickling my earlobe.

I pull my face just enough away from Timur's body to answer, "Yellow," before plunging my forehead back into the folds of the old man's clothing.

"Good," says Khalaf. "Yellow is the color of the sun, and what could be better than that? So I shall be the blue sky, and you shall be the sun in the heavens."

Thankfully, I have my face pressed into Timur's back so that no one can see the blush that paints itself across my face.

Khalaf announces, "You have chosen yellow, so I will tell you the story of 'How Bahrâm Sat on a Sunday in the Yellow Dome' and listened to 'The Tale of the Greek King's Daughter' as recounted in the *Haft Paykar* by Nizami Ganjavi."

"That's a mouthful," Timur mutters.

"And I've only just begun," says Khalaf.

"Must you?" sighs his father.

"I'm afraid I must."

With disarming cheerfulness, Khalaf begins to tell his tale.

Once upon a time in the land of Iraq, there lived a great king, a man whose brilliance of mind and body were like the sun, lighting up all the world. And yet he was lonely. When he was born, his horoscope dictated that should he ever marry, he would live in conflict and misery with his wife.

The simple solution to his problem was in the purchasing of slaves. He bought many lovely girls in the hope that he would find his soul mate among them. In each case, matters would begin well, but within a week, the girl would forget her place and put on fine airs and demand gifts of him.

It happened that a hunchbacked old witch worked in the king's palace, a hag who would whisper poison in every girl's ear so that each slave in turn would grow in pride and see herself as better than she was. Week after week, month after month, year after year, the old witch meddled and taught these slaves to disdain their master and shirk their duties.

Each girl for whom the king had woven love's mantle had no love in her heart for him. He searched for his love so long, bought and sold so many girls, that the people began to call him the Slave Dealer. Eventually, he tired of his search and despaired. Since he could not marry, nor could he find a fitting mate to love, he gave up the fruitless endeavor.

"Are you listening, Jinghua?" Khalaf asks me.

"Yes," I whisper, already missing the way his storytelling voice rumbles in his body and hums against the skin of my back.

"It's not like you gave either of us a choice," Timur points out.

"Do you like it so far?" Khalaf asks me, ignoring his father.

"I don't know yet."

The sound of the oars slapping against the water beneath us sets my alarm bells ringing.

"Then I had better keep going," Khalaf says.

One day, a trader arrived from the east with a thousand slaves in his train, pure women from the farthest reaches of the world. The king, growing hopeful again, observed among these beauties the loveliest creature he had ever beheld, a girl with the face of an angel. But when he asked the slave trader to name his price, the merchant told him that despite the flames of passion she lit in men's hearts, she refused to requite them. And so whoever bought her would return her the following day in bitter disappointment. The king, disregarding the slave merchant's warning and following his heart, bought the slave anyway.

In his harem, she served him as quietly as his shadow. She admonished the old witch for her ugly words, and the king finally understood how it had transpired with all the other slaves. Fired by love, he called her his life, his pearl, his dew-petaled flower.

"This is the sappiest piece of rotting carrion I have ever heard," Timur interjects.

"Shh!" I hiss into the old goat's back. Khalaf's voice up to this point has been hypnotic, helping me to forget that nothing but a leaky plank of wood stands between me and a watery death, and I'm not letting this arrogant mountain of a man ruin the effect for me, khan or not.

"It would appear that you have been overruled, my lord," says Khalaf.

"Ugh," says Timur.

When the beautiful slave refused his advances, the king sensed in her a terrible secret. He begged her for her honesty and, obliging slave that she was, she told him that her tribe suffered from a curse, that all the women in her family who gave their hearts to men died when giving birth. "Why give up life for the pleasure of a single moment?" she asked him. "Why taste honey when it has been poisoned?" Having laid her secret heart bare to him, she asked that he, in turn, always be as honest with her.

But the king did not repay this favor. So desperately in love was he that he asked the old witch to help him. The hag told him to take a new slave as a lover, to shower her with praise and gifts to incite the jealousy of the woman he truly loved. And, lovesick fool that he was, he did as she bade.

The angel-faced slave, upon seeing her king behaving as if he loved another, saw through his shameful ruse, but it did not lessen the pain she suffered as she watched him make love to another.

"You once gave me the joy of sunrise," she admonished him, "and now you bring me night's sorrow. Who sent you down this crooked path? What deception do you play at?"

Ashamed, the king admitted to his trick.

"You were as clear as the light of the candle's flame with me, and yet I was like the smoke of the flame to you. With unpardonable deceit, I tried to soften you with the burning of my heart."

He spoke to her of his love and with such gentle words touched the heart of the unblemished pearl until she accepted him at last. And when he removed her veil, he understood

*that he had unlocked a treasure more valuable than a
thousand caskets of yellow gold.*

There's a pause. The oars shush their way through the water,
and I wonder when this nightmare will end.

"What?" says Timur. "That's it?"

"I'd say it follows a pretty consistent story arc, so yes, that's it,"
Khalaf replies.

"Is this what they teach you at that university of yours?"

"That and a few other things."

"I want my money back," says Timur.

"Is there a blue princess?" I ask into Timur's back.

"Hmm?" Khalaf hums in my ear.

I pull my face away but keep my eyes shut tight, which may
or may not help in quelling the way the bobbing of the boat
makes me want to scream. "You told us blue is your favorite
color. Is there a blue princess?" I press my forehead into Timur
once more.

"Ow," says the old goat. "You're so scrawny, girl, even your
forehead is sharp."

"There's a turquoise princess," says Khalaf. "Will that work?"

"Yes," I say.

"Please, dear God, let it be a better story than the last," Timur
gripes, but I suspect that he liked the first story better than he lets
on or else he would have told his son to shut up by now.

Khalaf announces, "'How Bahrâm Sat on a Wednesday in the

Turquoise Dome: The Tale of the Princess of the Fifth Clime.'"

He tells the story of a naive prince who is led astray into a terrible desert by a demon, but is saved from peril many times over because he has a kind and trusting heart. It's an allegory, reminding the listener that life's garden has both roses and thorns, and yet the Muslim god is ever present, even to those without friends or hope. Timur only interrupts him twice, and, before my terror can devour me, Khalaf's voice manages to carry me across the river.

PART THREE

THE SECOND RIDDLE

The City of Khanbalik, Khanate of the Yuan Dynasty

Autumn 1281

15

TURANDOKHT SAYS,

"She is the dragon with an iridescent wing
Stretched taut across the bleak and yawning void
To whom the hollow human heart must sing
When, with it, like a cat with prey has toyed.

"She only lives in shadow's heavy hue
When, invoked by man, is night her reign.
So every dusk gives birth to her anew,
And every dawn destroys her once again."

"Seven minutes," Zhang announces.

Seven minutes.

Khalaf might only have seven minutes to live.

I think of the months upon months we traveled the world together on a hard road, and it wasn't enough. It will never be enough.

Seven minutes.

Seven minutes is nothing.

"Rotting carrion," Timur curses in my ear, and for once it seems completely appropriate.

The crowd is silent as Khalaf bows his head and digests the riddle. His eyes are closed, and his back and shoulders move ever so slightly with the even expansion and contraction of his lungs. I can hear a heartbeat thudding the seconds away in heartsick impotence. I'm not sure whether it's Timur's or my own.

"Six minutes remaining," Zhang calls out.

I despise my powerlessness in this moment, my complete and utter inability to do anything to help him. I had months and months to change this outcome, but I did nothing to stop it. I let myself feel my culpability. I allow my self-berating to eat me up from within.

"It lives in darkness and dies in light," Khalaf thinks aloud.

"Five minutes."

"No," I breathe. Timur holds me tighter.

"And yet it helps the human heart," Khalaf continues, unsnarling the riddle bit by bit. "It saves a man from the bleak void."

The crowd is absolutely silent. Khalaf inhales, exhales.

"Four minutes," Zhang announces. A wolfish smile spreads across this face. He smells blood.

"No," I whisper again.

Khalaf raises his head and gazes up at Turandokht where she sits as lovely as an illuminated manuscript high above him on her carved throne.

"My khatun, it is hope," he says, his voice as soft and calm as ever while my entire body feels like it's screaming for him. "The dark night of the soul gives birth to hope, who stretches her helpful wing across the void of despair. And so this night, hope is reborn in me, that I may live to see the dawn."

His reasoning makes sense, but logic has fled from me. I'm operating on raw emotion here, my fear for Khalaf's life eclipsing all rationality. *He answered too soon,* I think in a panicked blur. *He should have deliberated longer, waited until he was certain.*

Turandokht goes stony and still.

"Did he get it?" Timur nudges me with his shoulder. "Dammit, girl, did he get it?"

"Shh! You can hear just as well as I can!" I hiss, slamming him back with my own narrow shoulder.

The three scholars up in the tower confer with Zhang. The chancellor steps forward wearing a frown that pulls his face downward as he announces, "It is hope. The contestant has successfully answered the first riddle."

Timur groans with relief and lets his forehead fall against the top of my head. Even the crowd bursts into cheers and applause and catcalls. My own relief is so great that I feel like it might crush me.

"Lamb's balls, my lord," I commiserate with Timur.

"You've got that right, little bird. How does he look?"

I haven't taken my eyes off Khalaf yet. To the untrained eye, he holds himself erect and his face remains calm and serene. But I know him. I can see the way he rubs his thumb against his first finger, and I know he's itching to burnish his lower lip in concentration. There's a tautness in his shoulders, too, a readiness in his muscles as if he were about to fight to the death.

I tell Timur, "He's bearing up well," but to myself, I say, *You did this to him, Jinghua.*

"One down," says the old goat.

"One down," I agree.

Neither of us says anything about "two to go." Apparently, there's an unspoken agreement between us that we will only celebrate the small victories at this point.

"Silence, please, for the second riddle!" Zhang calls.

As the hubbub softens, Turandokht tells Khalaf, "Hope has a way of disappointing the foolish."

"I have not found that to be the case, my khatun," he replies.

She keeps her poise, but anyone can see that Khalaf has her rattled. I know the feeling.

"How many men have made it this far?" Timur asks the man next to us.

"None," he answers with an incredulous laugh, and a hysterical giggle bubbles up from my lungs.

"Rotting fucking carrion," says Timur. I nod in agreement and take his hand in mine.

When the crowd is silent again, Zhang declares, "The contestant has successfully answered the first riddle. The second riddle is about to begin. The contestant will have seven minutes to answer. Do you understand, sir?"

"I do," Khalaf says with a curt nod.

I want to shove my way through this crowd and run to him and drag him out of Khanbalik, all the way to . . . where?

Where?

Nowhere in the world is safe for him. He wouldn't be here if he had seen another way, and I can't help but consider exactly how much of that is my fault.

Turandokht regards him with a cold-blooded gaze and says, "The second riddle is this:

> "From the fountain in the palace courtyard flows
> A liquid flame that is no flame at all.
> At times pours out an icy stream of woes,
> At times pours hot with passion's burning call.

> "When hot, it is delirium and ardor,
> The heat of battle, the rusty hue of conquest.
> When cold, it is a dull and aching torpor,
> A longing, or your marble-encased rest."

Khalaf bows his head again.

"Seven minutes," says Zhang.

On her dais high above, Turandokht shines, lovely as the full moon, while I, the invisible new moon, watch helplessly from my dark corner.

PART FOUR

BLOOD

Chagatai Khanate

Summer 1281

16

KHALAF SKETCHES IBN AL-HAYTHAM'S explanation of the moon's phases with the point of his saber—a gift from Abbas—in a bare patch of earth in the caravanserai's courtyard. He expounds on the projection of light from the sun and the angle at which it strikes the moon through every phase. His voice sounds the way velvet feels to the fingertips.

The city of Bukhara is a jewel, and Khalaf glitters more brightly than ever against the Kalyan minaret from which he is called to prayer five times each day. Since the caravanserai is located inside the city, the structure lacks the heavy fortification of those along the trade routes. It feels more like someone's home than a fortress, which makes it all the more comforting. Safe in the Chagatai Khanate, by the courtyard fires, our university of two carries on as if civilization didn't matter, as if rank and circumstance could not separate equal minds.

I let myself enjoy it, all of it. Why not? Who knows how much longer we'll have together, especially if Timur insists on heading north to the Kipchak Khanate once we reach Samarkand? Or if the old goat finds a way to sell me despite Khalaf's promises? Or if we make it far enough east for me to strike out on my own?

Or if Khalaf goes to Khanbalik to die for Turandokht?

Or marry her?

It's all so hopeless and depressing. Home is farther away now than it has ever been. All I can do is live in the moment. And the moment, despite the odds, is full of joy.

"Does al-Haytham's diagram account for the spherical nature of the moon, though?" I wonder aloud as I examine Khalaf's series of circles and the pathways of light from the sun.

"What do you think?" he asks.

I've read Shen Kuo's *Dream Pool Essays*, in which he explains his argument for the spherical nature of both the sun and the moon, and, without thinking, I hold forth on what I know. "The moon must be a ball, not a disc. When it first begins to wax, the sun's light strikes it from the side, giving the illusion of a crescent shape, whereas when the moon is full, the sun's light strikes it head-on, giving it the appearance of a circular disc."

I'm still staring down at Khalaf's drawing, and for one stupid moment, I'm as lit up as he is. And then I remember with a crushing dread who I am, or who I am supposed to be, at any rate. I raise my head to look at him.

He slides the saber back into the scabbard and crosses his arms in front of his chest.

"Jinghua?" he says, drawing out the second half of my name in one long syllable.

"Yes, my lord?"

His eyes narrow into the look that makes me feel skinned and flayed, as though he can see all the shadowy truths inside me.

"Who are you?" he asks.

I wipe all expression from my face. "What do you mean?"

"You just explained how the moon's phases prove the spherical nature of celestial bodies. You're very well spoken, even in a language that isn't your native tongue. And, in general, you sing and translate poetry that is far beyond a basic folk song. 'Deep in the silent inner room / Every fiber of my soft heart / Turns to a thousand strands of sorrow'? That's not peasant music."

"So?" My voice is cold, but inside I'm a churning mess. Even as I chastise myself for my carelessness, there's a part of me that wants him to see me, to know me.

"I'm only saying that the way you speak, the words you use, the things you know—it's unusual for a . . ."

He can't say it, so I finish the sentence for him: "Slave?"

Khalaf doesn't use the word, never calls me what I am. He casts his eyes down to his drawing and scrapes it out of the soil with the upturned toe of his worn leather boot. He takes a breath and brings his eyes back to mine.

"I wish that you didn't feel a need to hide who you are. I wish that you would let me know you as you know me."

I don't know how to respond to the sentiment that, to him at least, I'm not a slave. To him, I'm an actual human being. My tongue ties itself into a harder knot when he adds, "We're friends, aren't we?"

Yes, I think, but the boy who wants to know me is concealing just as much as I am. He's hiding the fact that his father has every intention of going back to the Kipchak Khanate. He's hiding the fact that he hopes to go to Khanbalik to face Turandokht and her riddles. Who knows what else he's keeping from me? I'm not the only one holding back.

And if he knew who I was, what then? Would it change anything?

Who am I kidding? It would change everything.

"What do you want to know?" I ask him cautiously.

"You never speak of your family, your ancestors."

"Neither do you."

He opens his mouth to speak but thinks better of it. It's terrible of me, but I love these moments when I catch him off guard, when I make him stumble or think twice. He crosses his arms more firmly in front of him and says, "My mother's name was Bibi Hanem. She died when I was six."

And now I feel like a horrible human being.

"I'm sorry," I say.

He shrugs, but the gesture doesn't ring true, and I know I've just stumbled into one of his own dark, sad corners.

"Do you remember her?" I ask.

"A little. She used to sing me a lullaby. *Like the white duck's little chick, I call to my mother when she is far from me.*"

His tone-deaf rendition makes the song all the more poignant. It's like he just forked over a piece of his heart, the part that belonged to his mother, and I have no choice but to do the same.

"My mother's name was Dongmei," I tell him. "She died when I was fifteen."

"How old are you now?" he asks.

"Seventeen."

"Only two years ago?"

Now it's my turn to shrug unconvincingly.

He leans in, his face closer to mine than it's ever been, so close I can feel his breath on my cheek. His gaze drops to my nonexistent breasts for an instant, and my whole body goes up in flames.

"What is it that you wear around your neck?" he asks.

Oh. The pendant. *Get a grip on yourself, Jinghua,* I think.

I finger the lump over my breastbone through the fabric of my black kaftan. I had no idea he'd noticed it. Not that I've tried to hide it, but it's like he's uncovered a secret, like I've been caught out. Before I can second-guess myself, I pull out the pendant and set it out on the palm of my hand for him to inspect by firelight.

He bends over my hand so that all I can see is the top of his turbaned head. "What is it?"

"It's a duck." A sad, broken, woebegone duck.

"No, I mean . . ." He cups his hands beneath mine to hold it steady.

He's touching me.

He's *touching* me.

I can hardly breathe with his skin against my skin, the warmth of his fingers seeping into my flesh. My heart threatens to explode or leap out of my chest or perform some other terrifying act in response.

"I mean, what is it to *you*?" he asks.

My mother drowned. And then I drowned, too. With those words, I opened a door and let him take the first step inside, and each day he takes another step and another. He's been rolling up the carpets and sweeping the floor and rearranging furniture, and now, all of a sudden, home doesn't look like home anymore. I no longer know where I belong or what I'm doing. And the thought of leaving him to go back to Lin'an feels like losing home all over again.

"It was a part of a larger piece," I tell him, "an incense burner from my family's ancestral shrine. It broke off. Obviously."

"How?"

I remember how it felt when I smashed it, how the slim shards of porcelain skittered across the floor, my entire world shattering right along with it. Khalaf's gaze drifts back to my face, and his dark eyes go liquid with sympathy.

"You don't have to answer that," he says gently.

"Thank you." I sniff a couple of times and pull myself together.

I don't want to remember how the duck's head broke free. That life and this one—the one I'm living with Khalaf in the present—I don't want them touching. I don't want him in any way associated with what came before.

"It's all I have left of my old life," I explain, taking my hand from his, tucking the pendant back into place, hiding it between my clothes and my heart.

"Thank you," he says. "You honor me with this."

I nod. I keep my gaze on the ground where he snuffed out the cycles of the moon.

"Will you sing tonight?" he asks after a moment. It's a purposeful distraction, and I cling to it for dear life. I sing Li Qingzhao's "Remorse" for him to the tune of "Rouged Lips," my voice so soft that only he can hear it in the caravanserai courtyard.

I fully admit to being snobbish when it comes to the kingdoms under Mongol rule. They pale so pathetically in comparison to Lin'an. But even I have to admit that Samarkand is beautiful, an oasis of blue domes and towers. This city looks like the sky cut off a piece of itself and set it down here on earth. The caravanserai courtyard boasts an ornate fountain at its heart with arched doorways surrounding it on all sides. Even the camels look elegant here.

I hate the sight of it.

This is where the present ends and the future begins. This is where the road diverges into many paths, and none of us wants to be on the same one.

I know it. Khalaf knows it. Even the damn camel trader knows it.

"The Kipchaks say this is where we part ways," Mazdak tells me as I help him stable the camels at the caravanserai. "I assume you're going with them?"

"That's right," I answer, but now that he's asked the question, I realize that I am also assuming I have a choice, that if I decide not to run away, from this point Timur and Khalaf will take me with them.

Assumptions can be wrong.

I leave Mazdak to finish up and head to our sleeping quarters. I've got my hand on the door when I hear Timur's voice on the other side say, "I know you're fond of the girl. I don't dislike her myself. But men in our position don't have the luxury of choosing what we do and do not want in this world. We have other, larger matters to contend with."

"I made a promise," Khalaf says. "I promised her that we wouldn't sell her. I'm not going back on a promise. And if you ask me, we have no right to sell her in the first place."

"Well, I didn't ask you, and it's time you learned that the promise of a khan is worth very little."

"Khan of what? Look at us, Father. Do we look like khans?"

"You owe it to your people to survive and prosper so that you can come back to liberate them."

If Khalaf answers, I can't hear him.

"We're heading into war. Do you want to take her into

battle? Is that what's best for her?"

Silence.

"We'll see that she finds respectable service," Timur continues. "We won't just sell her to some brothel. You'll be able to set your mind at ease on that point."

Silence again.

"Is the Kipchak Khanate really worth less than one girl?" Timur asks.

I step away because I don't want to hear Khalaf's answer.

The truth hurts.

I'm halfway down the hall formulating my escape plan when I hear the door burst open behind me.

"Jinghua," Khalaf's voice rings out, loud, bouncing off the stone walls. I turn around to find him storming toward me.

Timur stands at the door. "We're not through here."

"Yes, we are," Khalaf answers gruffly without looking back. He doesn't break stride but takes me by the arm and drags me along with him, saying, "Come on. We need supplies."

"Fine. Be angry. You know I'm right. Enjoy your outing, because it's going to be your last," Timur shouts after us, his voice echoing off the arched ceiling as Khalaf drags me out into the courtyard. The glaring sun hurts my eyes when we emerge from the darkened hallway, but Khalaf doesn't stop.

"My lord?"

It's hard to keep up with his longer gait, and his hand is too tight on my elbow. I pull myself free, and he finally stops. He rubs his eyes with the heels of his hands and says, "Sorry. I'm sorry."

I wonder for what transgression he's apologizing, but I don't ask for details. Honestly, I don't want to know. I'm terrified to know.

"Should we go to the bazaar?" I ask like the cowardly little mouse I am.

"Did you hear that?" he asks bluntly. "Back there, did you hear what we were talking about?"

I don't answer, but I guess I don't need to, because he says, "We are not going to sell you. You came with us by choice, and that means you stay with us by choice or you leave us by choice." He points his finger each time he says "choice" as if his hand were a dagger aimed at his father's intentions. "I made a promise to you that I had no right to make, because you never belonged to us to begin with. Do you understand?"

In this moment, he is the Khalaf I glimpsed in the Caucasus: pared down, intense, dangerous, and for reasons that are so far beyond me I can't even begin to comprehend them, I want to wrap my arms around his neck and press him against the courtyard wall and kiss him hard. I've never even wanted to kiss someone normally, much less hard. What on earth is happening to me?

Why taste honey when it has been poisoned? the slave girl in Khalaf's story asked her king. Why want something you absolutely cannot have? I don't *want* to want him.

But I do.

There's no denying it, not to myself anyway.

"What are you saying?" I ask him, my bewilderment on full display. "Are you giving me my freedom?"

He finally softens. His shoulders relent, but the intensity of my wanting doesn't.

"I'm supposed to walk the steep pass, remember?" he says. "I can't be a companion of the right if you are not free. Your freedom was never mine to give or take. That is the will of God."

His words melt me. Just when I think my life can't get any messier, it does. "Thank you," I tell him. It's like taking the apple out of his hand all over again.

"I know how much you want to go home, Jinghua, wherever home is for you. You've never said it, but I know."

To be known. To be unknowable. What does it matter? I have so few truths to give him anyway. I may as well give him this one.

"Lin'an. I'm from Lin'an."

"Lin'an," he repeats as if I've handed him a gift, as if the word itself were made of gold. "I wish I could take you there."

"There is no 'there' to go back to, my lord. Not for me." I wipe my face with my sleeve and let myself sink into the cold, hard truth of it. Even if I made it past the Pamir mountain range to the east, there's no way I'd survive the journey on my own. And if by some miracle I found myself in Lin'an, what then? I'd be a beggar on the streets or worse. Why did it take me two years and thousands of *li* to understand this? Maybe Khalaf would be alive and well and studying at university if I had realized from the beginning that home was dead and gone.

Now, home is crossing deserts and mountains and rivers beside Khalaf. I don't want to lose that any sooner than I have to, so I take his right hand in both of mine. It's heavier than I expect, rougher, harder. His eyes widen at the gesture.

"I choose to stay with you," I tell him. I deliberately do not call him *my lord*.

His chest rises and falls. He swallows so hard I can see his larynx bob under the taut skin of his neck.

I want to kiss that, too.

Jinghua! I scream at myself.

He blinks. He nods.

I release his hand and say, "Supplies?"

"Supplies," he agrees, clearing his throat. We head to the stables as Mazdak is coming out, and the trader rolls his eyes in irritation as we ask for a camel to load up at the bazaar.

17

THE MARKET SPRAWLS IN THE SHADOW of a mosque whose domes are covered in lapis lazuli. Khalaf and I stock up on melons, dried apricots, peppers, onions, and chickpeas.

"I thought you might want a change from the lentils," he comments to me as we watch the vendor shovel scoops of the latter into a huge cotton bag for us. His knowing grin makes my cheeks go hot. I wonder how long he's known the depths of my lentil-inspired despair.

"You don't miss much, do you?" I say.

"Really? I'd say I'm missing a great deal." His eyes skate across my lips before he looks away. Oh, my heaven, if his eyes make my skin burn like this, what on earth would his lips do?

Jinghua! I berate myself again.

As I struggle internally to overcome my pointless attraction to the prince of the Kipchak Khanate, Khalaf's focus shifts to a public notice pasted on the mosque. He hands me the reins of the camel and our coin purse, and he walks over to read it.

I pay the vendor when he's finished with our order, and I lead the camel over to stand beside Khalaf, who hasn't moved away from the notice even though he could have read it in its entirety ten times over by now. It's written in several languages, including Hanyu:

Let it be known that this is the law: No prince shall be allowed to wed Turandokht Khatun who shall not previously have replied without hesitation to the riddles that she shall put to him. If his answers prove satisfactory, she will consent to his becoming her husband. But if the reverse, he shall forfeit his life for his temerity. This the Great Khan has sworn to the Earth and to the Eternal Blue Sky.

Turandokht.

Her name hasn't come up in weeks, but she never stops haunting me, never relinquishes her death grip on my life, as malevolent as any evil spirit. My hand strangles the camel's reins as I seethe at the sight of her name.

There at the very bottom of the page is more salt to rub into the wound: *Edict of Chancellor Zhang by order of the Great Khan of the Great Yuan Dynasty and the Empire of the Mongols.*

I curse under my breath before I realize that Khalaf still stands beside me, only now his eyes are no longer on the edict. They're on me, noticing things I wish to hide.

Like the fact that I can read.

"What does it say?" I ask clumsily.

His eyes remain narrowed. "Nothing."

I'm about to try to wriggle my way out of this blunder when I look over Khalaf's shoulder and notice a group of Mongol warriors milling about in the area of the market we just vacated.

"My lord, what is Hulegu Il-Khan's standard?"

He grows very still. His lips hardly move when he answers, "Red on a yellow background."

I nod to the men interrogating the chickpea seller we visited not five minutes ago, soldiers wearing the standard of Hulegu Il-Khan, as brazen as you please in the Chagatai Khanate. Khalaf surreptitiously peers over his shoulder, then turns back to me. He takes the camel's reins from my hand and says, very quietly, "Stay calm. No one has seen my father in town except maybe the caravanserai keeper. We walk back to our quarters, and we stay there, inside."

"Have you seen a Kipchak merchant—an old man—possibly traveling with a grown son?" one of the soldiers is asking the farmer.

They know Khalaf is alive. This is getting worse by the second.

The farmer laughs. "Every other man who comes through here is an old Kipchak merchant with a grown son. Now, do you mind? I'm running a business here."

That response doesn't go over well. I flinch as one of the warriors kicks over the cart, sending the round beans sailing through the air and spilling over the dirt. The leader yanks the vendor by the front of his tunic out into the main thoroughfare in a kicking, screaming cloud of dust. Now that they've created a scene, now that all buying and selling has come to a full and complete halt, the warrior holding the vendor announces for all to hear, "We speak for Hulegu Il-Khan by the blessing of Turandokht Khatun. We are looking for an old man—a Kipchak Mongol posing as a merchant. He may have his grown son with him."

I'm frozen in place. There must be an *arban* of ten hunting Khalaf down, him and Timur. The Il-Khanids aren't just waiting on the border. They're right here. With Turandokht's approval. Her long arm reaches halfway around the world to slap me down. I want to throw my head back and howl my outrage to the Mongols' Eternal Blue Sky.

"How about you, girl?" the leader says to me, dropping the skinny chickpea seller off to the side. "Seen an old Kipchak and his son? He's a big man, hard to miss."

I'm so alarmed that my ears start ringing.

"Go," I whisper to Khalaf without moving my lips, praying he can hear me.

"No!" he hisses, loud and clear even though his back is to me.

I don't give him a choice. I step forward and answer the soldier. "No, sir." To my relief, I can hear Khalaf moving on behind me, taking the camel with him.

The soldier swaggers a few paces in my direction. "Are you sure about that?"

I piss myself, just a tiny bit, and nod.

"Why are you bothering with her? She's not even a little pretty," one of his fellows calls over his shoulder, and the other men laugh.

"She's got an air about her. She's striking," the leader argues.

"Forget this. We'll catch them on the road north before they make it back to the Kipchak Khanate. What are they going to do? Outrun us *and* Turandokht's men?"

They all laugh again and find a prettier girl to torment, leaving me sweating out my panic with a carpet of chickpeas beneath my feet.

I want to run. I want to go tearing back to the caravanserai to make sure Khalaf is alive and well and still in the world. But I know that would draw attention, so once I'm certain the soldiers aren't looking, I make myself walk back to the caravanserai on a meandering route.

My feet may wander, but my mind does not. Or maybe it's simply my heart informing my mind that the decision has been made, and logic be damned.

I'm not going home.

My goal has moved outside myself.

I'm going to keep Khalaf alive. That's it. Pure and simple. He's not going to follow his father's mad plan to return to the Kipchak Khanate. He's not going to Khanbalik to face Turandokht's riddles. He's going to find this Qaidu person, and he is going to live out his life in relative peace. And I am going to make that happen.

If he isn't dead already, I think in sick terror.

A good half hour has passed by the time I get back. When I step into our quarters and find Khalaf and Timur playing a game of cards with Mazdak as if they had nothing better to do to pass the time, my knees nearly give out with relief. Khalaf closes his eyes when he sees me walk in. His cards vibrate with the shaking of his hands.

Mazdak serendipitously excuses himself to pee, leaving me, Khalaf, and Timur alone for a few minutes. It's clear that Khalaf has managed to fill in his father about the fact that Hulegu Il-Khan has sent men here to catch him with the approval of Turandokht Khatun. I add the nail in the coffin and pray he doesn't shoot the messenger.

"They said they would capture you on the northern road to the Kipchak Khanate, my lord."

"Rotting carrion!" Timur points an accusatory finger at Khalaf. "If you say, 'I told you so,' I will rip your balls off."

I can see Khalaf offer up a prayer to his god before he says calmly, "What now?"

Timur tosses his cards on the floor in disgust. "We stick with Mazdak. We keep heading east, and we try to find Qaidu. You can't tell me Hulegu Il-Khan is going to follow us past the Pamirs."

Yes, yes, and yes. This will all be excellent news if we manage to escape from Samarkand with our lives.

"Are you sure Qaidu will ally himself with you at this point?" asks Khalaf. "Why not appeal directly to the Great Khan, tell him your side of the story? What do we have to lose?"

Of course Khalaf wants to go to Khanbalik. Why run away from Hulegu Il-Khan when he can run toward perfect, beautiful, brilliant Turandokht Khatun, who, apparently, wants to kill the Kipchaks, too? It's ridiculous how much the very idea makes my chest hurt. Well, it's not going to happen. I won't let it happen.

"Are you kidding me?" says Timur. "With his daughter sending men after us? Who knows where the Great Khan stands?"

Khalaf narrows his eyes to the point where I wonder how he can even see. I'm glad I'm not the one on the other end of that suspicious gaze for a change. "You've been avoiding the Great Khan from the very beginning," he says, "and now his daughter has sent men to hunt you down, too. Why?"

"Don't be so dramatic. I'm not worried about some girl's milk-blooded army. We'll try Qaidu. I have my reasons."

"Would you care to share those reasons with me?" Khalaf asks.

Timur answers with stone-faced silence. His son shakes his head and rises to his feet. "I need some air."

"Did you have a better plan?" Timur challenges him.

I think of Khalaf standing in front of the edict before I saw the il-khan's men. *Let it be known that this is the law.* . . . He licks his lips, but he says, "No, my lord."

"Then stop sulking."

Khalaf peeks his head out into the hallway. He must not see

Mazdak returning yet because he tells Timur, "There's one more order of business we need to discuss."

Timur crosses his thick arms over his even thicker chest. "Oh, here we go: the slave."

I love it when they talk about my fate in front of me. "I'm right here," I say.

"That's three times Jinghua has demonstrated her loyalty to us and twice she's saved your life," says Khalaf. "She stays with us."

Timur glares at me. A few months ago, that look alone might have killed me. Now, considering all the things that might kill me, Timur's glare is pretty relative. I glare right back at him.

"Fine," he grunts.

"Thank you, my lord," Khalaf says, sounding less than gracious as he steps out into the hall.

"Where do you think you're going?" Timur calls after him.

Khalaf is already out of sight. We hear his voice say, "Courtyard," as the door swings shut, and Timur and I are left sitting alone together in a thick silence.

"Shut up," he says to me.

The sheer injustice of Timur's scolding makes my voice shoot up the musical scale, so high I'm surprised dogs don't start scratching at the door. "I didn't say anything!"

"Shut up anyway."

"Ugh!"

I rise to follow Khalaf out into the courtyard.

"Tell him to come in," Timur orders me. "He shouldn't be seen."

I'm on the verge of making a smart-mouthed retort, but the fact that he's displaying concern for his son's well-being softens me. "Agreed, my lord," I answer grudgingly, and the old goat actually gives me an appreciative nod.

By now, the sun has set, and it takes me a moment to find Khalaf. He leans against one of the walls and watches the clear night sky. I walk over to him and lean on the wall beside him.

"You know, al-Biruni postulated that the earth is not a fixed point but moves through the heavens," he says, still staring upward. "More recently, in *The Limit of Accomplishment concerning Knowledge of the Heavens*, Qutb al-Din al-Shirazi refined Ptolemy's principles on planetary motion and even suggested a heliocentric model. It's fascinating. You should read it sometime. Because you can. You can read."

This day will not stop being terrible. I sigh and answer, "I never said I couldn't."

"You never said you *could*." He finally looks at me, and I can see that he's just as angry with me as he was with Timur earlier today. "Who are you, really? Can you just tell me the truth for once?"

And now I'm mad because he's mad, and he has no right to be mad at me, not for this, anyway. "You're not asking me who I am. You're asking who I was."

"They're one and the same."

"No, they're not."

"You're no slave, Jinghua," he insists.

"'Tell that to heaven,'" I quote him, and, just to piss him off, I add, "my lord."

We stand there, side by side, each of us leaning against our own patch of wall. As my fuming starts to dissipate, I ask, "Why are you so mad?"

Khalaf pushes himself off the wall and steps in front of me, and it is clear that his own fury has not dissipated in the slightest. "Are you joking?" He glances to each side to make sure no one's listening. "Today? In the bazaar? Il-Khanid soldiers hunting us down? You deliberately put yourself in harm's way."

My anger surges right back up. "I got the soldiers' attention off you so you could get away. I was protecting you . . . and your father. You're welcome."

"I don't need your protection."

"Don't you?"

He's back in pointing mode, his finger jabbing the air as he speaks. "You could have gotten yourself killed today. Don't you see? You don't get to make decisions like that."

I pull myself up straight and tall, as regal as I can manage. It's a side of myself I've never let him see before. He blinks and even looks cowed.

"You told me my freedom—my *life*—was never yours to give

or take," I remind him. "So yes, I do. I do get to make decisions like that. And your father commands you to return to the room, by the way."

I leave him stammering in the caravanserai courtyard behind me.

"My lord," I tack on without looking back.

18

FOR THE NEXT FIVE DAYS HEADING east out of Samarkand, Khalaf hardly speaks to me aside from things like "Pass the
stew." For five days, I suffer Smoldering Khalaf and His Furious
Lip Rubbing (although, to be honest, even *that* is pretty). I'm not
sure if it's because he's still angry with me or if he's too busy looking behind us every ten seconds to do much else. Probably both.
In either case, once again, Hulegu Il-Khan doesn't materialize,
nor do Turandokht's soldiers.

It gets steadily colder as we rise in elevation, an apt reflection
of the Jinghua-Khalaf relationship. What does he expect me to
do, I wonder? Apologize for saving his life? Nope. Not going to
happen. I absolutely out-anger him on this.

By the sixth day into this leg of the journey, the Pamirs form a wall of mountains in front of us as far as the eye can see.

"How the hell are we going to get around that?" Timur asks Mazdak with more than a hint of accusation in his voice.

Mazdak laughs. "We're not going around it, my friend. We're going through it." He stands beside Timur, closes one eye, and aims his hand at a dip between two behemoth white peaks. "Right there."

Khalaf and Timur stare at that dip thousands of feet above us.

"Oh," says Khalaf.

Timur better captures the sentiment when he utters, "Cancerous, rotted, weeping lamb's balls."

Mazdak laughs again and slaps Timur heartily on the back. "Welcome to the Roof of the World," he says.

Timur said the il-khan's men wouldn't follow us into the Pamirs, and I can see why. There are not enough coats and blankets in the universe to make this place bearable. Cairns of sheep skulls reach out of the snow to mark our way, their huge curled horns acting as skeletal signposts. Local men, bundled head to toe, trudge behind their herds of yaks, whose shaggy coats are frosted with snow. The jagged white peaks surrounding us look like teeth ready and waiting to eat us alive.

"Why do I do this to myself?" Mazdak grumbles under his breath. "This is the last time I'm making this crossing."

When Mazdak complains, I know we're in trouble.

Three days into the pass, we sleep in a fort, high above the river valley below us. The view would be stunning if I didn't already hate the Pamirs from the depths of my soul. Even so, it's a huge improvement over our sleeping conditions of the previous two nights, although that's not saying much. Tiny stone hovels don't do much to keep out the cold.

Swathed in my inadequate blanket, I fall into sleep the way one steps off a cliff, slamming hard and fast into a dream of my brother. Tonight, he is not the ghostly creature he has become but the brother I remember at around age ten, his plait flying out behind him as he spins to kick a shuttlecock and keep it airborne.

It's summer. The air is thick and wet, sticking to my skin. Every breath itches with pollen.

I want to play, too, I tell Weiji, but he laughs and kicks the shuttlecock away from me. When I lunge for it, he takes it up in his hand and holds it high, out of my reach.

Let me have it! I yell at him, furious.

Come and get it! he taunts, running away down the garden path, still giggling.

No matter how fast I run, he's always faster, and I can't catch him.

The following day, we've reached the highest point of the pass, the Roof of the World, where it's so high and so prohibitively cold that we can barely get a fire started, and the fire we do start doesn't give off enough heat to boil a pot of water. I've heard of this place before, but I always assumed it was more metaphor or hyperbole than actual fact. I stand corrected, which makes me even grumpier.

I huddle in my blanket on the women's side of the way station in which we're spending the night, a tiny square of stone slabs pasted together with clay. I face the tepid fire and pray for sleep that does not come.

"Jinghua?" Khalaf calls to me from the men's side. It's the first time he's said my name since we left Samarkand.

"Yes, my lord?" I'm so cold that the word "lord" earns four extra syllables through my shivering.

"Are you all right?"

A peace offering. That's warm, at least.

"Yes, my lord," I answer. My chattering teeth barely allow me to answer. Even my voice is frozen. Even my breath is frozen.

"That has to be a bald-faced lie, because I am beyond freezing, and if I'm beyond freezing, you must be half dead over there by yourself."

The next thing I know, he has come over to my side of the fire, wrapped in his blanket.

"What are you doing?" I ask him, alarmed. I glance across the cabin to where Timur and Mazdak are sleeping.

"Making sure neither of us dies tonight."

"Shut up," Timur grumbles.

"But . . . but my lord . . . ," I protest.

"I'm freezing. You're freezing." Khalaf settles down right next to me, bumping against me with his backside.

"My lord!"

He stops. He sits. He looks down at me. "Jinghua, there are rules, but there is also a benevolent God. And I'd like to think that God in His infinite benevolence would prefer that we use our common sense and live rather than follow the rules and freeze to death in the night."

"But what about Mazdak? Won't he be offended?"

"Mazdak can go hang if he doesn't like it," Khalaf answers, spreading his blanket over both of us.

"I heard that, and all I can say is that God is watching, young master," says Mazdak, but he sounds more amused than offended.

"'As for anything wherein you differ, judgment thereof lies with God,'" Khalaf quotes back to him as he lies down beside me and snuggles his back against mine so that he's facing the outer stone wall and I'm sandwiched between him and the fire. I wonder if he can feel my heart clanging against him. I am suddenly wide-awake, my body humming with the awareness of his body's proximity to mine.

"Ah!" he sighs with pleasure. "You are so much warmer than you look."

"Thank you?"

"That didn't come out right," he admits.

Khalaf's warmth seeps into my spine and finally makes me drowsy. My full-body shaking transmutes into shivering and, eventually, stops altogether. His heat radiates against me under the combined power of both our blankets, but given the circumstances, it's hard to relax. For a time, there is only the wind outside and the weak crackle of the fire and the expansion and contraction of Khalaf's lungs.

"Jinghua?" he murmurs into the night.

"Yes, my lord?"

"Cancerous lamb's balls. Go. To. Sleep," groans Timur.

"If I am going to die on this mountain, I think I'd like to hear you sing one more time."

I'm waiting for a snarky remark from Timur, but he goes curiously silent.

"You want me to sing, my lord?" I ask, what little resentment I had left fizzling out in the freezing night.

"If it pleases you."

His voice wraps me up, the way his arms held me when I sobbed all over him beside the Oxus. I remember how his voice carried me across the river a few weeks ago.

Yes, it pleases me. *He* pleases me.

So I sing "The Beauty of White Chrysanthemums" for him. My voice rises and falls in the darkness. Khalaf's breath in and out is like the sea, and my voice is the boat that bobs in it.

> *Heaven ordains you will wither*
> *And your faint fragrance disappear.*
> *No matter how much I love you*
> *You will fade but be remembered in this poem.*

Timur's snoring and Mazdak's thick breath from across the fire greet me at the other end of the song. I assume Khalaf has fallen asleep, too, until he speaks, only it's neither Mongolian nor Hanyu coming from his lips but a string of unfamiliar syllables that I take to be Persian.

"What was that?" I whisper in the quiet that follows.

"It's a quatrain from the *Rubáiyát* of Omar Khayyám."

"What does it mean?"

He doesn't answer.

"My lord?" I ask, wondering again if he's fallen asleep, but his voice comes to me in the night as he translates the words:

"A book of verses underneath the bough
A flask of wine, a loaf of bread, and thou
Beside me singing in the wilderness
And . . ."

"And?" I press.

"Forgive me," he says, his voice low and warm like the embers in front of me. "I don't remember the rest."

"You remember everything."

He doesn't answer me, though, and I can't help but think that he's lying, that he does remember the rest and doesn't want to tell me. Now I desperately, desperately want to know how it ends.

"Jinghua?" he whispers one last time.

"Yes?" I ask, half amused, half exasperated.

"Thank you for putting up with me."

"You're welcome, my lord," I tell him in a stunning display of understatement. And not long afterward, I fall asleep.

There is a small pond surrounded by bamboo. I can't see it, but I know it's there. The bamboo sways overhead as I shove myself through the growth, the leaves punctuating a colorless sky in sharp points, the stalks reaching out to eternity. I catch glimpses of the water now, but I can't seem to get there.

The world is soundless. Nothing sings. No crickets saw their music. No fish ripple the water's surface. Everything has gone silent as my brother, Weiji, wounded and bleeding, tramps through the bamboo at the water's edge. He holds a falcon on his arm. Gaunt and lost, he looks for me between the reeds, but he does not see me. He cries out, "Look at her, Jinghua. She's beautiful. I mean, she's really, really beautiful."

Part of me wants to rush to him, but my more cowardly instinct is to hide. And so I become a crane. My gawky legs make the water shush as I move freely now through the bamboo and cattails. My intent was to make myself disappear, but it is Weiji who is gone while I am still here.

Now there is a tiger on the other side of the pond. The slick surface of his pelt shimmers moonlight as he moves with sinuous grace through the reeds on the opposite bank. I disappear farther into the bamboo on my side, quietly, carefully. The tiger breaks the surface of the pool with one enormous paw followed by another until the animal is submerged. The water ripples around him, his back shining wet, and he swims toward me until he is nothing but a great head bobbing on the surface.

The light is much brighter now, as if dusk has become morning. There is an explosion of music. Beetles and frogs and sparrows. Seed pods float by on white tails. The tiger swims toward me, his limbs propelling him forward without a splash. When he can touch the bottom, he begins to rise up out of the pool, and I can see he is no tiger at all, but a man. He is naked, and as the inches of his body rise out of the water with each halting step, he is inexplicably dry.

The water music has been saying his name, but I've only just now heard it and understood.

I am hiding in the bamboo. I want to see him, but I don't want to be seen. It's ridiculous, because he already knows I'm here. He finds me in the bamboo, where I pretend that I'm invisible. I jitter and twitch in the way of birds, my long neck taking me away but not away from him. He offers his cupped hands to me. He calls to me in the soft language of birds. He speaks the language of all things. He reaches out between the stalks, and I let the tips of his fingers trace the patterns of my feathered crest, unable to move from a combination of terror and wonder. He comes closer and with his lips brushes the feathers along the length of my neck, down one side and up the other, slowly, as if he would taste and feel each one.

And when he pulls away to look at me, I am no longer a bird.

And when his lips touch mine, when he presses me against the soft bank, when I push myself against his body in a nest of cattails, I know what I am.

When I wake, I'm breathing Khalaf.

In the night, our bodies have turned front to front rather than back to back, and my face is burrowed into his ropy neck. His skin smells of rust and smoke and earth. His arm is draped over my waist. There is an unremembered dream shimmering at the edge of my consciousness, and in my sleepy haze this all seems reasonable, lovely.

Perfect.

Until reality comes crashing in.

Our legs are tangled up, our bodies pressed together, and against my abdomen I feel something rocklike pushing against me. My eyes go wide, and I stop breathing.

Oh. My. Heaven.

Terrified that he'll wake to find me nuzzling him or find himself . . . in his current state, I take Khalaf's arm and carefully lift it so that I can scoot out from underneath its weight. His arm is much heavier than I would have thought, but I manage. I gently set it down in front of him on the ground. Only once does he stir, a little sound of protest at my taking my heat away, but he never wakes, never opens his eyes.

Outside the blankets, the icy air stabs through skin and muscle, straight to the bone. This is how newborn babies must feel, one moment warm and dark and protected, the next thrust into a frigid world full of light.

I want to crawl back beneath the blanket.

I want.

Why shouldn't I lie beside him? Why shouldn't he lie beside me? I ask myself in the darkest, loneliest part of my heart.

Because, my better self answers, and I let my dark, lonely heart fill in the rest.

My hands are shaking with a combination of cold and embarrassment. It takes me a long time to relight the fire, but when I do, I notice Khalaf, still curled on the ground, looking at me with half-opened eyes. He closes them when our eyes meet.

19

SINCE OUR NIGHT OF UNCONSCIOUS CUDDLING,
Khalaf has been walking beside his father for the most part, and
even when we carry on with our lessons, he's been guarded, careful, polite.

"How does the intonation sound again?"

"Which word would I use in that circumstance?"

I wonder if he remembers curling up to me with greater clarity
than I realized. Maybe he's as embarrassed and confused as I am.

One morning, as I'm taking a bite of a dried date, I catch him
watching me as I bring the fruit to my mouth. He's wearing that
glassy-eyed expression that makes my pulse pound in my veins.

"How do you say 'date' in Hanyu?" he asks, as if that's why he's
staring at me, at my mouth. And who knows? Maybe it is.

"'*Zăo,*'" I tell him.

"*Zăo.* Good. Excellent. Thank you."

He returns his attention to his own breakfast, but I'm reluctant to let him go so easily. I say, "When couples marry, people tell them '*zăo shēng guì zǐ,*' which means 'May you give birth to a son.' "But since '*zăo*' also means 'date,' and '*huāshēng*' means 'peanut,' sometimes people give the couple dates and peanuts as a joke."

And for a moment, I have him back. He smiles, enjoying the play on words. But then he glances over his shoulder at Timur, and his cool demeanor returns.

It's stunning how quickly the landscape changes once we exit the Pamirs, from stubbly steppe country to desert once more, all in less than a week's travel. By the time we arrive at Kashgar, it's been a month since we left Samarkand—a month of stilted awkwardness between me and Khalaf, punctuated briefly by one night of warmth on the Roof of the World. If I never see the Pamirs again, it will be too soon. Tonight, I will sleep in a nice, warm, dry caravanserai, and I will remember those freezing stone shelters in the mountains with no fondness at all. Whatsoever.

Although, truth be told, I can't quite expunge the memory of Khalaf's lying beside me, back-to-back. Or waking with my face pressed into his neck. Or the scent of him. Or the way his entire body felt against mine. Or his voice in the night.

. . . and thou

Beside me singing in the wilderness . . .

He lingers in the caravanserai stables, fussing with his camel's pack long after the rest of us are finished and ready to head to our sleeping quarters. Maybe I'm delusional, but I could swear he's avoiding me.

I walk several paces behind Timur and Mazdak on our way to the room with my pack weighing down my arms like a fat baby when I decide to turn back.

"Where are you going?" Timur calls behind me.

"Forgot something."

I hear him make that throaty protest behind me that forcefully reminds me of my mother. It seems impossible that Timur and my mother could have anything in common, but I suppose to a certain extent parents are parents. He doesn't want me going near Khalaf, and my mother probably wouldn't either. But he's not my mother, and there's nothing he can do about it.

As I walk back to the stables, it occurs to me that just this single act would have been impossible in my old life. In some ways, I'm freer now than I have ever been.

When I turn the corner, I find Khalaf already walking toward me from the opposite direction. He stops when he sees me, so I'm the one who closes the distance between us.

"Is everything all right?" he asks.

"Yes, my lord, it's only . . . Have I done something wrong?" His demeanor is still distant. He's standing right in front of me, and yet I miss him terribly.

"No, of course not." He doesn't elaborate. Even his eyes have walled me out.

My throat swells. "Then why are you being like this?" I ask, my voice wavering pathetically.

"I don't know what you mean."

"Like"—I take one arm away from my bundle and flap my hand at him—"this." I fumble with the sack and catch it up again with both arms.

Khalaf takes the bag from my arms even though he's carrying a bag of his own. "Jinghua," he says quietly, "look, I'm sorry. I know I owe you an apology."

"For what?"

"In the Pamirs, when I . . . when I slept next to you. It wasn't right. I'm a . . ." He looks around as people pass by us along the hallway, eyeing us with raised eyebrows and curious glances. "I am who I am," he whispers. "And you . . ."

I burn with anger and humiliation. "And I'm a slave," I finish for him. "Just say it."

"No. That isn't what I meant." His face twists. I think he might start bawling right here in the hallway.

Good, I think viciously.

My eyes catch a tiny glint of light coming from a darkened doorway right behind Khalaf, the reflection of light on metal.

Any and all indignation I may have felt half a second ago

drains out of me faster than lightning streaks across the night sky.

I launch myself at Khalaf. He's caught off guard, and we both go tumbling to the intricately tiled floor as the blade intended for Khalaf's back sails over us, clanks against the opposite wall, and clatters on the ground just inches from our tangled feet.

I'm spread-eagled on top of Khalaf's torso, but I'm so relieved he's still alive that I don't have the decency to be embarrassed. Khalaf raises his head off the floor and stares at the dagger with wide eyes before he turns his attention to the shadowy doorway from whence it came. A man bolts out of the darkness and runs pell-mell down the hall toward the courtyard. Khalaf squirms out from beneath me, snatches up the dagger, gets back on his feet in a blur of motion, and goes sprinting after the assassin.

I'm still trying to sort out why in the name of all that is good and holy Khalaf is running *toward* his killer rather than *away* from him as I get to my own feet and pelt down the corridor after them. I'm already ten paces behind Khalaf when I slam into a pair of merchants who dart out of Khalaf's way as he bullets past them. Now I've dropped too far behind to catch up. I leave the two merchants to scold my backside as I dart down an adjacent hallway, hoping to close in on the assassin from the opposite direction.

And do what? I wonder as my lungs ache and my muscles burn. "This is such a bad idea," I gasp as I take a corner heading to the market stalls that will lead me back toward the courtyard. Even this late in the afternoon, the bazaar is bustling with people, and now I'm pushing and shoving as well as running.

I see Khalaf on the other side of the market, racing toward me, but I don't see the assassin anywhere. Khalaf and I close the distance between us and stop to look for the man we were chasing as we gasp for air. Nothing. He's managed to disappear in the market crowds.

"Get somewhere safe before I kill you myself," I pant at Khalaf.

"Father" is Khalaf's only reply, and he goes racing off again, this time heading back toward the sleeping quarters.

I whimper, but I follow his lead, sprinting after him. He bursts into our room just a few seconds ahead of me.

"Oh, thank God," he breathes once he sees that his father is still alive. He closes the door behind me and leans up against it to catch his breath.

"Where the hell have you been?" Timur asks.

"My lord—Father, we need to leave. Now."

I watch as the reality of our situation weighs down Timur's eyebrows. "What? They're here? In fucking Kashgar?"

Khalaf glances at Mazdak and nods at Timur.

"How many?"

"Just one, but he ran and we lost him in the bazaar. We have to assume there are more."

"Rotting carrion!"

Mazdak chooses this moment to insert himself into the conversation.

"Look, I don't know what's going on here, but I don't want any trouble."

Timur doesn't even glance at the man. "We'll have to kill him," he says with a jerk of his head in Mazdak's direction. It takes the camel driver a moment to catch on, but when he does, he makes a mad, scrabbling rush toward the door, tripping over his own feet in the process.

"We are not going to kill him," Khalaf informs his father, and calls to our panicked companion, "We are not going to kill you."

Mazdak goes still, and his eyes dart back and forth between father and son. He's trying to figure out who's in charge. I think we're all trying to figure out who's in charge.

Khalaf strides past his father without a glance and gives the camel driver a hand up. "We'll need camels. Can you do that for us, friend?"

"We need speed," says Timur. "We need horses, not camels."

"We don't have horses, and we won't last more than a couple of days in the Taklamakan Desert without camels." Khalaf turns back to Mazdak. "The camels?"

The man glances nervously at Timur. "I won't tell. Whoever you are, I won't tell anyone."

"I know."

"I don't want any trouble."

"I know. Thank you. The camels?"

The man's eyes dart to Timur one more time and then to the door. He turns back to Khalaf and lets out a tension-filled breath. "Two," he says. "Abbas specified that two would belong to you. That's all I can do. Really."

"What?" Timur spits.

"Two." Khalaf nods in agreement. He places a hand on each of Mazdak's shoulders and kisses his cheeks. "Thank you."

We never really had the chance to unpack, so it's easy enough to gather up our few belongings. Timur, of course, doesn't lift a finger to help. He turns to stone as he did back in Sarai, a statue dedicated to resentment and cold fury. Five minutes later, we follow Mazdak to the stables, where the camel trader culls out the two camels designated for us. Khalaf kisses the man's cheeks once more and tells him, "I won't forget this, Brother."

"I know, my lord." It's the first time Mazdak has called Khalaf by his title, and the last, I suppose. "I'm heading southeast. You'd do best to take the northern road."

With that, Mazdak leaves the three of us on our own once again. Well, on our own with two camels. Khalaf walks over to Timur, who refuses to look at him, choosing instead to glare at the stable wall.

"We'll talk about this later," Khalaf tells him with a cold edge to his voice. "We need to get moving. I'll give you a leg up, Father. Jinghua, you can ride with me. We'll try to travel parallel to the road, but we'll need to go farther north than that to stay out of sight. We should run into Qaidu's camp within a couple of weeks, maybe three."

If the il-khan's men don't overtake us remains unsaid, but it hovers in the air like a ghost.

20

THE SUN SETS AND THE MOON rises. We travel for hours
in darkness and silence. I keep looking behind us, expecting to see
the meager moonlight glinting off our enemies' helmets.

We don't stop until Timur dozes off and nearly falls off his
camel before jerking awake and grappling for the pommel at the
last minute. The camels are half dead with exhaustion anyway.
Khalaf takes first watch while his father sleeps. I sit with him
since I'm too anxious to sleep. If we're attacked tonight, I want
to be awake and sitting up for whatever good it will do me. We
haven't lit a fire, so I squint into the darkness in the direction of
Kashgar and shiver in the frigid night air.

"Go to sleep, Jinghua," Khalaf tells me. "You need to rest."

"So do you."

We're both speaking to the southwestern horizon, our voices dissipating along the road to Kashgar.

"Mazdak's an incredible liability now, you know," I tell him.

"I couldn't let an innocent man die simply that I might live."

"Most men would have killed him."

"I'd like to think that's not true," Khalaf says.

"You can think whatever you like."

"You wouldn't have killed him either."

"I'm not a man"—I sigh—"and I'm not very good at killing."

"Is that so terrible?"

Yes, I think. *Very terrible.* Aloud, I say, "All this time, you've protected your father, like he's the only one who matters. Why would you assume that Hulegu Il-Khan only cares about him? Why would you assume no one wants to kill you, too?"

"The insignificant third son who likes to discuss philosophy and play with astrolabes?"

"You almost died today. Do you still think you're not worthy of assassination?"

"No, I thought *other* people thought I wasn't worthy of assassination."

"You underestimated your importance, my lord." My annoyance with his staggering ignorance flares hot.

"Not true. I think I'm very important," he says, trying to lighten the mood.

"It's not funny." I feel like I'm going to burst, like I'm teetering on some precipice and I'm about to go over the edge. I give him a shove to the shoulder and repeat, "It's not funny at all."

"Jinghua." His tone is remonstrative, and I'm in no mood for it.

"You are the prince of the Kipchak Khanate and Timur Khan's sole heir—his *sole heir*, whether you like it or not. I'm sorry you lost your brothers, and I'm sorry they didn't hold a candle to you. I'm sorry you have to lead when you don't want to. But you are brilliant and you are charismatic and you are dangerous on the field of battle, among many other threatening attributes. So trust me when I tell you, my lord, that you grossly underestimate the extent to which other people think you are important."

A dense silence follows my tirade. We stare at each other, our features dulled and flattened in the night, but I can see his mouth gaping at my temerity.

"You would know," Khalaf replies at last, his voice thick. "You're the expert on that subject."

His biting tone makes my eyes sting with hurt. I wasn't even important before I was a slave, much less now. How could I underestimate that?

We both turn away from each other to face Kashgar again, sitting side by side in the desert grit with me fuming more at myself than at him and him thinking heaven knows what. We watch and wait. The sky begins to lighten to a dull pink to the east. Suddenly, I see Khalaf go tense out of my peripheral vision. He leans forward, intent on the horizon to the southwest.

"What is it?" I whisper. His hand goes up to silence me, and my whole body goes numb with panic. He watches for a heartbeat more and then leaps to his feet, pulling the saber Abbas gave him out of its sheath with a metallic *shink*.

I can see them now: five dots to the southwest like a line of black ants.

"Jinghua?" Khalaf says quietly as he watches the dots grow larger by the second. "Go wake my father."

"Yes, my lord," I breathe, rising unsteadily to my feet, my fear so acute my whole body hums with it.

He turns to me, grim faced, his eyes bright and burning. "After that, you hide. Do you hear me?"

My mind fills with all the things I want to say to him, each one jostling for priority, among them *I'm sorry* and *I love you more than my life* and, above all, *Please, don't die.*

Oh.

I'm stupidly, hopelessly, pointlessly in love with the prince of the Kipchak Khanate.

In hindsight, this is obvious, but the realization bowls me over all the same.

"My lord," I plead, for what I don't know.

He takes me by the upper arm, his hand dimpling the wool of my sleeve. He leans down so that his face is level with mine, and his eyes meet my eyes straight on. He grasps my arm tighter and gives me a small shake, saying, "You wake him up, and then you hide. You *live*, Jinghua."

I nod. He lets me go and turns to face the five men riding hell-bent toward us on galloping mares, so close that I can hear the horses' hooves and feel them trembling in the earth beneath my feet. I shake Timur awake. I don't have to say a thing. The old man lunges for his lance.

By the time I turn back around, they're on us, firing arrows, one of which sails just past my shoulder and lodges in the desert sand. I see Khalaf roll out of the way of another rider as Timur, standing his ground like a madman, hooks his attacker with the lance and yanks the man off his saddle.

I make a run for the camels. Khalaf told me to hide, and given the monotony of the landscape, I don't have a lot of options. I can die right now, or I can hide behind a camel and wait a little longer to die.

The camel bleats in terror as I peer over its hump. Timur is nearer to me and easier to see. He's got the man he's already killed in one of his meaty hands, holding the corpse in front of him as a shield. When another warrior shoots at him, the arrow lodges into the dead man's back with a nauseating *thunk*. Timur hurls the body at another horseman bearing down on him so that the animal stumbles and falls and sends her rider sailing through the air. When the soldier lands, there's a *crack*, and he screeches in agony, his leg bone jutting out from the shredded, bloody flesh of his thigh.

My hands curl into the camel's hair as I search for Khalaf with my heart pounding so hard it feels like it's pulsing in my throat. I find him launching himself atop a riderless mare and flying across the desert with his saber out. Another man speeds toward him on his own horse with a bow nocked and ready to fire. This is no bandit; this is a trained Mongol warrior. And while the man's skill may not match that of Khalaf, he's fully armored, and Khalaf's body is as vulnerable as a baby's.

I stand up and scream as the man releases his arrow.

And misses.

Khalaf is on him now and shouts with effort as he uses the full force of his body to strike the enemy in the neck and throw him off his horse, sending a constellation of blood spurting from the man's throat.

I'm standing completely defenseless in the middle of a battlefield as one of the il-khan's men comes toward me on foot with a dagger in his hand, ready to cut me to shreds.

It all comes back to me, that moment my world ended in Lin'an, the way the word "run" pulsed through my entire body as I fled the men who had come to kill me. Terrified, I startle backward and trip over the camel. The man's shadow covers me. His eyes are cold, calculating.

I kick up at him, but my foot only bangs painfully against his armor. The will to live sends me spinning onto my stomach and scuttling away from my killer like a crab. He easily catches up and turns me onto my back with his toe.

I'm going to die. I'm really going to die this time.

I close my eyes and see Khalaf crouched before me the first time we met, his hand outstretched with an apple on his palm.

Nothing happens.

I open my eyes. The man still stands over me, his arm pulled back, ready to jab the dagger into my heart. But the arm falls. The dagger drops to the desert sand. A metallic point juts out of the hardened leather of the man's armor, then protrudes farther until several inches of a bloodied lance push past his stomach. The blade withdraws with a slick suck, and as the man falls, he reveals Timur towering behind him, murderous and terrifying.

Timur nods at me. It's a question, his way of asking me if I'm all right. I'm not, but I nod anyway. He turns back to survey what's left as the stunning fact that the old goat just saved my life hits me.

I'm shaking too hard to stand up, so I get to my hands and knees in time to watch Khalaf chase after the last remaining warrior, who is now fleeing back toward Kashgar. The man turns back, aiming an arrow at Khalaf behind him as his mount thunders forward. Khalaf pulls the bow from the saddle and an arrow from the quiver and takes aim as his legs grip the galloping mare beneath him. He sends the arrow sailing and hits his mark before the other man fires. The last of our assailants falls from his saddle, and his horse races off without him. Khalaf rides out to the fallen soldier, dismounts, pulls out his saber, and drives it into the man's body.

I count the dead to be sure: one-two-three-four-five. Exhausted with relief, I fall onto my ass and slump my head onto my knees, trying to get a grip. When I hear a horse galloping straight for me and feel its staccato beat in the ground, my head snaps up.

Khalaf is heading for us on horseback at full speed. I scramble to my feet, ready to roll out of the way. He pulls up to a stop at the last minute and slides off the horse in one fluid motion, running to me and taking me by the arm again, just as he did before the battle began.

"Are you all right? Are you hurt?" he asks in a rush of words.

"I'm not hurt, my lord," I tell him, overwhelmed by his raw, frantic energy.

"Jinghua?" His face is next to mine. His eyes bore into me.

"I believe that was my three to your two," Timur boasts to Khalaf. "That'll teach you to doubt your old man."

Khalaf shifts his focus from me to his father, and in that instant, his face goes white with rage. Stark fury streams off him like steam as Timur continues to brag, oblivious.

"I may be three times your age, young mustang, but I can still tear a man from the saddle," he gloats.

Khalaf releases me and walks over to his father so slowly, so deliberately, that I think he's trying to contain the urge to strangle Timur at last. "What is this?" he asks, his soft voice as menacing as cracked ice atop a river.

"What?" Timur asks defensively.

"This. This makes no sense. Hulegu Il-Khan already has your throne. Why is he so hell-bent on hunting you down?"

It's a great question, but I'm wondering why, after everything that's happened in the past few hours, Khalaf is still saying "you" rather than "us," a clear indication that his healthy sense of humility has veered wildly into willful ignorance. My exasperation with him escapes in a throaty huff.

"Fine. *Us*," Khalaf corrects himself, his voice sharp with anger. "Why is Hulegu still hunting *us* down? Happy now, Jinghua?"

"Thank you," I mutter, flustered that he knew exactly what I was thinking. My whole body is shaking. There are so many emotions rattling around inside me right now I feel like I'm going to explode.

Timur says nothing, his silence as menacing as Khalaf's fury.

"What aren't you telling me?" Khalaf fumes.

"My lords!" I interrupt, stomping my foot, completely out of patience with the manly chest-beating. "There were ten men after you back in Samarkand, and there are only five here. We have no idea how many are tracking you. Can you please wait to have it out until *after* we manage to live through the rest of this day? Let's go!"

I stare down Khalaf first. He blows out a breath and nods. I turn on Timur.

"Damn you, girl," the old goat mutters, but he walks obediently toward the camels.

21

KHALAF IS BACK IN HIS TURBAN, and I'm in a makeshift veil because the Taklamakan Desert is a wasteland of sand, sand, and curved, billowing dunes of sand. I have never in my life seen a landscape so monotonous and terrifying. The name Taklamakan actually means *You can get in, but you can't get out.* Really, that's what it means. And we're *in* it.

I'm riding in front of Khalaf on one of the camels, even though we've taken two of the enemy's horses. "I want to keep them as fresh as possible in case we need to move quickly," Khalaf reasons.

"Mm-hmm" is Timur's doubtful response.

"Are you sure you're all right?" Khalaf whispers in my ear, so close his lips touch my veil. We rode like this yesterday, but it was different, stiff, formal. Today, Khalaf's hands on the reins are nearer, his arms closer, his torso pressed fully against my back, like someone has placed me inside a Khalaf envelope. Or maybe this is all just wishful thinking. All I know is that if I have to die, this is how I want to go.

"I'm fine, my lord," I tell him. "Really."

"I'm sorry. You wouldn't be in this mess if it weren't for us."

"I'd be dead if it weren't for you. You don't need to apologize to me." *I'm more than capable of making my own messes,* I add in my mind.

We're several tense hours into our journey across the brutal landscape when Timur wonders aloud, "Why am I still in the world?"

"Father," Khalaf says warningly, but Timur's voice drones on, his tone both passive-aggressive and mythic. "Wouldn't it have been better to have fought my enemy in my own khanate and to have died defending Sarai than to drag out this pathetic half life?"

I have to admit the man's got a point.

"You shouldn't speak like that," says Khalaf.

"I'm sick to death of enduring our misfortunes with patience."

"'Patience,' you call it?" I chime in. Oddly, Timur is the one who harrumphs with amusement while Khalaf sighs with exasperation behind me.

"Father, I have faith that God—" he begins.

"Don't," snaps Timur. "You can tolerate the decrees of heaven if you want to. I, for one, have no intention of suffering in silence."

As if Timur has ever suffered in silence a day in his life.

Khalaf's irritation with his father simmers in his answer. "We'll find Qaidu, and then maybe our fortunes will change. Maybe God is preparing some relief for us that we can't foresee."

Timur snorts. This time, Khalaf and I sigh in unison.

When the animals are so exhausted that we can go no farther, we set up camp off the road. Khalaf tries to rub our footprints out of the sand with his saber, but in the light of dusk, it looks like two men, two horses, two camels, one not-exactly-a-slave girl, and a drunk snake have decided to journey north of the main road. By the time he's finished, he looks so exhausted I want to tuck him into his blanket, lie down behind him, and wrap him up in my spindly arms. The fact that I can't do that, especially now that I've admitted to myself that I'm in love with him, is almost as depressing as the possibility that I might be slaughtered in my sleep tonight.

We're out of food and nearly out of water, so there's no dinner. We're not lighting a fire. Timur begins to unroll his blanket when Khalaf says, "What do you think you're doing?"

"What does it look like?"

"Oh no. No, no, no. You owe me some answers, and I intend to have them."

"I'm tired," Timur says.

"Too bad. Why is the il-khan so dead set on hunting you down?"

"He's a vindictive, milk-blooded piece of carrion. Abbas said as much."

"Abbas? The man who is probably dead right now because of us?" Khalaf lets that remark sink in before adding, "The term 'vindictive' implies that a man responds too harshly to the actions of another. What I'd like to know is what exactly did you do to inspire his vindictiveness?"

"I've done nothing wrong," Timur insists.

"You need to be more specific. To what 'nothing' are you referring?"

Timur looks off to the sunrise, where pinks and oranges spread across the clouds. His frown registers something other than his usual arrogance, as if some actual human emotion lived in his shrunken goat heart.

"It involves your mother," the old man says, his eyes shifting, looking anywhere but at Khalaf.

That, apparently, was not what Khalaf was expecting to hear. He visibly recoils as if Timur has punched him in the gut, and here I am wading into this family's dysfunction with the current growing stronger by the second, threatening to pull me under.

The old man glances at his son and says, "It's complicated."

"I'm aware of that," Khalaf answers tightly.

Timur gives a bitter laugh. "You're aware of nothing."

"You think I don't know? You think Miran and Jahangir kept that little gem to themselves? You think they didn't throw it in my face every chance they got?"

"Khalaf," Timur murmurs, trying to placate his son.

"You think I don't remember her?" Khalaf's voice sounds so

pained that my own eyes well up in sympathy. I have no idea what's going on, and here I am standing knee-deep in Khalaf's wounds, and maybe Timur's as well.

"You asked me a question," Timur says, the calm one for once. "I'm trying to answer it. Do you want to hear the answer or not?"

Khalaf nods stiffly.

"The Great Khan didn't appreciate the fact that I didn't show up to his election," Timur explains. "I didn't support his claim, nor did I support the coup d'état that took the rightfully elected Great Khan out of commission."

"I know all this," Khalaf interrupts. "What does any of it have to do with our current situation? Or my mother?"

Timur blows out a gust of air from his lungs. "The Great Khan sent Bibi Hanem to me as a peace offering. I had intended to send her back, but..."

"But what?"

"But then I changed my mind."

By now, Khalaf is rubbing like mad at his lip. He stops and says, "What are you saying? Are you trying to tell me you were actually in love with my mother?" When Timur answers with a frown, Khalaf throws up his hands. "Will you just tell me once and for all what's going on here?"

"All right. Before the Great Khan sent him to retake control of Persia, Hulegu knew your mother in Khanbalik and was under the impression that she was intended for him. So when the Great Khan sent her to wed me instead, Hulegu wasn't exactly thrilled."

"So *he* was in love with her?" Khalaf clarifies.

"I guess that's what you'd call it. She was an uncommonly beautiful woman, your mother."

I sit back on my haunches, taking in this whole exchange in depressed wonder. All the strife of the world, armies battling armies, and hovering behind all of it like a ghost is one failed love story after another.

"So why now? Why is he attacking you now?"

"Us," Timur corrects him. "He's attacking you, too."

"I told you so," I mutter.

"I don't matter in this equation," Khalaf insists.

"You, the son of Timur Khan and Bibi Hanem, have always mattered . . . especially since, when I first learned that the Great Khan was dying, I sent a secret emissary to Khanbalik to broker a marriage between you and the Great Khan's daughter."

There's a long, long pause during which both Khalaf and I gape at Timur. My guts go leaden.

"You tried to marry me off to Turandokht?" Khalaf says.

Timur shrugs.

"I thought you said that was an idiotic idea!"

"No, I said that it was a *fucking* idiotic idea. That doesn't mean it wasn't worth a try. And keep your voice down. Sound probably carries for five *li* out here."

Khalaf throws his arms up again. "So what happened to the emissary?"

Timur scratches at his beard. "Well, it would seem the

emissary was intercepted by Il-Khanid spies, because it was shortly thereafter that the il-khan sacked Baghdad and then sent his own emissary to the Kipchak Khanate demanding a tribute he knew we couldn't pay."

"Purposefully drawing us into war," Khalaf says, rubbing his lip.

"Because there's no earthly way Hulegu Il-Khan is going to let the son of Timur Khan and Bibi Hanem become the next Great Khan," I finish off for him.

"Smart girl," Timur says.

"Oh please, this isn't about me," Khalaf snipes at his father. "This is about you. It's always been about you. You were using me to take over the empire yourself. No wonder Turandokht wants you dead."

Timur doesn't refute it. Khalaf rubs his eyes with the heels of his hands before asking, "Did either of my brothers know about this? Miran? Jahangir?"

Timur shakes his shaggy head.

"Did anyone know about this?"

"The men I sent," Timur jokes. No one laughs, of course. He clears his throat and adds, "And, er, Qaidu knew. He said would support me as long as it worked. But it didn't. Obviously."

"Qaidu was in on this, too?" Khalaf asks in disbelief.

Timur nods.

"Playing it pretty deep, Father," Khalaf assesses grimly.

"Aren't we all?" I add under my breath and start chewing on a

dirty fingernail. I can't believe what a snarling thicket this mess has become.

"It was a gamble," Timur admits.

"If we have nothing to lose, why are we still trying to ally with Qaidu when we could appeal directly to the Great Khan?" Khalaf demands, exasperated.

"I knew at the time that the Great Khan was dying. I did not know that all the princes trying to marry his daughter were dying as well. Now that I do, I've determined that I'm not sending you into a death trap."

Khalaf clamps his lips shut. He bows his head and takes a deep, audible breath in and out through his nose. "So now we're heading into Qaidu's camp facing God knows what kind of welcome."

"Yep."

It's too hot in the Taklamakan to travel during the day, so we stay out of the sun in our tiny tent as we wait for night to fall again. And this is all assuming that any assassins on our tail will be traveling at night as well. I've gone outside in the heat, ostensibly to scrub out a cookpot with sand, but I can't keep my eyes off the horizon behind us. Eventually, Khalaf comes out to find me.

"I have something for you," he says.

My pathetic excuse for a veil is off, and I wipe my sweaty fore-head with the back of my arm, leaving a swath of grit in its wake. "You have something for me?"

Me, the girl whose only possession in the world is a broken chunk of porcelain on a piece of twine around her neck.

Khalaf holds out a dagger, hilt first. I startle in surprise at the sight of it.

"I was not expecting that," I tell him.

"Go on. Take it."

I grasp the hilt in my hand, and he lets go of the blade. It feels awkward and useless in my grip.

"Oh," I joke, "do you give daggers to all the girls?"

Khalaf responds with a baffled look followed by another expression that's more difficult to read. His earlobes turn pink.

"Sorry," I mumble. "Isn't this the weapon that almost killed you in Kashgar?"

Khalaf shrugs. "Now it's the weapon that will protect you."

I tighten my grip on the handle. I move the blade through the air—nothing extravagant, but I still feel like an idiot.

"Thank you for this, my lord," I tell him, trying to hand it back, "but I'll never be able to use this thing."

He crosses his arms. "You can if you must."

"I can't kill anyone. Trust me."

"You need to be able to protect yourself. Think of Samarkand, Kashgar. I should have given you a weapon ages ago."

"My lord"—here, he rolls his eyes—"I'm fairly certain that things would be much, much worse for us right now if I had pulled out a knife on the il-khan's men. I'm more useful hiding than trying to help."

"Please"—he sighs—"at least do me the honor of accepting this gift, keeping it on you, and knowing how to use it. Do we have a deal?"

Now it's a "gift." Khalaf could hand me a lump of dirt; if he called it a "gift" and presented it to me with that earnest face of his, I'd treasure it all the days of my life.

"Deal," I relent.

"Thank you," he says, all velvety and genuine, and I know that I'm in way over my head. "Here's your first lesson."

"First? There's going to be more than one?"

"Okay, here's a lesson. If there are more, great. If there aren't, at least you'll have a clue as to what you're doing with a dagger."

"I have no clue what I'm doing with a dagger."

"Jinghua," he admonishes, exasperated.

"Sorry. I'll be a good student."

"Thank you. This weapon is very sharp on both edges. You can swipe it back and forth and cut your opponent. It'll hurt, but it likely won't stop him. The blade is short, and you're small, so you don't have much leverage. That means you'll need to develop some skill with it for it to do you any good. Does that make sense?"

"Yes."

"A dagger is for jabbing in close contact, which means you'll only really use it if you're desperate. That should make you feel better, right?"

"That's supposed to make me feel better?"

He laughs a little, smiles a little, makes me feel like jelly a little.

"Right, so . . . it's best to go for places where your opponent is vulnerable. The eyes are good. The abdomen is also soft, but depending on the size of your opponent, it may be difficult to hit an organ or any arteries. There's also the . . . uh . . . groin."

"Groin. Right," I say. *Shut up, Jinghua!* I scream at myself. I'm not sure which of us is more likely to melt of embarrassment on that one. It will probably be a tie.

"If you want to kill a man—"

"I definitely don't want to kill a man, my lord."

He looks up at the sky in prayer. "If you find yourself in a life-or-death situation, you may need to stab your opponent in the heart. But the heart is hard to get to. There's bone over the heart."

Here, Khalaf pounds his breastbone with the flattened palm of his hand, resulting in a solid, reassuring thud. I'm giddily tempted to thump him on the chest as well.

"You'll need to go under the breastbone with an upward jab. Here."

He takes his palm and hits the area of his torso underneath the arch of his rib cage. This time, it makes a slapping sound. He reaches for my hand that holds the dagger and wraps his fingers around mine.

His skin against my skin is very distracting.

"So, you would draw your arm back—no, bend at the elbow, like this."

He moves my arm into place, which means he has to step in close to me. I inwardly chastise myself for enjoying this so much.

"Use the momentum of your whole body, not just your arm," he continues, "and stab upward right here."

He brings my armed hand up quickly, stopping the blade just short of its target. Panicked that I'm about to stab him for real, I drop the dagger. It clunks on the dusty ground between us, and we're left to just stand there staring at each other, our faces scant inches apart.

My mind empties. Any thoughts of khans and empires vanish. The only idea I can cling to at this moment is the fact that I want to kiss him or he to kiss me or both of us to kiss each other.

He looks away as he picks up the dagger and dusts it off on his sleeve.

"I wasn't going to let you stab me," he informs me.

"That was cutting it a little too close, in my opinion."

He presents the weapon to me over his arm. I reach for it reluctantly, and I'm surprised when his hand doesn't let go. Instead, his face deadly serious, he takes my newly armed hand in both of his, and I am robbed of what little air I had left in my lungs. Every time he touches me, I feel like I'll detonate, an explosion of wanting and not having.

"Promise me you'll use this if you have to," he says.

"My lord—"

"Khalaf."

I don't think I can say his name without saying *I love you* in the same breath. The feeling wraps itself around the very word itself.

He leans in. "Promise me."

His voice gets me. Every. Single. Time.

"I promise," I say, and I mean it. I do. I promise.

I step back, escaping from his touch and his eyes. "Where do I put this thing?"

"Wrap it in your belt, and be very careful how you sit." He grins at me.

"Yes, my lord." I find a fold inside my belt to house the dagger. Focusing on the dagger is much safer than focusing on that grin.

"Khalaf," he corrects me for the millionth time. "And thank you for not wanting to kill me."

A strangled giggle escapes me. Honestly, my parents should have named me Irony instead of Illustrious Capital City.

22

"CHARITY? YOU *BEGGED*?" TIMUR ASKS.

"As you see." Khalaf dumps a cup of mare's milk curds and some kind of jerky on a blanket next to the brazier.

We fell in with a Mongol horde called the Barlas near Turpan two weeks ago and have followed them north and east away from the trade routes and onto the steppes, where not a single tree breaks the grassy landscape.

There are Mongols, and then there are *Mongols*. The Barlas, like the Kipchaks, are the real deal, with homes made of white felt. They cover themselves in mutton fat during the winter months not, as I originally thought, because they think it's pretty and smells nice (which it doesn't) but because if they didn't, they'd freeze on the spot in the brutal wind of the steppes.

My family thought they were so much better than these people, but now that I'm clinging to life in the paupers' *ger* of a Mongol encampment, I'm starting to understand how a bunch of nomads managed to conquer the world. If this landscape can't kill them, nothing can.

The Barlas have met up with Qaidu's horde just as our meager funds are running out. Overnight, a city of pale felt domes has popped up on the green steppes, laid out in a perfect grid with the door of each *ger* facing south to keep out the harsh northern winds. We're trying to figure out how to move past the clan's suspicious glares so we can present ourselves to Qaidu. Khalaf's begging probably doesn't further our cause, but I don't care. I'm hungry.

"This is unacceptable," says Timur.

"So is starving." Khalaf tears off a chunk of dried meat and hands it to me. I'm not as picky as Timur. I start to gnaw on it with my back teeth. Starving will do that to a girl.

"Did you even bother to ask after Qaidu?"

"No."

"Why not?" Timur demands.

"I look like a scarecrow."

"You are a prince. When do you intend to start acting like one?"

Khalaf tosses the remainder of the meat onto the blanket. "Are you serious? Do you really think either one of us is ever going to sit on a throne again? Look at us." He holds up the remnants of his tunic and shakes it at his father. "We're seeking asylum. Period."

"You need to keep your head on straight, boy."

"There's a word for this, Father—" says Khalaf.

"We are going to meet with Qaidu."

"—and that word is 'denial.'"

"And we are going to raise an army," Timur insists.

"How are we going to fund that army? Tell me that. We can't even afford to feed ourselves."

Timur opens his mouth and promptly shuts it again. Angry veins slowly pop out on his neck and forehead.

Khalaf rubs his eyes with the heels of his hands for the millionth time since we left Sarai. "Look, tomorrow I'll try to get an audience with Qaidu. I could make myself useful as a warrior in his army, work my way up the ranks."

"Unacceptable."

"Dying is also unacceptable!" Khalaf shouts.

Khalaf.

Shouting.

It feels like shattering glass, like porcelain pieces breaking apart on a clean-swept wooden floor.

He storms out of the *ger*. I hurry after him, but I don't get very far. The rigidity of his spine makes it clear he needs a moment alone, so I'm left to listen to the dried grass of late summer crunching beneath his feet as he stomps away.

Timur pokes his head out of the door that Khalaf didn't bother to shut behind him. "Where do you think you're going?"

Khalaf doesn't even bother to turn around. "To think. To pray," he calls into the air. "At least God listens to me."

I watch him trudge off toward the forest line at the foot of the Tian Mountains.

"Oh, well done, my lord," I snipe at Timur.

"Shut up, girl."

I don't bother to glower at the old goat. I keep my eyes on Khalaf until he disappears into the trees. I know he just needs to blow off steam, but it seems to me that father and son are so at odds at this point that something has to give. I can't quash the feeling that one or the other of them is on the precipice of doing something rash, and that our fortunes are about to change, and not for the better.

An hour passes.

Timur lies by the brazier. I think he wants me to believe that he's sleeping, that he's not worried, that his pride is more important than his feelings. I don't know why he should care what I think, and it's a vain attempt anyway. I can see right through him. He's a ball of regret and anxiety.

We don't speak.

I scrub cups that don't need scrubbing with old broth, and I lead the camels to pasture in some grass, even though they were just fine where they were. One of them spits in my hair.

Stupid camel.

I'm wiping camel spit off my head with my sleeve when I see

Khalaf. He steps out of the trees like a miracle, holding a large object up on his arm. His turban is off and his hair hangs loose. I squint at him, wondering what on earth he's carrying. It looks enormous from this distance.

He must see me, because he beckons me to him with his free hand. It's not until we close the distance between us by half that I see he's got his turban wrapped around his left arm, and on that arm perches a falcon.

"Look at her," he calls to me, and the bird's head swings toward his voice. "Isn't she incredible?"

He's glowing like a party boat on the West Lake as he holds up the bird for my inspection. The falcon's breast bulges powerfully under a downy field of snow-white feathers dappled with brown and fawn. Her beak curves downward in a glossy black hook. But this is no run-of-the-mill falcon. There's a gold chain around her neck that bulges with diamonds and topazes and rubies, and her jeweled jesses glint in the sunlight. She turns her head so that one enormous eye can stare me down.

"Where did you find her?" I marvel. "How?"

"I prayed," he tells me. "And when I finished my prayers, there she was on the branch just above me. I wrapped my turban around my arm and held it up, and she came right to me."

He doesn't look at the bird, only at me. His eyes are rimmed by dark, stubby lashes. He's so close. I stop breathing.

"What is it? What's going on?" Timur says from the doorway of our *ger*.

I think I might hate that man.

"The prince has found a falcon, my lord," I tell him as I step away from Khalaf. The words tumbling out of my mouth seem disconnected, as if such a collection of awkward sounds could not possibly belong in the same realm as Khalaf and his falcon.

"Can you see her, Father?" he asks excitedly.

"Of course I can see her. I'm standing right here."

"This is an omen, a good omen. God has sent us His blessing. Don't you see?"

Timur strokes his beard, but he doesn't seem to be looking at the bird, which is odd since she's so magnificent that I'm finding it hard to tear my eyes away from her. The jesses strapped around her legs glitter with lapis lazuli and rubies. Her talons hug Khalaf's arm in a way that makes me a little fearful. She's breathtaking. Every aspect of her being has been honed to hunt and kill, and somehow it makes her beautiful beyond words.

"Call it an omen if you want," says Timur. "All I care about is the fact that this bird is our ticket into Qaidu's *ger*."

"I think you're right. Even if she doesn't belong to Qaidu, she'll be valuable to him."

Timur wastes no time and starts to limp off toward the center of Qaidu's camp.

"Ready?" Khalaf asks me.

"Am I going?"

"Of course."

I'm not ready—I'm never ready—but I follow Timur anyway

as Khalaf strides beside me with the falcon steady on his arm. It's like walking next to the sun.

We draw the attention of the watch, who approach on horseback, one of whom sees Khalaf and exclaims, "That's Qaidu's falcon! He has every available hunter out looking for this bird. There would have been hell to pay if we didn't find her. You've done us a huge favor, sir."

The man dismounts and rushes forward to take the bird, but he backs off when the falcon flaps her wings in distress. Khalaf holds her steady. The guard sighs with disappointment and tells Khalaf, "You'd better come along, then." He swings back up onto his horse, and our little kingdom of three follows the guard through the grid of *gers*.

News of the falcon moves faster than we do, and by the time our ever-growing crowd reaches Qaidu's great tent at the center of the encampment, the khan himself comes out to greet Khalaf with a wide smile spread across his face. Qaidu is the quintessential Mongol: stocky, short-legged, hard-muscled. His tent is large but not particularly extravagant, and he is rather spare himself, a man whose strength and intelligence are his only adornments.

"My glove," he calls to no one in particular, but the glove appears all the same. He slips it on, holds out his arm, and takes the bird from her savior, gazing at her with the kind of soft fondness most girls dream of and never receive. I suppose a falcon is more useful than a girl, though, in the eyes of most men.

"To whom do I owe my thanks?" Qaidu asks.

Khalaf looks to his father, who nods his head. He stands a little straighter and suddenly he's a prince again, sliding back into
his destined role as easily as one might step over a puddle. And
if Khalaf is a prince again, that turns me back into something
I don't want to be. Loneliness sinks its cold teeth into me as he
openly declares his identity for the first time in months.

"I am Khalaf, son of Timur Khan and prince of the Kipchak
Khanate."

Qaidu raises his eyebrows and shifts his gaze from Khalaf to
his disheveled father.

"Eternal Blue Sky," he says.

"Not quite," Timur answers drily, "but I appreciate the compliment, cousin."

Qaidu bursts into a belly laugh and Timur laughs with him.
They grasp hands and thump each other on the back so heartily,
they sound like a pair of drums. I had no idea Timur was capable
of genuine laughter. I glance at Khalaf, who appears to be as surprised as I am. When our eyes meet, he shrugs.

"Is this your daughter?" Qaidu asks Timur, gesturing to me. "I
didn't know you took a Song wife."

I'm so stunned by the assumption that I nearly let my disgust
flash across my face.

"She's . . . ," begins Khalaf. "Well, she's . . ."

I look at him. He looks at me and turns his head away just as
quickly.

"No, she's no child of mine. The girl's just a servant," says

Timur with no little asperity.

Servant? I guess I'm moving up in the world.

"Nice of her to stick with you," says Qaidu.

"Exactly," Khalaf says under his breath to his father.

Qaidu claps Timur on the back again. "Well, come in, Timur. You and your son and even your servant shall dine with me tonight."

Qaidu is an impressive man, far more genteel than I would have thought. I spent my childhood among people who spoke derisively of these illiterate Mongols, and I still find large social gatherings where men and women mingle freely distasteful. Even now, my instinct is to retreat behind a curtain where I can remain unseen. But Qaidu is both unpretentious and courteous, and I find myself having to readjust, rather uncomfortably, my assumptions about the free Mongols living on the steppes.

Khalaf and Timur sit in a place of honor beside their ally eating red-legged partridges as delicately as they can given the fact that their hands shake with hunger. Khalaf seems to be doing a fine job impressing the de facto khan of the Chagatai Khanate, because Qaidu inclines his head toward him and says, "Prince Khalaf, I'm glad that it's you who found my falcon."

Prince Khalaf. It's as though Qaidu has lobbed the phrase directly at me where I watch on pins and needles from the women's side of the tent, a reminder of who and what Khalaf is. I should never have let myself think of him in any other way.

You'd think that in a tent full of Mongols already tipsy on *qumiz*, one man's voice would be drowned out in a sea of boisterous chatter, but Qaidu is the kind of leader who demands attention with little effort. Everyone watches him. Everyone listens. His slaves stand rigidly behind him like a wall reflecting his innate power.

"I'm glad to have returned her to her master," Khalaf replies.

"It's a miracle you made it here in one piece. I thought you were dead, you and your father. This business with Hulegu Il-Khan . . ." Qaidu shakes his head. "The il-khan pretends that he does nothing without the Great Khan holding his hand and egging him on, but he'd happily stab his brother in the back to get his hands on the throne of the empire. And the *Great Khan*, as he calls himself, can tell his ill-gotten empire whatever he likes; he can't protect any of us worth a damn. His daughter is running the show these days, and who knows where her allegiance lies? She's got a stranglehold on the trade routes now, I can tell you that. Makes it infinitely more difficult for me to raid the caravans when she's done such a damn good job securing the roads. Do you know she's killed at least twelve princes with those riddles of hers? And those are just the ones we've heard about."

"It's hard to credit the intelligence of any man who would enter that contest," Timur comments, needling Khalaf. I want to stand up and cheer. I can't believe there was a time when I thought Khalaf's going to Khanbalik might be a good idea.

"Do you know why Turandokht would support Hulegu Il-Khan's actions against the Kipchak Khanate?" Khalaf asks Qaidu as he ignores his father. Timur clears his throat loudly.

"Has she?" says Qaidu.

"The il-khan's men who caught up to us in Samarkand said they were there by her blessing."

"It sounds as though your bride-to-be dislikes the wedding bower your father has constructed for her, Prince Khalaf," Qaidu jokes. Timur smiles politely, and I'm oddly proud of him for not diving over his son to pummel his former ally.

Qaidu shakes his head again as his laughter dissipates. "The Il-Khanids and the Yuan Dynasty of the Great Khan are Mongols who have forgotten who they are, where they came from. They'd rather plant themselves beside their seeds than take their horses to the best pastures. They'd rather build cities of stone than camps of felt. And now the Kipchak Khanate is infested with Il-Khanid hordes raping their way through the countryside and taking over their trade routes."

Khalaf sets his dinner back down in his dish. He looks green. "Is it as bad as all that, then?" he asks.

"If the reports we hear are true, yes. I don't know what that fool Hulegu Il-Khan is playing at, but it seems ridiculous to destroy a kingdom that you plan to rule. It just goes to show you how far those so-called Mongols have strayed from the true path of Genghis Khan."

"So we have your support?" Khalaf asks.

"I'll ally myself with whoever and whatever brings the most fortunate alliance for the descendants of Ogodei Khan, who are the rightful rulers of the empire."

Timur starts coughing loudly.

"Is your father unwell?" our host asks Khalaf.

"Nothing a bit of *qumiz* won't cure. Have a drink, Father."

Khalaf as usual is far subtler than I would have been. I just glare at Timur even as I marvel at his pride. Honestly, can't we just eat one decent meal before he invites someone else to kill us? The tent is enormous, but I feel cramped and panicked.

"By the way, Prince Khalaf," Qaidu drawls casually, "you should know that I swore to grant to the man who found my bird whatever two things he might ask. You have only to tell me what you desire, and if what you ask for is within my power, I will grant it to you."

It was relatively quiet before, but now a hush falls over the room. Maybe this is why the Mongols have comported themselves so softly this evening. Maybe this is the moment they've been waiting for.

Timur leans across Khalaf and says, "That's very generous."

"Thank you, cousin," Qaidu replies, "but with your forgiveness, this offer is for your son alone, since he is the one who found the falcon."

Timur falls silent. It must be killing him to keep his mouth shut.

Khalaf glances around the tent at the rapt audience. He swallows his mouthful of game bird. "With your permission, my lord, I'd like to think on this gift before I answer."

"That's fine, but don't put your request off too long or I won't be drunk enough to remember that I offered it."

Khalaf laughs along with everyone else, but his eyes aren't in it. "Tomorrow morning, then, my lord," he says.

23

IN OUR NEW *GER* LINED WITH gold brocade like a much smaller version of the khan's *ger* back in Sarai, I try to block out Timur's voice as he plots what to do with Khalaf's wishes. With a stomach full of food and a new blanket furnished by Qaidu, I feel sleep close in on me.

"We should think about asking for horses," he says. I look at him with bleary eyes from across the coals and will him to shut up.

"Do we have to talk about this right now?" Khalaf asks as he crawls under his own blanket.

"Or we could turn the tables on him and ask for his army. Serve him right for letting Hulegu Il-Khan trample all over the Kipchak Khanate. I can't believe how quickly that gutless, milk-blooded bastard wrote us off. After years of alliances, he didn't even try to stop Hulegu. We should get out of here. I don't trust him."

"I'm going to bed," Khalaf says.

"We could just ask for money, I suppose. How much do you think he'd be willing to give? How much is that falcon worth?"

"Can we please just go to sleep? I'm exhausted."

Timur breathes out through his nose. "Fine, but let me be clear on one point. *We* might go to Khanbalik and seek an audience with the Great Khan, but *you* are not going to Khanbalik to face Turandokht. Is that understood?"

The old goat has finally laid it all out, the thing I've been worried about since Rasht. Suddenly, I'm awake and alert, listening carefully.

Khalaf sits back up and pushes the blanket away. "With all due respect, my lord, we are quickly running out of alternatives."

He as good as admitted it.

I've already lost my family and my home, and now, just when I've let myself fall in love with Khalaf, I'm about to lose him, too.

To her.

"Lamb's balls," says Timur. "I knew it. I knew the second Abbas's slave starting blathering on about Turandokht back in Rasht."

"Just hear me out," says Khalaf.

"There is nothing to discuss. You are not going to stake your life and the future of the Kipchak Khanate on some ridiculous riddles."

"The Kipchak Khanate needs us. Now. You heard Qaidu. You heard what the il-khan is doing to our people. We've run far enough."

Khalaf's logical arguments line up behind him like good little soldiers, although his demeanor lacks the passion I would expect from him in a moment like this. His focus never veers from Timur, and I get the feeling that he is very distinctly *not* looking at me. "Perhaps God has given us a means to an end," he adds.

"Exactly. Turandokht is the means to *your* end."

I am nodding emphatically in agreement with Timur—much good it does me since Khalaf won't even glance in my direction. His determination to face Turandokht—to *marry* her—cuts me like a dagger.

"You keep talking about raising armies," says Khalaf. "You think we can only see our way out of this mess with war. But what if I have something else to offer, a better weapon?"

"What, your philosophy? Is that going to get us back to the Kipchak Khanate? Your poetry? Are you going to recite your way into the Great Khan's coffers? Are you going to woo his generals with fine rhetoric? Bribe his ministers with the stars in the heavens?"

"If that's how you think of using one's mind rather than one's bow, then yes, I am speaking of my mind."

"Your mind," Timur scoffs.

"Am I or am I not an educated man?"

"You are a spoiled child, and you are going to get yourself killed."

"This isn't helpful, my lords," I interject from my bed on the other side of the fire, trying to put the brakes on a conversation that's veering toward calamity.

"You keep out of this," Timur fires back. "You've caused enough trouble already."

For the first time since the discussion began, Khalaf lights up, only this time, it's with anger. "This is between you and me. Don't you dare go after Jinghua."

"Oh balls, this again? Please. She's a slave. You're a prince. You know this. She knows this. You want to bed her? Fine. But that is the one and only possibility of what could happen between the two of you."

Timur's brutal honesty freezes me with humiliation. I don't know where to look or what to do in response. Khalaf goes completely silent. I can't bear to look at him.

"And when you're finished with that," Timur continues, "we will still need to get down to the business of figuring out how we're going to use Qaidu and his wishes to our advantage."

"I'm only saying this one more time," Khalaf rasps at his father. "Leave Jinghua out of this. This has nothing to do with her."

"Doesn't it?"

"Of course it doesn't," I whisper, heartsore, but of course, no one hears me but me.

Khalaf rises to his feet so he can exit both the *ger* and this disaster of an argument.

"We're not finished here," says Timur.

Khalaf's hand already is on the door, but he stops and faces his father. "You were the one who had me tutored, who sent me off to be educated in Isfahan, and now you don't want me using the education you took the trouble to give me. You were the one who wanted to marry me off to Turandokht in the first place, but now when the decision is mine to make, you *don't* want me to marry her. Tell me, my lord, is there one thing I can do that will meet with your approval?"

"You can start acting like my son and heir. That would be a nice start."

"Ugh," I direct into the air to any god in the vicinity who might be listening.

"Oh, warmongering, you mean?" Khalaf says, his voice dripping with uncommon irony and blatant anger. "Because that seems to be your definition of what it means to be a great man. Would you really rather I die in some pointless battle like my brothers? What exactly did their deaths accomplish? They died. They gave their lives for you, and for what? So that we can skulk across the countryside while Hulegu Il-Khan takes whatever he wants? Is that glory? Is that honor?"

"My lord," I say, sitting up. I may not love his father, but I don't relish watching Khalaf stoop so low.

"You shit," Timur says thickly. "You ungrateful little prick."

Khalaf nods. "That's right. I know what you think of me." He turns and pushes through the door and out into the night.

Timur and I sit in silence on opposite sides of the fire until

I say, "That could've gone better."

"Go suck your used tea leaves."

"Why do you have to be like that with him? It's like you're deliberately pushing him in the wrong direction. You may as well pack his bags for him."

"What should I have said? *Son, stay here and marry a slave and live in squalor all the days of your life?*"

I hate how he can see through me, right into the dark, sorry places in my heart. It's like he's found a sharp stick and is now prodding at all my tender, pointless desires with it. I glare at him across the fire. "You might have mentioned that you care about him. You might have mentioned that while you'd love him to rule the empire, it's slightly more important to you that he live. That would have been a lot more persuasive than criticizing a girl he's never looked at twice."

"And you say *I'm* blind. Fine, then. You talk him out of this holy quest of his, if you're so smart. But I'd lay even money that you won't be professing your undying love for that ungrateful brat either, coward."

I glower at him and start to bury myself in my blanket.

"Well?" asks Timur.

"Well, what?"

"Go on."

"What? You really want me to go talk to him? Now?"

He stares off to the side as if he can't look me in the eye, and he nods.

"What good will that do?"

"We need to stop him before he does anything rash, and the state he's in, he's far more likely to listen to you than to his own father, the idiot."

"Oh, thanks for that." I wonder if Timur will ever manage to put two words together that don't comprise an insult in my direction.

"Please," he says.

Please? From the khan of the Kipchak Khanate? That I was not expecting.

Timur is still gazing off to my right. I used to think of him as a statue, a carved slab of stone, but seeing him now with his bluster all melted away, he seems to be an actual human being, and one who cares about his son as much as I do. So I rise and wrap the blanket around my shoulders before going after Khalaf.

Outside, the cool night air is a slap to the face even though it's late summer. Khalaf is nowhere in sight. At first, I try to follow his tracks in the broken grass, but after a while, I give that up as futile and head back to our *ger* to wait for him.

And there he is, sitting on the ground just outside the door with his knees pulled up to his chest. He looks small, childlike, curled into himself like a ball. When he sees me, he raises a hand in greeting and says, "*Hǎo jiǔ bú jiàn*, Quiet Flower."

"My lord," I say in a way that communicates many things, like *Why are you sitting out here?* and *This is annoying* and *Go to bed.*

He shakes his finger at me and says, "Khalaf."

"What are you doing out here?"

"I am sitting upon my throne and thinking the great thoughts of a mighty prince." He makes a sweeping gesture with his right arm. "Behold my power and tremble."

This is when I spy a skin flopped on the ground beside him. The telltale odor of *qumiz* cuts through the crisp air.

"Wait. Are you drunk?"

"Yes, ma'am."

"You?" I laugh, because seriously I never could have imagined this. "You're drunk? *You're* drunk?"

He picks up the skin and raises it in toast. "That I am, Quiet Flower. That I am." He drinks, and when he pulls the skin away, he says, "Beautiful Jasmine Flower." His voice is throaty, husky. He draws out the last syllable like a long sigh after a hard day.

"I didn't know you could drink that stuff. I thought it was . . ."

"I believe the word you're looking for is 'haram,' and you would be correct."

I crouch down beside him, but he stares straight ahead. "This isn't like you, my lord."

A bitter and very un-Khalaf-like laugh issues from his *qumiz*-dampened lips. "This is exactly like me. Abandoning the field of battle? Haram. Disrespecting my father at every turn? Haram. Listening to you sing? Haram. Other things I don't care to mention? Haram. I am haram on two legs."

I feel very careful of him suddenly, as if he were a fine vase placed dangerously close to the edge of a table.

"You really are going to Khanbalik, aren't you? You're going to face the gods know what in the Yuan on the off chance that you might—*might*—solve those stupid riddles."

"Well, when you put it like that . . ." He turns back to me to give me a rueful grin. "Did my father really stoop to sending you to talk me out of it? He's been lecturing me on acting like a prince for years, and now when an opportunity presents itself, he backs down. And here you are, supporting him and not me."

"I don't think this was the opportunity either one of us had in mind," I tell him.

"This is exactly the opportunity my father had in mind. You?" He tilts his head, his eyes narrowed and a bit glassy with drink. "I have no idea what you have in mind. I can't even begin to fathom what you want."

I guess that makes two of us.

"What I want doesn't matter," I tell him.

"It matters to you." He opens his mouth as if he's going to add something to that, but he thinks better of it and takes another drink instead.

This is the exact conversation I cannot have with Khalaf, because one of the things I want very badly is him. I also want very badly to go home, or at least I did at some point in time. I can't have either one of those things without losing the other. I certainly can't have both. And since this conundrum is a non-starter, I remind myself to focus on the issue at hand.

"What about what you want?" I press him.

He shrugs.

"You don't want to be khan of the Kipchak Khanate, much less the Great Khan of the Mongol Empire. You never have."

"I know."

"Then why are you doing this?" Desperation has started to seep into my voice.

"Because I have to. Don't you see that?"

"No, I don't."

He slumps back against the felt wall of the *ger*, brings the skin of *qumiz* to his mouth, and takes another swig.

All at once, I feel hollowed out with exhaustion. I'm sick to death of standing out here in the dark as I try to reason with a drunk philosopher. At the end of the day, he won't disobey his father. I'm certain of it. So I dust off the snow that's fallen onto my shoulders and reach a hand down to Khalaf to help him up. "Look, just come inside. We'll sort it out in the morning."

He stares at my hand but makes no move to take it. I sigh with impatience and shake my hand at him. When he finally reaches for me, his grasp is surprisingly warm. We don't progress beyond this. He doesn't use my grip to leverage himself to his feet. He just sits there, studying our joined hands. His thumb brushes over the tops of my knuckles, slowly, touching each hill and valley of my hand, first in one direction, then the other.

Gods and ancestors help me.

He looks up at me and says, "Why don't you want me to go to Khanbalik, Jinghua?"

"Get up. Please, my lord." I tug at his hand, and this time he lets me pull him to his feet, which is awkward given that I'm on the tiny and bony side and he's on the tall and muscular side. Even so, he's remarkably steady for a drunk man, and now he's standing very close to me, all height and broad shoulders and distinctly male.

Beautiful.

"Give me a reason to stay," he challenges me, still holding on to my hand. He focuses on me with all his distinctive intensity, and my mind goes as white and empty as the Kipchack steppes in winter. The only thing I can think to say is "Come inside."

"The fate of my khanate rests on my shoulders. If I can answer Turandokht's riddles, I can take back everything and return my father to his rightful place. I could rule the empire. Give me one reason not to try."

"There are plenty of reasons," I say. "Lots of reasons."

"All I need is one."

I can't bring myself to look away. He moves in just a little closer. A bare inch separates the toes of our worn boots. The *qumiz* on his breath tinges the air with its sweet and sour scent. I don't know how to handle this, how to handle him. My heart swells large and fills the back of my throat with the threat of tears. I try to pull my hand free of his, but he holds tight to me, and I only manage to pull him closer. My eyes can no longer focus on any one part of his face. There's just an expanse of Khalaf and nothing but Khalaf before me.

"Come inside," I plead with him.

He leans in, bends down. His lips brush the corner of my mouth, and I freeze like a rabbit when the fox gets too close.

I want this.

I *want* this.

I know I can't have it, but I want it—him—with an iron will, a longing so strong and hard I could pound it with my fist and break my fingers on it.

He kisses me.

His lips against mine are dry and soft.

And I want more.

I *want*.

He kisses me again.

His lips against mine flood the world with possibilities, what-ifs that have nothing to do with riddles or khanates or disapproving parents.

When he kisses me a third time, I respond at last, kissing him back even though I have no idea what I'm doing. Instinctively, I make the embrace deeper, opening my lips to his, and he moans into my mouth. His hands cup my face so that he can kiss me even better, even more deliberately.

My blanket falls to the ground around my ankles, and I'm kissing him and kissing him as my fingers twine through the hair at the base of his neck. And it isn't awkward, and I don't mess it up. His hands feel warm and rough against my skin. His thumbs brush my cheeks. I slide my hands down to rest over his chest, where I feel his heart beating inside him.

There are entire lives in this one kiss, a river of futures that could belong to both of us.

Suddenly, he jerks his head back, taking his lips from mine. He grasps my hands in his, pulls them off his chest, and pushes me back. I stumble over the blanket at my feet as he gazes at me in stunned horror.

"I'm sorry," he gasps, letting go of me. He gapes at me as if I've sprouted horns out of my head. I feel like I've been slapped across the face. Mortification sears me to the point where my ears start ringing.

"I shouldn't have done that," he says. "I'm so sorry."

Hurt and anger well up inside me, pouring out of my mouth in a wave of ruthless honesty to which I have never before treated Khalaf.

"You're sorry? How could you do this to me?" My fingers clench. I want to wrap them around his neck and tear his flesh away with my jagged fingernails. I am a feral dog, cornered and ready to spring.

"I know. It was wrong of me."

"You think I'm your concubine, your little slave girl, and you can do whatever you want with me? Well, I'm not. I don't belong to you. I've never been yours."

"Jinghua—"

"Shut up." I'm freezing. I reach down for my blanket, slap bits of grass off it, and wrap it around my shoulders once more.

"You're so smart, aren't you? Brilliant, they said. You think you know everything. Well, I can promise you this, *my lord*: You don't know me. You don't know who I am. You don't know what I am. You don't know the first thing about me."

"It was just a mistake. Please, Jinghua."

He's so wretched and pathetic, wringing his hands and begging me for forgiveness. A casual observer would have no idea who was the servant and who was the master here.

"You know, your father was right about you," I tell him. "You are a prick. And you are an ungrateful little shit."

I turn my back on him and storm back inside the *ger*, burning with fury and abject humiliation.

"Let me guess," Timur says. "That could've gone better."

"Go suck your used tea leaves."

"Fair enough."

I lie down and curl up on my side with my back to the door, and I bury myself in the blanket that now smells of earth and grass and Khalaf.

"He'll come around," says Timur. "He always comes around." I think he says this more to comfort himself than me, which is just as well, since I'm too pissed off to care about anyone.

Or so I tell myself.

Khalaf stands right outside the entrance for a long, long time. I can feel his presence there. I lie very still so he'll think I'm asleep when he finally comes in.

Only he never does come inside.

Time stretches on until, at last, I hear him move. His feet crunch in the brittle grass as he walks away. The sound of his footsteps fades and then disappears altogether.

It was just a mistake, his voice echoes in my head.

I bury my face in my blanket so Timur won't hear me blubbering.

Khalaf's kiss is so fresh that my lips are still swollen with it. I wish I could wipe away the sensation of his mouth on mine with the back of my hand, but I know I'll burn with that memory for the rest of my life.

There used to be ten suns in the sky, scorching the earth until the archer Houyi shot down all but the great light that now rises in the east and sets in the west. I feel like one of the fallen, blazing and bright one moment, dark and defeated the next.

I thought I could guard my heart, but I might as well have tried to dam a river with a handful of pebbles.

24

WEIJI ENTERS THE FAMILY SHRINE, WHERE he bows twice to our ancestors.

Cups of wine, offerings of rice and pork, the incense burner—they all clutter the altar's surface. And now a falcon lands there as well, knocking over the ancestral tablets and sending thick, sweet wine spilling to the floor.

My brother kneels before the bird. When he holds his arm out to her and calls to her with a clicking of his tongue, she comes to him. Carefully, he gets to his feet and walks over to me.

"Look at her, Jinghua. Isn't she incredible?"

I open my mouth to warn him, to tell him that she's dangerous, but flower petals fall out of my mouth instead and float away in the oddly buoyant air of the shrine.

"She's beautiful," he tells me.

Let her go, I think, but I can't speak. Flowers continue to pour from my mouth like vomit, filling the air with the scent of jasmine.

Weiji doesn't see me anymore. It's like I've ceased to exist. For him, there is only this falcon.

She looms over him, enormous. She draws him into her wings like an embrace, even as she rakes and tears at his chest with jeweled talons.

And all I can do is scream in silence with flower petals falling around me like snow.

The next thing I know, Timur is waking me with a none-too-gentle nudge of his toe into my rib cage. I snort awake, still groggy. My head throbs.

"He never came back." Timur's deep voice echoes in the pain chambers of my sinus cavities. A wave of regret and embarrassment gives me a solid emotional wallop as I recall in vivid detail the disaster of the previous evening. I glance over to where Khalaf should be sleeping by the fire. His bedding lies in the same crumpled heap where he left it last night.

"Well? Where is he?" Timur demands.

"I'm not his keeper. How should I know?"

"Because you watch him like a starving man watches a rat."

I snort again, this time deliberately, and make a big show of throwing the covers over my head, signaling my derision as well as my intention to go back to sleep. He nudges me harder.

"Ow!" I sit up to avoid further onslaught.

"Let's go," Timur says, yanking my blanket off me.

"Where?"

"Qaidu's tent. That boy's not making a move without talking to me first. And I want breakfast."

"Fine," I huff, because, let's face it, it's hard to argue with breakfast.

Timur waits while I straighten out my rumpled clothes and attempt to comb and replait my hair. This process takes me all of five minutes, but the old goat says, "No one's writing a poem to your glorious beauty, girl, so give it up. Move it!"

I glare at him, but I head outside with him. Suddenly, it occurs to me that what I'm seeing is wrong, very wrong. The Mongols are pulling down their *gers* and loading them onto huge carts.

"My lord, I think they're packing up," I tell Timur.

"What? Lamb's balls!"

My mind whirs, trying to process what's happening, when Qaidu himself rides up to us atop a brown mare. "Good morning, cousin," he calls with a little salute.

"What is this?" Timur growls back.

Qaidu grins. "You are infinitely charming, Timur. I'll give you that. It's been a pleasure to see you again, but here, I'm afraid, we must part ways. I've come to bid you farewell."

The man's cheeriness serves as a stark foil to the icy dread that Timur and I share. Frantic, I search the steppes in all directions, but I don't see Khalaf anywhere.

"Where is my son?" Timur demands.

"He left at dawn. Didn't you know?"

Qaidu is clearly more than aware that we didn't know, and his joviality makes the gut punch hurt even more. The pain of it is like a sheep's bladder, limp and shapeless at first but growing larger and larger as it's inflated into a ball and kicked around in some brutal game.

Khalaf left us.

He left me.

Qaidu is enjoying himself now, and it makes me want to spit in his face. "He came to me late last night to redeem his two wishes," he says. "First, he asked that I have him outfitted for a long journey. Second, he asked me to take care of his father and his 'friend' that they may live in comfort among my people all the days of their lives should he fail to return. And, no offense, I do think it highly improbable that he will return given the direction of his journey."

Timur and I stand side by side, as cold and dead as a pair of graves.

"I bear you no ill will, Timur," Qaidu says. "Our armies have cooperated against a common enemy on more than one occasion, and I'm grateful to you for that—truly I am. But, you see, there's a hefty price on your head, literally and politically, and I won't risk the lives of my tribesmen to harbor you."

"You're cutting me loose?" Timur spits. "After what you promised my son? I saved your ass, you cowardly son of a bitch. You owe me."

Qaidu keeps smiling—honestly, genuinely smiling—which, given the situation, makes him look like a scary son of a bitch to me, not a cowardly one.

"Shut up," I warn Timur under my breath.

"Did you let my son go, or did you send your men after him to kill him?" Timur asks him.

That thought hadn't occurred to me, and terror for Khalaf's life takes hold of me.

"No, I didn't have him killed," Qaidu answers to my unspeakable relief. "That one has as good a chance as any to rule the empire. I want to make sure I'm on his good side in the unlikely event he wins Turandokht."

"You think leaving his father to die on the steppes will get you on his good side?"

"He won't ever know, will he? Besides, I'm doing him a favor. He'll never amount to anything with this father's stranglehold on him. The world needs a young prince. It does not need an old khan, especially a deposed old khan."

"You can't leave me behind. We're allies, you and I," Timur says. It's starting to sound like begging. Where is the bottom, I wonder? Where is the absolute rock bottom?

"You always tried so hard to emulate our common ancestor, the great Genghis Khan," Qaidu tells Timur. "Let this be an opportunity for you. He, too, was abandoned by his tribe, yet he rose up to rule the world. Maybe you will survive and do the same. Then, cousin, shall I bend at the knee to you. Until that time . . ."

Qaidu shrugs.

"Why not just kill me now, then?"

"I have enough integrity to give you a fighting chance, and I honor you enough to let you keep your blood inside your skin."

"And when I do rise up with my son, I will spill your blood onto the sacred earth and pick my teeth with the bones of your children."

Qaidu's horse fidgets, but the man only smirks at Timur. "I'm not overly concerned about that," he says. "And you, girl, the 'friend,' what will you do?"

It takes a moment for me to register that he's talking to me.

"What? What do you mean?" I stammer.

"I did promise the boy that I would keep both of you safe. I have had to rescind one promise, but I dislike reneging on two. If you stay with my people, I swear to Tengri, the Eternal Blue Sky, that you will live well."

"A half promise is worth nothing," I tell him coldly. "I'm sticking with my lord."

I'm not sure who's more shocked by my answer: me or Timur. Qaidu inclines his head and says, "As you wish," before he turns his horse away from us and trots off to oversee the packing up of camp.

Timur and I spend the next hour sitting back to back, huddled with our few earthly belongings as we watch the Mongols load their carts. I'm stuck with Timur for all eternity. Kill me. But since he's all I have now, I get up and move so that I'm sitting beside him. He just hunkers there, staring at nothing.

"What are you looking at? You can't even see."

He raises a skin of *qumiz* in my general direction and says, "Cheers," before guzzling it.

"Oh, seriously? Are *you* drunk now? Where did you get that?"

"It takes a hell of a lot more than this to get me drunk." He offers me the skin with a belch.

"Nice. Great. That's great."

"It's just you and me now. Have a drink."

Since getting drunk seems to be de rigueur these days, I shrug, take the skin, knock back a swig . . . and promptly choke on it.

"This stuff is disgusting," I inform him between coughing fits. "You drink that on purpose?"

Timur throws his head back and laughs at me. He may as well start prancing around in a country dance for as much as it startles me. His laughter, like his personality, is mammoth. I almost don't hate him when he's laughing like this.

"Shut up," I mutter at him.

He wipes away jovial tears and giggles. "I didn't say anything."

"Shut up anyway."

"Touché, little bird.'"

I don't know why I don't tell him not to call me a little bird. I just don't. Instead, I say, "Can I ask you something?"

"Could I stop you?"

"Why are you just sitting here when you could be chasing after your son so that he doesn't get himself killed in Khanbalik?"

Timur's little bout of hilarity evaporates. "Why are you sitting here talking to an old goat when you could be doing the same thing?"

"He won't listen to me. Obviously," I tell him, wondering how he's figured out that I call him "old goat" in my mind.

"Or me." Timur shakes his head. "My own son just threw me away. He left me—"

"I noticed."

"—dependent on a milk-blooded turncoat."

"He left me, too," I point out.

"It's different for you."

"How?"

Timur reaches across me and grabs the *qumiz* skin. He takes another drink before he answers, "Because you may do as you please."

I grab the skin back from him and take a drink without choking (although I want to very desperately). "Too bad no one ever bothers to ask me what pleases me."

"I know *he* pleases you."

What can I say to that? I take another gulp and cough again.

"And I can see, by the way," Timur tells me.

"What?"

"You asked what I was staring at since I can't even see. And I'm telling you that I *can* see."

"No, you can't," I sigh. "We've been down this road already."

"Yes, I can."

I almost take another drink of the *qumiz*, but I think better of it. It tastes like death, and it hasn't done Khalaf or Timur any good, if you ask me. And what am I doing here, anyway? Timur's not my father—thank heaven—and at least one of us should be racing after Khalaf, even if there's almost no chance whatsoever we'll catch up to him.

"Forget it," I mutter.

"I can see," Timur insists. "It's like someone burned a hole in the middle of my sight, right in the center, as if my sight were a piece of parchment and someone held it over a candle and scorched it. All around the edges, the world is still there, but if I look directly at a thing, I can't see it."

"Oh," I say lamely. This really is a heart-to-heart, and I have no clue what to do with it.

"I can only see my son's face if I don't look at him."

"That's awful," I say with actual sincerity.

"Yes, it is."

We sit there, side by side, soaking in our sadness, until Timur says, "If you tell anyone what I just told you, I'll punch—"

"You'll punch a hole in my chest and rip out my innards and take a bite of my still-beating heart, blah, blah, blah," I finish for him. "There's the lord and master I know and love."

By now, the Barlas and Qaidu's people have begun to head off to the south in a long train. Many of them stare at us with piti-less eyes on their way out. Some of the children make faces. I give them nothing in return, no emotion, no grief. If they remember me at all, they'll remember my face as cold and hard as stone.

When they're all gone, when they're nothing but specks on the horizon, Timur turns to me and says, "Come on, little bird."

It's hard to loathe a man who calls you "little bird."

"Khanbalik or bust?" I ask.

"Probably bust, but what the hell?"

He takes my hand in his enormous grasp, and I let him, because I'm feeling unmoored and small and alone out here on the steppes and his hand is big and warm and callused and real. But he doesn't move right away, and we just stand there holding hands. It's starting to feel awkward.

"Uh, my lord?" I ask.

"Rotting carrion, which way is east?"

"This way, my lord." And with clear eyes, I pull Timur Khan east to find his son.

PART FIVE

THE THIRD RIDDLE

The City of Khanbalik, Khanate of the Yuan Dynasty

Autumn 1281

25

TURANDOT SAYS,

"From the fountain in the palace courtyard flows
A liquid flame that is no flame at all.
At times pours out an icy stream of woes,
At times pours hot with passion's burning call.

"When hot, it is delirium and ardor,
The heat of battle, the rusty hue of conquest.
When cold, it is a dull and aching torpor,
A longing, or your marble-encased rest."

Khalaf bows his head again.

"Seven minutes," Zhang announces.

Standing here, powerless, watching Khalaf think as the seconds tick by is even more excruciating than it was for the first riddle.

Time is so fickle. It moved at a sluggish pace during our journey across deserts and plains and mountains, so slow and ponderous that it felt like we were traveling across eternity. Now, on an autumn night in Khanbalik, time moves like a rocket, swift and soaring and dangerous. All too soon, Zhang calls, "Six minutes."

Clearly, I didn't appreciate all the time I had, didn't make the most of it, didn't use it wisely. If I had, we wouldn't be trapped in this nightmare, and Khalaf wouldn't be fighting for his life and his khanate at the feet of Turandokht Khatun. I'm so panicked for him that I feel incorporeal, as if I might just float away if Timur's hand weren't anchoring me to the earth.

By the time Zhang gets to "Five minutes," my whole body is wound so tightly, I don't know how I'm ever going move again. The crowd starts to call out to Khalaf, some with jeers, some with words of encouragement. Khalaf keeps his eyes closed. He breathes in. He breathes out.

I have wasted so much time, and not just the moments I shared with Khalaf and even Timur. I spent the first fifteen years of my life sulking my time away, squandering every single breath before the Mongols came and turned me into what I am now, before I lost my home and my family.

Before I lost Weiji.

I think of the moment just over three years ago when the catastrophe first began to creep into our lives, as quietly as a spider, although we didn't realize it then. Weiji and I knelt side by side before our parents, the picture of filial propriety. *Nice going,* he whispered from the side of his mouth when Father wasn't looking, teasing me for the way I had brought our parents' disapproval upon myself.

What on earth would he say now if he could see just how badly I've messed up everything?

"Four minutes," Zhang calls.

"No," Timur begs any god who will listen as I shake uncontrollably against him.

Khalaf shuts his eyes tighter, making the skin pinch in at the corners. "A 'marble-encased rest' is a tomb," he says, thinking through the puzzle out loud. "What burns in battle and freezes in death?"

"Three minutes."

The crowd grows louder, and so does Khalaf as he presses his palms against his eyes and says, "'Ardor' is love, but so is 'longing.' What runs both hot and cold with love?"

The answer could be me. I burn with regret, and I am frozen with fear, all because I was stupid enough to let myself fall in love with the prince of the Kipchak Khanate.

"Two minutes!"

Khalaf takes his hands away from his face, draws his head up, and opens his eyes. His chest heaves with life.

"Blood," he declares, the echo of his voice ringing through the hall. "The answer is 'blood.' Blood is red like a flame. The heart pours blood through a man's body as a fountain pulses water. It burns feverishly both in love and in battle, and grows cold in longing and in death. The answer is 'blood.'"

Every head turns to the stunned scholars, who are gaping at Khalaf.

"The answer!" a man shouts from somewhere in the crowd, and someone farther away yells, "What's the answer?" The three men in the tower shake themselves and confer with the chancellor.

"Please," I pray, to whom I don't know.

"'Blood,'" Zhang concurs, not bothering to mask his disgust. "The answer is 'blood.' The contestant has won again."

The audience roars with approval, almost as if Khalaf were their representative rather than Turandokht. I stare at Khalaf as if I can make him successful one last time by the sheer force of my will. While his initial successes have raised the crowd's confidence, the second riddle seems to have had the opposite effect on him. His serenity and confidence have ebbed, replaced by tense cords of muscle along his neck.

His neck, which smells of rust and smoke and earth.

I have failed him so badly.

Zhang and the guards have a harder time silencing the crowd this time, but they do manage to get the job done. When the noise of the gathering softens to a dull roar, the chancellor shouts, "The contestant has successfully answered the second riddle. The third riddle is about to begin. The contestant will have seven minutes to answer. Do you understand, sir?"

"I do," Khalaf says before clenching his jaw shut. His nostrils flare as the square goes quiet again.

Turandokht rises to her feet. She towers over her father. She towers over Khalaf where he stands at the bottom of the stairs. She towers over the empire.

"Who are you?" she demands, her voice sharp as a knife.

He asked me the same question. Does he remember? Can he think of anything in this moment except for his duty to the Kipchak Khanate? Or Turandokht? Or his own mortality, so close it brushes his skin?

Who are you?

The way you speak, the words you use, the things you know . . .

I wish that you didn't feel a need to hide who you are. I wish that you would let me know you as you know me.

Who are you? Really?

How much time did I waste hiding from him? I spent nearly a year beside him crossing the wide world, and for what?

"The third riddle, please, my khatun" is all he says to Turandokht. He's smooth as a placid lake on the surface, but I know he's a mass of jangling nerves beneath.

"You will die today," she assures him. "The third riddle is this:

"It is a prison of snow, a graceful cage of ice,
Though pale you burn inside its darkened heart.
Raging hot, your fire cannot suffice,
Nor can you prize its icy bars apart.

"As on the mountain's peak, so useless is your fire
That from your flame grows colder still its ring.
Before you lies a choice: What's your desire?
Break free and be slave? Or remain and be king?"

"Seven minutes," calls Zhang.

Seven minutes is not enough.

I had a year to tell him everything, and I chose to tell him nothing.

Why didn't I just tell him who I was?

PART SIX

PRINCESS

The City of Lin'an, Song Empire

Autumn 1278

26

MY FATHER'S EYES FEEL LIKE A load of bricks on my shoulders as I prepare the tea. I cut off a chunk of the pressed cake and crumble it into the wide, shallow bowl. He loves the way the black porcelain shows off a well-prepared tea to its best advantage.

The problem is that it shows off imperfectly prepared tea as well.

I point the steaming water into the cup, take up the whisk, and begin to beat the concoction into submission. With a few flicks of my wrist, I can see that I have somehow failed before I've really even begun. The froth is not forthcoming, and I end up placing the sad excuse for tea, yellowed and sickly against the smooth black of the bowl, before my father.

I serve my mother next, creating another spectacularly terrible beverage before I step back to kneel beside my brother, both of us in attendance on our parents. My head is bowed, but I sneak a glance at Father. His bowl remains before him, untouched, and he's frowning into it.

Father sighs. He picks up his tea, rises from his richly lacquered chair, and dumps the contents out the window. As he sits beside my mother again, he says, "Hopefully, that won't kill the chrysanthemums."

"You are too particular," Mother replies.

I bow my head and wither in shame.

"Nice going," Weiji whispers to me out of the corner of his mouth. I guess his teasing is the only way he knows how to show solidarity with me, and I appreciate it, mortified as I am.

"I understand that her embroidery is equally dreadful," my father continues as he makes his own tea with deft hands. "Her cooking is mediocre, and she can barely spin silk."

"She will have servants who will do those things for her," says Mother.

"And she must know how to do these things so that she can manage those servants. Just look at her. The poor girl doesn't shine at all, does she?"

"She's shy," says Mother. "That's all. She's quiet and respectful. She's dutiful and obedient. That's what a man wants in a wife."

"Certainly, if his wife is pretty, but this one isn't. How old is she now? Ten? Eleven?"

I am acutely aware of my body's failings, the way the bones of my spine form a series of bumps underneath my silk gown.

"She's fourteen, Husband."

"Has she had her courses yet?" Father asks.

I don't know how to endure this humiliation. I had no idea men even knew of such matters, and the fact that my father is discussing these intimate, female subjects in front of my brother makes me wish the ground would open up and swallow me whole. Weiji makes a low, guttural sound that only I can hear to express his nausea.

"No, she hasn't," my mother answers.

"Well, that's something, at least. Maybe she'll find herself with a decent bosom when all is said and done. I doubt it, though."

My shame deepens. When will this trial end?

"She has small feet," my mother points out.

"No man has ever married a girl for her feet."

I sneak another glance of my father. He's a slight man, but from this viewpoint he looks like a giant swathed in black, his cap placed perfectly atop his head. He dabs at his tea-dampened lips with his sleeve and tells my mother, "Do something with her. She needs to marry well."

Mother bristles. "She's the daughter of the prince regent and a princess of the Song Dynasty. Of course she'll marry well."

"She's the fourth daughter of a second son, and she owes it to her family to be respectable. Do something with her."

Mother's eyes drop. "Yes, Husband."

Being in my father's presence is like staring into a mirror. All my faults are cataloged for me in his eyes: fat lips and beady eyes, cheeks too round for such a small frame, and wispy hair that flies loose of its elaborate coif.

"My daughters," Father says. "Four daughters you have given me, Wife, and not one of them worth a damn: one married to a fool fifteen years ago and two dead in their graves. This last one must do better. She must strive to emulate Turandokht, who is her better a thousand times over."

I have no idea who Turandokht is, but it seems to me that there are so many girls in the world—pretty girls, accomplished girls, elegant girls—who exist for the sole purpose of pointing out how ugly and inept and awkward I am.

"Turandokht?" my mother asks, forgetting her passivity. "You wish your daughter to comport herself like some gauche Mongol?"

"That 'gauche Mongol,' in addition to being unspeakably beautiful and refined, speaks five languages, studies astrology, and is learned in philosophy."

I've always thought of myself as smart. Reading and learning are the only things I've ever been good at. But while I've studied some astrology and even less philosophy, I don't speak five languages, and I'm certainly not pretty or refined. *Does she have to be beautiful* and *brilliant? I wonder. Couldn't she just be one or the other? Couldn't I be one or the other at least?*

"Forgive me, Husband, but what good will all that learning do her? What man would want a wife who is more learned than he is?"

"It is my dearest hope that this man will desire just such a wife." A rare grin thins Father's full lips as he nods at my brother.

"Me?" asks Weiji.

My father's grin widens. The smile looks unnatural on his stern face.

"You wish me to marry Turandokht?"

"I have sent the best portraitist of our kingdom to Khanbalik to take her likeness. Her portrait will return in the hands of Chancellor Zhang, who will arrive in the flesh to make the marriage arrangements."

Father awaits my brother's joyful response.

He doesn't receive it.

"But the Mongols are our enemies," Weiji protests. "You yourself have fought against them. How can you ask me to marry one?"

Father's smile dissipates. "Yes, I have fought them, you ingrate! And I know better than anyone how they will decimate the Song if we don't make peace with them now. With this marriage, we will unite Zhongguo, the north and the south. Not even the Han could achieve such glory."

I cringe and shrink under Father's anger, and it isn't even directed at me.

"But," begins Weiji.

"There is no 'but.' You will join yourself with the most powerful empire in the world, and you will get a beautiful and virtuous wife in the bargain. You will thank me in deep obeisance for this honor, and you will prostrate yourself before our gods and our ancestors in gratitude. Do you understand?"

Weiji stares down at his knees. His shoulders quiver in his attempt to hold back his tears. "Yes," he says weakly.

"Do you understand?" Father shouts. I feel myself growing even smaller.

"Yes," Weiji repeats, steadily this time. He gives my father a low bow. "Yes, thank you, Father."

My father rises and brushes out his robe. He makes his way to the door.

"And what is our son to do with such a wife?" my mother fires at his retreating backside, tears of anger evident in her voice.

Father halts. "What nonsense. You are a learned woman, Wife. You can read and write, and you know all manner of things."

"Yes, but I do not presume to rule."

"That is a matter of opinion," Father comments drily. "Do something about your daughter, woman, and leave the only son you've given this family to me." He leaves, heading off to do whatever it is important men do when they aren't carrying out diplomatic missions or discussing the finer points of Confucian philosophy.

Weiji, Mother, and I are left in silence. I don't understand how my humiliation turned into an unwanted wedding arrangement for my brother, but I feel somehow at fault. And it quickly sinks in that if my brother marries this perfect girl, this perfect girl is going to come live here with us. I'm going to have to live side by side with perfection.

At last, my brother says, "Excuse me," gives Mother a cursory bow, and skulks off.

Mother looks at me, and her lips thin. "Come. It's time to make an offering anyway." Mother calls over a servant girl and orders her to fetch wine and a plate of rice cakes. I don't even glance at the girl; she's as much a part of the house as the walls and furniture.

When the offerings arrive, I follow Mother to the ancestral shrine, watching my little feet as I scuff along the clean-swept floor. I start to sing a few bars of "The Boat of Stars" under my breath to the rhythm of my steps before my mother admonishes me.

"Honestly, Daughter, have you never read the *Classic of Filial Piety for Girls*? Or *Admonitions of Girls*? A lady does not sing."

I close my mouth.

"You disappoint me," she says as we continue to walk. "Where are your priorities? You take so little interest in your appearance or in your feminine development. You'll shame this family. You mark my words."

"Father says I'm to be educated," I point out hopefully. I may take little interest in my appearance—which is hopeless to begin with—but I do take great interest in learning.

"You *are* educated, too much so, in my estimation," Mother snaps. I bite my lip, chastened. "Your father means that you should be accomplished and refined. A head full of words and learning does you little good without the grace to put them to good use."

"What does it matter?" My small voice scurries like a mouse to my mother's ears. "A man will only appreciate my father's value, not mine."

"Your father's value is your primary value, just as it is mine, and you should be grateful for that. But your husband may one day come to appreciate the value that is all your own . . . if you ever get around to developing it. Heaven knows, if that little viper Turandokht can land a catch as good as your brother, there's no telling what prize you may capture."

We've arrived at the shrine, and with an impatient jerk of her head, my mother motions for me to offer my respects before the altar. I bow four times and Mother does the same. She lights incense and places it in the burner, a porcelain duck sitting atop a lotus blossom, white with a jade-green underglaze. The duck's head is tilted back and its bill is open, leaving a little hole into which Mother places the joss stick as it burns. It looks so cheery perched there on the altar shelf, keeping our ancestors company, a reminder that death is a part of life and not something to be dreaded or feared.

Mother pours wine into cups on the altar to quench our ancestors' thirst, and she places the cakes before their wooden tablets as an offering. She lights candles to either side of the burner.

"You need to start learning your duty," Mother tells me when we've finished and we make our way back to the women's quarters. "Someday, you will be the one making offerings to your husband's ancestors. No man wants a woman who fumbles her way through the rituals."

I don't say anything. Mother gives me an austere look as I follow her across the threshold beyond the red curtain.

"You're not pretty," she says. "Fine. But you are not exactly ugly either, Daughter, and you are wiser and in many ways more accomplished than most girls will ever be."

"Pretty girls don't need to be accomplished."

"They do, actually, and so do you." Mother's voice strains with frustration.

I stare longingly at the courtyard garden through the window, missing the days when I used climb a tree or hide behind the quince shrubs when I wanted to be alone with my thoughts.

Mother makes a feral sound of frustration from the back of her throat. "You're not listening. Go on. Off with you."

She shoos me out of her sight and into the garden.

"Yes, Mother." My voice is apologetic. The rest of me is filled with relief.

Freedom.

I walk to the pond. The goldfish burst through the water's surface before my reflection has a chance to form, their mouths kissing at the air. I watch a stand of bamboo sway in the breeze, and after a while, bored, I begin to sing.

Jasmine flower
Your willowy stems clustered with sweet-smelling buds
Fragrant and white, everyone praises your beauty
Let me pluck you down
And give you to the one I love

My voice starts strong, but it trails off as I see Weiji step along the garden path to come sit beside me. Whereas I am plain and shy, my brother is handsome and glowing with self-assurance. Today, however, he burns a little less brightly as we crouch side by side watching the goldfish slip though the water below us.

When the song is over, I look at my brother, who frowns back at me.

"Older Brother?" I say with a face full of sympathy.

"Yeah?"

I shove him over into the dirt, spring to my feet, and sprint to a three-yard head start before he even knows what hit him.

"You're it!" I whoop in triumph.

"No fair!" Weiji laughs. He chases after me, and my fine hair flies loose from my combs as I run as fast as I can.

27

MY FAMILY HAS COME INTO TOWN to meet the Yuan
entourage that arrived at the palace two days ago.

I'm sitting in an old, gnarled plum tree in the imperial gardens
on a branch that gently lilts in the breeze. My skirt is bunched up
in an undignified manner, my knees bent up to my chest. Weiji,
who is larger and heavier, sits in a crook where a thick branch
meets the main trunk. The tree stands just outside the Song
emperor's audience chamber, and snatches of the conversation
inside float up to us.

"Let us move on to the subject of the succession," my father
says.

"He's going to kill us," I whisper to Weiji.

"Not if we don't get caught."

"But what if he does catch us?"

"He won't if you shut up," Weiji hisses back. "You're the one who insisted on tagging along. Now be quiet, will you?"

I cling to my branch as the voices from within continue to waft up to us.

". . . assumed that any sons produced from the happy union will be considered eligible heirs to the Son of the Eternal Blue Sky," says an unfamiliar voice.

"Son of the Sky?" says the emperor of the Song, my cousin Bing. "Is that the same thing as the Son of Heaven? I thought *I* was the Son of Heaven."

Bing is sweet, but he's six years old and has no clue what's going on.

My father, who is the prince regent, sallies forth: "The Son of Heaven assumes that before any children are produced from this happy union, Prince Weiji would be the likely heir."

"Let us hope for the best, sir. I do not think we should plan on such an event."

"But if—"

"But if the Great Khan passes before a son is born, we shall deal with that when the time comes," that new voice answers with a steely grace. I can't believe anyone would have the temerity to interrupt Father.

Weiji curses in apparent agreement.

"Perhaps we should discuss the bridal gifts," says my father.

A courtier drones on about bolts of silk, gold jewelry, and the provision of a wardrobe.

"This is a lot less interesting than I thought it was going to be," I whisper to my brother.

"Shh! It's starting to get good," Weiji answers as the stranger's voice pipes up again.

"Turandokht Khatun, as the daughter of the Great Khan, will live in the beating heart of the Mongol Empire in Khanbalik. The home is the realm of the Mongol woman. It is for the man to come and live with her in her home, not for the woman to trot off to the hinterlands to live with her husband."

"Are we to understand," says my father, "that a son of the eternal house of the Song Dynasty is to act as a subservient to a woman?"

"Are we to understand that you dislike the offer of peace from the Son of the Eternal Blue Sky, the Great Khan of the Mongol Empire?" says that smooth, unfamiliar voice.

"Of course not, sir," my father answers, his voice tumbling awkwardly over his words. "You misunderstand me."

Weiji curses again.

I'm sitting on a low chair with a high, carved back in the grand palatial hall of the Song emperor. The other women and I stay out of sight behind a large screen the vibrant green of a kingfisher. I always feel so small and stupid in such a crush of people, but there is to be a poetry reading tonight meant to impress the Mongol entourage, and I am very fond of poetry. A scholar, probably dressed above his station for this occasion, reads a Tang Dynasty poem with great fervor at the front of the room. I perch on my seat, listening attentively.

It's the story of a woman's life, each stanza capturing a decade. As a girl, she is as lovely and delicate as a tree's blossoms in the rain. By the time she is twenty, her parents have arranged her marriage, and the groom carries her away like a goddess in a myth. But the woman's worth deteriorates as the poem continues. She may still be attractive at thirty, but by age fifty, her husband's affection diminishes as her beauty fades. Year by year, her skin wrinkles and her joints crack. She goes deaf and blind. At ninety, she is all alone, ailing in her solitary bed. By the time the scholar reads the last stanza, I feel wrung out.

At a hundred, like a cliff crumbling in the wind,
For her body it is the moment to become dust.
Children and grandchildren will perform sacrifices to her spirit,
And clear moonlight will forever illuminate her patch of earth.

A smattering of polite applause meets the end of the poem, but it seems an insufficient response to the depth of the poem's message. To everyone else, it was only a collection of words, prettily told. To me, it was an arrow shot through the heart, a hard truth I had never been able to articulate to myself before. I feel almost naked sitting here in a room full of people who either didn't understand the poem or didn't care enough to try.

There's to be music next, but I rise from my seat in the intermission and cross the opulent hall, stepping on several toes and tiny, bound feet in the process. I make my way outdoors into one of many imperial gardens even as I sense my mother's sharp eyes boring into the back of my head, warning me of my impropriety.

The garden is lit with paper lanterns, casting a gold light against a man-made hillock and a twisted pine tree. A brook plashes under a nearby wooden bridge. I lean against a post that holds up the awning above me, my left arm wrapped around it as if the carved wood could offer affection.

"Dreadfully hot in there." A heavyset man in a lavish green robe steps out into the garden and drifts across the porch to lean against the post opposite me. His skin is pale and delicate, his mustaches as thin and smooth as the handles of two fine paintbrushes.

Alarmed, I draw my arm up to my eyes so that my long sleeve covers my face. A concubine might be seen, a dancer, a servant, a slave. But a princess? Absolutely not.

"Forgive me," says the man, indicating his own face, a reflection of my gesture. "It's been so long since I've lived among my own people, I forget some of these niceties."

I recognize his voice as the one Weiji and I overheard earlier that day, when we eavesdropped on the wedding arrangements. One or the other of us should step away immediately, but he seems disinclined. This man is clearly from the Song, but he's with the Mongol entourage, and as I understand it, the Mongol court allows noblewomen to mingle freely with men despite the clear vulgarity of it. I drop my arm away from my face and offer the stranger a half bow, hoping I haven't blundered.

"Tell me, did you like that poem just now?" he asks, unconcerned by my decorum or possible lack thereof.

I shudder to think what my mother would say if she caught me having this conversation. My eyes shift to each side before asking, "Me?"

"Yes, you." He looks amused, and now I feel awkward and stupid.

"I don't know." As a general rule, no one asks for my opinion or cares what I think about anything. This man may be the first human being who has expressed any interest in what transpires inside my head.

"Do you know what I think?" he asks.

I shake my head, marveling at the fact that this conversation is happening.

"I think you liked it. I think you liked it a great deal. Tell me why."

I finger the carvings on the post. "Because it's true," I answer before I clamp my lips shut, worried that I've said more than I ought, shown too much of who I am on the inside.

"Is it?"

"I think so," I whisper, my eyes downcast.

"How so?"

I rub the tips of my fingers along the twin moles that dot my neck, that sit there like two burping frogs on a lily pad. In a fit of reckless bravery, I reply, "Because it seems to me that a woman's beauty is everything. And when she loses it—if she ever had it to begin with—she no longer has value in the world."

"And yet her beauty isn't her only source of happiness," the man counters, speaking as if he takes his conversation partner seriously. "She has her husband, her children, the industry of her hands, and in death she has the prayers and sacrifices of her family."

"But the poem is about change and sorrow," I soldier on, meeting his eyes this time. He gazes back at me attentively. "At twenty, her husband carries her away as if she were a treasure. But by fifty, as her beauty dissolves, so does her husband's love for her. And her children bring her sadness and worry, too. When they're young, they give her trouble, and when they're grown, the sons make poor marriages and the daughters leave her to start households of their own. She's left to die alone."

My bravery leaves me breathless. The man's eyes narrow, but he doesn't seem angry or offended. If anything, he seems pleased with my response.

"It's a Buddhist concept with which you may not be familiar, Princess. It is Princess Jinghua, yes?"

I nod, wondering how he knows who I am when he's never seen me. He gives me a gracious, handsome bow. "I am Zhang, chancellor of the empire of the Eternal Blue Sky. I am pleased to make your acquaintance, most pleased. Now, as I was saying, it is the idea that life, like happiness, is fleeting. The woman's life, then, is a metaphor, a representation of a spiritual idea."

"But it's also a man's concept of what it means to be a woman." I glance toward the open doorway into the splendor of the great hall. What if someone sees me talking to the chancellor or hears me speaking so boldly? Is there no end to my shame?

"Good," he says. "Yes, that's quite good. Go on."

His approval opens like a flowering bud inside me, pushing aside my reticence. I say, "In a man's view, a woman is something to be valued, like a silk painting or an ornate vase, until she becomes dingy with time and utterly without value. It's not how a woman sees herself."

He runs the right half of his mustache through his thumb and forefinger before saying, "Do you know, I had not thought of it quite that way before, Princess."

My heart races. I try to keep a pleased smile from spreading across my face in an unseemly manner. How exciting to be heard. How dangerous and thrilling to be understood.

"Perhaps when next we meet, it would be interesting to examine a poem that explores the sorrows of a man's life," he offers.

"Perhaps," I answer shyly.

"If you don't mind my saying so, you have a good mind, my lady."

An adult's approval is as rare as a pearl for me. I give Chancellor Zhang a genuine and truly indelicate smile.

28

FOR ALL THE EXCITEMENT GOING ON with the wedding arrangements these days, I'm incredibly bored, sitting here in the inner chambers. I have too much time on my hands, which means that I have nothing better to do than think about the conversation I had with Chancellor Zhang and the fact that I should not have had that conversation and that I wish I could talk to him again anyway.

I'm seated at a lacquered desk, reading the *Analects* in self-imposed penance. My heart isn't in it, though, and eventually, I rise and walk over to the courtyard window. From my home's situation on Phoenix Hill, I can see the West Lake in all its perfection below, bordered by lotus blossoms and crossed by ornate bridges. To the south lies the imperial palace with Lin'an glittering at its feet. The city and the mist-shrouded hills that surround it are framed by the window like a picture hung on a wall.

"Princess Jinghua?" says voice from the next room.

A male voice.

"Princess Jinghua, are you there?"

I look around, frantic that no one see or hear this, the scandal of a man calling to me inside the women's quarters. Thankfully, nobody is about. I hurry into the next room, where I see Chancellor Zhang's head poking around the side of the red curtain that separates the inner and outer chambers of my home. My arm is up, my sleeve covering my face.

Zhang tsk-tsks. "Oh, not all this again. I have spent considerable time in the presence of ladies, you know."

Embarrassment floods me from toe to head, like someone filling a cup of wine to the brim, but I let my arm fall to my side.

"You shouldn't be here," I whisper, standing just on the other side of the curtain now.

"But I've come to pay a call on your father, and what a dishonorable wretch I should be if I didn't deliver that poem I promised you."

I glance behind me, terrified that a servant or, worse, my mother will come in at any moment and see this exchange.

But I want that poem.

"All right," I say, still whispering as I hold out my hand. "But then you have to leave."

He tilts his head and gives me that amused expression from the night before. "You misunderstand me, Princess Jinghua. A poem is not an object to give the hand but a treasure to give the mind. Observe."

To my utter bewilderment, he draws back the curtain even farther, revealing his round figure. He gestures elegantly as he recites his poem. It's one I know well enough, a piece from *The Book of Songs*. My panic gives way to the timbre of the words, the sorrow of the tone as the poem describes a soldier's life, a man taken from his wife, restless, living at the whim of his lord.

Are we buffaloes, are we tigers
That our home should be these desolate wilds?

In my world, the soldier is a sort of man I have neither seen nor contemplated. The men of my sphere live in a world of words and ideas, art and scholarship. I have barely been beyond the red curtain that hangs halfway between me and Chancellor Zhang, but if I close my eyes, I see a world of tall grass through which men must push themselves like spare, hungry foxes.

When his voice drifts away, I open my eyes. My heart yearns for something I can't identify.

"So what do you say to the condition of men, Princess Jinghua?" he asks me.

"I think we should pity the poor soldier," I reply, but my answer seems inadequate.

"His lot does seem reasonably pitiable," Zhang agrees.

"Do you sympathize with him, Chancellor?"

"I do, yes."

"But you aren't a soldier, I think."

He still holds back the curtain, and the red silk clashes with the bright violet and gold of his elaborate jacket. It's strange to see a man wearing so much color.

"Certainly not," he says. "I have lived a privileged life. I am a scholar and statesman. Does that mean I cannot feel empathy for the plight of the common man?"

"Not all soldiers are common, though. For the Mongols, their greatest warriors are also their greatest men, like Genghis Khan."

"But a great warrior does not necessarily a good leader make. The Great Khan is no warrior. His grandfather, Genghis Khan, might be the exception rather than the rule."

"And my father, too. He has been a great general, and now as prince regent he is a great leader, too."

"Of course," Zhang agrees with a gracious nod.

"Chancellor?"

"Yes, Princess?"

"May I ask you something?"

"I believe you just did," he quips.

"You're from the Song, aren't you?"

"As you see."

"But you live in Khanbalik, and you work for the Mongols."

"Yes."

"But . . . how?" I stammer, looking behind me into the women's quarters and then beyond Zhang into the outer chambers to make sure we remain unseen. "Why?"

I suddenly feel as if I'm speaking with a mouth full of stones. I have no business asking him something so personal, and yet I badly want to know how an eloquent, educated man ended up in the imperial court of the backwater Mongols.

He leans against the doorframe, less formal than he was a moment ago, and rests his free hand over his belly, his elegant nails long and white and clean.

"Forgive me, Chancellor," I say in a rush. "I should not have asked that."

"No, no. It's quite all right. Do you really want to know?"

I nod.

He gazes wistfully into the distance. "Like so many young men of the Song court, I had passed the examinations and earned a place in our beautiful bureaucracy. When I was sent on a diplomatic mission to Kaifeng, the Mongols chose to hold me captive rather than treat with the Song Empire." He pulls his gaze out of the past and grins at me. "They appreciate usefulness, the Mongols, and apparently they found me useful. Turandokht Khatun had many tutors, but none of them were Song. As a general rule, the Song are not allowed into the imperial court, as you know, but the Great Khan thought his daughter ought not to be ignorant of the people she might one day rule. And so I was brought to Khanbalik to be her tutor."

"And you were glad?" I ask, relieved that I don't seem to have offended him.

"Oh no, not at first. At the time, I thought I'd sunk as low as a man can sink. But then I met her. And as the years passed, I began to understand the gift that heaven was kind enough to bestow upon me."

"What gift is that?"

"That 'gift' is an extraordinarily apt student. In all my years at the academy, I never met a man who could compare to Turandokht in intelligence and learning. In teaching her, I have had to learn just to keep up with her. She has made me a better scholar and a better man."

"And so you are loyal to her."

"I am. I would gladly fall on my sword for her—well, if I had a sword to begin with." He strokes his elegant mustache thoughtfully. "But a person—especially a woman—of that intellect is often lonely. And despite her learning and her position in the world, I do often wonder if she would do better to have a companion of her own rank and intelligence at her side."

He smiles at me, and my lips turn up sympathetically.

"I should be off," he says. "Sadly, I have come to Lin'an for matters that have little to do with poetry. Until we meet again, Princess."

He gives me a stately bow and finally releases the curtain, but not before I see, to my utter horror, my brother coming up behind him. The red silk is still shifting into place as they greet each other on the other side.

"Prince Weiji."

"Chancellor Zhang." I can hear the evil glee welling up in Weiji's mouth with each syllable, and I know I'm about to be teased mercilessly. A moment later, he sticks his head into the room with a sly grin plastered across his handsome face.

"Well, Jinghua, it's nice to see you getting friendly with boys."

"Be quiet," I retort, glancing around furiously to make sure no one overheard him. "It isn't like that."

"I wouldn't get my hopes up too high if I were you. He's probably three times your age. You wouldn't find that very fun."

Again with the embarrassment. "That's disgusting," I tell Weiji.

"You're right. That *is* disgusting." He shudders with revulsion.

"What are you doing here anyway?" I ask. I can't help but notice that he looks uncommonly pleased with himself, too, in a way that has nothing to do with catching his sister whispering with a man at the inner quarters curtain. "And what are you grinning about?" I add.

"Am I grinning?"

"Yes, witless, you're grinning like a madman."

By now, his grin has grown positively stupid. He pushes the curtain aside and says, "I wanted to show you this." He reaches into his sleeve pocket, pulls out a small portrait, and shows it to me. I take the portrait gingerly into my hands and study it. The girl staring back at me is lusciously beautiful.

"Turandokht?" I guess as I hand it back to him. He nods and stares down at the painting in his hand with that ridiculous smile still spread across his face.

"You like her?" I ask with a teasing grin of my own. "You like her picture?"

"Maybe."

He's beaming.

"What happened to all that Father-is-marrying-me-to-the-enemy business?"

"I know, but look at her." He holds the painting up for me to see and fully appreciate. "She's beautiful. I mean, she's really, really beautiful."

He turns the portrait back to face him and gazes at it moonily.

"And smart," I remind him. "Don't forget smart."

"Brilliant," he corrects me.

"Brilliant." My smile fades. My sense of my own inadequacy looms large. How can a girl feel herself anything but inadequate when placed side by side with such brilliant, beautiful perfection?

Just because she's one way doesn't mean you're the other, I try to tell myself. *Her beauty doesn't make you ugly. Her intelligence doesn't make you stupid. Her value doesn't make you worthless.*

But I don't really believe that.

"Do you think she'll like me?" Weiji asks.

"She'd better like you, or I'll spit in her eye."

This time, Weiji grins at me rather than at the portrait. "Thank you."

"You're welcome."

It hits me that I might never see Weiji again, and I'm going to miss him terribly. But that's not the sort of thing you say to your big brother, so in the end, I tell him, "I'm very happy for you."

"Thanks. Hey, can I tell you something?"

"Yes."

"You smell funny."

I reach beyond the curtain to box his ears, but I'm really just hiding the urge to cry. Because for the first time I understand that what I took for brotherly torment all my life was, in point of fact, affection.

29

"YOU WRITE TOLERABLY WELL, YOU KNOW," Mother tells me as I practice calligraphy.

"Thank you," I answer, even though the compliment is tepid. I pick up a brush, dip it in the ink, and finish Li Qingzhao's "A Morning Dream."

My heart knows I can never see my dream come true.
At least I can remember
That world and sigh.

It was the last poem Chancellor Zhang and I discussed before he left for Khanbalik ahead of my brother and my father to prepare for the wedding.

Before everything fell to pieces.

Mother comes around the table. She stands behind me and leans her chin on my shoulder. She's not tall, but I'm so petite that it's easy for her to peer over me and examine the calligraphy.

"See there?" she says. "When you're beautiful on the inside, your beauty finds a way to show itself on the outside. There are men who can see that sort of beauty, who value it."

This compliment is less tepid, but it still falls flat in my ears. The poem may be beautiful. The shapes of the words may be beautiful. But none of that has anything to do with me. I stare down at the parchment.

"I enjoy calligraphy," I say, "but shouldn't we be doing something useful?"

"Like what? Besides, your father wanted you educated, and so you shall be."

"But that was before . . ." My voice trails off. I don't need to finish. We are both more than aware that Turandokht rejected my brother before he ever reached Khanbalik. The girl never laid eyes on him, never gave him a chance. When the Song wedding delegation reached Kaifeng, they were greeted by Chancellor Zhang and a *zuun* of Yuan soldiers who forced them to turn back, an insult so grave that now the Mongols and the Song are at war over it. It's a fact that permeates our lives like a fog that has set in and stayed. It grows heavier with each passing week, knowing that Father and Weiji are off fighting battles against the greatest empire in the world.

And I hate the fact that Zhang was the messenger.

Ostensibly, even with a war going on, my life has changed very little in Lin'an, yet everything feels different now, dimmer. The only change of note is that Mother has become fanatical about my father's command that I be educated like Turandokht. It makes no sense on the surface, but I suspect it's her way of reproaching him, as if to say, *You wanted your daughter to emulate the girl who rejected your son and ruined us all? Fine.* I have more tutors now, more subjects to learn, more tracts to read. I'm ashamed of myself for enjoying it so much when Weiji's life has taken such a turn for the worse.

A servant comes into the women's quarters. She gives my mother a low bow.

"Rise," says Mother.

The girl glances warily at the curtain.

"What is it?" Mother snips.

"General Chen has just arrived, my lady, with a small contingent of men. He says your husband, the prince regent, sent him."

To my shock and against all propriety, the man himself comes barging into the women's quarters. Mother is still trying to formulate a comprehensible response to this intrusion when the man gives her a deep, ponderous bow.

I've seen General Chen only two or three times before. He has always been impeccably dressed and groomed. Today, I hardly recognize him. His beard is a scraggly mess. His clothes are stained and even torn in places. He still wears his armor, and it looks as if

someone has taken an ax to it.

"Forgive me, madam." His formality is stiff, his eyes cold and distant. "I come under inauspicious circumstances. It is imperative that I speak with you. I regret to inform you that your husband is dead."

Mother grows still as a statue. "What?" she breathes, her hand fluttering to her chest.

"Your son, Prince Weiji, is also dead. The Mongols overtook us. They cut through our men like a knife. We've lost. All is lost."

Weiji is also dead. The words push me down an abyss, into an empty well, only there's no bottom. There's only falling and falling and falling.

"No," Mother whispers with lips gone bloodless.

"I'm here on your husband's last orders," Chen tells my mother. "You'll come with me, madam. You and your daughter."

"Of course," Mother says, trying to pull herself together. She orders the servant to start packing our belongings.

"There's no time for that, my lady."

"But we'll need our clothes, our shrine—"

"There's no time!" His voice cracks through the air like a whip.

"What? Why?" she cries, her voice sharp with pain.

"The Mongols are coming. Now. We barely made it here alive."

My mother covers her face with both hands. She breathes once, twice. I stare at her, willing her to make this better somehow, to reach out to me, comfort me.

I'm falling, falling.

Mother draws herself up, haughty. "I understand," she says, her voice clipped. She tells the servant to let the others know to evacuate the estate. Then she turns to Chen and asks, "Where are we going?"

"The river."

"Right. Come along, Daughter."

I don't know how she is able to hold herself together when I feel so broken and afraid. I can barely walk, I'm shaking so badly.

We follow Chen through the outer chambers and into the courtyard garden toward a side entrance I've never used before. I'm trying hard to emulate my mother, to remain calm, to stuff my grief and terror into some dark corner inside myself, but I can already feel myself failing.

The garden is full of memories, and Weiji burns brightly in each and every one.

Weiji is also dead.

Falling and falling and falling.

"We'll come back, won't we?" I whisper to Mother.

"Of course," she assures me, but I know she's lying. We might never return. And I've never even left Lin'an before.

Chen's men are waiting for us on the other side of the gate. They have brought my little cousin Emperor Bing with them as well. Out in the open now, we're as exposed as ants on a picnic blanket.

"So few men?" Mother asks.

Chen nods grimly. The soldiers surround us as we make our

way down to the dock. Even though they're Song soldiers, it feels like a forced march, like we're prisoners of our own people. I can't think. My mind is a searing white wall that protects me from the overwhelming grief and fear welling up behind it. The tips of my fingers have gone numb. It's not until we near the river that I realize something is terribly wrong.

"Where's the boat?" I ask no one in particular, and no one answers me. "Mother, where's the boat?"

Mother squints ahead at the water rushing past the empty dock. She stops, turns to Chen, and repeats the question: "Where is the boat?"

Chen doesn't answer. He doesn't need to. He simply takes my mother by one arm to drag her to the water. Mother wails, tearing at Chen's arm, dragging the fingernails of her free hand down his cheek, but it does her no good. He won't release her. "Why?" she keens as one of Chen's men grabs hold of me, too. "Why? Why? Why?"

Chen squeezes her hard until her lungs are crushed into silence. "Do you want the Mongols to get their filthy hands on you? Or to take your one remaining child? Do you want her to live out her life as a slave? Let her death be honorable, woman."

Her death.

My death.

We're all going to die.

Mother grows limp with despair and lack of air, and Chen drops her, letting her fall to the ground like a wilted flower.

"Run!" I scream, as much at myself as at my mother and Bing. I knee my captor in the groin until he releases me with a grunt of pain. "Run!"

I bolt from the group, but one of the soldiers catches me, grabbing my upper arm with a hard, bruising hand. I bite him like a feral dog until I taste blood and break loose again. The word "run" drums in my head with the percussion of each footfall on the ground. *Run-run-run-run-run.* I'm just a skinny girl, but I'm faster than they are. I know where I'm going, and I'm not weighed down by armor or weapons. I run back to my house, the only home I've ever known. The salon, the dining hall, the women's quarters, my bedroom: these comprise the sum total of safety in my universe, so that's where I go. I flee to the safest place of all, my family's shrine.

I don't have time to light the joss sticks. I pick up the porcelain duck and cradle it against my heart. "Save us," I beg my ancestors, but they either can't or won't intervene.

Running footsteps clatter across the hall beyond the shrine.

"*Zhǎngxiōng!* Older Brother! Help me!" I plead.

Two men enter the shrine where I've trapped myself in front of the altar with its diminutive cups of wine.

My entire life, I have been a mouse, tiny and weak and insignificant. But like any creature cornered by threat, it isn't terror I experience at the prospect of death. It's rage. It's fury. It's a stone-cold will to live.

I lash out at the closest soldier, striking him in the shoulder with the incense burner. He's completely unhurt, but the lotus flower breaks free and goes rolling across the floor, sending little porcelain chips scattering across the wood. I wave what's left at the other man, who merely catches it in his hand and breaks it off so that only the duck's jolly head remains in my fist. One of them grabs me under the arms while the other scoops up my legs.

Rage.

Fury.

The will to live.

I kick and scream to no effect, but that doesn't stop me. I pull at the first man's arms with my free hand and hit him with my other hand fisted around the duck's head. I try to shake free of the second man. They stagger back to the river with me, cursing the entire way. We pass through a gauntlet of grave-faced soldiers, here to carry out their sad duty of honor, to kill the royal family before the Mongols do something far worse to us. I stop thrashing long enough to search frantically for my mother, but I don't see her. I only see General Chen nod to my captors, who take me to the edge of the dock.

"No!" I struggle against them. "No!"

The man who clutches my legs eases back so that he has me by the ankles, and the two men swing my body between them like a sack.

Once.

"No!" I scream.

Twice.

"No!"

I hear a hissing sound and a *thunk*, and the man who has me under the arms cries out and releases me. I have just enough time to see an arrow jutting from his chest before my upper half careens through the air as the other soldier tosses me into the river by my ankles.

I crash through the water's surface as if it were a wall of ice. My gold brocade robe rips away from my body and billows around me while the water pulls me under and sideways. I hold my breath and clutch the duck's head, praying to gods and ancestors, anyone. My robe dances lithely in the current. For an odd moment I'm calm, watching the pretty thing sway and swirl in front of me like a jellyfish, its excruciating beauty soporific.

The will to live.

My foot touches something solid and I push against it with all my might. I burst through the surface and gasp air and water. I sputter and cough and plunge once more under the water's violent surface. Somehow the mad movements of my arms and legs push me upward once more, and this time, there is a thick strong hand that lifts me out of river and flings my half-dead body into a boat. I cough up water and turn my head just in time to see my cousin Bing as the river hurls him past me. His eyes are as dead and empty as those of a fish on a platter.

My mind goes somewhere else, somewhere far away from here, and I begin to sing.

Jasmine flower
Your willowy stems clustered with sweet-smelling buds
Fragrant and white, everyone praises your beauty
Let me pluck you down
And give you to the one I love

My voice wavers. I can't stop shivering, and my lungs haven't quite adjusted yet to breathing air again. The sky above is unforgivably clear and beautiful. When the peasant who fished me out of the water leans over me, I no longer know whether I want to live or die. I clutch the duck's head. The jagged edges where it broke free of the incense burner cut into my palm. Blood streaks across my skin and leaves diluted red droplets on the rocking floor of the boat.

When we reach shore, the peasant lifts me out of the boat and hands me over to a group of Mongol warriors on the bank. Money changes hands, but I'm too cold and hazy to care. The Mongols' foreign words twang in my water-clogged ears.

I can't stop shaking. One of the Mongols slips off his rough wool outer robe and ties it around me. My skin grows drunk on his residual body heat. The man takes my hand and pries my fingers off the duck's head. My fingers snap back and clutch at what's left of my life, the entire sum of strength left in my body dedicated to this one act. The Mongol says something to one of his companions, and the other man hands him a length of twine. He pulls a knife from his belt, and fear flickers inside me. But he uses his knife to cut the twine, not me. He puts the knife back, takes my hand again, and gently unfurls my fingers.

And he takes the duck.

"No!" I scream. My limp body springs into action. My flaccid mind focuses on one burning purpose. Hands become claws. Teeth become fangs. I attack the man who took my duck, but one of the other warriors grabs me about the middle and clamps my arms to my sides.

The man looks at me with raised eyebrows, his expression one of amusement, which makes me rage all the harder. He takes the duck's head and runs the twine through the hole in the beak and out the hollow, broken neck. He ties the ends of the twine together, steps over to me, and places the makeshift necklace over my head so that the duck rests over my heart. He steps back and looks at me, trying to say something with his face that he can't communicate to me with his strange language.

My last fit of rage has sapped every ounce of energy I had out of me, and I hang in the warrior's arms. The man takes my hand again and, meeting no resistance, begins to clean and bandage my cut.

And just like that, in the blink of an eye, between life and death, I am transformed from princess to slave.

In Khanbalik, I lie on the ground with my back pressed against the earthen wall of the small room where slaves sleep. We're packed together like bundles of firewood, twists of rope, our bodies rank

with labor, our breath rough with exhaustion. The Great Khan's slaves. Turandokht's slaves.

Me.

A slave.

I hate myself for accepting it. I hate myself for resisting it.

I roll onto my side, fetal on my mat, curled like a fern before it unfurls. I whisper my name into the darkness. I say it over and over again, my breath as thin as a string.

Jinghua.

I'm so afraid I'll forget who I am.

30

I STAND NEXT TO A BOILING vat filled with silkworms ready for harvesting and stir the carcasses with a long paddle. Steam rises from the cauldron like a frenetic ghost as it sifts itself through the bamboo awning above, and I stop to wipe condensation and sweat from my forehead. My rough, woven trousers and linen shirt chafe my sweat-sticky skin. Take away the silk and what am I? A slave. How perfectly simple.

A man clears his throat to get my attention. I look up from my work to find Zhang standing between the awning posts. It's the first time I've seen him since I came to Khanbalik to work in the Great Khan's palace three months ago. He's dressed in flamboyant violet clothes while I sweat over my work in a cheap uniform, a visual reminder of just how far I have fallen. It feels like a slap to the face.

I register no emotion on my face before I return to my work. I've been a slave for three months, and yet I still have to resist the urge to hide my face. Anyone may see me now if he chooses, Zhang included.

"They said they only managed to fish one member of the Song royal family out of the river alive," he says in his typical conversational manner. "I somehow knew it would be you. Clever girl."

"I'm not clever," I say. "Just lucky." I run the paddle around the pot once, twice, before adding, "Or not."

"And the Great Khan didn't want you in his harem? I thought he might take you for a wife or at least a concubine, a symbol of his dominance over the Song."

I pull out the paddle, pick up a sieve off the mat beneath my feet, and begin to remove the dead worms from the vat. My voice is devoid of feeling. "He said that if I'd been part of a peace deal he might have taken me, but since the Mongols had defeated the Song, he had no use for me."

"Ah, I see." Zhang's tone is inscrutable, ever diplomatic.

"The Mongols who rescued me were disappointed. They were hoping to get a lot more for me. Turns out I wasn't worth much." I dump a dripping load of cocoons onto a tray and dip the sieve into the cauldron again.

Zhang switches to Mongolian. "Are you learning to speak the language?"

"Well enough," I reply, also in Mongolian.

Zhang nods, hesitates, and then says, "I'll see what I can do for you, little Jinghua," before he saunters off.

The word "princess" is noticeably absent from this statement.

It's funny, but until this moment, I didn't really believe that I was a slave, hadn't accepted it, as if it were all a bad dream and I would wake up someday back in Lin'an. But now a man whom I once outranked calls me "little." I can taste the bitterness of the moment on my tongue, like biting into rotten fruit.

"What?" I call to his broad backside, not bothering to mask my resentment. "No poetry today?"

He turns. His smile is kind but sad. "Another day, perhaps." He leaves me to unwind the softened cocoons heaped in the tray.

In the scullery of the imperial palace, I'm drying a freshly washed platter. It's a beautiful piece, this enormous porcelain circle, white, hand-painted with dragons and lions and lotus blossoms in blue paint. Unaccountably alone, I allow myself the liberty of tracing the brushstrokes with a work-ruined finger. A year ago, I would have been the one eating off this platter. Now I'm the one cleaning it.

I'm still tiny, still girlish, but there is a suggestion of womanliness in my body, the way a bud hints at the flower within, although I am no flower. It does me no good now. I'm the bud that will never bloom.

"I have a job for you" comes a voice from the doorway. It's Zhang, his hands folded in his sleeves. I haven't seen him in several months, not since he came to see me while I was softening the silkworm cocoons.

"I already have a job." I hold up the platter. "See?"

"If you succeed in this job, there's a chance you could go home."

I wipe at the platter and tell him, "I don't have a home anymore."

"Lin'an is still there. Your family's estate is still there."

"So I'd be a slave where I used to be a princess? Thanks, but no thanks."

But already I'm intrigued, tempted. Even a slave can see the water lilies in the West Lake. Even a slave can watch the fog dissipate over the green hills beyond.

"You'd be mistress of that estate," Zhang tells me, his tongue sweet and smooth as honey. "You'd be married to a very powerful man, one very much in favor with the Great Khan."

I know I shouldn't listen to him, but I can't help myself. I want so desperately to go home, to go back to my old life. I hunger for it. I hold that dream so close it nuzzles me.

"Rich and married—you'd want for nothing," Zhang presses unctuously.

I could fall back on my principles, the sort that would never allow me to make a deal with a snake like him. But the truth is that I no longer have any principles to speak of, and he knows it.

"I hate you," I tell him.

"I don't really care."

"Why should I trust you?"

"What else are you going to do?"

I glower at him for several long, uncomfortable seconds, even as I cave. I lower my eyes and scowl. "What would I have to do?"

Zhang opens the door to the scullery and gestures for me to follow him.

"I'll be whipped if someone catches me outside the kitchens," I inform him.

"You let me worry about that. Now be a good little slave and follow me."

I curse him under my breath, but he pretends not to hear it.

Zhang leads me through the corridors of the imperial palace. Once we're out of the kitchens, my surroundings become dizzyingly rich and unfamiliar: ceilings covered in gold leaf, paintings of the hunt or serene landscapes on every wall, a hall lined with bronze dragon statues, all there to remind me of what I've lost. I compare everything I see to my home in Lin'an, and I think with bitter satisfaction that the Mongols' ostentatious display of their wealth makes the vanished elegance of the Song Dynasty shine brighter, even in death.

We encounter no one. Zhang eventually takes us to a wing with rooms on either side of a passageway.

"Guest chambers," he explains before opening a door and ushering me inside one of the rooms.

"What are we doing here?"

"You know of Turandokht's riddles, of all the suitors who come to Khanbalik to die?"

"Of course I know about them—suitors just like my brother."

I'm boiling with grief and anger, but Zhang blithely ignores the reference to my loss.

"It was her hope that the riddles and the accompanying death penalty would deter the hordes of princes who insist on flocking to Khanbalik to marry her," he says. "But it isn't working. The prince of Kyrghiz asked to try his hand just last month, and now another suitor has beaten the drum this morning to signal his intent."

"And what does any of that have to do with a slave girl in Turandokht's kitchens?" I ask, crossing my arms.

"You are no longer standing in the kitchens, and you are no ordinary slave girl." Zhang strolls around the room as if he were taking a walk in a garden rather than skulking around the palace with the help. "Honestly, it's all worked out infinitely better than I could have imagined. In the end, we did not need the Song alliance to rule all of Zhongguo, and with the Great Khan feeling under the weather these days, I am positively indispensable to my khatun. So you see, I'm not too concerned about all the princes who descend upon Khanbalik for her hand. No, it's just one man who worries me, the one man my khatun fears most, the one who might actually be able to solve Turandokht's riddles."

He stops strolling and gives me a knowing look.

"What?" I ask, and then I begin to catch on. "You want me to kill this man?"

"'Kill' is such a distasteful word."

"I can't. I can't kill anyone."

"Then you can't go home," Zhang tells me. "And you'll be a

slave all the days of your life."

I look down at my work-roughened hands. My skin is dried out from scrubbing dishes. My knuckles are cracked and bleeding.

"I'm fond of you, little Jinghua," Zhang says. "You're very bright, and I had once hoped that you might serve as a companion to my khatun. But now I see how you might serve her in a much larger capacity."

A companion to the girl who rejected my brother? Every feeling revolts. "And if I refuse?" I ask.

"I will have you sold to the nearest slave trader. Do you know what happens to most girls sold into slavery?"

The threat isn't lost on me. I'll end up in a brothel. Or worse. I can feel myself falling into the very possibility, like plunging down that well of grief again and wondering when I'll hit the bottom, what cold death is waiting for me in the darkness.

But there's another part of me that still clings to what I was, *who* I was, the part that now says, "Yes. I know. I'm not stupid, *little* Zhang."

He arches one eyebrow at me. "Now, now. I can free you once it's done, and until then, I can make sure you end up in respectable service. But only if you agree to do this one small thing."

"Killing a man is no small thing."

"Fine, then, this one enormous thing. Do this one enormous thing, and you can be free, and you can go home. You can go back to the life you deserve."

"Why me?" And here it is: the crying. The useless, pathetic

crying. I loathe myself for crying so easily.

Zhang steps closer to me and speaks in a kind, paternal way. "Because you're small enough and plain enough to be invisible. Because you're clever enough to be inventive and take initiative. And you're motivated, very deeply motivated."

I'm silent for a good long time. Zhang waits patiently for my answer. My eyes glaze over, and I imagine what it means to kill someone, how I even go about that sort of thing, the impossibility of the task.

"What choice do I have?" I ask.

"You're a slave now, my dear," says Zhang. "You don't have a choice."

I nod helplessly.

"Excellent." He crosses in front of me to a large silk-screen painting of misty hills and a lake. I realize with a sickness in my stomach that it's a picture of Lin'an, of home. He lifts the screen to reveal a door, which he slides open. A dark, cramped passage lies beyond.

"We use this for purposes of state security. It leads to the stables," Zhang explains.

"You mean if you need to assassinate someone and remove his body in the dark of night," I say coldly.

"Among other things. My man is waiting on the other side. He's a merchant headed for Sarai. He knows to take good care of you."

"Sarai? Where's Sarai?" It seems like the room is spinning.

"In the Kipchak Khanate."

"The Kipchak Khanate? That's on the other end of the empire. How long will it take to get there?"

"At least six months, I should think."

"Six months?" I ask incredulously.

Zhang smiles. How can he smile at this moment?

"How do I get back?" I ask.

"You'll have a *gerege*. It's already in the possession of one of the prince's friends. He'll be your contact in Sarai and will escort you back to Khanbalik once your mission is complete."

"He doesn't sound like a very good friend."

"No man up to his eyeballs in debt can be counted a good friend," says Zhang. "Now, when you make it back to Khanbalik—"

"*If* I make it back to Khanbalik," I say.

"Fine. If you make it back to Khanbalik, you'll approach the stable gate of the imperial compound, and you will tell the guards, *Success*. Just that one word. They will then escort you to the door on the other end of this passage. My quarters are located in the corridor just to the east of this one, next to the imperial library. When you find me—"

"If."

"When you find me, our deal will be complete, and I will send you back to Lin'an, where you belong."

I nod, cataloging this information, burning it into my brain so that I won't forget.

"And who am I supposed to . . . ?" Oh, my mother, I can't even say the word.

"One of Timur Khan's sons, the bookish one. He's purported to be brilliant, even at his tender age."

"If he has noble blood, why shouldn't he marry Turandokht?" I challenge Zhang as grief for my brother stokes my acrimony. "Why shouldn't she marry any of them?"

At first, Zhang shows a rare spark of anger, but then he softens. "You wouldn't understand, the way you were raised to marry, to obey. My mistress has risen above such expectations. She's like the ice at the mountain's peak, the snow on the Roof of the World, where men can't even light a proper fire. And underneath all that ice is rock. The good of the empire is her only passion. For the most part, she does not require a man to hold her hand and do her business for her. And when she does require a man, well, she has me."

I hate him for his arrogance, and I hate myself more for having let him pull aside the red curtain and wriggle his way into my life.

"And what would your precious khatun say if she knew you had arranged the assassination of a worthy suitor?" I ask him.

"What makes you think this is anything other than her own order?"

"You just told me I was clever. Do you really think I don't see the game you're playing here? Your dedication to your khatun and the empire only goes as far as it benefits one man: Chancellor Zhang."

"Fine," he says, not bothering to deny it. "This is a matter of public relations. I'm fairly certain my khatun has no intention of marrying, so even if somebody manages to answer the riddles,

she'll have him killed one way or another. That's all rather . . .
messy. Or worse, she might actually marry him. From time to
time, she is too honorable for her own good, and where would
that leave me?"

"In the dirt, where you belong," I answer.

He waves away my resentment. "I act on behalf of the empire.
The khan of the Kipchak Khanate is Genghis Khan's great-
grandson, even if his grandfather was illegitimate. Some have the
audacity to argue that he has more right to the title Great Khan
than the Great Khan himself does. And he's an ambitious man,
more than willing to take advantage of his son. It's for Turandokht's own good that we nip this threat in the bud."

I could stand here and quibble with Zhang all day, and I
wouldn't be any closer to home.

"What's his name?" I sigh.

"Who? The son? Oh, I don't recall. Pilaf. Kumar. One of those
unpronounceable Turkic names."

"You don't even know his name? How am I supposed to know
I have the right person?"

"You'll know," Zhang assures me.

"But how?"

Zhang takes me by the shoulders in that repugnant, fatherly
way of his. He says, "My dear, he's the really, really smart one."

PART SEVEN

THE LAST RIDDLE

The City of Khanbalik, Khanate of the Yuan Dynasty

Autumn 1281

31

TURANDOKHT SAYS,

> "It is a prison of snow, a graceful cage of ice,
> Though pale you burn inside its darkened heart.
> Raging hot, your fire cannot suffice,
> Nor can you prize its icy bars apart.
>
> "As on the mountain's peak, so useless is your fire
> That from your flame grows colder still its ring.
> Before you lies a choice: What's your desire?
> Break free and be slave? Or remain and be king?"

"Seven minutes."

Khalaf doesn't close his eyes or bow his head as he did before, and I swear that the first minute goes whizzing by in the span of a mere heartbeat.

"Six minutes," calls Zhang.

Rub your lip, I beg Khalaf. *Press the heels of your hands to your eyes. Raise your face to your god. Do the things you do when you're thinking.*

"'It is a prison of snow, a graceful cage of ice,'" Khalaf repeats breathily, "'though pale you burn inside its darkened heart...'"

"Five minutes."

My heart begins to break, the first fissure snaking its way down my chest. Timur and I have squeezed our palms together. My hand grows numb in his grip, but I don't care. I feel a tear splash against my neck, and it isn't my own. The mountain is crying.

"Four minutes."

Turandokht doesn't gloat. She doesn't move. She watches and waits. If the breeze didn't buffet the feather of her headdress, I might think she had truly turned to stone.

You can't have his life, I seethe at her. *He won't die for you. You can marry him and even love him, so long as he lives.*

"Three minutes."

Let him live.

"You don't know the answer," Zhang says triumphantly from the bell tower. "The icy prison where your fire is useless—what is it?"

I think of Zhang standing at the red curtain, the way he barged into my life and never left it. And I let him.

This is all my fault, all of it.

Khalaf concentrates, the skin around his eyes puckering with stress. He breathes in and out, trying to work through it. "'As on the mountain's peak, so useless is your fire . . .'"

He's bursting with life. Every heartbeat, every breath, is as rare and precious as pearls. I think of his back against mine, his warmth wrapping me up on the Roof of the World, his voice like embers in the dark night.

> *A book of verses underneath the bough*
> *A flask of wine, a loaf of bread, and thou*
> *Beside me singing in the wilderness*
> *And . . .*

And.

My eyes widen with understanding.

His last words to me at the foot of the drum tower, the line he quoted as Turandokht's men were escorting him away.

"'And wilderness is paradise now,'" I finish aloud.

"Shh!" Timur hisses in my ear.

I sang beside him in the wilderness, and wilderness is paradise now.

Did he love me?

Could he still?

My heart aches with the possibility, curling around the

memory of Khalaf pressed against me in the frigid night in the Pamirs.

On the Roof the World.

I gasp, my lungs pushing my panic away in all directions as I remember the words Chancellor Zhang said to me in a darkened room.

She's like the ice at the mountain's peak, the snow on the Roof of the World, where men can't even light a proper fire.

I know this.

Break free and be slave? Or remain and be king?

I know the answer.

"Two minutes," says Zhang in a voice infused with noxious glee at Khalaf's floundering.

The people on the ground surrounding the dais are packed in and restless. They're talking to Khalaf now, words of encouragement from all directions.

"Come on!"

"The answer! What's the answer?"

"One minute!" Zhang crows.

He won't die for her. I let go of Timur and step forward.

"Little bird!" he whispers behind me like a lost child.

I ease my way to the front of the crowd and lean into the lamplight, my face visible for anyone to see, and I will Khalaf to look at me.

"Thirty seconds!"

Look at me, I think.

Khalaf buries his face in his hands, his back hunching over in growing hopelessness.

Look at me, Khalaf!

"Fifteen seconds!"

My insides scream, an incomprehensible wail that feels as if it's turning me inside out. Slowly, Khalaf lifts his head from his hands as if he can hear me. He looks right at me. He finds me with wild, panicked eyes.

"Ten seconds!"

I mouth a word to him. He shakes his head. He doesn't understand. I mouth it again. One word, one message passed between us through the torchlit night. For the span of one breath, it's as if we were alone, sitting across the fire from each other on the vast steppes between Sarai and Khanbalik.

"Five-four-three-two—"

"Turandokht!" he exclaims, turning to face her. "The cage of ice that enslaves you and makes you king. It's you, Khatun. 'Turandokht' is the answer."

Khalaf's voice echoes through the silent square. The scholars in the bell tower forget to confer with Zhang. They turn their heads in one synchronized movement to gape at Khalaf.

"Well?" Zhang asks them.

One of them nods.

Bone-crushing relief crumbles my spine like a clump of dried-out rice. The only thing that keeps me upright is the crowd all around me. I grip a complete stranger by the shoulder, a woman who glares at me and shakes off my hand in disgust as if I were a spider that had landed on her.

Zhang's round face becomes drawn, old even. He straightens the front of his robe, gives his khatun a pitying glance, and announces to all of Khanbalik, "The answer is 'Turandokht.' The contestant has successfully answered all three riddles."

I expect the gathered masses to explode with noise, but the silence stretches on following the announcement of Khalaf's victory. The realization that this unknown boy, plainly dressed and softly spoken, is now the heir apparent to the throne of the empire begins to sink in. Khalaf draws himself up and stands erect and dignified, the hero, the saintly victor of Turandokht's game.

He won. He'll live. And who knows but I might even get to go home now. It occurs to me that for all these reasons I should be happy. But I'm not. I am the antithesis of happy.

An apple. A choice. A song. A kiss.

And wilderness is paradise now.

He might have loved me. And I wasted it. And then I lost it. And I never deserved it to begin with.

This is the moment of being airborne, the body caught between earth and sky before it hits the water's cold edge.

Zhang clears his throat and returns his attention to his scroll. It gives a brittle creak as he unrolls it to its full length. He's never made it this far into the decree before.

"No prince shall be allowed to wed Turandokht Khatun who shall not previously have replied without hesitation to the riddles

that she shall put to him. Today, this man has succeeded. The sacred oath of the Great Khan has been fulfilled. The Eternal Blue Sky smiles upon him. Glory to the victor, and ten thousand years to the Great Khan."

What begins as a flutter of applause after this proclamation grows exponentially, and soon the crowd is whooping and cheering and pounding on any surface they can find.

Turandokht stands alone atop the marble stairs. In her pale rose silk, she reminds me of the moon, shining and solitary at dusk. She belongs to Khalaf now, just as he belongs to her.

My heart's fissure becomes a valley.

This is where I disappear, I think. There are other things that could happen to me, worse things. Disappearing is definitely one of my better options at the moment. But it doesn't feel better. I don't want to be invisible anymore.

Turandokht finally moves. She steps before her father and bows in deep obeisance to the Great Khan. "Son of the Eternal Blue Sky, my father, I beg that you will not hand me over to this stranger."

Zhang's words come back to me like a knife in the gut.

I'm fairly certain my khatun has no intention of marrying, so even if somebody manages to answer the riddles, she'll have him killed one way or another.

"No," I breathe just as Timur pushes his way to the front and grabs my arm. He must have had a terrible time finding me in the crowd with his bad eyes, and he is livid.

"Rotting carrion, where have you been?" he chides me, and one of my neighbors, the woman I unintentionally grabbed, shushes us, sending a spray of saliva against my round cheek. "Go suck your used tea leaves!" Timur spits back at her.

"My vow is unbreakable, Daughter," says the Great Khan, and Timur shuts up to listen. "Would you defame a promise made to the Earth? To the Eternal Blue Sky himself?"

"Am I chattel?" she counters. "No, I am your sacred daughter, not some worthless slave to be handled like cheap goods."

That cuts me hard. She has no idea—no idea whatsoever— what it means to be worthless, to be handled like cheap goods.

A horse? A camel? Chattel? That's what she is. Me, the one and only asset to be liquidated.

"You are more precious to me than all the world," says the Great Khan, "but this man has bargained his life, and he has won."

Turandokht rises to her feet and fixes Khalaf with a piercing glare. "No man will ever possess me—not you, not anyone."

"I have no wish to possess you, my khatun," Khalaf tells her.

"I am not *your* khatun. I will never belong to you."

It's almost verbatim what I said to Khalaf when he kissed me in Qaidu's camp and then pushed me away. *I don't belong to you. I've never been yours.* Is Turandokht so determined to take every- thing from me that she must steal my words as well?

Khalaf's eyes find me where I stand at the front of the crowd, and for once I don't try to mask who I am or what I feel. The face he sees in this moment is my honest face, brokenhearted, full of longing, and completely terrified for him. What do I have to lose? His veneer of cool indifference shows its cracks. He's still looking at me when he says, "You asked me three riddles, Turandokht Khatun. I'll ask you only one."

My internal alarm lights the signal fires. I have no idea what he's doing, but I shake my head at him.

He looks up at her and dares to plant one foot on the bottom step. He says,

"Rich in mind but poor in purse,
A prince who is a beggar called
For nearly a year has suffered this curse.
Took care of his father. For months has hauled

"His woes upon his troubled back.
Across the mountains and desert sand
Fought his way, survived attack.
He rules no men. He has no land.

"If by dawn his name you say.
You decide the price he'll pay."

32

"WHAT IS HE DOING?" TIMUR HISSES in my ear. I'm still shaking my head.

"Your offer is completely unnecessary," the Great Khan says to Khalaf.

"It's as I wish it, Son of the Sky," Khalaf replies, shifting his gaze back to me.

And wilderness is paradise now.

I can't bear to look at him, nor can I bear to turn away. I feel like I'm breaking into pieces.

"Zhang." The Great Khan summons the chancellor.

"My lord?" Zhang says as he steps forward on the tower, lapdog that he is.

"Is there precedent for this?"

"No, my lord, but I believe the stranger's riddle must stand."
The chancellor eyes Khalaf with loathing. He wants Khalaf dead
and gone. I can see it even from here.

This is the nightmare that will not end.

"Hear this now," Turandokht declares over Khalaf's head to
her restless audience. "No one shall sleep tonight until the stranger's
name is discovered, and whoever unearths his name will be
richly rewarded."

Greed oozes through the crowd. How many of them saw
Timur and me speaking with Khalaf at the foot of the drum
tower? Half of Khanbalik will be looking for us, I realize with a
sick lurch of my insides.

"Five hundred silver ingots to the one who discovers his name,"
Turandokht declares.

It feels like a death sentence.

The mob begins to tear apart. People dash off in all directions to
find the name as if it were something you could discover by turning
over a stone. Within a minute, the market square has cleared out
considerably, and Timur and I are no longer able to fit in with the
crowd. Timur especially stands out, the size of him.

It speaks to the urgency of the situation that he has no snide
remarks. He lets me drag him out of the square and into a nearby
alley. I take us as far into the darkness as we can go. We find our way
into a cramped, smelly corner and stand there, catching our breath.

"Will this do, I wonder?" I ask Timur. "Should I find us a better hiding place?"

"What's wrong with this one?"

"It's too close to the market, and it smells."

"Then it's perfect. What idiot would hide here? Besides, it's more dangerous to be out in the open at this point, even if it is to find a better place to hide."

He's got a point.

"What do we do now?" I ask him. My heart won't slow down.

"We stay hidden. Hidden and silent." His voice is uncommonly quiet and soothing. He reaches out and strokes my hair with his huge hand. The tenderness of the gesture plus Timur's utter lack of prickliness magnifies the gravity of our circumstances. His hand is meant to comfort, but the unfamiliarity of his affection makes my nerves scream in fear.

Timur's gruff voice breaks the moment. "That riddle was too easy. How many landless princes are running around the empire these days? Fetid, stinking lamb's balls!"

"Your 'insignificant third son who likes to discuss philosophy and play with astrolabes' thinks Turandokht has no idea who he could be," I answer. Guilt washes over me, drowning me in remorse. "This is all my fault. I did this to him."

"Don't flatter yourself." He leans against the wall behind him and says, "Do you really want to know why he offered up that damn riddle? Maybe it's time you heard some truth from me for a change, little bird. Maybe you should know what kind of a man stands beside you."

His eyes are hollowed out. I feel suddenly careful of him, as if

I were handling something fragile, like transplanting an orchid or cleaning a precious vase.

"I think a good man stands beside me, my lord," I answer.

"I think a flawed man stands beside you."

"We're all flawed."

"We are all as flawed as our sons think we are," he answers bitterly. "And how flawed does that make me?"

I open my mouth to reply and find myself closing it without having said anything.

"Aha," he says, pointing that thick finger at me. "There's no arguing with that."

"There's no arguing with *you*."

"Everyone argues with me."

"But nobody wins," I snap. He doesn't understand what's happening here, and I'm breaking under the strain of my own lies and secrets.

"Did he ever tell you about his mother?"

Timur's abrupt change in subject throws me off my guard.

"A little. Not very much," I say.

"Then let me tell you a story. Twenty years ago, the Great Khan sent me a bride, a girl named Bibi Hanem. She was a peace offering, a contract between nations, because he knew I didn't support his claim to the throne of the empire. When Bibi came to my court, I was ready to cut her head off and send it back to the illegally crowned Great Khan with a bow wrapped around it and a great big note saying, *Go suck your used tea leaves.* But then I saw her."

"And she was beautiful," I supply. Of course she was beautiful. This story could never have happened if she had looked like me. If the Great Khan had sent me, I'd be headless by now, and my head would be wrapped with a bow and a great big note saying, *Go suck your used tea leaves.*

"She was beautiful," Timur agrees. "And so young. And I was already, well, not young. My first wife was dull and practical, a nice enough woman. And I had plenty of other women. . . ."

"I'm sure you did," I sigh. Leave it to Timur to boast of his sexual prowess at a time like this.

"But I had never loved before," he finishes, and now, against my will, I find myself sympathizing with the old goat.

"You say that like loving someone is a bad thing," I tell him.

"It is. It's like being enslaved, if you'll pardon the expression."

I give him a mirthless laugh. "I can't disagree with that."

He answers with his noncommittal grunt. The air goes thicker, more serious.

"Did she love you?" I ask.

"No."

"Oh. Sorry." The words sound pathetic even before they exit my mouth, but out they come all the same.

"She did her duty by me for a few years. I went away to strangle the Great Khan's tribute out of the Seljuks, and when I came back, she had a baby boy in her arms for me."

"Khalaf," I guess.

"I held that tiny thing in my arms and looked into his eyes, and

I knew what he would be."

I want to ask Timur why on earth he had never bothered to mention any of this to Khalaf, why he never let his son see his raw father's love. But I can't bring myself to ask it, probably because Timur is so troublingly delicate at this moment.

"What happened to her—Bibi Hanem?" I ask.

Timur's crevices and hollows deepen, grow darker. His is a face full of chasms. "My next campaign was longer, bloodier. While I was gone, my wife decided to have a mosque built in my honor."

"That's good, right?"

"Not when the architect is a pretty boy who imagines himself in love with the khatun of the Kipchak Khanate."

"And she . . . ?"

"And she," Timur agrees. The unspoken completion of that thought gallops through our stinking alley. "When I came back, and I heard of the situation, I had the man executed. I had his filthy mouth stuffed with stones until he choked on his own rank breath. And two days after I had the bastard killed, my wife climbed to the tallest minaret of the beautiful mosque she had built for me, and she jumped."

In my mind, I hear Khalaf's tuneless rendition of his mother's lullaby. *Like the white duck's little chick, I call to my mother when she is far from me.* Another crack snakes along my heart, this one for both the khan and his son. I put a hand on Timur's arm knowing full well that anything I might say in response would be an insulting understatement.

"So if you wanted to know why he asked his own riddle," Timur says, "you have your answer. At the end of the day, he couldn't wed a woman against her will. He didn't want to be a monster like his father. He didn't want to be me."

I take one of Timur's hands in my own and hold it to my cheek. "You are not a monster, my lord." His rough thumb brushes my face. "And you're wrong. I told you, this is all my fault, all my doing."

"Don't be ridiculous." The gravel of his voice rubs painfully against my conscience.

"You don't understand. *He* doesn't understand. Zhang wants him dead. Turandokht, too, riddle or no. The chancellor will stop at nothing. I have to see—" I stop myself. Even in this pungent alleyway, I don't dare speak his name. "I have to talk to him," I finish.

"How do you propose to do that? You can't just saunter into the imperial compound. You'll never get past the palace gates, much less make it to wherever it is they're keeping him."

I step back. I look at him long and hard, and I assure him, "Yes, my lord, I think I can."

"You can get into the palace?" He snorts, but I'm not laughing.

"Yes."

Now I have his full attention.

"How?" he asks.

I want desperately to not answer that question. Timur assesses me—whatever he can see of me in the darkness—with those piercing eyes shifted to the side. I watch as the understanding washes over him. "Cancerous lamb's balls, I don't want to know who you really are, do I?"

My face bloats with the urge to cry. "No, my lord, you don't want to know who I am."

"So I was right. Back in the Caucasus, when I told him to leave you dead in a ditch, I was right about you. You're a rutting spy."

"Something like that, yes."

Timur breathes out a great gust of air, like someone just punched him in the gut. "And you can get into the palace? You're sure?"

"Pretty sure."

"Dammit!" Timur kicks a stone and sends it flying into the wall behind me. A dog starts barking somewhere nearby.

"My lord," I warn him.

"And damn *you*," he says, pointing at me with a finger that shakes with anger. He may as well take the dagger from the folds of my belt and stab me with it. "That boy is going to live another day. He's going to live many, many more days. And do you know why?"

I shake my head and let the tears fall.

"Because I deserve the opportunity to tell that little shit *I told you so*. That means you are going to help me keep that boy alive. Do you hear me?"

"Yes, my lord."

He takes me by the shoulders with his huge hands and bends his face in front of mine. "Say it with me: I am going to keep that boy alive."

"I am going to keep that boy alive," I repeat.

"Again."

This time we say it together like a chanted prayer. "I am going to keep that boy alive."

"Got it?" he asks.

I nod, and then I throw my arms around his thick middle and tuck my head into his shoulder and squeeze him with all my might.

"All right," he says gruffly, unwrapping me from his bulk. "I know the ladies have a hard time keeping their hands off me, but this is ridiculous."

"Yes, my lord. I'm sorry, my lord."

"Now, you get in there and bring my boy back to me."

I sniff and dab at my nose with a dirty sleeve. "Yes, my lord. I'll come back for you. We'll both come back for you," I promise him with everything that I am, however little it may be worth.

As I walk away from him, Timur calls after me, "Jinghua."

It's the first time I've heard him speak my name. It feels like a seedpod ready to burst inside me. I turn back to him. "Yes, my lord?"

"Whatever it is, whatever you've done . . . I forgive you."

By now, I'm bawling. "Thank you, my lord," I say before I run out of the alley and into the streets of Khanbalik.

33

"WHAT'S A TINY THING LIKE YOU doing out this late at night?" one of the guards at the stable gate asks as I approach.

"She's looking for the name, same as everyone else," one of his companions answers for me.

"I know that," the first guard answers drily. "I was flirting. You should try it sometime. With a girl." He returns his attention to me. "You wouldn't happen to know the stranger's name, would you? Split the reward with a nice fellow like me?"

Some of the other men laugh. I'm so nervous that I wonder if I'm going to do anything other than squawk nonsensically the second I open my mouth.

"Success," I say, my voice low and breathy.

"She speaks!" the first guard says with a huge smile. He turns his ear toward me and asks, "Now, what was that, sweetheart?"

I clear my throat and feel the sting of bile. "Success," I repeat.

With that, I have all the guards' attention. The flirtatious leader makes no bones of looking me over head to toe. "You must be joking."

I shake my head.

He looks to his colleagues. One of them shrugs. "All right," he says doubtfully. He takes a set of keys proffered by one of his companions, unlocks the gate, pushes one of the huge doors inward, and says, "After you, my lady."

Once we're inside the imperial compound, he leads me to the stables, where he dismisses the stable boys, but not before sending one of them off to retrieve a lamp. Once the lamp is in hand, he takes me to an empty stall and pushes on the back wall to reveal a dark passage.

"I assume you know where you're going?" he asks.

I nod.

As he hands me the lamp, he leans in and says, "My name's Bekter. Feel free to put in a good word for me with Chancellor Zhang."

I take the lamp from him and enter the passageway. "I don't think a good word from me would take you very far in life," I tell him as I push the door closed in his face.

The lamplight surrounds me like a bubble in the corridor that stretches fathomlessly before me. There's just enough light to see a few feet ahead of me and a few feet behind. Beyond the bubble, the darkness slumps heavily against the light. I arrive at a set of

stairs leading to an underground tunnel. The temperature drops with each step, and the air grows damp and moldy. My light flickers in the chilly darkness. I find myself on level ground once more, and I walk and walk and walk.

I can feel Weiji behind me even before he speaks.

Jinghua.

I don't gasp. I'm not surprised or afraid. There's so little left to fear anymore. I turn around, and there he is dressed in dark silk rather than armor. He wears the black cap that signifies his manhood, and his braid drapes handsomely over his shoulder. He's all arms and legs, the Weiji I remember, not the ghost he has become.

"Hello, Older Brother," I say.

He's so incredibly real. I reach out a hand to touch him, but it passes right through his chest, straight to where his heart would be if he still had a life beating inside him. An illogical sense of disappointment stabs at me. As I pull my hand away, his wound returns. I watch as it splits his body in two. Blood seeps out of the divide, staining his dark silk.

"I'm sorry," I tell him. "I'm so sorry."

I'm hungry. He's like a kitten yowling at the door to be let in.

"Don't you think I know that by now?"

The weight of his need—and of Timur's and Khalaf's, too, for that matter—pushes down on me so hard, I'm tempted to just lie down right here in this dark corridor and never get up.

"I have nothing left to give you," I tell Weiji without

bothering to mask my frustration. "My whole life is nothing. Can't you understand that?"

Feed me, he begs.

"I can't!"

I'm so tired. His eyes go black and hollow as he speaks. His fingers become bony hooks. He's turning into a ghost to haunt the living right before my eyes.

"So am I," I tell him, frazzled to the point of breaking. "I can't help you anymore. I can't even help myself."

Yes, you can.

"How?"

He fades until there is nothing left to see in the lamplight, but his voice remains a second longer, echoing in the passage.

You'll see.

Ten minutes' walk takes me to a set of stairs leading up, after which I reach the door at the other end of the passage. I put my ear to the panel and hear the scuffing sounds of movement across a wood floor, the splashing of water in a basin, the rustle of fabric.

"My lord?" I whisper.

The sounds of movement continue. What if it's not Khalaf on the other side? Then again, what do I have to lose at this point? I slide the door open a crack and repeat, "My lord?"

"Who's there?"

I can barely see him across the room through the gap between the painting and the wall. He's wound tight like a spring, his eyes

sweeping the room in my direction.

"It's only me, my lord."

His body straightens. He looks stunned.

"Jinghua?"

I open the door and step out from behind the landscape painting of Lin'an. Khalaf's eyes go wide. He rushes to me but stops short of touching me. He pulls back the painting and takes in the passageway beyond.

"What—?" he asks. "How did you—?"

"My lord, please, there's no time for questions. I need you to listen to me."

"Is my father with you?"

"No, he's hiding in the city. My lord—"

"You have to leave," he tells me, his worried face leaning in close, and I can taste the memory of his lips on mine.

"I can't, not before I speak with you," I tell him.

"You saved my life tonight. Again. We owe you everything. Everything. I have to get you out of here."

I grasp at the air with hands that want to grab hold of the boy standing in front of me. "I'm here to get *you* out, not the other way around. And trust me when I say you owe me nothing."

He won't listen, though. "I know it was a gamble, but even if she doesn't solve my riddle, I've at least proven my goodwill and my respect for her mind and abilities."

"And if she does solve it, she's going to kill you!" I hiss, trying to keep myself from shouting or shaking him until his brilliant brain rattles in his head.

"Or we're both free, Turandokht and I."

"She's not going to set you free!" I burst, but Khalaf keeps talking over me.

"And now the entire city is on the hunt for anyone who might know me. I've put my father in terrible danger, and you. I'm so sorry. I wasn't thinking. I just—"

"You just didn't want Turandokht to be condemned to the same fate as your mother. Or me." I finish for him more brusquely than the situation demands, but there isn't time to coddle him. He needs to understand his predicament. "And no, you weren't thinking, but I put myself in danger a long time ago."

"Jinghua—"

"Stop," I tell him, holding up my hands. "Just stop. Because I'm not setting one foot outside this room until you hear what I have to say. Do you understand?"

An ember of the princess I was flares and burns inside me. Khalaf nods in mute awe.

"Turandokht will likely have you killed no matter how this plays out. And if she doesn't, Chancellor Zhang will definitely have you killed. He'll never let you win. Never."

"But I've already won," Khalaf argues. "I'm a prince of the realm. Zhang can't touch me."

"He can and he will kill you. Your riddle is no riddle at all."

"I don't understand."

"My lord, when I say that he wants you dead, I mean that he's wanted you dead—specifically you—for a long, long time."

"That's ridiculous. How can that be? He probably didn't even know I existed before today."

Here it is: the last moment I'll possess Khalaf's good opinion and respect. I'm about to blow it all to hell.

"Your brilliance precedes you. You were the only threat out there, the only one who might be able to solve Turandokht's riddles. That's why he sent me. You're the only thing that stands between him and his beloved khatun."

"Sent you? Who sent you? Zhang? How could he have sent you?" Khalaf's perception of the universe hasn't caught up to reality yet, but I can see his mind whirring behind his eyes, trying to make sense of what I'm telling him. Or maybe he's doing his best not to make sense of it.

My eyes and nose and lips swell with truth and tears. "I'm not yours," I tell him. "I've never been yours."

He shakes his head.

"I belong to *her*."

"No," he says. His eyes are enormous.

"I was sent to Sarai to kill you."

"No."

"On Zhang's orders," I insist.

"That can't be."

"And when you went into exile, I had to follow. Don't you see?" I pull back the silk painting and show him the tunnel again. "How could I know about this? How could I possibly get in here if I'm not exactly who I say I am?"

His face goes shockingly pale. "The tea," he says. "Back in Sarai, you served me tea."

"Yes."

"It was poisoned."

I hesitate, but I make myself say it. "Yes."

"Oh my God," he says, backing away from me. I don't know if he's praying or blaspheming, but he keeps repeating it over and over. "Oh my God. Oh my God. Oh my God."

I drag myself out of my selfish pool of despair and remind myself that I'm here to save him, that the truth will set him free even as it slams my own prison door shut. "I'm telling you that Zhang will make sure she will not accept your rule. I'm telling you that one of the most powerful men in the Yuan and the entire empire has wanted you dead for a long, long time. And I am telling you that if you value your life, you will come with me and escape Khanbalik right now."

He gazes at me with a face that is a mask of hurt and fury. "Value my life? What do you care? You've wanted me dead from the beginning."

My whole body shrinks in on itself. "That's not true."

"I don't think I know anything about you that's true." His eyes are red and brimming.

Now that the truth is out, I feel oddly light, free. I stop cringing, and I stand before him as dignified as Turandokht. "Now you do."

Khalaf and I stand in silence, divided, as if we had been flesh and a saber had rent us apart like the gaping hole in my brother's body.

"Then why am I still alive?" he asks, his lovely voice made rough with barely contained rage. He can't even look at me now. "You could have let me drink that tea back in Sarai before this nightmare even began, but you knocked it out of my hand. You could have left me to the bandits in the Caucasus. You could have let the assassin's dagger hit its mark in Kashgar. You could have killed me a hundred times over by now. But you didn't. Why?"

I stare at him. A second ticks by. Two. Three. Five. Seven. He refuses to look at me. What am I supposed to say? *I love you?* What good would that do? He hates me now.

Finally, I answer, "I told you once before. I can't kill anyone."

Timur would have grown still and stony right before my eyes. Khalaf, on the other hand, burns hot. If I tried to touch him now, I think his skin would scald my hand.

"I'm staying," he says. "I've chosen my fate, and I will honor my word. This ungodly night will end eventually. The stars will set, and when the sun rises, I will be either dead or victorious." He finally looks at me, a hard glare that empties my heart. "Go."

"My lord—" I plead.

"I am not your lord. I am nothing to you." I stand before his hatred, powerless and hollowed out. "You promised me that you would take care of my father. I'm holding you to your word. No matter what happens to me, you will take care of him. Promise me that."

"I promise."

"Can I trust your promise, or is it just another lie?"

"It's the truth," I say, not bothering to wipe my face. The truth is all I can give him now.

"Then go." He pulls back the painting to reveal the corridor beyond. "And keep your promise well, because no one is sleeping in Khanbalik tonight."

I step into the corridor.

"My lord?"

"Don't call me that," he says through clenched teeth.

"Prince," I say. There is a distinctive lack of subservience in my voice. I can fall apart later. Right now, I need to save his life one last time. He acknowledges me with furious eyes. "You need to barricade this door behind me. Do you understand?"

His whole body betrays his hurt and anger. He trembles visibly. His nostrils flare with ragged breath. His red eyes are about to brim over.

He nods once and closes the door on me.

I wait a long time until, at last, I hear him push a heavy piece of furniture in front of the entrance. As he barricades himself against any potential assassins, myself included, he walls me out of his life.

Forever.

I knew this day would come, no matter how hard I fought

against it. But that knowledge doesn't lessen the blow. I need to return to Timur, but I give myself a moment to press my hands against the door, to let myself feel all the cracks and fissures that have been building up in my heart break open at last.

It's all I have left now.

34

I FIND TIMUR SEATED IN THE alley where I left him with his back propped up against a dirty hovel. I collapse in a defeated heap next to him.

"You couldn't find him?" he asks.

"No, I found him." My words are slurred as if I'm drunk on failure.

"And he wouldn't come?"

"No." I let my head fall back against the hard wall behind us.

"You didn't tell him the truth, did you?"

I turn my head away from Timur.

"Dammit!" he says. "That was a dumbshit thing to do."

"Thank you, my lord, but I managed to figure that out on my own."

I feel like crying again, but the tears are all wrung out of me. I look at Timur, the boulder of a man sitting next to me in a filthy alley. We are homeless, landless, nationless beggars, and for my own part, I am lost and broken. I wonder how he's managing to hold it together, because my own hysteria is screaming inside me. He pats my knee and says, "There's nothing left to do now, little bird. We'll just have to wait for morning."

It would seem that I am not wrung dry. I sag against Timur and weep into his musky chest.

"Now, don't go losing your head," he murmurs into my greasy hair. "That boy has proven me wrong more than a few times. This may be just another example of his superiority over me."

His big arms wrap around me and he rocks me like a baby. The dethroned khan of the Kipchak Khanate comforts the slave and would-be assassin on a hard-packed street. Incredible.

"My lord?" I whisper.

"Hmm?" The sound rumbles in his chest. I half expect him to repeat Khalaf's words: *I am not your lord.* The fact that he doesn't turns me into a weeping puddle.

"I'm grateful to be your little bird," I tell him. It's a stupid thing to say, but at least it's sincere.

"Ugh. Stop being so damn sappy," he says, but he makes it sound affectionate somehow. He rocks me gently until we drift off to sleep.

That's how the city guards find us three hours later when a dutiful citizen reports two strange people hulking in a stinking alley. A few months ago, Timur would have crushed his first opponent's face with his enormous fist. He would have knocked the second assailant's short curved blade from the man's hand like a child's toy. He would have been a lion. Now, after weeks crossing the desert with next to nothing to eat, his fight is pathetic, but not as pathetic or ineffectual as my own. At least they bothered to get Timur bound up around the torso. They only tie my wrists together.

"Thanks for the help," Timur says as the guards frog-march us out into the street to stand before the man who escorted Khalaf away from the foot of the drum tower. If I weren't mute with terror, I'm sure I'd cough up some kind of pithy comeback.

"That's them," the guard says with a nod. "Saw them talking to the stranger right after he beat the drum."

The guards are merciless in their handling of us as they push us through the throng of people who have gathered in the market square, the place where Turandokht intends to watch Khalaf's body be trampled by horses.

I've made it through this latest ordeal with just a few scratches. Timur, on the other hand, is a mess. Both his eyes are puffy with bruised flesh, and the knuckles of his right hand are split to the bone and bleeding. His hair flies crazily from his head like a lion's mane as Turandokht's guards drag us toward our imminent demise. I think I've never loved him as much as I do at this moment.

A swarm of people follows behind us like a parade, growing

and swelling as we make our way into the heart of this tragic opera playing itself out in Khanbalik.

"So, do you actually know this Turandokht bitch?" Timur asks me out of the side of his mouth.

"No."

"I guess that means you can't put in a good word for us?"

"I don't suppose I could, my lord. I've managed to screw over pretty much everyone by this point, including her."

"Good girl," he says, and then grimaces. I think a few of his remaining teeth were knocked loose in the altercation. His gums are bleeding. I reach for his left hand, which pokes out from underneath the ropes that bind him, and I clasp his fingers in mine.

"Sunrise isn't far off, little bird," he says. "Let's try to live another day."

I look to the eastern horizon as the guards drag us through the jeering crowd, but the sky is black as iron.

"Out of the way!" one of the soldiers shouts. The market square is so packed with bodies that we have come to a full stop. He uses the blunt side of his spear to push past the people blocking our way. When that doesn't work, he switches to the sharp end. A woman in the crowd screams, and the masses slowly separate to make room as we push forward.

Any hope I was entertaining of the sun rising before we made it to our destination disintegrates when we arrive at the foot of the dais. The braziers still burn. The drum tower looms above us. The only difference now is that the moon is gone, making the entire scene dimmer.

Khalaf is already here, wreathed by a guard unit as he awaits the arrival of Turandokht. He doesn't bother to look over at us. I'm sure he got wind of our arrival, but he fixes a bored expression on his face, pretending that he doesn't know us.

Zhang also waits for his perfect mistress in the square, and his eyes gleam when he hears our guards call, "These people know the stranger's name!"

We're all going to die. All of us. I promised Khalaf that I would keep Timur safe. I promised Timur I would keep Khalaf alive. I've failed them both. Everything I've done, the sum total of my life, has ended in failure. And I'm scared. I'm so, so scared now.

Zhang comes over to confer with our captors. He glances my way but doesn't seem to recognize me. He was right when he said that I am so small and plain as to be invisible. How ridiculous that even now it hurts my feelings.

"Where did you catch them?" he asks the guards, who have already begun to celebrate with a skin of *qumiz*.

"They were hiding in an alley just off the square."

Zhang nods and ambles toward Khalaf with a nasty grin spreading across his face. He can hardly contain his smug superiority.

"What is it?" Khalaf asks, as if he has no idea what's going on.

Zhang inclines his head in our direction. "Your friends."

Khalaf looks over Zhang's shoulder at us. "I don't know them."

"Don't you?"

Khalaf's faux serenity shows signs of disintegrating when he sees the soldiers push me and Timur forward. I keep my chin tucked tightly against my chest in a desperate attempt to escape recognition.

I am a dead woman.

"Those poor people don't know my name any more than you do," Khalaf insists. "Let them go."

"I think not." Zhang turns and points at Timur. "You, what is this man's name?"

Time stops. Timur stands straight and tall next to me, defiant, saying nothing. The guards jostle him, and he grunts in pain. He falls forward, and since his arms are bound, he lands face first on the ground.

"No! Leave him alone!" I shout as they heave my beloved old goat to his knees. Timur is not going to die for my mistakes, and neither is Khalaf. I'm not hiding my face anymore. "*I'm* the one you're looking for," I tell them all.

My eyes meet Zhang's, and his lips thin with a cold, murderous rage as he recognizes me at last. I'm terrified, but I'm not sorry. Not even a little. My fiery rebelliousness fuels a courage I didn't know I had. The war of wills has begun, and sunrise will determine the victor.

"Bring the girl forward," Zhang commands my captors.

The entire population of Khanbalik stares at me as the guards push me forward, but it's Khalaf who breaks the horrid silence.

"You know nothing, slave," he says with a voice that cuts like honed steal.

Slave.

The word is a slap to the face.

Khalaf glares at me with a hatred of which I never thought him capable. He truly believes I'm about to sell him out.

And it makes me livid.

I raise my head and look him straight in the eye as I both promise and admonish him, "I'm not going to tell them your name, my lord."

I watch his face blanch as understanding begins to dawn on him. His hate and anger slowly evaporate, and stone-cold fear takes their place. He's still looking at me when he tells Zhang, "Let her go."

"Hmm," Zhang answers, beginning to enjoy himself now. "No."

My eyes are still locked with Khalaf's. I can see the moment he comprehends what it is I'm willing to sacrifice for him, as visceral as a stab wound. He turns so violently on the chancellor that a couple of guards have to jump in to hold him back.

"I swear, she doesn't know me!" he shouts desperately at Zhang while Timur bellows, "Let her go!" But it's too late.

"Gag them both," Zhang orders with a lackadaisical wave of his smooth hand, and the guards obey his command. They try to bind Khalaf up, too, just like his father, but he struggles hard against them. Timur, still kneeling on the ground, turns his head to the side so that he can see what's happening.

Zhang never takes his eyes off me. It's clear he didn't expect to see me here, now, and it's equally clear that he has every intention of breaking me to pieces until he has what he wants. It's crazy, but I've been worried about this moment for so long that, now that it's happened, I feel relieved, unburdened.

"The name," Zhang commands in a dangerously soft voice.

"No," I answer just as softly. It feels so good to tell him no, to deny him what he wants.

He grasps me by my frazzled braid and twists my head back to look at him. We stare at each other nose to nose. He may not know exactly what I've been doing since I left Khanbalik, but he does know that I failed him and his khatun and that I must be punished for it.

"You don't know his name," I tell him, reveling in my defiance even as his tight grasp brings tears to my eyes. "You never have and you never will."

He swings around to look at Khalaf, yanking me so hard by the scalp that I cry out in pain. Khalaf shouts in protest through the cloth tied over his mouth as he struggles to free himself from the men who hold him. And all the while, Zhang's mind is hard at work behind his clever eyes.

Pilaf. Kumar. One of those unpronounceable Turkic names.

Zhang turns his attention back to me. I think I see fear in his eyes.

"Maybe I should tell your perfect khatun about what you've

been up to, little Zhang," I taunt him recklessly, luxuriating in this new power I hold over him.

He lets go of my hair and swings his arm, striking me full in the face with the back of his hand. He's no soldier, but it doesn't take much to send a hollow-boned bird like me floundering across the dirt. A high-pitched buzzing noise balloons in my ear.

"The name!" he shouts.

I was right. He is afraid. I roll to my knees and, growing drunk on his fear, I tell him savagely, "I don't have to obey you. You're nothing to me."

Zhang grabs me by my braid again. It feels like he could tear my skin from my skull. He points to one of the guards and says, "You there. Your dagger."

"My lord?" the man asks.

"Your dagger. Give it to me."

My newfound bravery evaporates as quickly as it appeared, and all I can think is *No-no-no-no-no.*

The man takes a dagger from his belt and hands it to Zhang, who drags the point of the blade down my left cheek. I scream as my flesh splits open in agonizing increments. Somewhere beyond the buzzing in my ear, I can hear someone rage in helpless protest, Khalaf or Timur or maybe both.

Zhang throws me to the ground. The pain of the cut reaches far beyond the line he carved into my cheek. It spreads like oil over the left half of my head, burning, nearly unbearable. Blood trickles down my chin and drips to the dirt. He grabs my shoul-

ders with hands like talons, but a commotion from the other end of the square stops him. A path forms in the crowd, and the masses give birth to an ornate sedan chair, carried from the palace by slaves. A unit of bodyguards surround the palanquin on all sides, pushing onlookers back to make room. Zhang releases me and hurries forward to head up the welcoming committee as the slaves set down their burden. Turandokht steps out from behind the silk curtains like the sun emerging over the dark horizon.

"My khatun, we have the name," Zhang says over her hand as he grasps it subserviently in his own.

"What is it?" Her own desperation is palpable.

"This slave knows." He indicates me as two soldiers pick me up under the arms and carry me forward with my feet dragging across the dirt. "I will personally rip the name from her throat."

Hot urine pours out of me. My face throbs and bleeds.

"Let her go," Turandokht tells my guards.

"But my khatun . . . ," Zhang begins.

"Enough. I said let her go."

The two men reluctantly obey, moving aside as Turandokht approaches. Unsupported, I fall to my knees.

"No," I croak. I don't want to kneel before her.

Khalaf's struggle against his captors carries on to my left, but she doesn't bother glancing in his direction. That's how little he means to her. It kills me that he's nothing to her when he is everything to me.

"I've already solved the riddle," she tells me. "I know he must be the son of Timur Khan. I simply need his name. Save yourself. Your freedom in exchange for one name. But if you refuse, my men will have you whipped to death."

My defiance rebounds. "Then whip me," I say as I struggle to my feet. I'm not addressing her by title. I'm not showing obeisance. I won't bow and scrape to her. We're equals, she and I.

"There is no need for this. If you tell me his name, we will both be free."

In the most ludicrous example of incongruity, I begin to laugh. If my face didn't hurt so badly, I might have slipped into hysterics. "Oh no," I tell her, giggling. "I'm going to keep that boy alive."

"Why? What could you possibly have to gain? The future of the empire is at stake. Can't you see that?"

The lack of recognition in her eyes as she regards me kills my laughter. I worked in her house, served her food, washed her dishes, but she never saw me.

No one ever saw me except Khalaf.

He cries out, guttural and incomprehensible behind his gag. His face is flushed with effort as he strains against the men who can barely contain him.

"I don't care about countries and empires," I tell Turandokht. "I love him. And that's all that matters."

How simple it is, so easy to say now that it is said. In this moment, everyone, everything grows still and silent, even Khalaf. The very air is listening to me.

"I love him enough to give him up," I say, and since there's nothing left to lose, I allow myself to look at Khalaf, to love him without hiding it. "He's a gift. And now he's my gift to you."

His face above the gag is a constellation of emotions, so muddled I can't read any one of them.

I turn back to Turandokht with unaccustomed bravado rising giddily inside me. "You have taken everything from me—my family, my home, my freedom. Now you will take him, too. And you don't even know my name. Well, you won't have his name either. His name belongs to me as much as my own."

Turandokht hardens as if she has turned to ice in front of me. "I want that name," she breathes.

It's all the permission Zhang needs. "Let her be whipped. Let her be flayed. I'll tear the name from her skin if I have to."

Torture.

My words were brave. My body isn't. I can't face this.

Khalaf rages against his bindings once more. Three men try to hold him captive, and it's not enough. He's screaming through the gag, the same muffled word, over and over and over as his bindings grow looser against his fight.

Two syllables.

One word.

Khalaf!

He's saying his own name, weeping it, soaking the gag with spit and tears.

He's trying to save me.

He's willing to die so that I may live.

Khalaf! he screams.

He fights hard. He almost has the muzzle off, and then what? I didn't come all this way to watch him die for me.

I look to the east, but there's no hint of sunlight there to greet me. I rise to my feet and take a few steps toward Khalaf before two guards step in front of me and halt my progress.

Khalaf wails into his gag. The tendons of his neck strain against his skin. He struggles until he slumps with exhaustion. His eyes find me, screaming his apologies and his regret and his agony.

And his love.

He loves me.

We look at each other, *see* each other, unhidden and unapologetic. It's like bursting from the water's surface and taking that first breath of air when you thought you were going to drown.

He hangs limply in his captors' arms, pouring out all the love he never let me see until this moment.

A gift.

A gift, my mother whispers in my ear. I turn to find her standing beside me, as lovely and graceful in death as she was in life. I'm so relieved to see her here, now. I'm so grateful to have her at my side when I need her the most. *Remember your gift, Daughter,* she tells me.

My mother's words stir up the memory of Khalaf in the desert, holding out a dagger to me. *Promise me you'll use this if you have to.*

All my ancestors are here now, standing at my back, silent and

peaceful. My father steps forward, the lines of his body comprising a softer man than I remember in life. I never realized until this moment how much I resemble him, how much of him lives in me. He extends a ghost hand that I can't hold. *It's time to come home now.*

I hear the memory of singing. *Jasmine flower, your willowy stems clustered with sweet-smelling buds.*

I know what I have to do. I stand up straight and hold myself the way my mother taught me to do, and I face Turandokht.

"You'll see," I assure her. "Someday, you'll understand what it is I gave you."

I look at Khalaf one last time. "'And wilderness is paradise now,'" I tell him.

"No!" he begs me in a hoarse, muffled voice through the slipping gag. He shakes his head. His whole soul is telling me no, but there is only one way I can save any of us now, and he knows it.

They only tied my wrists, so I can reach the dagger with ease. I pull Khalaf's gift from my belt.

"No!" he screams through the gag.

All this time I thought I couldn't kill anyone, but I was wrong.

Come home, Daughter.

Come home.

My ancestors reach out, stroking gently at my arms, my undamaged cheek, my soft, fine hair.

Weiji's voice is last, floating somewhere nearby, separate and alone.

I want to go home.

I take the dagger and shove it as hard as I can up underneath my breastbone and into my heart, just the way Khalaf taught me. I watch him burst free of the guards as the blade sends pain searing through my chest. Khalaf cries out, and I collapse in anguish at his feet. He's there beside me, ripping off his gag and stuffing it against my wound as if it could possibly stanch the blood. His hand is on my heart.

I didn't know anything could hurt like this. I begin to go blind with pain. My vision grows gray around the outside edges, but I can still see him leaning over me. One of his braids has come loose, and his hair tickles my cheek, the one that isn't ruined.

I sing.

Fragrant and white, everyone praises your beauty
Let me pluck you down
And give you to the one I love

"Jinghua," Khalaf says so gently to me in that lovely voice of his, the sweet sound of my name in his mouth.

I breathe a single word so that no one can hear but he and I.

"Khalaf."

It begins with an explosion and ends in a whisper.

And then I die.

35

I DRIFT OUT OF MYSELF AND through Khalaf's body, swimming across his grief and that huge expanse of love, like a bottomless reservoir. I thought it was only a trickle when, in fact, he carried an ocean inside him. There's so much of it.

I hover over the scene, billowing in death like gauze in a soft breeze. I see Khalaf's head bent over my tiny body. It's incredible that something so small and insignificant could mean anything to anyone.

"Jinghua," he calls to my body. He lays his hands on my skinny arms and gives me a gentle shake. "Jinghua," he calls again, plaintive. He shakes me harder, as if I were only asleep, but of course I don't wake.

"No," he tells my body again and again. "No. No. No. No!"

He wraps his arms around my body and lifts it against his. His loose hair grows damp in my blood. He holds my shell in his arms and releases wracking waves of grief into the crook of my neck, nuzzling his face against the dissipating warmth of my body as if his love could bring me back to life. I experience the sensation like a boat bobbing on the waves of the sea.

The crowd stands in cowed silence as a gust of wind blows through them. I can't feel it, but I can see it tugging at their robes and ripping at the Great Khan's crimson banners. The eastern sky grows pale with pinks and oranges, and my spirit starts to stretch and thin.

Only the dead can see me now. They gaze up at me expectantly as I float higher and higher.

Someone has set Timur free. He staggers over to my body and falls to his knees next to his son. Timur picks up my limp hand where it hangs free from Khalaf's embrace. My eyes are open, empty.

"Jinghua," Timur says, coaxing, even as my soul stretches thinner, even as I float farther away. "Jinghua, come on now. The sun is rising. Wake up, little bird."

"She's dead, old man," Zhang tells him, his own spirit radiating fear of me, of what I might become to him in death.

Imagine, fearing me.

Or me, says my brother beside me above the world we leave behind. I take his hand in mine.

Timur throws back his shaggy head and cries out, a sound so primal it speaks to the falcon in the sky, the buffalo in the desolate wilds. He lunges for Zhang, but the guards kick him back down as the chancellor darts out of the way.

Khan no more, utterly powerless, my old goat pushes himself back up onto his aching knees, his shoulders stooped in defeat. He places a hand on his son's shoulder and urges him to ease the burden of my body back down to the ground. When Khalaf reaches for me again, Timur holds him back.

"She's gone," he says softly. "She's gone now."

Khalaf can't hide the wet tracks streaking down his cheeks, the grimace of his mouth, the shaking of his chest. He remembers the feeling of my hands stitching him back together in the mountains.

Don't tell him I cried.

I won't, my lord, I promise him.

From all around, silent prayers weave into a great spirit song that buoys me and Weiji farther upward and outward. The only voice that is absent is Turandokht's. She's all hollowed out. Her utter isolation and loneliness pour into all her empty places.

I want to go home now, Jinghua. Can you take me home? Weiji asks me.

Yes, I tell him. *I know the way.*

The men come forward then, the guards who had been keeping me and Khalaf apart. One of them picks up my little body and carries it out of the square and toward the palace while the other one hovers at his shoulder as if I were someone who mattered.

Khalaf and Timur stay where they are, kneeling side by side in stunned disbelief by the puddle of blood that once pulsed within my body.

What remains of me stretches two ways: the part that longs for the body and the part that longs for the people I leave behind, like a slingshot, pulled and unreleased with only Weiji's hand to anchor me.

Another imperial guard unit arrives on the scene with five foreigners dressed in the yellow standard of the Il-Khanate.

"Forgive us for intruding at such a delicate moment, my khatun, but we have the name you seek," says one of Hulegu Il-Khan's men.

"Yes?" she says flatly. "Speak."

"This man is Khalaf, son of Timur Khan of the Kipchak Khanate."

"You're certain?" she asks the guard.

"Yes, my khatun."

Turandokht watches my body grow smaller and smaller as her guards carry me away before she strides to Khalaf where he kneels on the ground, staring at my blood. "Khalaf, son of Timur," she calls down to him.

The face he raises to look up at hers is filthy and streaked with tears. He is sick with failure and grief.

You died for nothing, his soul cries to mine.

No, I didn't, I answer, but he can't hear me now.

"Khalaf," says Turandokht, "I have unriddled you."

"Then may you triumph in my death." With the lithe grace of a tiger, he leaps to his feet, takes her by the back of the head, and presses his lips hard on hers. There's nothing tender about it. It's a vindictive gesture and a self-excoriation. He smears my blood on her robe, her cheek, her lips.

The guards land upon him, ripping him from her as Turandokht orders, "Don't hurt him! I want him alive!"

Khalaf doesn't fight the guards who jostle and bind him again. He only regards Turandokht with a cold hatred.

Her victory tastes like ashes in her mouth. She looks to the east, where an eyelash of sun glints over the horizon. Zhang, sensing victory, oozes up behind her and says from his respectful distance, "It's dawn, my khatun."

"It's dawn," she agrees wearily, regarding Khalaf, who glares back at her. If a man could kill with his eyes, Turandokht would be dead.

"After all this, you give away your life so easily?" she asks him.

"Take it," says Khalaf. "I'm not afraid to die."

In his heart, for this one terrible moment, he wants only to join me where I have gone.

Not yet, I tell him.

There's one last stretch of my spirit, taut as a drawn bow. As the sun rises, slaves arrive with one more imperial sedan chair. They pull back the curtains to reveal the Great Khan, who struggles out of his transport with their assistance. Turandokht's sickly father surveys the scene and marvels at the macabre sight before him.

"I know his name, Father," Turandokht tells him without shifting her gaze. She nods to the bloodied prince of the Kipchak Khanate and announces, "This day, I will wed Khalaf, son of Timur."

The bow snaps. I hold my brother's hand and together we scatter into eternity.

And I am everywhere and I am myself and I am nothing and I am changed.

And I am what I have never thought to be.

EPILOGUE

A VOW IS A VOW. THEY married. Throughout the known world, people are calling it the golden age of the empire. How could it be otherwise with two such rulers?

He is who he is, so he's forgiven her. He has always sought to learn what he could not understand. She is no different. She was a puzzle, and now he understands her, and he respects her.

He doesn't love her, though.

He'll never love her.

His father chooses neither to understand her nor to respect her. He does tolerate her, and that's pretty good for the old goat. He's completely blind now and nearly deaf as well. Sometimes, when he's not busy goosing the plum-cheeked maid who pushes his wheelchair along the gravel path, he thinks of me. He finds my voice somewhere in his cloudy mind and holds my hand in his. When his bones ache in the darkness, he calls to me. He tells me how he longs to follow me to where I have gone. When he calls to me, I come to him quietly in the breeze that billows in his long, white beard and tickles the thick hairs of his outrageous eyebrows.

And sometimes, she calls to me, too. I am, for her, the sole recipient of her sadness and loneliness, her love for a man who can hardly bear to look at her. When she calls to me, I am the lily in the pool, the rustle of leaves. I ride before her on a fast horse.

One day, she's brave enough to speak of me. They are walking side by side in the garden. They're so rarely alone like this.

"I never even knew her name," she says.

He remains silent for a few paces before he answers, "Jinghua. Her name was Jinghua. It means 'illustrious capital city.'" But in his mind, he still calls me *"jinghuā."* Quiet Flower.

He walks ahead of her. He remembers that he kissed me once, and his lips turn up at the memory, and then they fall again. He still feels the dull ache of grief.

He's forgiven her, but he hasn't managed to forgive himself yet. I wish he would, but his hair grows gray at his temples now, so I doubt he ever will. Not in this life, at least.

In his private chamber, he had a woodworker from Lin'an install a little altar carved with a motif of jasmine flowers. He places a small, finely painted porcelain cup on its polished surface and fills it with steaming tea or rich wine. He sets out offerings of rice and cakes on a pretty saucer.

And apples.

Always apples.

After his evening prayers, he cleans the dishes himself and dries them carefully with a square of fine muslin.

When he calls to me, I am the scent of jasmine in the garden, the word on the page, the birdsong at his window, his name on the wind.

When he needs me, I am there.

AUTHOR'S NOTE

One day during the summer of 2008, I was listening to the opera *Turandot* and bristling over the slave girl's tragic demise when, for reasons I cannot begin to fathom, I suddenly thought, *Hey, this story would make a great young adult novel!*

Because nothing says *great young adult novel* like opera.

Ten years and ninety-two thousand words later, my outrage over the death of a fictional character has turned into a reinterpretation of an eighteenth-century French tale set in the thirteenth-century Mongol Empire. There's a little fact and a whole lot of fiction in these pages. Should you care to separate the two, read on.

THE ORIGINS OF THE STORY

The Bird and the Blade is a retelling of "Prince Khalaf and the Princess of China," which first appeared in a collection of tales called *The Thousand and One Days*. The author, a French scholar named François Pétis de la Croix, claimed that the book was a translation of a Persian text given to him by a dervish.

The story bears a strong resemblance to a tale from *Haft Paykar* by the medieval Persian poet Nizami Ganjavi. In this version of events, a beautiful princess with too many suitors walls herself up inside a mountain fortress. Any man who wishes to marry her has to make his way past killer automatons, then answer three riddles correctly. The point here is that a great king, in addition to being a military badass, must also possess wisdom.

Pétis de la Croix's tale has been adapted into many plays and operas, most notably by Carlo Gozzi, Friedrich Schiller, and Giacomo Puccini. These Western versions view the story through a more misogynistic lens. Here, Turandokht is a viper, a female full of pride who must be brought to heel by her male counterpart, Khalaf. The retellings tend to pick up the story at the point when Khalaf arrives in Peking (Khanbalik in my version), ditching the long journey and great suffering that preceded it.

The slave girl character appears in every iteration of the tale. In most cases, she is Turandokht's slave and the instrument by which the princess learns Khalaf's name. While she's not a very likable character in these stories, she is, in my view, the most complicated and compelling. A princess-turned-slave who loathes Turandokht for destroying her family, she still forks over Khalaf's name to the ice queen when she realizes that he'll never return her love.

Puccini and his librettists did something different with this character: They made her the loyal servant of Timur and Khalaf. Complicating matters further is the fact that Puccini died before finishing the work. Composer Franco Alfano completed the score, but when the opera premiered at La Scala on April 25, 1926, the conductor, Arturo Toscanini, set down the baton after the slave girl's funeral procession, turned to the audience, and announced that this was the point at which the maestro had died.

That night, the opera ended right there, and if you ask me, that's where it should have ended anyway.

THE MONGOL EMPIRE

The Mongol empire, which began in the early thirteenth century and extended well into the fourteenth, grew to envelop most of the Asian continent as well as parts of Europe. While I set *The Bird and the Blade* in this particular time and place in history, it's important to understand that I took many liberties with the facts in the telling of this tale. For instance, while the Il-Khanate and the Kipchak Khanate fought against each other, the Il-Khanids never defeated the Kipchaks or vice versa. Additionally, Timur and his older sons would have had multiple wives and many children, but I have chosen to omit them for the sake of narrative clarity. Khubilai Khan, who was the Great Khan of the Mongol Empire at the time, had several children and was succeeded by one of his grandsons. And Zhang would not have counted down the minutes and seconds after Turandokht posed each riddle, since the basic unit of time measurement was the kè, roughly equivalent to fifteen minutes. These are just a few examples of the many, many liberties I took with history for the sake of fiction.

I should also mention that the story of Khalaf's mother, Bibi Hanem, is anachronistic to the time period. This legend is linked to Amir Timur (better known in English as Tamerlane), a fourteenth-century Turco-Mongol conqueror who may have inspired the character Timur. The blue domes of Samarkand were built under Amir Timur's rule, which makes them anachronistic to the story as well.

That said, many people and events referenced here are real, although I have condensed several decades of history into a span of three years. The descendants of Genghis Khan's son Tolui did stage a coup d'état to take over the position of Great Khan. Qaidu, a descendant of Genghis Khan's son Ogodei, did fight against the Toluids (and his daughter Khutulun is thought by some to have inspired the character Turandokht). The sacking of Baghdad did kick off a war between the khan of the Kipchak Khanate and Hulegu Il-Khan, although that event occurred in 1258, not 1281. Finally, the route taken by Jinghua, Khalaf, and Timur across the Mongol Empire closely resembles that of Marco Polo's famous journey.

One final note on the Mongols: They were remarkably tolerant of others' spiritual beliefs, and they financially supported a wide variety of religious institutions. Some of the early rulers of the empire were Nestorian Christians, but the Mongols of the Yuan Dynasty eventually adopted Buddhism while the Kipchaks converted to Islam. Pétis de la Croix makes it clear that Khalaf is a devout Muslim, but subsequent versions of the story tend to erase this facet of the tale. I thought it important to reinsert the prince's unwavering faith into the story as one of the character traits that makes Khalaf the stellar human being he is.

THE SONG (SUNG) DYNASTY

The Song Dynasty of China is generally divided into two eras: the Northern Song and the Southern Song. The Northern Song

Dynasty existed from 960 to 1127, when it was defeated by the Jin Dynasty. The Song moved their capital south to Lin'an (modern-day Hangzhou) and were conquered by the Mongols in 1279. The Song period is associated with a strong adherence to neo-Confucianism, a renewed dedication to living by secular Confucian ideals within a highly stratified social structure.

Once again, taking any part of this novel as historical fact would be a bit like viewing "Hansel and Gretel" as a tract on German history. For example, Jinghua would probably have had her feet bound, but since that would make her journey across most of the Asian continent impossible, I have omitted it from the story. Also, Jinghua could never have accessed the Song or Yuan palaces as she does in this novel. Only the ruler and his consorts could live in a palace, which was heavily and carefully guarded. Although the Mongols did conquer the Song, events did not transpire as described in this book. In reality, the Mongols were the aggressors, not the Song, and the surviving members of the Song imperial family were allowed to live out their lives in exile, not slavery.

Poor little Emperor Bing did drown, though. When it was clear that the Song had lost their last battle against the Mongols—a naval defeat—a Song official carried the boy over the side of the ship rather than let him fall into Mongol hands.

LANGUAGE AND LITERATURE IN *THE BIRD AND THE BLADE*

In an attempt to anchor *The Bird and the Blade* in the thirteenth-century Mongol Empire, I have had the characters in the novel use non-English terms on occasion. While I have tried to incorporate elements of both Hanyu (Mandarin Chinese) and Mongolian into an English-language novel, I have made a few word choices that don't translate well. I'm afraid "old goat" just isn't something a Song girl would call even the most crotchety of overthrown khans.

The characters also frequently refer to poetry and other works that would have been available to them during this period. In chapter 10, Khalaf quotes several lines from Nizami's *Haft Paykar* to Abbas, paraphrased from Charles Edward Wilson's translation. In chapter 13, he quotes several Persian poems, including "The Newborn" by Farid al-Din Attar in my own wording paraphrased from Coleman Barks's translation; "The Parrot of Baghdad" by Jalal ad-Din Muhammad Rumi, translated by E. H. Palmer; "Guardians" by Saadi Shirazi, translated by E. B. Eastwick; and *Laili and Majnun*, the epic poem by Nizami, translated by James Atkinson. In chapter 14, Khalaf tells Jinghua two stories from *Haft Paykar*, which I have paraphrased with the aid of Julie Scott Meisami's translation, and *The Seven Wise Princesses: A Medieval Persian Epic* by Wafa Tarnowska.

There are references throughout the book to a quatrain from *The Rubáiyát* of Omar Khayyám, which I adapted from the translation by Edward FitzGerald. FitzGerald's translation is not terribly faithful to the original Persian text, but it is considered a great work of English-language poetry in its own right.

Khalaf also quotes the Qur'an on several occasions, including

94:5 in chapter 7, 90:12–18 in chapter 8, and 42:10 in chapter 18. All English translations were taken from *The Study Quran: A New Translation and Commentary*, edited by Seyyed Hossein Nasr et al. Additionally, Khalaf quotes *Sahih Muslim*, 2564, in the prologue, English translation found in *A Brief Illustrated Guide to Understanding Islam* by I. A. Ibrahim.

Jinghua sings excerpts from several poems by the Song poet Li Qingzhao, translated into English by Kenneth Rexroth and Ling Chung, including "Sorrow of Departure" in chapter 13, "Remorse" in chapter 16, "The Beauty of White Chrysanthemums" in chapter 18, and "A Morning Dream" in chapter 29. In chapter 27, she listens to a recitation of a Tang Dynasty poem called "A Woman's Hundred Years," translated by Patricia Ebrey and Lily Hwa. In chapter 28, Zhang recites "What Plant Is Not Faded?" from *The Book of Songs*, said to be compiled by Confucius, translated by Arthur Waley.

Throughout the book, Jinghua sings a Chinese folk song called *"Mòlihuā."* The song is anachronistic to the time period, but Puccini threaded this melody throughout his opera, which is why I chose to use it in the novel. I consulted several translations and tweaked the wording to suit the story.

Also in the opera, Turandot (Turandokht) sings an aria called *"In questa Reggia"* ("In this Kingdom") in which she delivers her argument for shunning men and marriage. It occurred to me that one of the most powerful women in Western history faced a similar struggle. For this reason, Turandokht's speech in chapter 1 borrows heavily from two speeches by Queen Elizabeth I of England: her "Marriage Speech to Parliament in 1559" and her "Response to Parliamentary Delegation on Her Marriage in 1566."

The riddles are, of course, the centerpiece of the story, and each version of the tale contains different puzzles. My favorites by far were those created by librettists Giuseppe Adami and Renato Simoni for Puccini's opera. I have rewritten them, but the tone and the answers remain very much intact.

GLOSSARY

arban: (Mongolian) a military unit consisting of ten men

Cān jiàn Diànxià: (Mandarin Chinese) It is an honor to greet you, my prince.

Chagatai Khanate: a khanate of the Mongol Empire, consisting of large swaths of Central Asia

deel: (Mongolian) an article of traditional Mongol clothing, similar to a kaftan, that clasps at the shoulder and under the armpit and is belted around the waist

dirham: a unit of currency dating back to pre-Islamic times and still in use today in several Berber and Arab states

ger: (Mongolian) a round housing structure constructed of felt over a wooden frame designed to be easily transported

gerege: (Mongolian) a flat tablet, made of metal, that rendered to the holder the ability to demand goods and services from civilian populations, particularly while traveling through the empire

Great Khan: the khan of khans, the elected leader of the Mongol Empire

Hanyu: the language of the Han, better known in the West as Mandarin Chinese

Hǎo jiǔ bú jiàn, xiōngtái: (Mandarin Chinese) Long time no see, brother.

huāshēng: peanut

il-khan: subkhan, maintaining a portion of the empire on behalf of the Great Khan

Il-Khanate: the khanate of the Mongol Empire to the south of the Caspian Sea, consisting of Persia, Iraq, and parts of central Asia

khan: king

khanate: a mini-empire, a portion of the Mongol Empire overseen by its own khan

khatun: queen

Kipchak Khanate: the khanate of the Mongol Empire to the north of the Caspian Sea, consisting of extensive lands in Russia, eastern Europe, and parts of central Asia *lǐ:* (Mandarin Chinese) a Chinese unit measuring distance, about a third of a mile

mòlìhuā: (Mandarin Chinese) jasmine flower

qumiz: (Mongolian) fermented mare's milk; sometimes spelled koumiss in English

shǎguā: (Mandarin Chinese) fool; literally "silly melon."

Song Dynasty, Empire of the: Specifically, the Empire of the Southern Song Dynasty, located in what is now southern China, which fell to the Mongols in 1279; sometimes spelled Sung in English

sukhe: (Mongolian) the standardized currency of the Mongol Empire, based on a silver ingot divided into five hundred parts

tumen: (Mongolian) a military unit consisting of ten thousand men

uurga: (Mongolian) a lasso made from a wooden rod and a loop of leather

xiàngqí: (Mandarin Chinese) a Chinese board game, similar to chess

Yuan Dynasty, Khanate of the: the Great Khan's khanate in the east, consisting of the Mongol homeland, China, and Tibet

Wǒ de tiān nǎ: (Mandarin Chinese) Oh, my heaven!

zǎo: date

Zǎo shēng guì zǐ: may you give birth to a son

zhǎngxiōng: (Mandarin Chinese) older brother

Zhongguo: (Mandarin Chinese) China; historically, a term that suggested a sense of cultural superiority felt by Chinese empires

zuun: (Mongolian) a military unit consisting of one hundred men

ACKNOWLEDGMENTS

My heartfelt gratitude goes to Meagan Condon, Katie Korte, L. L. McKinney, Kate McNair, Dennis Ross, and Meghan Stigge for their insightful feedback on early drafts of this novel. Thanks also to Kester "Kit" Grant, Peter Knops, Henry Lien, Myra McEntire, and Carrie Ryan for being incredibly helpful people. Bear hugs and fat kisses to Tessa Gratton and Natalie C. Parker for ALL THE THINGS.

Meyrnah Khodr and Jūn Aī were staggeringly generous in answering my many, many questions. Meyrnah and AJ, you two are wonderful. And to Associate Professor Anne Broadbridge of the University of Massachusetts Amherst, Assistant Professor Man Xu of Tufts University, Professor Morris Rossabi, and Shenwei Chang for their willingness to provide feedback regarding the accuracy and authenticity of this book: I can't thank you enough.

My critique partners, Jenny Mendez and Kathee Goldsich, have supported me and put up with my unending text messages and *Poldark* gifs for years. Jenny and Kathee, this book would not exist without you.

Let it be known that my agent, Holly Root, is an angel wrapped in kitten hugs and the new Defense against the Dark Arts teacher (in an excellent Professor Lupin kind of way). You are the absolute best, Holly. Thanks also to Heather Baror-Shapiro, who has championed *The Bird and the Blade* the world over.

Giant thanks to Renée Cafiero, Kelsey Murphy, Janet Robbins Rosenberg, Jordan Saia, Michelle Taormina, and the entire team at HarperCollins and Balzer + Bray. I'm ridiculously lucky to have you in my corner.

As for my editor, Kristin Daly Rens, there aren't enough words in the world to convey my gratitude. Her insight and guidance have made Jinghua's story a thousand times better than when she first laid eyes on it. I am eternally grateful to you, Kristin.

Lastly, I want to thank my friends and family for their unending support and enthusiasm, especially my sons, Hank and Gus, who have valiantly tolerated a mother who plays ukulele whenever she gets stuck on a plot point, and my husband, Mike, who, in addition to being smarter and better looking than Khalaf, offered fantastic feedback on the manuscript. I love you guys.

Megan Bannen is a librarian and author. In her spare time, she collects graduate degrees from Kansas colleges and universities. While most of her professional career has been spent in public libraries, she has also sold luggage, written grants, and taught English abroad and at home. She lives in the Kansas City area with her husband, their two sons, and a few too many pets with literary names. She can be found online at www.meganbannen.com.